MR WARREN'S PROFESSION

SEBASTIAN NOTHWELL

TABLE OF CONTENTS

ACKNOWLEDGMENTS

Thanks to Ang, Lou, Olivia, Marcella, Mary, Meagan, Mercutio, Siobhan, and the Rhode Island Romance Writers for the encouragement and feedback that made this book a reality, and thanks to Monica for getting the ball rolling.

CHAPTER ONE

Manchester, England, 1891

"WARREN? WHAT THE devil are you doing here at this hour?"

The voice, though gentle, interrupted the distant drone of the factory like a thunderclap.

Aubrey Warren snapped to attention. His pen slashed a line through a column in his ledger as he whipped his head up to regard the man in the doorway.

The hallway outside the office remained dark despite the weak sunrise fighting its way through the Manchester smog. Yet Aubrey recognised the barrel-shaped body perched on spindly legs as Mr Jennings, mill manager.

"Sorry, sir," said Aubrey. His broken nib dripped ink between the pages of the ledger. Aubrey whipped out an old rag—already more ink than cloth—to blot the mess.

Mr Jennings shut the office door and hung up his hat, exposing his balding pate.

"What time did you come in?" he said, approaching Aubrey's desk. "Five o'clock? Four?"

Aubrey held his tongue.

Mr Jennings sighed. "You never went home, did you, Warren?"

"There was work to be done, sir."

"Work ought to be done during office hours." Mr Jennings clasped his hands behind his back and bent at the waist to peer down at Aubrey's desk. "That's Smith's ledger, isn't it? Why are you working through the night in another man's ledger, Warren? Sabotage, perhaps—should I fear a mutiny?"

From any other man, the stream of questions would be an inquisition. But hearing them in Mr Jennings's resigned tone, Aubrey didn't feel attacked, only duly chastised. "No, sir."

"Then Smith has begged you to correct his work for him?"

Not so much begged as commanded, Aubrey thought. Aloud, he said, "Smith's work is perfectly adequate, sir."

"Then why are you here?"

"To confirm its adequacy."

Mr Jennings didn't bother to pretend he believed him. "I'd send you home, Warren, but I'm afraid I cannot spare you today."

Aubrey awaited further explanation. Mr Jennings offered up nothing more, merely ambled away behind the door of his own inner office, set apart from the common clerks. Aubrey returned to Smith's ledger.

Smith himself strolled in at quarter-past eight. While not a notably athletic specimen, he looked like Hercules next to Aubrey. Aubrey's flat, dark hair was a mere shadow of the light-brown locks Smith waxed into waves. Smith's bright copper eyes far outshone the black-brown of Aubrey's, and Smith's cheeks flushed warm and pink with life while Aubrey's sunk into a colour indistinguishable from the parchment he worked on. Though they were of a like age, only Smith carried the aura of youthful vitality. Aubrey, meanwhile, seemed to have died at twenty or so and somehow kept on with the bookkeeping.

Aubrey cast his own attention back down to his desk and tried to ignore the sounds of Smith tossing his hat and jacket onto their respective pegs. The sound of Smith's footsteps coming closer proved more difficult to disregard. The sound of Smith's voice, impossible.

"What, still at it, Warren?" Smith clapped a hand onto Aubrey's shoulder.

Aubrey watched in vain as the tail end of his 7 veered off into the next row. He lifted his eyes from the ruined page. "So it would seem."

Smith clucked his tongue in mock reproof and, much to Aubrey's relief, wandered off to his own desk, seeming content to let his ledger remain in Aubrey's more capable hands. Aubrey knew better than to attempt to return it to him. Left up to Smith, the entire mill complex would crumble around their ears.

No sooner had Smith sat down than Mr Jennings reappeared.

"Interesting news, boys," he said.

Aubrey snapped to attention. Smith deigned to remove his feet from his desk. Mr Jennings fixed the same placid look on both.

"The mill is changing hands," he continued. "Our new owner, Mr Althorp, requests a tour of the property. Today."

Short notice, yes, but Mr Jennings ran a tight ship. Whoever this Mr Althorp was, he would find no fault in the Rook Mill. Not if Aubrey had any say in the matter.

"We've an hour and three-quarters to prepare," Mr Jennings went on. "Make yourselves ready."

Aubrey surreptitiously rubbed the stubble on his chin. Mr Jennings returned to his office. The instant the door clicked shut, Smith put his heels back on his desk. Aubrey hoped he'd have the sense to adopt a more professional posture before Mr Althorp arrived. Not that Aubrey looked any better himself. A prickly jaw, ink-stained knuckles, and yesterday's shirt did not add up to a respectable appearance. Nothing could be done about the shirt—he wouldn't have enough time to walk home and back, to say nothing of what the sweat and smog of the return journey would do to a fresh shirt. His unshaven face was another matter.

Aubrey closed Smith's ledger and opened the bottom-right drawer of his desk. There, under a ream of parchment, sat a battered cigar box. Its contents rattled as he tucked it under his arm. Without a word, he deposited Smith's ledger beside Smith's ankles and walked out the door.

The office stood apart from the main body of the mill on the other side of a cobblestoned courtyard, with a water pump centred between them. Most of the water drawn from it went to thirsty mill workers. Several such men gathered around it now, talking amongst themselves. They fell silent as Aubrey approached.

"Good morning," said Aubrey.

A couple of the men responded in kind. After that, the group as a whole seemed to forget the oddity of a clerk coming down to mingle with the rest of the workforce. They moved back a bit to let him at the pump and struck up their conversation again as if he'd never arrived. Aubrey took no offense. He had little practice in the art of conversation, and work to do besides.

Out of his cigar box came a plain clay bowl with multiple hairline fissures running down its sides. Aubrey filled it with water, then stripped off his jacket, waistcoat, and shirt, and draped them over the pump handle. This caught the workers' attention again. The youngest one, a lad of fourteen or so, pointed at Aubrey's pale bare chest, but caught a slap on the back of his head from one of his elders before he could open his mouth to heckle. The rest of the workers turned back to their business.

11

Aubrey assumed they hoped ignoring him would make him stop being odd in their yard and go away. He wondered how their reaction might differ if they knew he hadn't been born to the middle-class status of a clerk. If they realised his origins were far lower than that, even lower than their own. Still, any shame he felt at revealing his naked flesh was nothing compared to the shame he would feel if he made no effort to appear respectable in front of the mill's new owner. To that end, he returned to his cigar box and drew out a bar of soap and a razor.

Aubrey knew his own face well enough to shave without a looking-glass. Today he used double his usual allotment of soap—all the while trying not to think about the cost—and pulled the blade over his cheeks with especial care. Once done, he washed his face and hands, beat the soot from his clothes, dressed, and returned to the office. He could still feel the mill hands' stares on the back of his neck as he left the yard.

He stepped through the office doorway at quarter-past nine. Contrary to his expectation, Smith had moved in the interim—he'd draped a handkerchief over his eyes. It fluttered in time with his snores. Aubrey, knowing Smith would accomplish as much asleep as he would awake, didn't bother trying to rouse him. Instead, he returned the cigar box to its drawer and took out his own ledger. He had three-quarters of an hour until Mr Althorp arrived. He intended to make them count.

Mr Jennings re-emerged at ten minutes to ten. He took in the sight of the sleeping Smith, then turned to Aubrey with a finger pressed against his inexpressive lips. Aubrey followed him out of the office in silence.

"Sir?" said Aubrey as they walked across the yard towards the mill. "Shouldn't Smith be present as well?"

"I find the more industrious employee makes a better impression," said Mr Jennings.

Aubrey thought it might have been a compliment.

☞

Lindsey Althorp boarded the morning train from Wiltshire to Manchester. One short tour of the textile mill to show his father he'd grown into sedate and responsible manhood, university or no university, then he could catch the very next train back to the country house and get on with the urgent business of reading the latest *Strand*. He would have brought the magazine with him, but reading on the train made him ill.

Even without it, he had plenty to occupy his mind. He'd never owned a mill before, which leant a novel air to the day's excursion. (His elder sister, Rowena, had predicted over breakfast he'd grow bored with it before the week was out. Because of this, she had not been invited along.) He'd won the mill off Clarence in a card game down at the club last week. He'd had every intention of giving Clarence the chance to win it back, but Clarence had declined all invitations to play. Seven days later, Lindsey supposed it was his to keep.

Lindsey had never visited Manchester before. He knew people there, or rather he knew people who did business there, or who hired people to do business there for them. But the city itself, boasting no literary significance or sporting society—at least, none Lindsey had ever heard of—did not play to his interests. So Manchester had remained a dull, smoggy haze in his imagination.

But as he stepped off the train in Manchester Central, the dull haze sprang to life with a clang that knocked Lindsey's preconceptions right out of his head. Manchester wasn't so downtrodden and depressed as Dickens and Gaskell had led him to believe. The street surged with crowds to match any in London. The air rang with the constant echo of rattling steam engines and screaming factory whistles. The smog of a thousand busy chimneys swirled around the hansom cab carrying Lindsey from the train station to his new mill. It would take more than a good brushing to clean the grime of Manchester from Lindsey's blue frock coat, but that was his valet's problem; rather than concern himself with it, he sat back in idle contentment to watch the industrious world go by.

When the cab pulled into the cobblestone courtyard of Rook Mill, Lindsey found himself disappointed. Clarence Rook, the dear old schoolmate who'd given up the mill, was a man of elegance, with a subtle-yet-stylish wardrobe and an impeccable eye for everything from silk waistcoats to horses. The mill's architecture reflected none of Clarence's good taste. Of course, Clarence hadn't built it—his paternal grandfather had designed and commissioned the mill complex, and it seemed the old man's vision had been red brick, as both construction material and inspiration for the shape of the mill complex as a whole, and its individual buildings. Straight lines and right angles dominated the mill, broken up by chimneys spewing dark plumes into the low-hanging smog. A massive clock tower rose up beyond the roof of the largest and most central of the buildings, likewise plain. Lindsey, who'd hoped for something more in the neo-Gothic line, withheld a sigh. Modern architecture might be good for business, he thought, but it did nothing for his soul.

The hansom stopped in front of the largest building. Lindsey stepped down into the courtyard and encountered a bizarre phenomenon. The cobblestones vibrated. He took an experimental step forward. The vibration continued. Lindsey suspected it might bear some relation to the faint roar coming from behind the tall, black, rectangular double-doors of the mill. He looked up at these doors just as the one on the left opened, allowing more of the roar to escape. A voice projected over the rumbling.

"Mr Althorp?"

Lindsey stepped closer. Two men stood in the doorway. The one who'd spoken looked the same age as Lindsey's father, dressed in a gray suit which matched his grizzled muttonchops. His round bulk kept the second, smaller man in shadow.

"You have the advantage of me," said Lindsey, sweeping his top hat from his head.

"Mr Jennings, sir," the gray man said with a deferential nod. "Mill manager."

"A pleasure," said Lindsey, not entirely sincere. From architecture to staff, this adventure was proving underwhelming. If Mr Jennings noticed, he disguised it well.

"My assistant clerk," Mr Jennings said, moving aside to let the other man into Lindsey's line of vision, "Mr Warren."

Lindsey stared.

Mr Warren, appearing scarcely older than Lindsey himself, stood a good head shorter. His heart-shaped face held a small, sharp nose, Cupid's-bow lips, and a spellbinding pair of large, dark, half-lidded eyes. He wore a black wool suit, which offset the china white of his skin as much as it matched the ebony gleam of his hair, combed back to reveal a high, intelligent forehead.

"Sir," said Mr Warren in a tone as mechanical as their surroundings. He gave Lindsey a clockwork-sharp nod.

Lindsey hardly heard him, though his hind-brain noted the gesture and may have responded in kind. Alternatively, he might have continued staring at Mr Warren with parted lips and furrowed brow. He couldn't say for certain.

"Mr Althorp?" said Mr Jennings.

"Yes," Lindsey replied, a half-second before he redirected his gaze away from Mr Warren.

"If I may," said Mr Jennings, standing back with an invitational gesture. Mr Warren mirrored him in silence. Lindsey stepped up into the mill, and the tour began.

From outside, the ground had vibrated. Inside, the floorboards quaked with tenfold violence. The muffled roar multiplied into the endless, thundering bellow of Leviathan rumbling through the deep. It deafened Lindsey. He hoped the effect was temporary.

The mill interior loomed larger than any ballroom he'd ever danced in. Clattering machines filled it from wall to wall. Lindsey couldn't tell where one ended and another began. To his eyes, it seemed an ouroboros of cotton and steel. Levers and wheels zipped back and forth, and a thousand criss-crossed threads trembled in the air. Every motion in the mill produced a fresh burst of lint. This lint floated through the room like a flurry of snowflakes. Lindsey inhaled a speck of it, quite by accident, and coughed. He couldn't hear his cough, could barely feel it reverberate through his own ribcage over the clamour of the room.

Dozens of women and girls tended the mechanical labyrinth, reaching in with narrow arms and small hands to adjust this or that, then retreating fractions of a second before steel came crashing down where their limbs had been. These constant brushes with disfigurement or worse didn't seem to alarm them. Lindsey turned to Mr Jennings to remark upon this, but found him already in the midst of speech, crisply gesticulating at various points of interest throughout the room. For all Lindsey could hear him, he may as well have merely mouthed his words.

"Pardon?" Lindsey half-shouted. Then, realising half-measures would get him nowhere, he repeated his inquiry at a bellow. Neither attracted Mr Jennings's attention.

Before Lindsey lowered himself to tapping Mr Jennings's shoulder like an impertinent schoolboy, Mr Warren's pale fingers reached out and performed the service for him. Mr Jennings gave a start and followed Mr Warren's nod to Lindsey.

Mr Jennings said a word. Given the context and the shape his mouth formed, Lindsey determined it to be: "Sir?"

Lindsey repeated his question. To his amazement, Mr Jennings heard him, and rattled off an answer. Lindsey couldn't hear a word. Still, he nodded as though he understood.

Mr Jennings started down an aisle of the labyrinth. Lindsey looked to Mr Warren for a cue, and for the simple pleasure of looking at Mr Warren. Mr Warren remained stone-faced—no, marble-faced, Lindsey decided, like

15

Michelangelo's David—as he waved Lindsey onward. Lindsey followed Mr Jennings. Mr Warren took up the rear, much to Lindsey's consternation.

Mr Jennings attempted to draw Lindsey's attention to various points of interest, shouting over the constant rattle. Lindsey caught none of it. He considered turning to Mr Warren again, under the pretense of asking for clarification, but then Mr Jennings wanted to show him the winding threads, and the rolling wheels, and a hundred other dreary things that weren't Mr Warren's face. Mr Warren remained behind them, or so Lindsey assumed. He dearly wished to turn around and confirm it, but Mr Jennings pointed to the rotating shafts and belts suspended from the ceiling, forcing Lindsey to tilt his head up and behold them.

Like Orpheus and Eurydice, Lindsey thought, his eyes still fixed on the ceiling. Forbidden from gazing upon Mr Warren, he could only trust Mr Warren yet followed him. He wondered if Mr Warren would find the parallels as amusing as he did. Likely Mr Jennings would not; he didn't seem the poetic sort. But Mr Warren was undoubtedly poetic. Surely a marvellous literary mind philosophized underneath his ivory brow. Multitudes of mythological references must teem behind those shadowed eyes. And his mysterious silence—why, he was clearly deep in thought, as far beyond the earthly realm of the mill as Lindsey himself.

This state of affairs continued up all four floors of the mill, down the steel spiral staircase, and out the same doors they had entered hours earlier. Lindsey's whole skull rang in the absence of the industrial roar. He turned back to the mill and, much to his relief, found Mr Warren standing there, with Mr Jennings beside him.

"Have you any further inquiries, sir?" said Mr Jennings.

At last, an opportunity to break Mr Warren's silence. Lindsey would have delighted to hear, in the relative quiet of the yard, the sound of whatever voice might issue from Mr Warren's beautiful bow-shaped lips.

"How many persons does the mill employ?" asked Lindsey, his attention fixed on Mr Warren's perfect, yet immobile face.

But Mr Warren's shadowed eyes flicked away to meet Mr Jennings, and it was the latter who replied, "One hundred and sixty-six at present, sir."

Lindsey made a second attempt. "And when was the factory complex built?"

"1844, sir." Mr Jennings again.

Lindsey racked his brains for a question which Mr Warren could answer but Mr Jennings could not. At length, his mind produced a suitably subtle solution. He withheld a triumphant grin, and asked, "How long have you been employed here, Mr Jennings?"

"Some six-and-twenty years, sir."

Lindsey hummed thoughtfully, then offered up the piece de resistance of his cunning plan. "And you, Mr Warren?"

Mr Warren's dark eyes widened. He looked to Mr Jennings, who raised his eyebrows. Mr Warren's expression flattened again. He turned back to Lindsey.

"Eight years, sir," he said.

Lindsey ruminated on this new information. He supposed the earliest a lad could start clerking in a textile mill would be fifteen. Add eight to that, and Mr Warren was at least twenty-three, to Lindsey's twenty-one. What he might do with this information, Lindsey couldn't say, but it was more of Mr Warren than he'd known five minutes ago, so he cherished it.

"Was there anything else you wanted, sir?" said Mr Jennings.

An excellent question. From Mr Jennings, nothing. From Mr Warren, everything. However, the two men had one thing in common.

"May I see your offices?" asked Lindsey.

After a good three second's pause, Mr Jennings replied, "The offices, sir?"

"Yes," said Lindsey. "I presume you and Mr Warren clerk in an office?"

"Of course, sir," said Mr Jennings. "Warren?"

Mr Warren nodded briskly and dashed off—the precise opposite of the outcome Lindsey had hoped for.

"If you'll follow me, sir," said Mr Jennings.

Lindsey did his best to disguise his crushing disappointment.

∽

THE NEW OWNER was insane.

This was the conclusion Aubrey drew as he sprinted across the yard. Mr Jennings, ambling along on his twiggy legs, would slow Mr Althorp down, but even so, Aubrey estimated he had mere minutes to get the mill office in order. He threw the door open and faced his first obstacle: Smith, still at his desk, still asleep.

Aubrey stopped in the doorway. The sound of the door alone ought to have woken him, and yet here they were.

"Smith," said Aubrey.

Smith snored. Aubrey didn't have time for this.

"Smith," he said again, louder.

Smith smacked his lips.

Aubrey dared not shout. Mr Althorp might arrive any moment now, and it wouldn't do for him to overhear Aubrey berating his fellow clerk. He considered chucking the apparently-comatose Smith out the window, but that was mere fancy. Smith's broad shoulders would never fit through the window frame. Besides, Aubrey didn't think he could lift him.

Smith mumbled something in his sleep.

Aubrey looked over the office for a solution and came across a crumpled paper ball by Smith's wastebasket. Having missed the bin, it flew a truer course to Smith's forehead.

Smith started awake. "What!?"

"Mr Althorp is here," said Aubrey.

"Already?" Smith rubbed his face and looked to the clock over the door.

"Yes," said Aubrey. "He wishes to see the office. Mr Jennings is leading him here as we speak."

"Oh, splendid," said Smith mildly.

Aubrey didn't reply, being far too busy emptying wastepaper bins into the corner stove, where yesterday's coals still smoldered. The papers flared up. An ember landed on Aubrey's thigh. He hurried to pat it out and brush it away, muttering oaths under his breath. A cursory examination showed minimal damage to his trousers; the ember hadn't stayed long enough to burn, and the black wool helped disguise charcoal smears. Still, Aubrey would know the blemish existed, and the knowledge had already begun driving him mad. Smith wasn't helping.

"So," said Smith, who remained seated at his desk, though he had finally put his heels back on the floor where they belonged. "What's Althorp like, then?"

Based on first impressions, Aubrey had determined several facts regarding Mr Althorp. First, he was young, much younger than Aubrey had expected—though according to rumour, the previous owner, Mr Rook, was of a like age. Mr Althorp was also aristocratic, judging by his crisp public-school accent and the long, aquiline features that seemed to come standard with a peerage. Such a lineage might explain his peculiar mannerisms; the staring, the selective hearing loss, the general air of sleepwalking.

"Warren!" said Smith. "Are you deaf?"

"Tall," said Aubrey.

"What?"

18

"He's quite tall," Aubrey elaborated. In fact, he thought Mr Althorp bore strong resemblance to a lamp post. A tall, narrow pole topped with bright blond curls like a yellow gas flame.

"That's all you know?"

Aubrey opened his mouth to retort. A muffled voice outside the office cut him off. He rushed to the door. In that instant, the door swung inward. Aubrey scampered out of the way to admit Mr Jennings, who held the door open for Mr Althorp.

The look on Mr Althorp's face suggested he saw something very different from the dreary chamber Aubrey toiled in six-and-one-half days per week. Indeed, according to his awestruck expression, one might suppose he'd entered a great palace or cathedral of ancient times.

Smith had jumped up from his chair when the door opened and stood at the ready beside his desk. It took some time for Mr Althorp to notice him. It might never have happened at all if Mr Jennings hadn't intervened.

"My other assistant, Mr Smith."

"How do you do, sir," said Smith in the smooth tone of an actor reciting from memory. He played the part of a contented servant well, Aubrey thought, when he bothered with the effort.

Mr Althorp didn't respond, his attention focused on the lint- and soot-smeared window on the opposite wall. When he did turn in Smith's direction, rather than look Smith in the eye, his gaze dropped down to Smith's desk, then wandered over to Aubrey's far cleaner one.

"And who works where?" said Mr Althorp to no one in particular.

"I set up shop here, sir," said Smith. He rapped his knuckles against his stained blotter, then jerked his chin towards Aubrey's desk. "Warren sits there."

Mr Althorp's manner transformed from bored to bright in an instant. "Does he, indeed?"

Aubrey tensed.

Mr Althorp approached his desk, folded his hands behind his back, and bent forward at the waist to examine Aubrey's work. He stood in silence for a long, uncomfortable minute, then moved a bit to the left and cocked his head to one side, inspecting the desk from all angles as if it were an artifact of some long-deceased civilization which he couldn't touch for fear it would crumble to dust. Aubrey resisted the impulse to offer Mr Althorp a magnifying glass.

"And what do you do here, Mr Warren?"

19

Aubrey restrained his expression of surprise to a raised eyebrow, which he wrestled back into its original position posthaste. "I assist Mr Jennings in keeping records of our raw material input, finished material output, orders filled, the accounts to which we sell, the persons we employ, and the expenses incurred in maintaining the mill. Mr Smith does the same," he added hastily.

But Mr Althorp's attention remained fixed on Aubrey. "Could you furnish me with a copy of these records?"

It took Aubrey a half-second to swallow his shock.

Mr Jennings, ever the consummate professional, required no such pause to collect himself before he cut in. "All of them, sir?"

Mr Althorp pursed his lips. Aubrey, refusing to believe anyone could give serious consideration to such a request, held his breath.

"No," Mr Althorp said. "Just the last month's will do."

Smith made a choking noise. Aubrey shot him a disapproving glare. It went unnoticed.

"Of course, sir," said Mr Jennings. "Mr Warren will be delighted to copy them out for you."

Aubrey, who'd assumed the task would fall to him the moment Mr Althorp had suggested it, put on a polite smile for his benefit. He couldn't imagine it looked at all sincere. But true delight lit up Mr Althorp's face.

"Would you really?" he said, looking between Aubrey and Mr Jennings as if he couldn't believe his good fortune. To see his grin, one would think they'd offered him a stable full of fine racing horses, or whatever it was rich young toffs desired most. Aubrey didn't pretend to know. Regardless, Mr Althorp's visage glowed almost as bright as his hair as he declared, "Splendid!"

The corner of Mr Jennings's mouth twitched. Behind Mr Althorp's back, Smith covered his mouth as faint hiccups fought their way out of his throat. Fortunately, Mr Althorp continued to not pay him the slightest attention.

"They should be ready by the end of next week," Mr Jennings continued. "We'll have them delivered to your residence."

"No need for that," said Mr Althorp. "I'll just drop by again to retrieve them."

Mr Jennings betrayed his astonishment with a slow blink. "Very well, sir. Will that be all?"

Mr Althorp's smile dimmed a little. His eyes flicked over to Aubrey just long enough for Aubrey to realise how astonishingly blue they were, like pure indigo dye. Before Aubrey could recover his senses enough to smile, or bow, or do anything intelligent, Mr Althorp spoke.

"Of course," he said, as if in answer to Mr Jennings's question. Then he added, "Good day, Mr Warren."

Aubrey couldn't stop his eyebrows from shooting up to his hairline, but he managed to echo Mr Althorp's sentiment aloud nonetheless. Mr Althorp beamed at him. For a moment it seemed as though Smith would be forgotten again, but Mr Althorp turned and offered him the same words of parting. Smith responded with a bow deep enough for Aubrey to suspect mockery in the gesture. If Mr Althorp noticed, he took no offense.

Mr Jennings led Mr Althorp out to his waiting hansom cab. Smith showed restraint for once in all the years Aubrey had known him and waited until they were out of earshot before he spoke.

"What d'you think, then?" said Smith. "Daft, or just stupid?"

Aubrey feigned hearing loss as he returned to his desk and started copying out a month's worth of accounts. With his head full of numbers, it would be far easier to forget the sight of those blue eyes.

CHAPTER TWO

UPON HIS RETURN to the country house in Wiltshire, Lindsey exchanged his morning suit for evening attire, then retired to the library. Hundreds of books sat on mahogany shelves, matched by a mahogany reading table, with an entire south-facing wall of ceiling-high windows for illumination. In the far corner stood a Wardian case full of ferns, installed by Lindsey's mother, the late Lady Althorp, some twenty-five years earlier. At the moment of Lindsey's entrance, the library's only occupant, apart from the ferns, was his sister.

Rowena Althorp, almost as tall as her brother and just as blonde, could have passed for his twin. In fact she was three years his senior and had spent much of their childhood reminding him of it. Now, she sat half-curled in on a settee next to the hearth, her skirts hanging down off the edge, and her gaze cast down into a magazine.

"How was the factory?" she asked, not raising her eyes from her reading material. Nor did she raise herself from the settee. In Lindsey's lifelong experience with her, this constituted a warm reception.

"Marvellous!" Lindsey answered her.

"I'm glad to hear it," she said, looking up at last. "Though I wonder what marvels one might find in a cotton mill."

"Oh, hundreds, I'm sure."

Rowena gave him a slow blink, a habit Lindsey thought she'd acquired from a particularly uncanny kitten she'd had as a girl. He supposed he should elaborate.

"I found it a trifle difficult to hear the finer points of the tour over the sound of the machinery," he said. "Mr Warren will clear matters up later."

"And who is Mr Warren?" asked Rowena.

"A clerk," said Lindsey.

"I see," said Rowena, in a tone suggesting the opposite. She fixed him with a queer look. "Are you quite well, Lindsey?"

"Tolerably so, I think. Why?"

"You've been home for nearly an hour and you haven't asked after *The Strand*."

"Oh!" said Lindsey. "Yes. Right. Where is it?"

Rowena lifted her magazine to put its cover within Lindsey's line of sight.

"Ah," said Lindsey. "So it is."

"Do you want it?" she said, replacing it in her lap.

"Later, perhaps."

"Later? Isn't it what you came in for?"

"No, no," said Lindsey. "I'm here for the encyclopaedia. Got to read up on textile manufacture, engineering, that sort of thing."

"Engineering," Rowena echoed, her voice flat.

"Yes, precisely that. There's rather a lot for me to catch up on." He approached the shelves and began his search. "Now that I think of it, do we have any books on engineering specifically?"

"Are you suggesting there's a single book in this room with which you're not intimately familiar?"

"You exaggerate," said Lindsey. He drew his fingertips along the assorted leather bindings for the sheer pleasure of their texture. "I only gave the works of Dr Johnson the most cursory glance. I'm sure there are many other volumes I've not yet skimmed."

"If you say so," said Rowena, and resumed reading *The Strand*.

Lindsey found the E volume of the encyclopaedia easily enough. He encountered difficulty when he flipped to the entry on engineering. He knew enough maths to keep track of his own expenditures, but this business confounded him. Furthermore, nothing on the page resembled anything he'd seen at the mill. He frowned down at it. This didn't help. Yet he kept at it, long after Rowena had tossed *The Strand* aside and left to dress for dinner. He was still trying to decipher it when a footman came in to call him to the dining room.

Dinner in the country house was served *à la Française* at the unfashionable hour of six. Rowena was already seated when Lindsey arrived, as was his father.

Sir Geoffrey Althorp, a tall, thin man of some sixty years with a close-trimmed grey beard, sat at the head of the table. In times gone by, his thick white hair had been a match for Lindsey's in its golden hue. Overall, father and son bore a great resemblance, differing in only three areas: age, athleticism (though Sir Geoffrey had been a ripping sportsman in his youth, rheumatism made him no match for Lindsey's effortless energy), and temperament. Lindsey owed his sentimental nature to his dearly departed mother. Likewise, Rowena's indifferent sarcasm derived from their father.

"Busy day at the mill?" said Sir Geoffrey after he carved the roast and dispensed it to his offspring. "Didn't work you too hard, I trust? Learn anything?"

"Indeed, sir," said Lindsey. "Thought not so much as I'd hoped."

Sir Geoffrey gave a sardonic smile. "You'll simply have to go back again tomorrow."

"I intend to," said Lindsey.

Sir Geoffrey paused, his fork halfway to his mouth. He lowered it and fixed Lindsey with a look of icy inquiry.

Lindsey hurried to explain himself. "That is to say, not tomorrow, but soon. I'm waiting on word from Mr Warren."

"Who?" said Sir Geoffrey.

Rowena piped up in her sweetest, most-helpful, least-natural tone. "The clerk."

"And why," said Sir Geoffrey, "is my son waiting on the word of a manufacturing clerk?"

"Because," said Lindsey, "he will be providing me with last month's records. Shipping and receiving and the like. Thought it would be best to keep an eye on things from the outset. Wouldn't want to do anything rash."

"I see," said Sir Geoffrey in the same unconvinced tone Rowena had used in the library.

"I do hope you hear from him before Saturday next," Rowena broke in. She held her chin high, but kept her eyes cast down on her plate as she cut a ladylike bite of roast. "It would be a terrible shame if you had to run out on your friends in the middle of shooting."

The shooting she spoke of was to be an informal affair between Lindsey and a few old schoolmates—Miller, Graves, and Clarence Rook. Lindsey didn't think it would be too difficult to reschedule, should the need arise.

"I'm sure," said Sir Geoffrey, "Lindsey wouldn't miss a minute of shooting for the world."

Lindsey finished his dinner in quiet complacency.

⌒

AUBREY STARTED COPYING out last month's records as soon as Mr Althorp left the office. He was a quarter of the way through them by six o'clock, when Smith stretched and yawned (for the seventh time that day) and announced his intention to go home. An hour and a half after Smith's departure, Mr Jennings emerged from his office, ready to retire for the evening, and insisted Aubrey do the same. Aubrey hated to leave a task unfinished, but Mr Jennings stood firm.

Mr Jennings went home by omnibus. Aubrey preferred to walk, though he lived in a more distant neighbourhood. He rented the garret of a ramshackle house, where he shared the ground floor water closet with five other lodgers. All were bachelors. Three were clerks. Mr Brown on the first floor was an evangelical tract writer with a habit of slipping said tracts under the doors of his fellow lodgers. Mr Halloway, in the rooms just below Aubrey's garret, was a painter. He'd invited Aubrey to model for him on the day he'd moved in, offering a modest sum for his trouble. Unfortunately for Mr Halloway, Aubrey was determined to lead a respectable life. Respectable gentlemen didn't allow their likenesses to be preserved in the nude, no matter how noble the scene or how handsome the preserver. Furthermore, the paint fumes required Mr Halloway to keep his windows open at all times for ventilation, and the prospect of standing naked in a cold draught for hours on end didn't appeal to Aubrey.

On a typical evening, Aubrey arrived home long after Mr Jennings had finished dinner. But it hadn't been a typical day, and Aubrey supposed himself a fool for expecting a typical evening to follow. He had made it out of the mill complex without incident when a figure in a flat cap, muslin dress, and standard-issue factory smock waylaid him.

"Mr Warren," said Miss Brewster, a young woman with a skeptical twist to her lips. She had one hand on her hip, the other on the brick wall beside her to block Aubrey's path.

"Miss Brewster," said Aubrey, touching the brim of his hat.

She removed her hand from the wall and crossed her arms. "I notice you've not brought word of a meeting between myself and Mr Rook."

"My apologies," Aubrey began.

It had evidently been a bad day at the mill, for Miss Brewster didn't allow him to continue. "Your apologies. That and twopence will give me a cup of the swill they call tea 'round here. I'm not interested in apologies, Mr Warren, I'm interested in action."

"I'm aware—"

"Are you? Because I'm getting an impression otherwise. Perhaps you've forgotten our demands—equal pay for equal work. There'd be far fewer babes with starving bellies if their mothers could earn as well as their fathers."

"Miss Brewster!" Aubrey interrupted as she paused for breath. "I am entirely sympathetic to your concerns."

"Then why haven't you let me bring them to Mr Rook directly?"

"Because he would have you arrested."

Miss Brewster fixed Aubrey with an incredulous squint. "If I were afraid of arrest, I'd hardly have begun this line of inquiry in the first place."

Aubrey would have pointed out how, with her imprisoned, there would no one to speak for the female workforce, but there were more pertinent matters at hand. "A meeting with Mr Rook would do you no good now. He no longer owns the mill."

"Who does?"

"Mr Althorp."

"Get me a meeting with him, then."

Aubrey stared at her. "I'm afraid you overestimate my influence."

"With all due respect, I overestimate no such thing. As the new owner, Mr Althorp will confer with Mr Jennings, and Mr Jennings already bends his ear to you."

Aubrey's throat went dry. His mind worked double to talk himself out of his panic. Just because Miss Brewster had noticed the peculiar bond between him and Mr Jennings, it didn't mean she knew the true nature of that bond, or how it came to pass. While observant and clever, she focused her energies on improving the lot of her fellow workers—not on collecting idle gossip. And just because she'd noticed something out of the ordinary, it didn't mean the truth looked so obvious to anyone else. Still, Aubrey resolved to be more careful in the future. He swallowed as surreptitiously as possible. "And now, I bend my ear to you?"

"Precisely," said Miss Brewster. "One meeting's all I ask. Name a date and time."

Aubrey felt too exhausted to remember the current date and time, much less the projected future schedule of a man he'd met not twelve hours ago. But he'd brushed off too many off Miss Brewster's requests already. From the look she gave him now, he wouldn't leave the factory yard alive if he tried to run for it.

"A week," he said. "Let me talk to him first, get him warmed up to the notion. He's new at this."

Miss Brewster considered his terms in silence, then nodded and stuck out her hand. Aubrey shook it. She stepped aside to let him pass.

"I'll be holding you to your word, Mr Warren," she said as he walked by.

Aubrey touched the brim of his hat again and escaped while he could.

CHAPTER THREE

AUBREY FINISHED COPYING the records two days later, around nine o'clock in the morning, and sent a telegram to Mr Althorp announcing the completion of his task. Rather than send a return telegram, Mr Althorp himself arrived at the office at three the same afternoon.

"Sir!" was the best Aubrey could manage on such short notice. He gave silent thanks for Smith's failure to come to work that day, though Smith's empty desk made a glaring eyesore.

Mr Althorp didn't seem to notice. He directed his inquiring look at Aubrey alone.

"Mr Warren," he replied in a chipper tone. "May I come in?"

"Of course, sir," said Aubrey, and stood to greet him.

Mr Althorp smiled and stepped over the threshold. Aubrey had the copies—two folios' worth—ready on his desk before Mr Althorp reached it.

"Here you are, sir," said Aubrey, attempting to hand them over.

"Splendid," said Mr Althorp. He made no move to take the folios from Aubrey. "Could I ask another favour of you?"

After a moment of hesitation, Aubrey set the folios back down on his desk.

"Of course, sir," he said, careful not to let any bitterness seep into his words. He'd only stayed up half the night making copies Mr Althorp apparently no longer wanted.

"I'd like another tour of the factory," said Mr Althorp.

Aubrey limited himself to a single blink of confusion. "If you'll wait here, sir, I'll fetch Mr Jennings."

"Forgive me," said Mr Althorp, holding out a hand to stay Aubrey's progress towards the door. "I'm afraid I've been unclear. I'd like you to direct the tour, if at all possible."

Aubrey didn't raise his eyebrows at his new employer, no matter how much he wished to. "If you found Mr Jennings's tour insufficient, I fear mine wouldn't suit much better. His knowledge of the mill is unparalleled. A tour directed by myself would be far less informative."

"Perhaps," said Mr Althorp. "But in my experience, the more knowledgeable the speaker, the drier the speech. Thus, in the presence of 'unparalleled knowledge,' one finds one's attention wandering, and one learns very little."

Aubrey suspected Mr Althorp's attention would wander if a stray dust mote floated into his peripheral vision. "Correct me if I mistake your meaning, sir. You believe my ignorance will prove advantageous to your purpose?"

"Yes!" said Mr Althorp with a triumphant grin. It quickly faded. "I mean, that is to say—not ignorance, precisely—"

Aubrey withheld a grin of his own. Doing so was only moderately more difficult than trying to ignore how Mr Althorp stammered and blushed when flustered. The scarlet flush clashed with the gold of his hair and oughtn't have looked as becoming as it did.

Mr Althorp took no notice of Aubrey's struggle. "—merely an understanding of how one who is not already possessed of all the facts might approach new information, as it relates to manufacturing. To use the common phrase, you can put it into layman's terms."

Aubrey choked back a snort of disbelief at the thought of Mr Althorp considering himself a layman.

"Are you ill, Mr Warren?" said Mr Althorp.

His gentle tone, combined with the knitting of his brows would, in any other person, represent grave concern. In a man of Mr Althorp's position, such and emotion was impossible. Particularly towards a mere assistant clerk.

"Not at all, sir," said Aubrey. "If you were still interested in a tour...?"

"Yes!" said Mr Althorp with more enthusiasm than the situation warranted. "If you have the time for it?"

"You are full owner of the mill, sir," said Aubrey. "My time is your object."

"Still, I should hate to infringe upon your hospitality, or impede your work in any way."

And yet, here you remain, thought Aubrey, though the sentiment lacked its typical bite. If nothing else, touring the mill with Mr Althorp would be a refreshing respite from yet another afternoon spent toiling in darkness. The latter reasoning silenced the guilty little voice in the back of Aubrey's head that demanded maximum efficiency.

"No imposition at all, sir," said Aubrey. "If you'll just let me notify Mr Jennings of my absence, we may begin our tour directly."

"Delightful!" said Mr Althorp, and sounded as if he meant it.

☞

As LINDSEY FOLLOWED Mr Warren across the yard to the mill, it seemed as if he walked not upon the vibrating cobblestones but on a cloud of bliss. This cloud began to dissipate as they reached the mill, and vanished entirely when Mr Warren opened the doors and the deafening roar of industry returned in full force.

In his eagerness to secure a tour from Mr Warren, Lindsey forgot the reason Mr Jennings's tour proved insufficient. Now it was too late to deter Mr Warren from gesturing at various industrial processes and giving detailed verbal instruction—all of it drowned out by the cacophony around them.

Lindsey, regretting the lost opportunity to hear Mr Warren's voice, yet happy for the chance to gaze upon his face, nodded along regardless of what Mr Warren was saying. This strategy worked until a nod from Lindsey produced a queer look from Mr Warren. Mr Warren repeated himself, his bow-shaped lips moving with slow precision. Despite this, the factory's rumblings swallowed up his words. Lindsey, having already failed with a nod, tried shaking his head. Mr Warren's queer expression deepened into a full-on frown of confusion. A handsome frown, but a frown Lindsey was loath to have caused. The game was up.

"I can't hear you," said Lindsey, with no proof in his own ears of whether or not he'd made any sound at all.

Mr Warren's frown disappeared. He brought out a notebook and pencil from his jacket pocket, scribbled in it, then held up the result for Lindsey to read. In clear, precise script were the words:

Will this do?

Lindsey laughed. "Yes, quite!"

The corners of Mr Warren's mouth twitched. He wrote more, then handed the notebook over to Lindsey.

Carding room. Straightens cotton fibre and removes impurities.

Lindsey looked up to find Mr Warren pointing at a particular section of the apparently endless machine. Men fed great bundles of cotton into huge cylinders of wire teeth, which devoured it, tearing it to pieces and remolding it into a cleaner more orderly shape. The cotton tossed from one cylinder to the next, growing brighter and finer at each stage, then the whole mess fell onto a conveyor belt. Lindsey watched in quiet fascination until Mr Warren tapped him on the shoulder—a touch Lindsey savoured—and indicated they should move on.

They followed the carded cotton into the spinning room, where Mr Warren's notes told Lindsey of the *self-acting mule*. It hunched on the floor like an enormous steel spider. Two men tended it. As Lindsey watched, the front of the mule lurched forward. Wheels ran along a track in the floor, presenting a long bar at waist-height with a hundred bobbins stuck on in a row, trailing threads behind. With a clatter and whirr, the bobbins spun and grew thick with thread. Then, quick as they'd started, they stopped. The mule folded back in on itself and the men sprang into action. The first scooped up the full bobbins and carried them off in a hand-cart. The second swooped in after him to refill the rack with empty bobbins. With a decisive thunk, the machine jerked into motion again. Boys—younger than Lindsey had been when his father sent him to Eton—ran under the mule between revolutions, ducking clacking beams to fiddle with the suspended strings. According to Mr Warren's notes, the men were *mule-spinners*, and the boys were *piecers*, repairing broken threads.

The bobbins went next to the weave room. Lindsey and Mr Warren went with them. Here worked the dozens of young women Lindsey recalled from his initial tour. They continued to ignore him, intent on their task as Mr Warren explained it. His notes, full of *looms* and *warps* and *wefts* brought to life all the diagrams and illustrations Lindsey had studied the night before.

More importantly, Mr Warren's face came alive, too. Throughout their tour, a smile threatened to overtake his bow-shaped lips and his dark eyes shown bright as he expounded on the industrial processes. Lindsey found it most distracting, and as a result, failed to memorise some of the knowledge Mr Warren endeavoured to impart. It didn't trouble Lindsey overmuch; if worse came to worst, he'd simply request a third tour of the mill.

Mr Warren drew Lindsey's attention up to the rafters, where a thick leather belt wrapped around a spinning shaft, connecting it to the loom on the floor. Lindsey turned back to Mr Warren with a quizzical expression. Mr Warren scribbled in his notebook.

Power transferred from engine to shaft to belt to loom.

"And where is the engine?" shouted Lindsey.

Mr Warren motioned for Lindsey to follow him back to the stair.

∽

MR ALTHORP FOLLOWED Aubrey out of the mill like an amicable shadow. They circled the building to the engine house at the back. Aubrey introduced Mr Althorp to the two men on duty: Mr Cartwright, chief engineer, a heavyset fellow in his fifties with a gray broom-bristle mustache; and Mr Hepworth, second engineer, of a narrower build with thirty-odd years under his belt. Mr Althorp peppered them both with questions. Aubrey bit his tongue to keep from answering them in Mr Cartwright's place. They were more intelligent questions than Aubrey would've expected from a toff of Mr Althorp's calibre—along the lines of, "At what pressure does the boiler run?", rather than, "What is an engine?"—and Mr Cartwright responded with his customary dry, yet respectful, tone. Still, Mr Cartwright had a thankful nod to spare for Aubrey when Aubrey gently steered Mr Althorp away towards the mill yard.

They walked side-by-side, Aubrey taking a step and a half for every one of Mr Althorp's strides. Mr Althorp looked up at the rooftops of the mill complex. Aubrey looked at Mr Althorp. Weak sunlight filtered down through the clouds of Manchester. Each pathetic ray caught and bloomed brilliant in the blond waves escaping from under Mr Althorp's top hat. Aubrey felt some guilt—he wasn't paid to admire handsome gentlemen on the sly—but the sight captivated him nonetheless. If he were caught, he supposed he could pass off his behaviour as the natural awestruck gaze a posh twit would expect the lower classes to bestow upon the gentry.

"I've been reading up on textile manufacture," said Mr Althorp, startling Aubrey out of his reverie. "I've come across a curious item. I wonder—if it isn't too much trouble—could you tell me more about Jacquard looms?"

Aubrey stumbled to a halt.

"Jacquard looms?" he echoed, giving Mr Althorp a very unprofessional look of surprise.

"If it wouldn't be too much trouble," Mr Althorp reiterated.

Aubrey tried to stop gawking at him. "No trouble at all, sir. But I'm afraid the explanation is rather dull. I should hate to bore you."

Mr Althorp put on a grave expression, though his eyes continued to gleam with a suppressed smile. "I take full responsibility for my own potential boredom."

"Very well." Aubrey cleared his throat. "Jacquard loom is something of a misnomer. The actual mechanism is a head which one may attach to almost any dobby loom. It uses a system of punched cards to—please, stop me if I grow tedious."

"Not at all," said Mr Althorp. "This is fascinating."

From anyone else, Aubrey would have assumed the remark was sarcastic. But the look of rapt attention on Mr Althorp's face suggested otherwise. Aubrey couldn't decide which reaction was more unnerving. He swallowed his discomfort and spoke on.

"As I said, the punch card system enables the creation of much more complex patterns. Each card is fitted over the hooks of... One moment. We require a diagram."

He dug out his notebook and pencil, cast about for a flat surface, found the brick wall of the offices, and ran over to them. Only then did he realise how deranged he must appear to Mr Althorp's eyes.

Yet Mr Althorp didn't question his behaviour. He followed Aubrey to the wall and peered over his shoulder at the blank page. The faint heat radiating from Mr Althorp's chest, like a thrumming engine, washed over Aubrey's back as if his wool jacket were made of cobwebs. The warmth drove all thought of engineering from Aubrey's brain for several terrifying moments. He hadn't stood so close to another man—to another person— for more years than he cared to count. A weak and reprehensible part of him yearned to lean back. His rational mind reminded him he had a job to keep and a reputation to uphold. He forced himself to think upon the latter, found strength enough to steady his pencil, and began to draw.

It wasn't the best diagram Aubrey had ever produced. The texture of the bricks beneath his notebook gave his linework a bit of a wobble, and his pencil moved at speed to keep up with his words. Still, when he finished his explanation and looked back over his shoulder, Mr Althorp nodded in understanding.

"Fascinating!" he said again. "Might I keep that?"

Aubrey, caught in the midst of closing his notebook, paused. His left eyebrow shot up before he could stop it.

"The drawing, I mean," Mr Althorp added. "If it wouldn't be—"

"No trouble at all, sir," Aubrey finished for him. He tore out the page, careful to keep a straight edge to the paper. "If you'd like a more accurate diagram, an encyclopaedia might..."

As he held out the page to Mr Althorp, he trailed off, a thought having just occurred to him. An encyclopaedia would not only contain a more accurate diagram, but also a full and complete explanation of the Jacquard loom. In fact, Aubrey couldn't think of any source but an encyclopaedia from which Mr Althorp could have learned of the Jacquard loom's existence in the first place. Which made his desire for an explanation from Aubrey equal parts superfluous and unfathomable.

Mr Althorp took the drawing with a benign smile and folded it up to fit in his waistcoat pocket. "Thank you. You said something earlier about punched cards outside the textile industry?"

"Yes!" Aubrey replied with a bit too much vigor. "That is to say, Charles Babbage intended to integrate them into his analytical engine. He never managed it, of course, but just two years past, Herman Hollerith used punch cards to sort through census data..."

In Aubrey's experience, most people stopped listening by this point, if not long before. He knew he ought to keep his passions restrained, particularly when speaking to his employer. However, Mr Althorp gave no sign of impatience. On the contrary, his eyes widened as Aubrey detailed the latest advances in mathematics and the sciences.

"Extraordinary!" said Mr Althorp when Aubrey finished. "Most extraordinary indeed! Mr Warren, you're wasted as a clerk. You ought to be an engineer."

The cautious smile blooming on Aubrey's lips died at that remark. "I'm quite happy in my position, sir."

He meant to sound more grateful, but there it was. Any fool would be happy to be clerking rather than labouring, or starving, or on his knees before men of Mr Althorp's station. His frustrated aspirations didn't matter. Aubrey was lucky enough to have escaped the poverty of his youth. To expect more would be folly.

Mr Althorp frowned in confusion but said nothing beyond, "Of course."

Aubrey forced a smile in return.

CHAPTER FOUR

AUBREY.

The sight of Mr Warren's Christian name on the Rook Mill payroll sent a thrill through Lindsey's brain. Aubrey Warren. He wanted to say it aloud, to let it roll over his lips, to imagine how it might feel to address the clerk so. However, Lindsey sat in the country house library, where his father might come in at any moment, and so Lindsey didn't deem it prudent to take the risk.

Apart from Mr Aubrey Warren, the factory records puzzled Lindsey. Not as badly as the engineering, thank God, but they furrowed his brow nonetheless. From what little he understood of economics, it ought've run thus: profits decreased, wages decreased; profits increased, wages increased. However, while Rook Mill profits seemed on a steady rise, no corresponding increase had occurred in wages. Instead, wages had stagnated across the board, from overseers to sweepers, for the last five months. Then, in the week preceding Lindsey's acquisition of the mill, wages dropped, with the office staff—Mr Jennings, Mr Smith, and Mr Warren—taking the deepest plunge. Most confusing, particularly given what Lindsey had observed of Mr Warren's work ethic.

"Good heavens," said a dry voice from the doorway. "What a magnificent mess you've made."

Lindsey looked around at the factory records spread out across the library table, his lap, and the floor, then lifted his eyes to meet his sister's gaze as she approached. He opened his mouth to explain himself, but she cut him off.

"If I hear another word about Jacquard looms or self-acting mules," she declared, "I will scream. Isn't the whole enterprise supposed to be self-regulating? I don't recall Clarence ever giving it so much attention."

"Why should he?" said Lindsey. "It's all old hat to him."

"Whilst for you, it's a novelty."

"Not a novelty, Ro," Lindsey protested. "Merely... something new."

"You just defined the word novelty."

Lindsey bristled. "To call it a novelty would imply my interest is frivolous at best."

Rowena looked skeptical.

"Which it most certainly is not!" Lindsey added.

"Of course not," Rowena replied in her most patronising tone. "Still, I've never seen you so excited over anything outside the pages of a penny dreadful."

"Lies and slander," said Lindsey. "I'm a fair sportsman, for one."

"Then what on earth are you doing in here while your friends go out shooting?"

Lindsey blinked at her, turned to the towering grandfather clock, then pulled out his pocket-watch to confirm its grim tidings. "By Jove. That late already?"

"Clarence is waiting for you by the stables. Miller and Graves went ahead with Tanner. Will you be joining them before sunset or after?"

Lindsey ignored his sister's sardonic smirk as he hurried from the room.

True to her word, he found Clarence at the stables, leaning against a fence and craning his elegant neck to watch a groom put Sir Geoffrey's best hunter through her paces.

Clarence, yet another old Etonian, came from manufacturing stock. His grandfather had ascended from mill hand to mill owner, and his father from mill owner to multiple mill owner. Clarence would inherit the whole when he came of age in another year or so. In the meantime, he had the original Rook Mill to practice on—until he'd put it up as collateral in a casual game with Lindsey.

Despite his grandfather's origins, Clarence looked the gentleman. He was among the few men who could stand eye-to-eye with Lindsey, though Clarence had broader shoulders. Auburn waves of hair tumbled over his brow, and his grey eyes changed their tint from green to blue depending on the light. These features had proved most distracting for Lindsey at Eton. Clarence had turned this distraction into an advantage by tutoring Lindsey in mathematics, which Lindsey had been hopeless at before Clarence's interference. Beyond academics, they'd bonded over cricket, where they both excelled, and had become inseparable.

At university, Clarence had studied the Classics, as befit a man of the station to which his family had ascended. His father would have preferred he study mathematics, but the old fellow had passed on before the end of Clarence's first term. Clarence's uncle became his legal guardian, but failed to govern him. The best he could do was withhold the bulk of Clarence's inheritance until Clarence reached his majority, sticking to the letter, if not the spirit, of the entailment. Clarence made do with a small allowance and his winnings from games with friends.

Lindsey had often hoped Clarence might become his brother-in-law; *Rowena Rook* had a delightful ring to it, and it would be dashed convenient if his sister married his bosom friend. Clarence agreed, but Rowena did not, so Lindsey let the matter drop. Clarence had a sister of his own, two years their junior, and had hinted at a possible union between her and Lindsey. Lindsey laughed him off. Emmeline Rook was a pale slip of a child. Lindsey hadn't given much thought to what he wanted in a wife, but he felt certain Miss Rook didn't possess the desired qualities.

At present, whilst Clarence admired the mare, Lindsey admired Clarence. A minute or so passed before Clarence's chimerical eyes slid sideways to meet Lindsey's, and Lindsey realised his presence had not gone as unnoticed as he'd assumed.

Lindsey coughed. "Shall we be off, then?"

A wicked smile wound its way up Clarence's cheek. "Indeed."

He took up two guns propped against the side of the stable, handed one off to Lindsey, and led the way towards the woods. Throughout their journey, they remained silent. While they were the sort of friends who didn't need to fill the air with chatter, today's silence put Lindsey on edge. He and Clarence hadn't discussed the mill since Lindsey had won it. He wished to bring it up, to have Clarence's opinion of the place, its staff, and one particular clerk. At the same time, he remained wary of upsetting his dearest friend. He'd just made up his mind to broach the subject when the gamekeeper drew up to them.

Tanner, the gamekeeper, was rather young for his position—hardly older than Lindsey himself. Lindsey supposed Rowena had hired him for his handsome face and considerable height, which precisely matched the footmen. True to his station, Tanner greeted the gentlemen with a doff of his tweed cap and fell into line behind them, near enough to be of use if called upon. While Lindsey didn't think Rowena would ever hire the eavesdropping sort, Tanner's presence was enough to quell all desire to speak with Clarence on the delicate subject of the mill.

The last day of shooting before the London season had a maudlin air about it, despite nature's best efforts to insist spring had arrived and the world was born anew. The trees had budded and the grass had turned from brown to green, but an echo of frost hung in the air. Most of the fauna remained in hibernation. Rabbits, however, were always a plentiful nuisance.

Sir Geoffrey's favourite hound, Belle, stuck close to Lindsey's side. She'd grown a bit spoiled in her old age, but she remained capable of flushing game out from the underbrush and retrieving it once it had fallen. The rabbits she brought back for Lindsey were all shot clean through the neck. As the shooting drew to a close, Lindsey ended up walking along the edge of the wood with Roderick Miller.

If Lindsey were blessed with an elder brother, he would have wished for someone like Miller. Miller was two years Lindsey's senior, with a ruddy complexion, strawberry-blond mustache, and a hearty, if rare, smile. He stood almost as tall as Lindsey, and twice as broad. The bulk of him was muscle, though if he were anything like his father, it would all turn to fat by the time he saw forty. His father, grandfather, great-grandfather, etc., were bankers. The senior Miller was Sir Geoffrey's personal financial advisor. That was how Miller introduced himself to Lindsey at Eton, where he took him under his wing. Miller not only pulled Lindsey into his established circle of acquaintances, but insisted Lindsey step outside his books and try his hand at sport. As a result, Lindsey thrived at Eton well after Miller left for university. At Cambridge, Miller bucked the banking tradition by studying law. Fortunately, his father came to terms with it by the end of his university career.

"Miller," said Lindsey, adjusting his grip on the gun over his shoulder. "I should like your advice on a personal matter."

"And you'll have it," Miller assured him. "Just as soon as you tell me what it is."

Lindsey had rehearsed the problem over and over in his head since he'd left the library. Yet he found he couldn't say it out loud while looking Miller in the eye, so he dropped his gaze. Between them, the barrel of Miller's gun brushed the grass back and forth with every stride.

"I've made a new acquaintance," said Lindsey.

Miller firmed up his grip on his gun. "Oh?"

The forced casual tone didn't fool Lindsey. It confirmed his instincts to keep the details of his problem as vague as possible. It wasn't that he didn't trust Miller—after all, Miller had been his friend, his confidante, his mentor at Eton. But even Lindsey knew cultivating a friendship between a gentleman and a clerk was not the done thing. An upstanding fellow such as Miller would certainly disapprove.

"It's..." Lindsey coughed. "It's something of a delicate issue."

"Delicate issues are my speciality," said a voice behind them.

The voice belonged to Lord Cyril Graves, the third son of an unremarkable marquess. His brown locks hung down into his eyes, giving him a habit of tossing his head back to clear his vision. The first time Lindsey saw him do it at Eton, the gesture reminded him of a mighty and impatient stallion. To others, Graves was merely horse-faced. He'd sported a well-waxed handlebar mustache at university, but sacrificed it on the altar of the Aesthetes soon after. In his post-university career, he wrote infrequent, acerbic literary reviews.

On the present excursion, Graves hadn't shot a thing. He hadn't even aimed his gun, much less fired it, despite a Hellenic devotion to Artemis and the rest of the Olympian set. Lindsey suspected he'd come along only to pose in picturesque woodlands and pretend he was attending a Bacchanal.

Graves threw an arm across Lindsey's shoulders and demanded to know the issue. Lindsey hesitated to divulge the details—Graves tended to carry tales—but Miller had no such reluctance.

"Althorp," said Miller, "has made a new acquaintance." He punctuated his remark with a significant lift of his bushy brows.

Graves mirrored the expression. "Who?"

"No one you'd know," Lindsey demurred.

"Don't be coy," said Graves, tossing his head. "Let me guess—animal, vegetable, or mineral?"

Lindsey smiled in spite of himself. "A man, our age, though... not of our sort."

Graves widened his eyes and turned to Miller, who appeared to suffer the same surprise, though with less theatricality.

"He has rendered me a great service," Lindsey continued, ignoring Graves's immediate inquiry into just what service had been rendered. "I should like to reward him for it."

"A shilling or two should suffice," said Miller. "Ten, if the service were extraordinary."

"Too extraordinary for shillings," said Lindsey. The thought of courting Mr Warren's friendship with mere money repulsed him. "I want to further the acquaintance, not cap it off."

"A further acquaintance with a man of another sort who has performed extraordinary service," Graves murmured, a little too loud to be talking to himself. Lindsey pretended he couldn't hear him.

"A gift, then?" said Miller, raising his voice over Graves's ongoing speculation.

"Surely Althorp is gifted enough already." Clarence emerged from the woods with the gamekeeper in tow.

Graves explained Lindsey's predicament with more dramatic speculation than Lindsey had suggested.

"The solution is obvious," Graves concluded. He turned back to Lindsey. "Give him a book."

Lindsey shook his head. His friends stared at him.

"Are you feeling quite the thing, Althorp?" said Miller.

"Clearly not," Graves interrupted Lindsey's reassurances. "He's suffering from a brain fever if he thinks a book isn't the solution to this and every other problem."

Lindsey hurried to explain over Graves's elaboration on the brain-fever theory. "It's precisely because it's the obvious solution that I know it isn't the correct one. I don't wish to do the obvious."

Graves appeared unconvinced, but Clarence nodded sagely.

"It ought to be a small, practical item," said Clarence. "A knife?"

"Too pedestrian," Lindsey replied.

Graves barked out a laugh. "I'd like to meet the man you think is too good for a knife!"

"One assumes gloves are likewise pedestrian?" said Clarence, smiling along with Graves. "And cuff-links as well?"

"A handkerchief, unthinkable!" said Graves.

"A pack of playing cards, then," said Clarence. "Personalised, of course."

"Why stop at cards?" said Graves. "Why not a mill?"

Lindsey bolted upright, fearing he'd been far too transparent in his inquiries, but a glance between Clarence and Graves showed his fears were misplaced. Clarence looked down on Graves with cold, hard, unforgiving eyes. Graves shot him a furtive, mischievous look in return.

Miller cleared his throat and smoothed his mustache. "That's not cricket, Graves."

Graves opened his mouth to retort, but Clarence cut him off.

"That reminds me, Miller," Clarence said in an arch tone. "How many rabbits did you bag?"

Miller gave his number. Clarence claimed a higher one and received a guinea from Miller after the gamekeeper confirmed it.

Lindsey hardly noted the transaction. His mind churned with his friends' suggestions. Books, knives, gloves, cuff-links, handkerchiefs—none seemed suitable. Yet there was something to Clarence's aside about cards. Something personal might do. In fact, Lindsey resolved nothing else would suit.

When Lindsey arrived at the mill the next morning, he found Mr Warren alone in the office, the other clerk being gone for reasons Lindsey didn't bother asking after. He gave Mr Warren an enthusiastic greeting and would have given him more besides, but the moment he let slip any hint of a question regarding the factory records, Mr Warren jumped up to fetch Mr Jennings. Lindsey swallowed his disappointment and put on a smile as Mr Warren ushered him into the manager's office.

Mr Jennings's office was small but not cramped. Fastidious, meticulous organisation prevented claustrophobia. File cabinets flanked his desk and bookshelves stood behind it, turning his seat into a fortress of industry. The matching chair in front of the desk stayed at an angle to facilitate entry into the room. Lindsey took this seat as Mr Jennings closed the door.

"Now, Mr Althorp," said Mr Jennings as he returned to his desk. "What may I do for you?"

Lindsey brought out the folio and explained his concerns. As he spoke, Mr Jennings's fingers clenched and unclenched, tapped their tips together, and finally lay flat upon the desk to give full support to their owner.

"Can you shed any light upon these discrepancies?" Lindsey asked. "I'm certain I'm missing something—new to the business and all that."

Mr Jennings's right forefinger tapped once more, then fell still. "No, sir, I'm afraid you haven't missed a trick."

Lindsey frowned, confused. "Beg pardon?"

"Cant expression, forgive me." Mr Jennings cleared his throat. "As to the discrepancies... The previous owner required maximum yield from the mill—that is to say, it had to run as profitably as possible at minimum cost."

Lindsey frowned harder. Clarence Rook was among the kindest men he knew. Surely it wasn't Clarence's idea to strangle his employees to line his own pockets. His late father and his uncle had advised him on the business. Clarence was a Classics man; commerce might be in his blood, but his

40

brain turned towards higher pursuits. No, Lindsey felt certain Clarence wasn't to blame for this mess.

"I was forced," Mr Jennings went on, "to cut corners wherever I could. When the workers' wages could be slashed no further—there's a point where even the Irish won't bother coming in—I had to find another solution. The workers are paid by the hour. But the office staff are salaried. Which is to say, the same sum per annum regardless of what hours we keep. So I discharged the under-clerks and office-boys and made do with Mr Smith and Mr Warren. They've risen to the occasion admirably. Then when Mr Rook demanded—forgive me, asked—that we cut costs even further, I chose to cut the office staff's pay rather than risk a riot from the mill hands."

Lindsey raised his eyebrows. "They've threatened to riot?"

"They've attempted to unionise," said Mr Jennings. "Nothing you need worry about, sir."

All Lindsey knew of unions came from an aborted attempt to read *Mary Barton* at Rowena's behest. (In her own words, "Lady Pelham has foisted it upon me, and I refuse to suffer alone.") He didn't get past the first few chapters of children starving to death. He preferred more fantastical fiction. However, if the reality were as gloomy as *Mary Barton* claimed, he couldn't condemn the Rook Mill hands for their dissatisfaction.

But none of his reasoning was any concern of Mr Jennings. To him, Lindsey said, "You didn't approve of how Mr Rook directed you to run the mill?"

"No, sir, I did not," said Mr Jennings. "But I'm a company man, and I do as I'm bid."

"How would you run it if you had your way?"

Mr Jennings's eyes blinked wider. "Well, sir, to start, I suppose I'd raise wages to reflect the mill's profits, as you said."

"Including your own salary?"

Mr Jennings looked abashed. "Including all the office staff, yes."

Lindsey sat back and considered. "What would it cost to do things your way?"

Mr Jennings named a sum. Lindsey thought it acceptable and said as much.

"Sir?" said Mr Jennings, as if there were any confusion about the matter.

Lindsey had already picked up his hat and stood to leave. He turned back, one hand on the door handle.

"Make it so, Mr Jennings," he said, and opened it.

41

AUBREY HAD JUST shooed Mr Althorp into Mr Jennings's office when another knock sounded. Aubrey went to answer it. Mr Althorp was already here, and Smith never knocked, so Aubrey assumed it must be one of the floor overseers coming to report.

He opened the door. On the other side stood Miss Brewster. Aubrey wished he'd left it shut, but it was too late now.

"Good morning, Mr Warren," she said, stepping over the threshold. She brushed past him and strode to the centre of the office, looking the whole of it up and down as if she were an empress come to survey her empire.

"Miss Brewster." Aubrey closed the door behind her. "I'm afraid this isn't a good time."

"Have to disagree with you there," she said, peering over Smith's desk to inspect his empty chair. "Now is the only time. Where's Mr Althorp?"

Aubrey hesitated, to his peril. Miss Brewster barreled on.

"Don't try to palm me off with an excuse. I know he's here. I saw him come in not ten minutes past."

She focused her keen gaze on Mr Jennings's closed door and stepped towards it. Aubrey half-ran to block her path.

"Mr Althorp is meeting with Mr Jennings," he said.

The left side of Miss Brewster's mouth quirked up, the closest to a smile Aubrey had ever seen on her face. "Figured that much out for m'self, thanks."

Aubrey withheld an exasperated sigh. "If you return to your station, I'd be happy to fetch you once they've finished."

"And give him a chance to escape? No, thank you." She leaned against the edge of Smith's desk. "I'll just wait here till he's done."

Aubrey swallowed. "Miss Brewster, please—"

"Too distracting for you, having a woman in the office? Just keep your hands and eyes to yourself, Mr Warren, and I'll be quiet as a churchmouse."

Aubrey refrained from rolling his eyes. If there was one thing she needn't fear from him... Though he could hardly admit as much aloud. And true to her word, she kept remarkably still after she crossed her arms and turned her head towards Mr Jennings's door, with her chin up and eyes unblinking. But regardless of her behaviour now, he had to consider the inevitable explosion of her impending contact with Mr Althorp.

42

The crux of Aubrey's dilemma was this: she wasn't wrong. Rook Mill's wages were the lowest in the city. Its machinery was out-of-date, much of it in need of repair if not outright replacement. A deadly accident was only a matter of time. Miss Brewster and her working girls had threatened to walk out three times in the last year. Mr Jennings placated them with breaks, leniency, and the implied threat of a dozen other women happy to step in and take their places. Mr Rook, with his insatiable craving for profit, cared not for the literal hunger of his workforce.

Mr Althorp, on the other hand...

Aubrey tried to derail that train of thought, but it had already left the station and was well underway to its terminus. Compared to his predecessor, Mr Althorp showed far more interest in managing the mill. Given the chance, it was entirely possible Miss Brewster could win him over with her arguments. Throwing Mr Althorp into her path would mean the sacrifice of any good impression Aubrey had made on him thus far, but Aubrey couldn't justify never taking the chance. His pathetic desire for the attentions of a handsome gentleman meant nothing in the face of true progress.

Aubrey returned to his ledgers and did his best to pretend Miss Brewster wasn't there. His resolve didn't have to hold for long.

"Make it so," declared Mr Althorp as the door swung open and he returned to the main office. Miss Brewster leapt in front of him.

"Mr Althorp," she said, thrusting out her hand before Aubrey could do more than stand up and lurch impotently towards her. "Miss Brewster, weaver."

Mr Althorp appeared stunned as he took her hand. Mr Jennings emerged from his office in time to witness the transaction, but too late to prevent it.

"How do you—" Mr Althorp began.

"Quite well, thanks," Miss Brewster replied. "Mr Althorp, are you aware of the earning disparity between male and female mill hands?"

Mr Althorp blinked at her. Behind his back, Mr Jennings shot a horrified look from her to Aubrey. Aubrey wanted nothing more than to drop his forehead into his palms. He settled for a small shake of his head.

"I'm afraid not," said Mr Althorp.

"Then allow me to enlighten you. All the mule-spinners in Rook Mill are men. As are the overseers. And the foremen. And the clerks. Every job with an inkling of a living wage belongs to a man. And before you tell me they must have earned that place—" she said as Mr Althorp opened his mouth to speak, "—let me finish. Mule-spinning, for example. One of the highest positions a man can attain, and only a man may attain it. What reason is given for this? Why, the weaker sex haven't the strength required to run the machine. This is nonsense. The self-acting mule is called such for an excellent reason: it is self-acting. All the heavy lifting, all physically taxing mechanical motions, are done by the mule. The spinner need only tend it. Therefore, any man or woman of average strength should find no difficulty. And yet, all mule-spinners are men. Does this not seem strange to you, Mr Althorp?"

Mr Althorp, after it became apparent her question wasn't rhetorical, spoke. "Miss Brewster, would it be possible for you to put your concerns in writing? I'd like to go over them in detail with Mr Jennings."

"I'd be happy to," she said, "if I thought it wouldn't be a wasted effort on my part. They've told us time and time again, sir, to wait patiently for all the big important men in the world to notice our problems and, eventually, solve them. I've had enough of waiting. I'd like your answer now."

"Yes," said Mr Althorp.

Three sets of eyes gawked at him. In the absence of a verbal response, he elaborated.

"Your foremost complaint is against low wages, correct?" He gestured to Mr Jennings over his shoulder. "Mr Jennings and I have agreed to raise them to a level better reflecting the mill's prosperity. It should take effect...?"

"At the end of the week, sir," Mr Jennings finished.

Mr Althorp nodded and returned to Miss Brewster. "By the end of this week, on my word as a gentleman. Which I hope you'll come to trust."

Miss Brewster continued to regard him with suspicion. Aubrey couldn't entirely blame her.

"In the meantime," said Mr Althorp, "your writings would be most helpful in moving forward with the mill. May I have that by the end of the week as well?"

Miss Brewster stared him down a few seconds more. His hopeful smile never faded.

"You may," she said at last, uncrossing her arms and holding out her hand for him to shake. Mr Althorp did so, still smiling.

"A pleasure meeting you, Miss Brewster. If you'll excuse me, I've some business to conduct with Mr Warren."

Aubrey jerked upright.

Miss Brewster gave a short curtsy and showed herself out. Mr Jennings bowed to Mr Althorp and returned to his office.

And so Aubrey and Mr Althorp were left alone. The reason for it remained beyond Aubrey's understanding. Mr Althorp, far from forthcoming, let an awkward silence settle between them. After half a minute, Aubrey could stand it no longer.

"What may I do for you, sir?"

Splotches of red appeared on Mr Althorp's high cheekbones. Aubrey gave serious consideration to inquiring after his health. Before he could, Mr Althorp blurted out a question of his own.

"Would you care to take a turn about the mill yard with me, Mr Warren?"

The words poured out all at once, the torrent sweeping over Aubrey and leaving him stunned. It took a moment for him to collect himself enough to reply. "Of course, sir."

Mr Althorp's tight smile relaxed in unmistakable relief. He remained silent as they left the office, though several times he bit his lip, and twice he opened his mouth as if about to speak, but caught himself, clearing his throat and adjusting his cravat. On one occasion he raised his hand to cover his mouth, rubbing his palm over the lower half of his face and on down his neck. Aubrey found his eyes following the hand's progress as it stroked that slender throat. He hurriedly looked away.

They walked on in silence, past the boiler shed behind the mill, and back around to the offices. Aubrey stopped beside the door.

"Was there anything else you wanted, sir?" he asked.

"Yes," said Mr Althorp, much to Aubrey's surprise. "I, er, have something for you."

"Oh?" said Aubrey, his bewilderment barring a more articulate response.

Mr Althorp, preoccupied with retrieving something from the inner pocket of his jacket, took a moment to respond. "A small token of my appreciation for your diligence."

Aubrey stared at the object Mr Althorp held out to him: a narrow rectangular receptacle with a hinged lid at one end, made of silver and embossed with intricate curlicues around the edges. These ornamental curls framed the central engraving of *WARREN* in elegant script. Aubrey didn't need to see it opened to know it was empty. The box itself was the gift, and an extravagant one. Impossible as it seemed, he couldn't deny the reality before him—Mr Althorp was attempting to present him with a calling card case.

What possible use Mr Althorp thought a clerk who scraped by on ten shillings a week could possibly have for such a thing, Aubrey couldn't fathom. And yet, there it lay in Mr Althorp's outstretched palm.

It occurred to Aubrey he should probably respond to this.

"I couldn't—" he stammered out. The expression of anguished disappointment on Mr Althorp's face silenced him.

"Oh, but you must!" Mr Althorp implored. "I insist!"

Aubrey hesitated. He could hardly hope to refuse his employer's insistence and retain his position. Besides, as useless as the trinket was, the thought behind the gesture seemed sincere.

"Thank you, sir," he said. A second or two afterward, he remembered to take the calling card case from Mr Althorp's hand. The metal felt warm in his fingers. He slipped it into his waistcoat pocket.

Mr Althorp nodded smartly, satisfied. "You're quite welcome, Aubrey. That is, if I may call you Aubrey?"

Aubrey gave a start at the first utterance of his Christian name. In Mr Althorp's aristocratic accent, it carried echoes of Aubrey's fantasies. But a twinge of bitterness followed. Of course Mr Althorp might presume to call him Aubrey. It was Mr Althorp's right as his employer and social superior. He could call him anything he liked—clerk, boy, you there, and a half-dozen ruder terms—and Aubrey would be obliged to answer.

By the second time Mr Althorp said his name, Aubrey had recovered his composure enough to respond with minimal venom. "As it suits you, sir."

"Lindsey," said Mr Althorp.

Aubrey allowed himself a confused frown. "Beg pardon, sir?"

"You must call me Lindsey. That is, if I'm to call you Aubrey. It's only fair."

It took a concentrated effort on Aubrey's part to keep his jaw from dropping open. Words failed him. He could only stare.

Mr Althorp, meanwhile, seemed blissfully unaware he'd said anything out of the ordinary. He maintained his placid smile as Aubrey stared in silence, his mind chugging along like an overworked engine to try and to understand what the deuce was happening. His heart beat faster, his pulse reverberating through the calling card case in his pocket.

"Very well," said Aubrey. Then he added, "Lindsey."

Lindsey's smile broadened into a grin.

CHAPTER FIVE

To LINDSEY, THE trip from Manchester to London felt as if the train were floating rather than rumbling over the steel track. He smiled to himself in the hansom cab between the station and the townhouse, the sound of his name on Aubrey's lips ringing in his mind. His cheerful mood continued all afternoon and evening, on through the night, and remained with him the following dawn. He greeted his valet, Charles, with unwarranted enthusiasm when the latter brought his morning tea and biscuit, and grinned at all the staff he passed in the townhouse's halls. He laughed louder than ever at Clarence's jokes in the club, laughed off Graves's criticism of his favourite novels over dinner, and laughed at Rowena's disapproval of his laughter throughout the day. For the rest of the week, nothing could persuade him that the world was anything but bright and beautiful and inherently good. It all ground to a halt the following Monday, when he entered the London house's library to find his father at the shelves.

Sir Geoffrey glanced up sharply at his son's entrance. Lindsey froze in place on the threshold.

"Good morning, sir," he said.

Sir Geoffrey turned back to his books. He had one in hand already, and was running his fingers over the spines of its shelved companions, searching for its proper place. "Good news from the mill?"

"Indeed," Lindsey replied too quickly, over-eager for any assistance in crafting the lie he needed. "The, erm, profits are quite satisfactory."

"And unnecessary," added Sir Geoffrey. "Still, I'm happy for you."

He neither looked nor sounded particularly happy, but Lindsey chose to take him at his word. His blood still sang with elation from his encounter at the mill. A little thing like his father's perpetual disappointment couldn't sour his mood. He wished he could pass on some of his cheer to Sir

Geoffrey. There'd never been much Lindsey could do to please his father, but he knew of one possible method.

"Would you care for a game of chess, sir?"

Sir Geoffrey's mustache twitched, and the corners of his eyes crinkled. He set his book aside. "Yes, I believe I would."

Lindsey hurried to fetch the board. Sir Geoffrey approached the table at a more sedate pace as Lindsey set the pieces up. Black went on his father's side, and white on his own, a tradition begun when Lindsey was a child just learning to play. Though Sir Geoffrey gave his son the advantage of the first move, his tactics were otherwise merciless. He never once held back to allow Lindsey to win. If his son desired success, he would have to earn it. And he had earned it, eventually. Over years of play, they had become more evenly matched, until Lindsey's chances of winning were as good as a coin toss. In recent times, he'd started to win a little more often than that—just by a hair, the smallest increase. As a child, he'd assumed such victories would bring him joy. As a man, they unnerved him. He wasn't used to having any advantage over his father, no matter how inconsequential. This new balance of power didn't rest easy on his shoulders.

But perhaps Sir Geoffrey would win today. Lindsey held onto that comforting thought as he made his opening move.

The game progressed slowly, with equal ground gained and lost on either side. Belle wandered in as Lindsey's queen took one of Sir Geoffrey's rooks. As Sir Geoffrey's favourite hound, Belle had the honour of accompanying him from country to town. She settled under the table between Lindsey and his father. Sir Geoffrey scratched behind her ears, then demolished Lindsey's bishop.

Halfway through the match, when Lindsey thought he might have regained the upper hand, Charles appeared in the doorway. Sir Geoffrey sat with his back to the door and didn't perceive the valet's approach. Lindsey, however, took immediate notice. While the chessboard arrested his father's attention, Lindsey dared to cast an inquiring glance at his valet. But Charles remained tight-lipped. Whatever his business, it was important enough for him to come find Lindsey, but not urgent enough to interrupt the match.

Distracted by curiosity, Lindsey suffered a sudden, crushing defeat. Sir Geoffrey sat back with a suspicious frown. Lindsey braced for his father to accuse him of throwing the match.

"You're too protective of your queen," said Sir Geoffrey.

Lindsey balked. "Sir?"

Sir Geoffrey shook his head, his stern gaze focused on the board. "I've told you time and time again, boy. You sacrifice everything to keep her in play when a calculated loss would give you an advantage—if not the outright win."

Lindsey relaxed. "Yes, sir."

Sir Geoffrey, apparently satisfied, moved to rise. Charles stepped backward into the hallway before entering the room, preserving the illusion of just now coming in. He passed Sir Geoffrey as the latter returned to the bookcase. Sir Geoffrey paid him enough attention to prevent a collision, but no more.

"What is it, Charles?" said Lindsey.

Charles flicked his eyes over to Sir Geoffrey—who continued ignoring them both—then returned to Lindsey and leaned in to answer in a low tone. "You've a visitor, sir."

Lindsey's hopes soared with the thought of Aubrey Warren, here, on his very doorstep.

"A Miss Brewster," Charles continued. If he noticed how these words crushed Lindsey's spirit, he gave no sign of it. "She claimed you were expecting her. She was most insistent. I had Timothy put her in the front parlour."

"Timothy?"

"The new footman, sir."

"Ah." Lindsey stood up. "I suppose I'd better see to it, then."

"Very good, sir."

Lindsey bid his father good day as he left the library. Sir Geoffrey spared him a nod, then returned to the shelves.

When Lindsey reached the front parlour, he found Miss Brewster standing in the centre of the room, a small carpet-bag in hand, her attention flitting between the lace-curtained windows and the tall mahogany mirror over the marble-topped mantle.

"Miss Brewster," said Lindsey. He left the door open for propriety's sake, wondering if he oughtn't call his sister in as well. It couldn't do Miss Brewster's reputation any good to be alone in a room with a bachelor. But she didn't seem to think anything of it.

"Mr Althorp," she replied. She continued examining the Oriental carpet under their feet, then met his eyes with a face stern enough to halt an oncoming train.

Lindsey likewise paused before responding. "Would you care to sit down?"

It felt like offering a seat to a lioness. Miss Brewster glanced over the pink velvet chairs sprinkled throughout the room. She didn't wrinkle her nose, exactly, but came very near to it. Yet she thanked him all the same and perched on the edge of a cushion, setting her carpet-bag by her boots.

Lindsey sat next to her. He didn't like looming over her—far from giving him the high ground, it seemed to expose his fleshy underbelly to her predatory stare. He cleared his throat. "Is there something I may do for you, Miss Brewster?"

"Many things, I'm sure." A smile flashed across her lips, a glint of bared teeth, then her stony expression returned. "But first, I must thank you for keeping your word."

"You find your new wages satisfactory?"

"It's a start," she conceded. "In return, I've brought what I promised."

She opened her carpet bag. Lindsey watched in fascination as she rummaged through its contents. At last, she produced a pamphlet and held it out to him. He took it dumbly, his lips pursed in confusion. They smoothed out into a grin as he beheld the words ROOK MILL WOMEN WORKERS' UNION printed on the top page.

"Thank you, Miss Brewster!" he said, flicking it open to peruse its contents. Her resulting silence induced him to raise his head and see her regarding him with one eyebrow elevated far above the other.

"You're welcome," she said, still giving him an odd look.

"Is something wrong?"

"No," she said, drawing out the word. "It's just... May I be frank, Mr Althorp?"

"Of course."

"Most gentlemen don't give two bits what their workforce wants, much less ask for their literature."

"But I adore literature!"

Miss Brewster looked yet more disturbed. Lindsey hastened to elaborate.

"That is to say, I'm most intrigued by your ideas—I'm rather new to this whole manufacturing business, you see. I'd like to do it right. And it can't be right if my workforce is unhappy. Indeed, I don't see how the mill could function in such a state. Surely the happiest workforce is the most productive. I certainly accomplish more when I'm happy with what I'm doing and feel it's worthwhile."

Miss Brewster continued to stare at him.

"I suppose so," she said at last, though her concerned look never wavered. Before Lindsey could add anything more, she rose. "Thank you for hearing our concerns, Mr Althorp. I'll not trouble you any further today."

Lindsey stood as well and pulled the bell-rope. A footman arrived to show Miss Brewster out. She eyed him warily before accepting his escort.

"If you've any questions," she said as she departed, "you know where to find me."

Once she'd gone, Lindsey picked up the pamphlet and wandered back down the hall to his own rooms, reading as he walked. The pamphlet employed a fiery breed of rhetoric. Lindsey couldn't help admiring its passionate language, though the charges laid out against the mill's previous owner felt somewhat harsh.

"Who was that?"

Lindsey stumbled to a halt. In the hall before him stood Sir Geoffrey.

"Sir?" said Lindsey, dropping the hand holding the pamphlet to his side and giving his father his full attention.

"That woman with the carpet-bag. Who was she? A new maid?"

"Yes," said Lindsey. Something in his chest twisted as he did so, as if he'd actually bruised his conscience by presenting Miss Brewster as anything other than her true self. Certainly the lady herself wouldn't approve. "Rowena meant to interview her, but it seems there was some confusion as to the time and place."

Sir Geoffrey gave him a long, inquisitive look. Lindsey stood firm under it. Experience had taught him it wouldn't do any good to flinch from scrutiny.

"You've sent her packing, then?" Sir Geoffrey said at last.

Lindsey swallowed. "Yes, sir."

"Good. She'd never last here if she can't keep track of the time."

With that, Sir Geoffrey passed by and was gone. Lindsey withheld his sigh of relief and hurried to the safety of his own chambers, Miss Brewster's pamphlet clutched in his fist.

⚮

THE TELEGRAM ARRIVED on Lindsey's doorstep not a moment too soon. He leapt into the family carriage and took off for the mill. The journey seemed shorter than ever before. Within the space of a blink, he'd arrived.

The office held Aubrey alone, bent over his work. Lindsey didn't question his good fortune. He made a beeline for the desk. As he approached, Aubrey looked up and stood to greet him with a warm smile.

"Lindsey," he said.

Lindsey reached across the desk to stroke the clerk's porcelain cheek. Aubrey leaned into the touch, turning to press a kiss to Lindsey's palm. Lindsey rushed forward—the desk had disappeared, he didn't know where it went, he didn't care—and claimed Aubrey's lips in his own.

Aubrey's thigh slipped between Lindsey's legs to brush against his stirring prick. Both their clothes had gone the way of the desk, leaving Lindsey's hands free to roam over the supple landscape of Aubrey's bare flesh. Their bodies pressed together, their hard cocks trapped between their bellies. Lindsey rolled his hips, Aubrey whispered huskily into his ear, *Lindsey*, and then—

Lindsey awoke with prick in hand, bucking into his fist. His seed spilled over his sheets as the name "Aubrey" tumbled from his lips onto his pillow. It left his mind in a haze.

Some minutes later, when the lovely languid feeling wore off, Lindsey had much to consider. Certain sonnets of Shakespeare and large portions of the Classical texts he'd studied at Eton made far more sense in light of his sudden self-discovery. He understood what compelled Zeus to carry Ganymede to Olympus and cast his image among the stars, what drove Hadrian to deify Antinous. New worlds bloomed into being, all revolving around the dark sun of Aubrey.

An anticipatory shudder ran through Lindsey's frame. He expended a tremendous effort to harness his imagination. As much as he wished to, he could hardly gallop to the mill and pounce on its clerk. A true gentleman would ask permission first. And for all he knew, he might be refused. This possibility cast a shadow over his sunny disposition, but not for long. He'd simply have to prove himself worthy of Aubrey's affections. And he was determined to do so.

◦

NOBODY BOTHERED AUBREY when he stayed at the office past eight o'clock. Everyone else, from mill hands to stationary engineers to his fellow office staff, left far earlier. To hear a knock on the door was most unexpected. And when he called out for the unexpected to come in, it doubly astonished him to see Mr Althorp enter.

"Good evening, sir," he managed despite his bewilderment. "What a pleasant surprise."

Even more surprising, Aubrey realised his idle comment was sincere. He put considerable effort into tempering his enthusiasm. It wouldn't do to let slip just how much he appreciated the visit. If Smith hadn't left hours ago, the humiliation alone would have struck Aubrey stone dead.

Mr Althorp—or Lindsey, as he allowed Aubrey to call him—showed no such restraint. His winning smile made it perfectly clear how delighted he felt to be in the mill office after hours, for reasons beyond Aubrey's understanding.

"I hope I'm not interrupting anything," said Lindsey.

He was, of course, but Aubrey would never tell him so. "Not at all. To what do we owe the pleasure?"

The moment the phrase escaped his throat, Aubrey wished he could snatch it back. It wasn't a *pleasure* for a mill owner to drop in on his employees without warning. He ought've asked what he could do for Lindsey—that would've demonstrated a work ethic beyond sycophantic flattery. But Lindsey didn't seem to notice the subtle difference.

"Is Mr Jennings available?" he asked.

The question caused Aubrey unaccountable disappointment. He refused to reflect on why this might be. "No, sir, I'm afraid Mr Jennings went home some time past."

"And the other clerk?" Lindsey asked before Aubrey could offer his services as a replacement. "Mr ...Smith, wasn't it? Is he in?"

Smith had gone home for lunch and never returned, though Lindsey didn't need to know that. Neither did he need to know how the thought of Smith as an acceptable substitute, preferable to Aubrey himself, made Aubrey queasy. Still, he replied in a level tone, "No."

To his astonishment, Lindsey grinned.

"Perfect," he said, and took the liberty of hanging his hat on the coat rack. "I'd hoped to make a request of you particularly, and in private."

As he talked, he advanced across the room until he came to Aubrey's desk and seated himself quite casually on the corner of it.

Aubrey, meanwhile, refused to accept this version of reality. Lindsey couldn't possibly mean what he supposed. Life didn't work that way. Surely Lindsey spoke in jest. Yet as Aubrey looked into his eyes—the too-blue eyes of a man who'd given him an expensive, if thoughtless, gift, along with words of praise and a request to be called by his Christian name—he found a shy, hopeful expression.

"I would be delighted," said Lindsey, "if you would do me the honour of accompanying me to the theatre."

Aubrey felt a slight pressure on his thigh. He glanced down to find Lindsey's hand upon it.

He buried his initial reaction of wild, inappropriate glee deep down where Lindsey would never see it. Yet while he could hide his joy from the outside world, he couldn't escape it within the confines of his own mind. His imagination presented a whirlwind of vignettes—Lindsey's fingers brushing the arm of his jacket as they walked to the theatre; once inside, Aubrey taking advantage of the darkness to rest his hand in Lindsey's lap; he and Lindsey sharing a cab home after the show, Lindsey undoing the buttons of his waistcoat, Lindsey's mouth on his throat, Lindsey straddling him, Lindsey—

At present, Lindsey's hand remained on his thigh. Aubrey reined in his fantasies, lest Lindsey encounter more than he'd expected there.

Or perhaps precisely what he'd expected.

Aubrey swallowed hard. Regardless of his tempting offer, Lindsey remained Aubrey's superior. If Lindsey tired of his companionship, Aubrey would be tossed back in the gutter. The alternate possibility, that Aubrey's own interest would wane, and Lindsey would demand continued affection as a condition of his employment, didn't sound any more appealing. And if by some miracle a third path appeared, as the stupider parts of Aubrey's brain hoped, wherein he and Lindsey remained inseparable in mutual bliss until the end of their days, Aubrey couldn't conceive of a world in which he became anything more than Lindsey's pet clerk, a filthy little secret. No. He'd moved on from that role long ago. He had no intention of returning to it now.

Then again, considering all he'd accepted from Lindsey, it looked as if he'd returned to it already.

Realising this uncomfortable truth left Aubrey with only one respectable option. He took a deep breath, gathering courage along with air, and spoke.

"Mr Althorp, I am not entirely comfortable with the position of your hand."

CHAPTER SIX

LINDSEY'S SEDUCTIVE SMILE fell away into an expression of terror. He snatched his hand back as if Aubrey had burned him.

"Yes, of course," he stammered. "Please forgive—forget I said anything."

He shot up from the desk, upsetting the ink-bottle. Grabbing for it earned him a splash of ink between his left thumb and forefinger. Aubrey, wary of his resolve in the face of physical contact, kept clear of Lindsey's flailing.

"I should go," Lindsey continued as he backed away toward the door. "I've an appointment, and I—well, best not trouble you any further. Good evening, Mr Warren."

He gave a stiff nod and fled.

His exit left the door in motion behind him, swinging between open and shut. It stopped a hand's-breadth shy of closed. Aubrey stared at where Lindsey had disappeared.

Without Lindsey's hand, his thigh felt cold. This chill spread throughout the office. The empty space loomed larger than ever before. Aubrey's breath seemed to echo in it.

He wrenched his gaze away from the door, rearranged the papers Lindsey had scattered in his flight, and returned to his bookkeeping. After the fourth elementary error, he realised his current temper was ill-suited for it, and stopped. It wouldn't do to lose his job over something so trivial.

It then occurred to him he may have lost his job already.

Aubrey stared at his ledger, his mind elsewhere. With his advances rebuked, Lindsey had no further reason to keep Aubrey in his employ and would no doubt sack him tomorrow. Aubrey's stomach growled as

55

if to remind him of the hungry times ahead. The abdominal pangs came alongside an ache in his chest with no physical cause Aubrey could discern.

Able to do no more work that night, and thoroughly ashamed of himself for it, he prepared to leave. As he retrieved his coat and hat from their respective pegs, he realised Lindsey had left his own hat behind.

Aubrey's brain struggled for a solution. The hat needed to be returned to its owner. A gentleman would return it in person—an impossible task for one so vulgar as Aubrey. Perhaps he could use an intermediary.

As he pondered his predicament, it dawned on him he'd spent the last few minutes stroking the smooth silk of the hat's brim. He jerked his fingers away and brushed them off on his trousers. The hat remained on the hook, taunting him. Aubrey cast a helpless gaze upon it.

Surely a man so wealthy as Lindsey wouldn't miss one hat.

Aubrey chastised himself for the thought as soon as it occurred, but it persisted nonetheless. Besides, he didn't intend to *steal* the hat. Just put it away for a while. Until he knew what to do about it. That would be enough for now.

He glanced into the hall, determined it contained no one, then whipped the hat off the hook, crossed the room, flung open the bottom-right drawer of his desk, and, after a moment's hesitation, gently laid the hat inside with a few sheets of paper balanced atop it. It was a poor disguise and would fool nobody, but for now it was the best he could do. Aubrey resolved to think no more on it, nor on Lindsey's proposal. He'd made the right decision.

He told himself so as he put on his own hat and coat and walked home from the mill. He told himself again as he choked down his tinned supper, tasting none of it. As he tried to unbutton the shirt he'd already removed and ended up jabbing his fingertips stupidly at his bare chest; as he crawled into bed and shivered beneath a threadbare blanket powerless to keep the night's frost from seeping into his skin; as he stared up into the darkness trying to will himself to sleep; as he twitched awake after dreaming of Lindsey naked and writhing on top of him, lying curled beside him, twining his arms around him—he told himself, over and again, he'd made the right decision.

He insisted upon the point even as he woke late, nicked himself twice shaving, missed breakfast and barely made it into the office before the bell tolled for first shift, all the while pushing the specter of Lindsey from his mind. Or trying to. It proved difficult to banish, particularly when Aubrey had to work at the very desk with Lindsey's hat secreted away inside it. By second shift, Aubrey had added the same column of figures thrice over and found a different sum each time.

That night, sleep eluded him. His mind raced, engineering formulae replaced by the repeating recollection of his encounter with Lindsey the previous evening. Lindsey, with his regal carriage and noble ancestry, who thought nothing of tossing social protocol aside to meet Aubrey where he stood. Lindsey, with golden hair and a smile made of sunshine. Lindsey, with his deep blue eyes focused on Aubrey's face and his hand on Aubrey's thigh. The memory of his warm, firm touch left Aubrey's skin afire in its wake.

Aubrey tried his utmost to think of anything but Lindsey. The only available distraction was his own prick twitching against his inner thigh.

He'd be awake until dawn if this kept up.

Aubrey let his hands wander under the hem of his nightshirt. He pulled it up to his navel and clenched it in one hand as he palmed his half-hard cock with the other. His hips bucked of their own accord. He took the hint and curled his fist tight. He imagined his hand were Lindsey's, recalled the softness of fingers unaccustomed to hard labour. Aubrey yearned to feel it again, a velvet touch to match velvet tones, sweet nothings murmured in an aristocratic accent. He hated himself for craving the sound, but desire won out. His mind filled with remembrances of blond curls and smooth hands and crisp speech. He imagined a whisper in his ear—*Aubrey*—and slender fingers wrapping around his length, releasing it to trail down his thighs until the teasing touch returned northward to his cock and circled its head—

Aubrey.

That delicious, detested voice, tripping off a toff's tongue. Surely such a tongue could be put to better use. And with his mouth occupied, Lindsey's elegant hands would be free to...

Aubrey had but an instant to imagine Lindsey's tongue on the slit of his cock and those fingers crooked inside him before the vision of Lindsey swallowing his whole length down overwhelmed his senses. He shot off, spending in his right hand while the left leapt to his mouth to muffle his cry of ecstasy.

The next morning dawned dim and dull. Aubrey woke late again, full of melancholy longing. He sat up and regarded his garret by Manchester's cold, gray excuse for sunlight. From the bare floor to the peeling yellow wallpaper to the low slope of the ceiling beams, all spoke of poverty and despair. This, then, was what Aubrey deprived himself of every joy to preserve. The thought nearly drove him back to bed. But he refused to succumb. He pushed through the motions of preparing for work. While his body obeyed, his mind continued to wander.

So what if Aubrey wanted Lindsey; Aubrey was used to never getting what he wanted. And so what if Lindsey wanted Aubrey in return; as a man of means, Lindsey could have whatever he wanted whenever he pleased. He'd probably already moved on to the next easy conquest. He would forget Aubrey within the week. Aubrey resolved to forget Lindsey first. But as much as he disliked the idea of being forgotten, he found he despised the prospect of forgetting Lindsey even more.

Regardless of his emotional turmoil, Aubrey couldn't take Lindsey up on his offer. Such a path lead to scandal, strife, and self-delusion. But he couldn't keep on as he was, either. Twice now he'd tied his bootlaces in accidental slipknots. Hellfire and damnation, at this rate Smith would arrive at the office before him. Aubrey, ready to pull out his hair in frustration, racked his brain for a solution. He needed a third option, something between throwing himself upon Lindsey's mercy and tossing Lindsey out of his life forever. Perhaps if he accepted Lindsey's offer, just the once, indulged himself just enough to take the edge off his unnatural impulses, perhaps then he could return to his accustomed equilibrium.

Aubrey tied a proper knot in his laces, and stood up, squaring his narrow shoulders. Very well. He would accept.

❧

"You're quite the talented sulk," said Rowena over breakfast.

She and Lindsey arrived late to the meal. Rowena had stayed out at a dinner party with Lady Pelham until the small hours of the morning. Lindsey had spent the night going over every syllable spoken, every gesture made in the course of his acquaintance with Aubrey, pulling his memories apart to find the point where it'd all gone wrong. Consequently, neither sibling was awake when their father rose at dawn to consult the elder Miller at his bank. Now, at half-past eleven, Rowena and Lindsey faced only each other.

Lindsey scowled at his eggs. He didn't consider Rowena's barb worth the trouble of a reply. Nothing seemed worth the trouble anymore. Getting dressed felt like an exercise in futility—Charles had managed to coax him into a fashionable outfit, but Lindsey still couldn't see the point. He had no one to impress. Certainly not Aubrey, who wasn't looking at him now and had never looked at him the way Lindsey wished he would. The memory of Aubrey's dark wool suit came to the forefront of Lindsey's mind with no effort whatsoever, yet Lindsey couldn't recall what Charles had clothed him in not an hour previous. He had no idea whether he wore the periwinkle paisley waistcoat or the robin's egg blue. He considered tipping his gaze down his front to check, then remembered he didn't care and huffed in disgust.

He was more than disgusted; he was enraged. Not at Aubrey of course, never Aubrey, the idea was inconceivable. No, Lindsey reserved all his anger for himself. Only a fool would've pursued Aubrey with such relentless passion. Lindsey had probably frightened the poor man. To match the stain his folly left on his pride, a corporeal stain from Aubrey's inkwell remained on his left hand. He'd half a mind to tattoo it in place as a permanent reminder not to transgress again.

"Has Mr Holmes failed to solve a case?"

Lindsey looked up from his hand to find Rowena smirking at him. Were he not a gentleman, he might've thrown his napkin in her face. He settled for glowering at her from across the table. She smiled wider.

"Nothing else could cause you so much grief," she continued. "Is it a robbery? Murder? Blackmail?"

Lindsey crushed his napkin in his unstained fist, dropped it into his runny eggs, stood from the table, and strode out of the room.

"Lindsey!"

He quickened his steps down the hall, determined to ignore his sister's cries. Just a few hundred yards more to the stairs, and he could climb up to spend the rest of his life moping behind the locked doors of his suite.

"Lindsey Marie Althorp, will you stop!"

Unfortunately for his plans, Rowena outpaced him despite the handicap of skirts. He could've run for it, but his mood wasn't dark enough to blind him to the indignity of such a scene. As such, he allowed Rowena to catch his elbow and whirl him around to face her.

"What is the matter with you?" she demanded.

Lindsey fixed his gaze on the ceiling as he contrived to put his tempestuous emotions into words. "I've offended my clerk."

Rowena remained silent, which forced Lindsey to look down to see her reaction. This vexed him. It vexed him double to discover she had one hand clamped over her mouth as the corners of her eyes pinched with restrained laughter. He wrenched his arm out of her delicate grip and marched off again.

"Lindsey, wait!" she called, her voice bubbling with mirth. "I'm sorry, I'm so sorry, please forgive me—"

"Your apologies would ring more sincere if you could refrain from giggling!" Lindsey spun to a halt to fix her with his fiercest glare. She ignored it.

"Will you join me in the morning room for reconciliation?" she said. "I do so hate quarrelling in the hall."

Upon reflection, Lindsey thought her suggestion prudent, and followed her there.

"Now," she said once the doors had shut and they stood together in an otherwise empty chamber. "What's this about your clerk?"

"I believe I've spoken to you of Mr Warren before?"

"Often and at length, yes."

"Then permit me to bore you again."

She inclined her head in a polite bow. He launched into a summary of his recent activity—acquiring the factory, meeting Aubrey, attempting to deepen their bond beyond what typically existed between employer and employee. Lindsey thought Rowena might do more than quirk an eyebrow at that last point, but she seemed far less surprised than he himself had felt at the discovery of his peculiar proclivities. Undaunted, he pressed on, culminating in a stuttered description of his final conversation with Aubrey.

Rowena remained silent for a minute or so after Lindsey concluded his tragic tale, deep in thought, with one hand held in a fist under her chin.

"What were his exact words?" she asked.

Lindsey blushed to repeat them, but did so regardless.

"'I am not entirely comfortable with the position of your hand,'" she echoed. A small frown creased her brow. "I suppose we must take him at his word. There's nothing else for it but time. You'll forget him eventually."

"Forget Aubrey!?"

Rowena's left eyebrow reached new heights. Lindsey belatedly realised his error.

"He's 'Aubrey' now, is he?" said Rowena.

Lindsey said nothing. Rowena tipped her head forward to pinch the bridge of her nose between two slender fingers.

"While I dread the answer," she said, her tone grim, "I must assume you are 'Lindsey' to him?"

"Until yesterday."

60

Rowena sighed and fixed her brother with a hard look. "Forget him. Don't sack him—"

"I could never!"

Rowena continued as if she hadn't heard him. "—it's already scandalous. Sacking him now would only set tongues wagging. He remains employed, you never set foot in the factory again—no, that's even more suspicious. Go on as though none of it ever happened. Don't speak to him unless absolutely necessary, which, given the disparity between your respective stations, should be 'not at all'. Throw yourself into theatre and have an affair with an actor or brood into your novels, I care not, but forget him. And for God's sake, be discreet."

"Rowena—!"

She cut him off. "Do you understand what's at stake? It might not be a capital offense any longer, but you're hardly suited for prison."

Lindsey jerked back, stunned. "What are you implying?"

"You must know whatever you desired between yourself and Mr Warren is illegal."

"Yes, but Aubrey would never—!"

"Mr Warren," said Rowena, enunciating the name with ferocity, "is an unknown quantity. I cannot assume what he may or may not do. Why couldn't you fall for any of the dozens of grooms I threw into your path?"

"The grooms you...?" Lindsey blinked. "What?"

Rowena gave him a disappointed look. "Surely you don't imagine I hired only the handsomest and most discreet young men for my own sake?"

"Didn't you?"

Rowena let her face fall forward into her pretty palms, muffling her voice. "Oh, Lindsey, you perfect idiot."

Lindsey struggled to maintain his composure. "If you're suggesting Aubrey could be replaced by any random gentleman you chose for me, you are quite mistaken!"

"It hardly matters now." Rowena lifted her head and fixed him with an expression of cool composure. "He has rejected your suit. Accept his decision with grace, forget him, and move on as you see fit. Should you seek to vent your frustrations, I can suggest several accommodating avenues."

"No, thank you," Lindsey replied curtly.

"Then the matter is closed. Good day, brother."

She swept out of the room without waiting for his reply.

Lindsey wished she'd left him in the library. There he might have found some distraction from his misery. Instead, he stood staring into space for a few minutes, then sat chin-in-hand in an understuffed armchair and stared at the wall for many minutes more. He wasn't brooding. No matter what Rowena would say if she'd stayed to watch him.

"Sir?"

Lindsey whipped his head around to the doorway, where Charles waited. "Yes?"

"Telegram for you, sir."

Lindsey took it and dismissed him with a nod. After Charles had gone, he opened it.

Mr Althorp
Warren
Please come to mill at 9.

Lindsey frowned at it, certain he'd misread. Aubrey wanted to see him—impossible. He'd made his opinion of Lindsey very clear at their last meeting. Perhaps something had gone wrong at the mill, though in that case the telegram would've come from Mr Jennings. If it wasn't an invitation for a liaison, nor notice of an emergency, only one possibility remained.

Blackmail.

Lindsey's heart plummeted to the pit of his stomach. He supposed Aubrey's presumption should enrage him, but all he could muster was profound disappointment. He'd thought better of Aubrey. Just yesterday, he'd have given him anything he desired.

And he still would, good sense be damned.

❧

AUBREY SPENT THE day in dread. Smith left the office at the unusually late hour of four. Mr Jennings likewise stayed late, departing at quarter-to-nine. Aubrey's heart stuttered in his throat as he watched Mr Jennings gather up his articles. He waited in dread for Mr Jennings to stop at the door and demand Aubrey leave with him—or worse yet, encounter Lindsey on his way out.

But neither occurred. Mr Jennings sighed and shook his head at the sight of Aubrey bent over three ledgers and left without further comment.

Part of Aubrey's anxiety left with him. The rest—fear of his telegram's interception by third parties, fear of Lindsey arriving with the police to arrest Aubrey for indecent solicitation—remained to prevent him from accomplishing anything in the quarter-hour between Mr Jennings's departure and Lindsey's earliest expected arrival. He endeavoured regardless.

The sun had set hours ago. Aubrey almost forgot what light was. Then, at ten-past, Lindsey appeared on the threshold and reminded him.

"Mr Warren," he gasped, breathless, as if he'd run all the way from London. "You wished to see me?"

For once, he wasn't smiling. Aubrey suppressed a surge of pity.

"Mr Althorp," he said. He'd risen from his desk the instant Lindsey arrived. Now he wavered, uncertain if he should approach him, or if he had any right to. He rapped his knuckles against a ledger. "Please come in."

Lindsey hesitated, then stepped into the office, his fingers clenched tight around the brim of his hat.

Aubrey's pity won out. He abandoned the shelter of the desk and came forward to stand within arm's reach of Lindsey. "Regarding the subject of your hand on my thigh..."

Lindsey's eyes flew wide. Aubrey realised his opening could be interpreted as a threat, and rushed to conclude his proposal.

"I've given it some thought," he said, stumbling over syllables in his haste, "and I find myself far more amicable towards the suggestion than my previous answer may have led you to believe."

Lindsey stared at him. Aubrey feared he'd overstepped, but then a slow smile crept across Lindsey's features.

"Then," said Lindsey, "might I make another attempt?"

He ended his inquiry by biting his lip. The sight stole Aubrey's breath. The best he could manage in reply was a nod.

With timidity Aubrey found painful to witness, Lindsey lifted his hand to Aubrey's cheek. His fingertips brushed against Aubrey's jaw, their touch even softer than Aubrey had imagined.

Lindsey halved the distance between them, then shut his eyes, tilted his head, and leaned in to close the final breach.

Lightning seemed to strike the office as Lindsey's kiss made contact. Aubrey fought to stay upright despite the shock.

The kiss remained chaste until Aubrey took Lindsey's lower lip between his own, drawing a gasp of delighted discovery from Lindsey's throat. Aubrey relished the sound. He cupped the back of Lindsey's head, pulling him in, determined to wring more pleasure from him.

He got his wish soon enough, he and Lindsey entangling like youths in the throes of a newfound passion. The force of Lindsey's affections pushed Aubrey back against the desk. Aubrey responded in kind, his hands slipping under Lindsey's jacket and shoving it off his shoulders. The sight of Lindsey's upper arms in nothing more than shirtsleeves made him want to tear the jacket in twain, desperate to feel the warm, solid flesh beneath.

Over those same magnificent shoulders, Aubrey could see the office door. It hung open a crack. All passion fled in the face of his horror.

"Stop!" he hissed, shoving Lindsey's sternum with both palms.

He'd expected to have to fight further to escape Lindsey's amorous clutches, but to his astonishment, Lindsey fell back the instant the command left his lips—looking confused and a little hurt, but not angry.

Aubrey had no time soothe his hurts or feel relief at the absence of rage. All his perception narrowed on the crack and the hallway beyond. He listened for any sign of possible witnesses. Hearing nothing, he stepped away from Lindsey—despite the cacophonous protests of his own fevered desire—to the door. He pushed it further open and peered up and down the corridor. It remained dark, silent, empty. No noise but the pounding of his panicked heart. He shut the door with a soft click.

"This cannot continue," he said.

An indignant sound of protest came from behind him. He turned to find the same look of confusion on Lindsey's face, though his hurt seemed to have progressed to anguish.

"Here, I mean!" Aubrey corrected himself as he hurried back to Lindsey's side, taking one of those magnificent arms in his grip. His mind went momentarily blank as he felt the strong sinew beneath the fine linen, then he shook his head clear and continued. "Here and now, impossible, but..."

"Somewhere more private?" Lindsey finished, a hopeful smile returning to his handsome features.

"Yes!" Aubrey agreed, though rack his brains as he might, he couldn't think of anywhere they could go. The local hotels couldn't be trusted. His own lodgings shamed him.

"Tomorrow?" said Lindsey, apparently untroubled by Aubrey's conundrum. "It's Saturday. You won't have to work, will you?"

"A half-day," said Aubrey. "But—"

"Then perhaps you could arrive in Wiltshire on the eight-o'clock train." Aubrey blinked. "Pardon?"

"It would give me time to open up the house before you arrive. No one's there at present. We'd have total privacy. And you're welcome to stay the night."

Lindsey looked very pleased with his plan as he waited for Aubrey's input. Aubrey struggled to wrap his mind around it.

"Forgive me," he choked out, "but do I understand... you're inviting me up to your house?"

"I believe I am, yes," said Lindsey with a cheeky grin.

Aubrey couldn't help it—he gawked. Goggled, even, at Lindsey's devil-may-care assessment of their predicament. "Wouldn't it attract suspicion?"

"I don't see how," said Lindsey. "What could be more natural than for me to discuss business with a clerk from my mill? And if I choose to do so in my own home rather than the office, why, then these are clearly urgent matters indeed, requiring utmost secrecy. It would be terribly rude and suspicious for anyone to inquire further. Do you accept?"

A rational and right-thinking man would take the time to weigh the risks and rewards of the proposal.

"God, yes!" Aubrey replied in a rushed exhale.

CHAPTER SEVEN

THE WILTSHIRE TRAIN platform was deserted when Aubrey arrived. By the gaslight leaking out the station windows, he saw a sleek, black-varnished carriage with a silver crest painted on the door, waiting alone in the road.

The coachman sitting on the box caught Aubrey's stare and nodded down at another man who stood ready by the wheels with his hands folded. The second man turned to Aubrey and began to approach.

"Mr Warren?" he said, his voice carrying in the still night air.

"Yes," Aubrey confirmed. He would've asked the man's name in return, but said man interrupted him by reaching for the messenger bag slung over Aubrey's shoulder.

"I'll take that for you, sir," he said when Aubrey didn't relinquish it.

The bag contained two ledgers from the office, chosen at random to represent the "business" Aubrey and Lindsey were supposedly conducting. The man gave no sign he found either the bag or Aubrey's hesitance suspicious.

Aubrey remained wary. "I'm sorry, but I didn't catch your name."

The dim light didn't give Aubrey a good look at the stranger's expression as he stepped back, but his tone, when he spoke, sounded apologetic. "Charles, sir."

"Is this Mr Althorp's carriage, Mr Charles?"

"Just Charles, sir. And yes, it belongs to the Althorp estate. Mr Althorp sent it down for you."

Aubrey, who'd assumed he'd walk from the station to Lindsey's house, tried to suppress his instinctive panic at the change in plan. "That's... very kind of him."

"If I may, sir?"

Charles reached for the bag again. Aubrey let him have it. With the bag under one arm, Charles performed a brief yet impressive balancing act to open the carriage door with his other hand. Aubrey climbed into the carriage and came face-to-face with Lindsey.

"Good evening," said the latter, unable or unwilling to disguise his grin.

The door shut behind Aubrey before he could respond in kind.

The carriage ride was equal parts luxurious and unbearable. The springs ensured few if any bumps in the road made it up to the plush velvet seats within. The matching curtains kept out the night's chill. Nevertheless, Aubrey's discomfort only grew.

Matters had cooled in the hours since his office encounter with Lindsey. Now, at leisure to enjoy each other's company in a more secluded setting, Lindsey acted shy. The barest touch of their knees seemed all he could initiate.

Aubrey counted the seconds in his head as the carriage lurched off. When he reached a hundred and twenty, his patience wore out. He took Lindsey's jaw in hand and kissed him. Lindsey rose to the occasion in every sense of the phrase.

"It's an hour's ride," he gasped into Aubrey's ear as they caught their breath. "Do we have time...?"

An odd question. Most men Aubrey'd known hadn't needed half as many minutes. Nevertheless, he assured Lindsey an hour was plenty, and let his hand slip beneath Lindsey's jacket.

Perhaps it was only his own fevered imagination, but Aubrey swore he could feel the warmth of Lindsey's flesh through his silk waistcoat. His fingers trailed farther down to trace the outline of Lindsey's erection. One had to admire the sheer heft of the thing. He couldn't wait to get his hands around it.

Despite the thick wool barrier, Lindsey squirmed under his touch. Needful noises escaped his throat. Aubrey, though he enjoyed the display, supposed he ought to give the poor man a reprieve.

He started unbuttoning Lindsey's trousers. The jostling carriage and Lindsey's rolling hips hampered him. Lindsey himself had his wrist in his mouth, biting it to keep quiet. Aubrey caught Lindsey's wrist in one hand, kissed it, then gently pushed it aside to recapture his lips in his own.

Lindsey cried out into Aubrey's mouth. His back arched, his hips bucked, his whole frame spasmed—then he fell back, limp, panting, his eyes fluttering shut.

Aubrey, still half in Lindsey's lap, stared at him. Surely he hadn't...

"Are you all right?" he said when Lindsey failed to show any sign of life beyond his ragged breaths.

"What?" said Lindsey. "I'm... yes, I'm fine." He laughed a little and opened his eyes, his cheeks flush with exertion. "Though I'm afraid I've quite ruined these trousers."

Aubrey knew he was good, but he didn't think he was that good. Fortunately, Lindsey took no offense to his shocked silence.

"Kiss me?" said Lindsey with a dazed smile. "It'll revive me, I think. Like a prince in a fairy tale."

Aubrey thought a lover's embrace revived fairy tale princesses, not princes. He kissed Lindsey anyway.

૭

THEY SPENT THE rest of the journey returning their rumpled selves to a state of respectability. The carriage pulled up to the house the same instant Lindsey smoothed the last ruffled curl of his hair back into place.

Aubrey stepped down from the carriage. Ahead, he couldn't see any proof of a house apart from a few windows twinkling with candlelight. Their distance from each other suggested a structure whose size rivaled the Rook Mill. Intimidating, to say the least. He flinched as Lindsey touched his elbow.

"Sorry!" said Lindsey, dropping his hand.

Aubrey wanted to explain himself, to have Lindsey's comforting touch return, but just then two small globes of light appeared in the distance, bouncing down from the presumed house. As they approached, Aubrey realised it was one servant carrying two lanterns.

Lindsey spoke to his staff—Charles, coachman, and newcomer alike— in smooth, self-assured, warm tones. In the space of a few words, too quick for Aubrey to catch, he had the coachman on his way to the carriage-house, the newcomer handing one lamp off to Charles and following the coachman with the other, and Charles leading the way up to the house with Aubrey's bag on his shoulder.

Through a pair of doors large enough to admit an elephant cavalry, Aubrey entered the house. He found himself facing a massive staircase, as wide as three London streets, in a hall that echoed like a tomb. Candles in wall sconces provided more flickering shadows than light.

"Shall I put this in the library for the morning, sir?" said Charles.

68

He'd spoken to Lindsey, who looked to Aubrey.

"That's fine," said Aubrey, not so concerned with his bag as with the house looming around him.

Lindsey nodded to Charles, who disappeared into the shadows. The lamp went with him.

Just as Aubrey's anxieties reached their zenith, he caught a candlelit glimpse of Lindsey's fond smile. This time, Aubrey put his hand on Lindsey's elbow. Lindsey's grin shone white in the dark.

Lindsey led Aubrey up the stair and down uncounted winding corridors until they reached a gaslit antechamber full of bookshelves, armchairs, and other accoutrements. A tall door stood at the far end. Lindsey opened it and revealed the massive bedroom beyond.

The bed alone, a great four-posted thing with crimson curtains and polished cherrywood feet carved into lion's paws bigger than a man's skull, would take up most of Aubrey's garret. A mountain of pillows lay at the head. The scarlet glow of the lamps glinted off the wardrobe handles, the drawer knobs, and the organic curves of the lamps themselves, all gold.

Aubrey stopped on the threshold. Lindsey strode into the room as if he'd been born to it—because he was born to it, Aubrey reminded himself. Aubrey knew he should follow. He meant to. But his legs refused to obey. He didn't belong here.

Lindsey, halfway across the room, realised he'd lost his bedfellow and looked back with a puzzled expression. "What's wrong?"

"Nothing!" Aubrey replied too quickly, still frozen.

Lindsey's concerned look continued for another moment, then in three long strides he returned to Aubrey's side and opened his mouth as if to speak.

Aubrey, knowing he couldn't answer whatever question Lindsey intended to pose, darted up to cover his open mouth with his own. Lindsey's surprise proved no match for Aubrey's passion. As they kissed, Lindsey spun them both around so he could shut to door behind them. With the door locked, Aubrey had no compunctions against steering Lindsey to the bed. They fell on it in a heap.

In all his experience, Aubrey hadn't yet found a way to make untying shoes and flinging them aside look enticing. But once they were gone, he could slide his hands up Lindsey's long, well-formed calves to unhook the garters holding up his socks, and linger on the firm muscles.

This done, Aubrey began untying Lindsey's cravat. In turn, Aubrey fumbled with Aubrey's necktie. Their wrists tangled. Aubrey bit back a frustrated oath. Lindsey laughed and brought him up for another kiss.

Cravat, tie, jackets, and waistcoats were tossed to the floor. Lindsey's hands fell to the buttons of Aubrey's shirt. Aubrey stayed out of it lest they tangle again. Unbuttoned, his shirt slipped off his shoulders. His undershirt went over his head and left him bare-chested beneath Lindsey's hungry gaze. No, not hungry. Curious. A look Aubrey hadn't seen in years. He coloured under its scrutiny.

Lindsey smiled shyly up at him and kissed his collarbone. It flickered through Aubrey's touched-starved frame like an electric current. Before he realised it, he'd clutched Lindsey to his chest. But Lindsey, who wriggled up and out of his grip to kiss him again, didn't seem to notice anything odd about Aubrey's behaviour.

Aubrey ignored the trembling of his own fingers as he unbuttoned Lindsey's shirt. He'd tired of self-denial; he wanted to see the flesh he'd dreamt of, to realise the fantasy.

Lindsey did not disappoint.

Underneath the fine linen lay a lean, lithe body. Sporting exercise had developed the muscles overlapping his ribs and outlining his abdomen. Aubrey traced them with his fingertips, resisting the urge to follow with his tongue. Lindsey shivered under his touch. Aubrey wanted to make him quake.

He hooked a finger through the top buttonhole of Lindsey's trousers. Lindsey's hips bucked. His simultaneous gasp suggested spontaneity. Aubrey, far too desperate himself, tore Lindsey's fly open and wrestled his waistband off his hips. By the time he reached into Lindsey's drawers to claim his cock, it was hard as iron. Aubrey felt much the same. He would've disrobed, but Lindsey pulled him in for another ravenous kiss which left Aubrey grinding his own clothed cock against Lindsey's bare hips.

"Please—!" Aubrey heard himself beg as Lindsey drew back. He managed to shut up before he said anything more incriminating.

Lindsey took the hint. His clever fingers made quick work of Aubrey's trousers.

Naked at last, Aubrey set upon Lindsey with the single-minded fury of a hound scenting a hare. He fumbled his cock into place to slide against Lindsey's with the lubrication their feverish undressing had provided. The slick stroke of hard prick on prick made both men moan. Yet Aubrey needed more.

"Do you have pomade?" he murmured into Lindsey's ear. "Something to ease the way?"

"The way to what?"

Aubrey stopped—the kissing, the groping, the grinding, everything. He could've sworn Lindsey was joking, save for his expression of total confusion. Lindsey's premature release, his uncertain caresses, his present bafflement, all facts led to one conclusion.

"You've never done this before, have you," Aubrey said flatly.

Lindsey's lips parted, but no answer emerged. The sudden scarlet hue of his cheeks and ears were answer enough.

"How!?" Aubrey cried before his better judgment could prevent him. "You went to public school, for God's sake!"

Lindsey's eyebrows swooped down from the heights of surprise to a defensive knot. "What the devil does that have to do with anything?"

Everything, Aubrey would've replied, but he'd not spent months fantasising about their encounter only to sabotage it now. He forced a smile and leaned down to run his thumb over Lindsey's sharp cheekbone. "Nothing. It doesn't matter."

Lindsey's blush of shame faded away to the flush of healthy exertion. "You don't mind, then?"

"Not in the slightest," Aubrey assured him. "Though we'll need some sort of grease to finish what we've started. I think you'll enjoy it immensely."

He rolled his hips to give Lindsey a hint. Their cocks slid together in his fist.

"Chest of drawers!" Lindsey gasped. "Top left!"

Aubrey leapt to retrieve it. As he returned to the bed, Lindsey sat up. "What do I do?"

Aubrey straddled his lap. "Just lie back, and I'll take care of everything."

Lindsey complied with a look of eager anticipation.

Truth told, Aubrey felt relieved it'd worked out this way. Lindsey's prick wasn't the largest he'd ever seen, but damn near to it, and Aubrey hadn't taken a cock of any kind in years. Far better for Lindsey to let Aubrey set the pace than to have Lindsey flip Aubrey onto his face and ravage him from behind with a cock that size. Aubrey banished the image from his mind as soon as he'd conjured it, lest his nerves get the better of him. If this was Lindsey's first time, Aubrey wanted to make it memorable.

Lindsey watched with open curiosity as Aubrey dipped two fingers into the pomade and slid one inside himself. He kept at it, adding more grease

71

and a second finger. When he thought he might be ready, he slathered Lindsey's prick with it. Lindsey bucked into his slippery fist. Aubrey grinned, then pulled himself up, arranged Lindsey's prick in line with his hole, and leaned back. The head slid around the point of entry. Aubrey would've liked to tease himself with it, but Lindsey's fascinated patience wouldn't hold forever, so he guided his cock inside.

Both men gasped—Aubrey at the welcome return of a familiar sensation, Lindsey at the discovery of pleasures he hadn't dared dream of. His eyes fluttered shut.

"Like that, do you?" said Aubrey, unable to keep the smile off his face.

Lindsey replied with a helpless laugh. "Yes, quite."

It took a few more shuddering breaths for him to gather the will to open his eyes. He tried to sit up, reaching for Aubrey's face. But Aubrey shook his head, so he lay back again, content to wait for whatever came next.

It astonished Aubrey to find Lindsey so biddable. He couldn't remember the last time he'd had a partner willing to consider his needs, much less let him take the reins.

Aubrey pushed out, opening himself up to let in a few more inches of Lindsey's massive cock. His insides burned as they stretched. He held off, torn between impaling himself and watching the look on Lindsey's face as he experienced it for the first time, or selfishly taking his prick at a glacial pace to drag out the marvellous feeling of being filled. The latter course seemed safer. Besides, judging by the groans arising from Lindsey's throat, Lindsey enjoyed it either way.

Inch by inch, Aubrey sank onto Lindsey's cock, till the tip grazed a certain sensitive spot inside him and his own prick twitched in response. There. That was what he'd missed all these years. A broken moan escaped him.

"Are you all right?" said Lindsey. His hands came up from where they'd rested atop Aubrey's thighs to stroke his hips as if soothing a skittish beast.

"Yes," Aubrey hissed through gritted teeth. "I'm fine."

He didn't make a very convincing case with his eyes screwed shut, sweat beading on his brow, and his legs trembling to balance in his precarious position.

Lindsey frowned. "Are you sure? Because you look a bit—"

Aubrey clenched around Lindsey's prick. Lindsey yelped. Aubrey grinned.

"See?" he said, then took a steadying breath and bore down. His arse met Lindsey's hipbones in one slick thrust.

Lindsey let out a blasphemous exclamation. Aubrey shuddered, gasping to restore the breath he'd driven from his body. To have Lindsey's whole length inside him—! He'd be lying if he called it painless, but it was the satisfied ache of accomplishment. The steady pressure on that certain point inside him helped considerably. He'd take full advantage of it soon. For now, he felt content to wait, breathe, and adjust.

And to soak in the look Lindsey gave him, which seemed rather as if he'd lassoed the moon or caught the stars in a net or some other poetic nonsense.

As it so happened, Lindsey's command of poetic nonsense in thought or speech left him as his eyes rolled back into his head. All awareness of the outside world was lost. Engulfed in soft, tight heat, his whole essence concentrated in his groin. "Exquisite" was the word he'd use for it when he regained his vocabulary. At present, he had only wild cries. He bit his lip to silence them.

In the midst of one such muffled shout, Aubrey bent forward—Lindsey's cock slid out a few inches, and by Jove, did Lindsey appreciate the sensation—and kissed him. Lindsey returned it hungrily. His hands rose to catch Aubrey's jaw, but Aubrey pulled back out of his reach. Ganymede teasing Tantalus.

All Lindsey could do was clutch Aubrey's waist and hold on for the ride. It didn't take long to come to its natural conclusion.

"Aubrey," Lindsey gasped. "I—I'm afraid I must—"

"Hold on," Aubrey groaned. "Just a little longer, please—"

He fell off talking and frigged himself desperately, his cock slipping from his fist in his haste. Before he could grasp it again, Lindsey's hand was upon him. Long, soft fingers twined around his twitching prick. They resolved into a fist and gently tugged. Aubrey almost sobbed in frustration.

"Harder," he begged, bucking into Lindsey's grip. It was almost enough, he was nearly there. "More, for God's sake—!"

Lindsey thrust into him, his hips driving upward, his hand pulling rhythmic and rough on Aubrey's cock. Then Lindsey rose up to claim Aubrey's lips in a devouring kiss, and—

Aubrey cried out into Lindsey's mouth. His hands scrambled for purchase on Lindsey's back, nails drawing furrows in virgin skin. His back arched as ecstasy shot from his groin through his entire body—then he sagged, trembling, half-laughing in relief.

73

Lindsey stroked him through his crisis, though his own thrust grew erratic. He balanced on the knife's edge of release. Then Aubrey lifted his head from where it'd fallen to rest on Lindsey's shoulder and whispered in his ear—

"It's all right. You can come now. Come for me."

—and he went off with a strangled yell and fireworks exploding behind his eyelids as he buried himself in Aubrey's flesh. He fell back onto the mattress, Aubrey collapsing in a heap atop him, both men gasping to recover their spent breath.

☞

WHEN THE MINDLESS euphoria faded, Aubrey grew conscious of his semen drying between their bodies and the discomfort his weight must exert on Lindsey's lean frame. He started to roll off him, but Lindsey's hands roamed north to trace lazy lines over Aubrey's ribs, and up further still, until his arms settled around Aubrey's shoulders in a gentle embrace—all with his eyes closed and a sleepy smile on his lips.

Aubrey wished he could feel even half as assured. Though he could break Lindsey's hold with a casual roll of his shoulders, he felt trapped.

Fucking, he understood. Intimately. To hold a cock, to suck it, and take it with professional ease, he knew well.

But this?

Lindsey, half-asleep and blissfully unaware of Aubrey's dilemma, softly stroked his sweat-slicked back.

Aubrey fought the panic rising in his chest. Most men would've shoved him off by now, washed their pricks, and left with no more of a backward glance than to say, "Same time next week, then?" As for those who stayed, who called him "beloved" and swore everlasting, smothering affection— he'd've done anything to get them out of his bed faster.

Of course, this wasn't his bed.

He considered pulling out of Lindsey's embrace and slipping out the door. But the bed was soft, and Lindsey's touch softer still, and a comfortable warmth surrounded him.

He supposed he could stand it a little longer.

By slow increments, Aubrey repositioned himself half on his side, half on Lindsey. A contented hum issued from Lindsey's lips. Then his eyes opened. His sleepy smile remained for an instant before his brow knitted in concern.

74

"You all right?"

Aubrey hurried to rearrange his own discomfited expression the moment Lindsey opened his eyes, but it seemed he hadn't been quick enough. He plastered an easy grin over his anxieties and affected an airy tone. "Of course."

Lindsey didn't appear convinced. His mouth opened. Aubrey, dreading further questions, put a stop to it with a kiss.

Thus distracted, Lindsey gave up his inquiries. He pulled away to nuzzle at Aubrey's jaw and on down his throat. Aubrey allowed himself to relax a fraction under the quiet, undemanding affection.

The downy duvet drew up over his shoulders. Another kiss, this time to his collarbone, then Lindsey's forehead came to rest upon it and seemed content to stay there. Aubrey let his own hand rise to come through Lindsey's well-tousled curls, untangling and twining them through his fingers.

He could get used to this, he thought drowsily.

He wouldn't, of course. Only a fool would dare to.

But he could.

CHAPTER EIGHT

LINDSEY AWOKE TO sunshine, birdsong, and absolute bliss. At first he didn't recall why. Then he rolled over and beheld Aubrey, curled in on himself like a cat, sheets clenched tight in his fists.

Even closed in sleep, dark bruises shadowed his eyes. His black hair fell half on the pillow, half over his face. With no expression to pull at its edges, his perfect mouth took on a bow shape, turned down at the corners.

Lindsey reached out to smooth a dark strand back into place. Aubrey's brow flinched, but he slumbered on oblivious. If he didn't look peaceful, at least he appeared less troubled. Either way, he remained the handsomest creature Lindsey knew.

He felt content to lie beside him for a thousand years, but his growling stomach demanded otherwise. Lindsey slipped out of bed and into his dressing gown, pulled the bedclothes back up around Aubrey's ivory shoulders, rang for Charles, and stepped into the hall to make arrangements for tea.

By the time the tray arrived, Lindsey had washed up, though he'd yet to exchange his dressing gown for more respectable attire. He spent another quarter-hour sitting up in bed, nibbling a biscuit and rereading his well-worn copy of *Lady Audley's Secret* by the sunlight streaming in through the windows.

One of these sunbeams crept over Aubrey's face at half-past ten. His awakening groan drew Lindsey's attention from the book.

"Good morning!" said Lindsey as Aubrey shook the sleep from his head.

Aubrey glanced up at Lindsey as if he'd only just noticed him. As soon as they locked eyes, Aubrey looked away. "...'Morning."

Lindsey's smile waned. If he didn't know better, he'd say Aubrey seemed ashamed. Discomfited, at the very least. Lindsey found the idea of Aubrey's discomfort unbearable.

"There's tea," he said, thinking perhaps hunger formed the root of Aubrey's ills. "And toast, if you're so inclined. It's all warm yet, I've kept it covered."

Aubrey turned away and reached over the edge of the bed for his clothes with a mumbled, "Thank you."

"...Or muffins?" said Lindsey. "I can arrange for muffins if you'd rather."

"Toast is fine."

Lindsey set his book aside. Perhaps Aubrey wasn't hungry after all. Something else must've upset him. Before Lindsey could inquire, Aubrey sat up.

"Do you have—" Aubrey still wouldn't meet his eyes. "I mean, is there a...?"

"Lavatory?" Lindsey guessed.

Aubrey nodded, his face pale as skimmed milk.

"Through there," said Lindsey, pointing at the door to his private bath.

"Thanks."

Aubrey rushed off, pulling on his trousers as he fled. Lindsey chastised himself for failing to offer a dressing gown.

"Are you all right?" he called after Aubrey.

The door slammed shut.

᧞

LINDSEY'S LAVATORY WAS a massive marvel of engineering and a testament to the aesthetic triumph of marble. Aubrey noted it only in passing. He sat down hard on the edge of the hip-bath, nearly slipped off, and took gravity's hint and settled down on the cold marble floor to consider his situation.

The aristocratic vice had come full circle. It'd trickled down through society's ranks to the lowest rung until he, pathetic urchin, doubled back up the ladder to retake one of the upper class. Aubrey would've laughed if he didn't feel so ill. For God's sake, what was he doing here? Who did he think he was fooling?

Someone knocked on the door. Aubrey jumped up, scrambling for purchase on the tiles.

77

"Aubrey?" The thick wood muffled Lindsey's voice.

Aubrey coughed out the squeak in his throat. "Yes?"

"I've a dressing gown for when you come out, if you need it."

Aubrey detected a note of disappointment in his tone. Perhaps Lindsey expected last night's festivities to continue through the morning. Aubrey thought he might be amenable to the notion, but it wasn't his place to suggest it. His place involved gathering his effects and getting out before the situation became embarrassing. Assuming it wasn't embarrassing already. Aubrey had a sinking feeling they'd passed the point of embarrassment long ago and were well underway to total humiliation. Still, he managed to summon up a small, "Thanks," as he hurriedly cleaned himself up and threw on his clothes.

When he opened the door, Lindsey stood on the other side, dressed for the day, leaning against the bedpost with a silk dressing gown thrown over one arm.

"Could I interest you in breakfast, at least?" he said.

Aubrey, who'd given serious thought to bolting past him, paused.

"It's downstairs," Lindsey continued with an apologetic air. "I could have it brought up if you prefer."

Aubrey swallowed. "Downstairs is fine."

Lindsey grinned, tossed the dressing gown on the bed, and led the way down.

❧

THE COUNTRY HOUSE had seemed grand in the night. Daylight made it resplendent.

The breakfast room alone—an entire room set aside for a single meal— was thrice as large as Aubrey's garret. French windows ran from floor to ceiling along the south-facing wall, wringing out every drop of sunshine from the overcast sky. The eggshell wallpaper reflected the light, doubling it, giving the whole room a warm glow. The table could sit six comfortably, ten in the settings Aubrey was used to, yet only four chairs surrounded it. Eggs, buttered toast, bacon, sausage, ham, soft rolls, marmalade, jams, and a tea service covered the mahogany sideboard. Enough for an army, laid out to feed two men.

"Help yourself," said Lindsey, as if this were normal. Aubrey reminded himself that, for Lindsey, it was normal. Absurdly normal.

Aubrey took what he considered a reasonable portion of eggs and toast. He ignored the temptations of bacon and ham. Best not get used to such luxuries. It would make it harder when it all came to an end.

"Would you like to see the house?" asked Lindsey after a few moments of silent consumption.

Aubrey lowered his egg-laden fork. The mill didn't require him on Sundays, but that was no excuse for sloth. A man focused on self-improvement would've gone home and studied *The Engineer*. Yet all Aubrey could focus on was the smile lighting up Lindsey's handsome features. "Certainly."

Lindsey looked out the window over Aubrey's shoulder. "The weather's fine enough. Shall we start with the gardens and work our way in?"

Aubrey supposed so, and said as much.

The air outdoors had a crisp quality. Aubrey indulged in deep breaths as Lindsey pointed out features of interest. Aubrey wasn't sure if Lindsey meant to impress or inform him. He was impressed despite himself.

"The house was properly built in 1731," Lindsey began. "Before that it was little more than a hunting lodge. Capability Brown designed the hedge maze, though we've let the topiary go since then. Would you care to see it?"

Aubrey hadn't the first idea who Capability Brown was, but he acquiesced to the plan and followed Lindsey across the property.

The hedge maze, with twelve-foot walls casting impenetrable shadows, gave him pause. Uphill from the house, its elevated position kept its coils hidden. The air of a trap hung around the entrance.

"It's not as complicated as it looks." Lindsey stepped into it and looked back at Aubrey. "Just keep making right-hand turns 'til you reach the centre."

"What's in the centre?" Aubrey asked as he caught him up.

"I suppose I ought to preserve the surprise. But since you asked: a folly."

Aubrey didn't wish to appear as much of a fool as he felt for not knowing what "folly" meant in this context, and so kept silent.

The path twisted, turned, and forked, yet Lindsey's stride never wavered. He kept his head high and his eyes forward. Aubrey, on the other hand, had a devil of a time keeping his own head from swiveling back and forth between the dark alcoves looming on either side. Some contained shaggy green figures—the promised topiary—most overgrown into an unrecognisable state, though Aubrey thought one upright creature with two fuzzy antennae might have been a rabbit.

Aubrey began wondering if they hadn't taken a wrong turn at some point. Then Lindsey, with a cheeky grin, brought him around the final corner and into what he could only suppose was the folly.

Six gleaming white marble pillars supported a domed roof over the larger-than-life-sized statue of a woman wearing a sheet and carrying a bow with a nocked arrow. She stood upon her pedestal with a hunter's readiness, her head turned from the altar before her towards the wall of the maze, as if she'd heard something over her shoulder.

"Temple to Diana," said Lindsey when Aubrey looked to him for explanation. "It's not original to the maze. Father had it installed as a wedding present for Mother. Rowena and I used to picnic on the altar."

"Rowena?"

"My sister." Lindsey stepped up to the folly as if it were no more remarkable than a public water pump. "Elder sister. Keeps me in line. You'd like her, I think."

Aubrey, about to follow Lindsey into the false temple, paused mid-step. None of the other men he'd fucked had tried to introduce him to their families. He'd certainly never met any sisters.

Lindsey looked back at him and, seeing his hesitation, added, "It's terribly pagan, I know, but I assure you it's quite harmless."

Aubrey laughed and approached the folly. Up close, he could admire how the sculpted marble mimicked flesh and falling cloth. He could also admire the smooth curve of Lindsey's throat as Lindsey craned his neck to point out the constellation map engraved in the ceiling.

On their way out, the path forked. Aubrey tugged Lindsey towards the shadowy right-hand path.

"That's a dead end," Lindsey said, a note of apology in his voice.

"I know," said Aubrey.

Then he pulled him into the alcove for a kiss, and had the satisfaction of leading a dazed Lindsey out of the maze.

Between maze and manor, Lindsey showed Aubrey a gleaming glass conservatory, the edge of the wooded glen, and the stables. Just as Aubrey had predicted, the stables held a variety of handsome steeds. Lindsey listed off their names with a fond glance at each. Aubrey endeavoured to remember them, but found himself distracted by the presence of a groom brushing one of the geldings. The groom didn't regard them, apart from a deferential nod to Lindsey when they arrived. Lindsey had answered him in kind and turned his attention to a chestnut mare.

"Do you ride?"

Aubrey, who was keeping a wary eye on the groom, gave a start and turned back to Lindsey.

Lindsey, petting the mare's neck, didn't seem to notice anything unusual in Aubrey's behaviour. He awaited his answer with a patient smile.

Aubrey struggled to formulate an appropriate response. Where Lindsey thought he'd found a horse to ride, or the space to ride it, he couldn't imagine. "I'm afraid I had to give up keeping thoroughbreds in Manchester. They didn't get on with the self-acting mules."

He'd meant to temper his sarcasm, he really had, but there it was. He braced himself for Lindsey's anger. He didn't dare turn to see what the groom thought of it.

Lindsey blinked, then brought a hand up to cover his mouth, lest his laughter spook the horses.

"Sorry," he said, when he'd recovered his composure. "That was rather stupid of me, wasn't it?" He shook his head and spoke on over Aubrey's protests. "Would you care to learn?"

Aubrey eyed the mare towering over him, watched her toss her mane and paw the ground with hooves as big as his face. "Another day, perhaps."

"I look forward to it."

Aubrey dared a glance up at Lindsey, who wore a sincere smile, and did his best to mirror it.

Beyond the stables and behind the house lay a fern garden with an artificial waterfall, installed by Lindsey's mother. As they followed its walkways to the front of the house, Lindsey apologised for not knowing the scientific names of all the represented species. Aubrey assured him he didn't mind.

"Are you hungry?"

Aubrey, distracted by the massive marble lions flanking the stairs from the front courtyard to the house, which he'd missed in the dark of the previous night, took a moment to realise Lindsey had spoken to him.

"It's about time for luncheon," Lindsey continued, undaunted, nodding towards the oxidized copper sundial in the centre of the ornamental water feature. "I'm afraid I didn't give Cook much notice of our arrival, but you'd be amazed what she can do with so little."

And so Aubrey went back in.

Luncheon in the breakfast room—Lindsey actually apologised for using the same room twice, as most of the household staff had moved to London with the family for the season—included chicken, more ham, fresh greens, and mashed potatoes. Lindsey filled Aubrey's plate with some of everything. With ample encouragement from Lindsey, Aubrey polished it off. Then, to his surprise, the cook herself, a rotund middle-aged woman with a scowl for everything but Lindsey, arrived with gooseberry tart. Lindsey tucked in as if he hadn't just eaten more food than Aubrey saw in a week. Aubrey picked at his tart with a silver fork.

"No good?"

Aubrey dropped the fork. His head jerked up to meet Lindsey's concerned frown.

"No, no, it's fine," Aubrey rushed to reassure him. "I'm just not terribly hungry, is all."

Lindsey nodded, though his brow remained furrowed. In an effort to smooth it, Aubrey scooped some tart onto his fork. Delicious, but his gut contracted when he tried to swallow.

"You don't have to finish it," said Lindsey. "I assure you, Cook won't take offense."

Aubrey doubted it, but he lowered his fork with a grateful smile all the same.

With luncheon under their belts, the tour continued indoors. Corridor on corridor, chamber after chamber, the house seemed endless. And all devoted to nothing more strenuous than an afternoon's light exercise. Compared to the ceaseless industry of Manchester, Aubrey could hardly justify it. Yet when he saw the delight on Lindsey's face at a fern in a terrarium, or his evident joy when Aubrey responded positively to the library, Aubrey couldn't begrudge him an inch of it.

"Do you read?" Lindsey asked as Aubrey took in the endless shelves. "For pleasure, I mean."

"Haven't the time," Aubrey replied. But Lindsey, head cocked with a listening look on his face, seemed to want more from him, so he continued. "Used to, though. When I was younger. Penny dreadfuls and such. Nothing like..."

He waved his arm to indicate the library entire. Lindsey followed the gesture and returned to Aubrey with a smile.

"You'd be surprised. It looks austere, bound up in leather, but the content is much the same."

Aubrey raised an eyebrow, but couldn't withhold a smile of his own.

At the other end of the house lay the music room. A harpsichord carved in last century's style and painted gleaming white sat at one end of the enormous, echoing chamber. Lindsey went straight to it and lifted its lid. A few delicate chords stirred the air, drawing Aubrey's eyes from windows taller than his whole lodging-house. Lindsey, realising he had Aubrey's attention, played some showier notes. Then a self-conscious smile stole over his lips and he stepped away from the instrument, sitting down on its bench with his back to it.

Aubrey sat down beside Lindsey and looked over his shoulder at the harpsichord. The last few notes still hung in the air. "Do you play often?"

"No, hardly at all. My sister's the real musician. She used to teach me her lessons as she learnt them, for practice."

"Used to?"

"Until our father sent me to Eton." Lindsey's smile waned. "He resisted the notion for years. Finally gave in when I was thirteen, only to call me home three years later."

"Why?" Aubrey asked before his sense of propriety could stop him.

Lindsey shrugged. "Didn't see fit to explain his reasoning to me." He reached behind himself and played half a scale, his long fingers ambling over the keys. "He's not terribly forthcoming at the best of times. I assume he was dissatisfied with my academic performance."

Aubrey, having no experience with parents of any kind, much less those who might care whether he succeeded or failed, changed the subject. "Did you enjoy school?"

"Oh, I adored it!" Lindsey abandoned the harpsichord to fix Aubrey with a look of purest joy. "The books, the sport—I found my dearest friends there."

"What sort of sport?"

As it turned out, every sort. Lindsey related them all, from cricket to football to rowing and back again, throwing in anecdotes of striking successes or failures in the field. It all lay outside Aubrey's purview, but even what he didn't understand seemed wondrous when delivered with Lindsey's enthusiasm. Bright blue eyes shone with glories of days past, and his hands moved with animated vigor as he described a close boat race. Aubrey pictured those hands clenched around oars, those lean shoulders pulling against the rushing river, bare skin gleaming in the summer sun.

"And you?"

The spell broke, leaving Aubrey stunned. "Pardon?"

"Did you enjoy school?" Lindsey asked with an expression of eager interest, which made it all the more painful for Aubrey to realise how inadequate his answer would be.

"Yes. But it was hardly so exciting as Eton."

The ghost of Lindsey's grin remained, but his eyebrows knit in confusion.

Aubrey hopped off the bench as if it'd bit him. "You said something about a portrait gallery?"

Lindsey looked no less confused than before, but stood up regardless. "I did, yes. Shall we?"

Aubrey wholeheartedly agreed.

Lindsey led the way to a grand hall with a high, vaulted ceiling. Originally built for indoor perambulation, thick curtains now covered its wall of impossibly tall windows. Every remaining inch of wall from floor to ceiling displayed framed portraits of blond, blue-eyed, aquiline-featured people. Several could've passed for Lindsey's doubles, costumes aside. These, then, were Lindsey's ancestors, stretching back through the centuries to William the Conqueror. Possibly beyond.

The entire Althorp clan stared Aubrey down. Aubrey, alone, with no gallery of compact, bow-lipped, large-eyed individuals behind him. Not a single living soul who bore any resemblance. No memory of a face like his looking into his own.

Despite his best efforts, he felt a bit small.

"My father." Lindsey pointed to a portrait of a man with a moustache set in a grim line. "He's gone a bit grey since. Well, entirely grey."

"I see." Aubrey didn't know what else he could say, apart from congratulations to Lindsey for having a recorded past.

"And here's their wedding portrait." Lindsey stepped aside to indicate a life-sized full-figure piece. A younger version of the man stood with a smile pulling up the ends of his moustache and crinkling the corners of his eyes. His hand rested on the back of a chair, in which sat a slender blonde woman with a long neck, a regal bearing, and Lindsey's own smile beaming down on them with the force of a thousand suns.

"Him and my mother, I mean," Lindsey added, as if it weren't immediately apparent. "Alice Althorp. She used to say her middle name was Alliteration. Took me ages to work out the joke. In fairness, it sounds a bit like a real name when one is four years old."

Aubrey wouldn't have known the difference at that age either, and told Lindsey so. Lindsey smile appreciatively.

84

"Is there a more recent portrait of her?" asked Aubrey.

Lindsey's smile vanished. A pathetic imitation replaced it, yet Aubrey felt its absence like an ice-cold draught blowing in through a broken window.

"No, unfortunately," said Lindsey. "She passed away when I was seven."

His gaze returned to the wedding portrait. Aubrey tried not to notice how ferociously he blinked to force tears back into his eyes.

"I'm sorry," said Aubrey. Inadequate words, he knew, but before he could add more, Lindsey cut him off.

"Don't be," he said, pulling his pained smile into something more sincere. "She wouldn't stand for it. Never could abide sorrow of any kind."

His right hand disappeared into his trouser pocket. His left twitched as if it, too, wished to hide. Aubrey caught it in his own. Lindsey, jerked out of his reminiscence, looked down to their joined hands, then up at Aubrey with a grateful half-smile. Aubrey drew closer, and Lindsey leaned his head atop Aubrey's own.

"Are your parents...?" Lindsey began.

Aubrey stiffened, felt Lindsey do the same against him, and forced himself to relax. "Both deceased."

"Forgive me, I didn't mean—"

"There's nothing to forgive. Happens to everyone eventually."

Lindsey squeezed his arm.

They wandered back through the house, Lindsey adding a few more interesting details he'd forgotten along the way, 'til he halted abruptly at the base of the entrance hall stair.

"By Jove!" he cried. "We never made it to the theatre!"

Aubrey'd forgotten all about it. "It's all right, I don't mind."

"Are you sure?" asked Lindsey. "I feel dreadful about it. I did promise, after all."

"Promise?"

"Offered, then. I fear I've lured you here under false pretenses."

"No," Aubrey replied quickly. "You didn't." He, of all people, knew a thing or two about false pretenses and luring.

Lindsey didn't notice. "Shall we go tonight? I could take you to dinner beforehand. Give Cook a break from us, and us a break from her cooking."

Only a fool would turn down a free meal. And it would take a better man than Aubrey to resist the temptation of such a handsome face, bearing such a kind smile.

Aubrey answered with a smile of his own. "Then I suppose we're off to the theatre."

⟿

NOTHING DISTINGUISHED LINDSEY'S club from the rest of Pall Mall until Aubrey entered. Though the staff welcomed him as Lindsey's guest, the other members fixed him with cold stares. Their everyday attire put Aubrey's best—and only—jacket to shame. Even the staff had more polish. But Lindsey didn't seem to see anything amiss with Aubrey's appearance. Aubrey gave silent thanks and turned his attention to the food, more than enough to sate his appetite. Then he and Lindsey left the club's indignant eyes behind for the glamour of the theatre.

St. James's Theatre was only marginally more opulent than the Althorp estate. Aubrey wasn't the worst-dressed man there. Plenty of other theatre-goers had similar attire. But none of them stood beside Lindsey in his tailored evening jacket and silk waistcoat. And they certainly didn't have Lindsey's gentle hand on their elbows, guiding them out of the lobby to the magnificent stone stair leading up, up, up to the private box reserved for the Althorp family. In Lindsey's words, both he and his sister adored the theatre. Aubrey assumed their father felt indifferent towards it.

The theatre's interior had cream-coloured walls gilded with gold inlay, framing murals of frolicking youths. Aubrey wondered how anyone could concentrate on the stage with the house so decorated, though his own interest lay in the electric chandelier far above the audience. He tried to restrain himself, but Lindsey caught him looking up.

"The, er, lights," Aubrey explained. "Electric."

Lindsey followed his gaze upward. "So they are!"

The lights dimmed soon after, much to Aubrey's relief. In the dark, no one could gawk at the shabby little man sitting beside the elegant Mr Althorp.

Aubrey hadn't heard of the play, *Lady Windermere's Fan*, but Lindsey assured him his friend Graves, a literary critic, had judged it acceptable. It proved better than acceptable. Aubrey laughed outright twice in the first act, surprising himself as much as Lindsey.

It could've been a terrible play for all Aubrey cared. The experience of sitting with Lindsey in the privacy of a dark theatre box thrilled him even more than he'd imagined. Their shoulders pressed together from the moment the lights went down, and Lindsey's hand meandered over to rest on Aubrey's thigh as the evening progressed. It left Aubrey giddy as the curtain closed for intermission. But whatever plans he had for entertainment between acts were dashed by the arrival of an usher bearing a note for Lindsey. Lindsey took the note, smiled at it, and gave an affirmative reply.

"Graves is in the box opposite," he said after the usher departed.

Aubrey peered across the house as if he could discern a specific stranger at such a distance.

"He'd like to stop by for a quick chat," Lindsey continued. His sunny serenity turned to concern. "You don't mind, do you?"

Inwardly, Aubrey panicked. Foolish enough to agree to accompany Lindsey in public, but he'd done it assuming no one would notice or remember him. An introduction to Lindsey's friend hadn't factored into Aubrey's calculations.

Outwardly, Aubrey assured Lindsey he didn't mind.

It took some time for Graves to arrive. Aubrey and Lindsey spent it watching the crowd below, until an usher behind them cleared his throat and announced, "Lord Cyril Graves."

Aubrey turned, and came face-to-face with Mr Halloway.

CHAPTER NINE

BESIDE MR HALLOWAY stood another gentleman. Lindsey took that gentleman's hand with a cheerful greeting, but Aubrey's attention remained fixed on his downstairs neighbour.

Halloway, wide-eyed, seemed equally off-put by the coincidence. Then the gentleman stranger put an arm around Halloway's shoulders in an affectionate squeeze, and Halloway's shocked expression gave way to a wry, resigned smile. Before Aubrey could respond, Lindsey stepped in.

"Warren," he said to Aubrey, "this is Graves, my friend I was just telling you about."

Aubrey stood—belatedly—and shook hands with Graves, a toff their age with a lock of flat brown hair falling into his eyes. A pair of lavender gloves poked out of his waistcoat pocket, and a green carnation adorned his buttonhole. His eyes swept over Aubrey, lingering on his frayed trouser hems.

"Charmed, I'm sure," said Graves. "Althorp, Halloway."

Halloway, quicker to catch on than Aubrey, gave Lindsey a charming, easygoing response. Aubrey quieted the turbulent whirlpool of fear, shame, and jealousy brewing in his guts and pasted on a polite smile. If nothing else, he could take comfort in how Halloway's costume resembled his own, with the addition of an emerald paint smear on his shirt-sleeve, so near the cuff as to show under his jacket when he moved his arm.

Lindsey and Graves fell to talking like the old friends they were, leaving Halloway and Aubrey on their own. Aubrey had half a mind to pretend he was meeting Halloway for the first time. Halloway didn't.

"What's a respectable chap like you doing in a place like this?" he asked with a cheeky grin.

"Taking in a show," Aubrey replied, unamused.

"I bet you are." Halloway's gaze fell on Lindsey, wandering up and down his lean frame.

"And you?" Aubrey said, as if Halloway hadn't just undressed Lindsey with his eyes.

Halloway gave a fond eye-roll towards Graves. "He had work to do, and he despises doing it alone. Prefers to mix it with pleasure. I'm the same way."

"Indeed," said Aubrey, his tone flat.

Halloway raised his brows and turned away to put his hand on Graves's shoulder. Graves, though still chatting, caught the hint and bid Lindsey adieu.

When they'd gone, Lindsey looked to Aubrey with a hopeful expression.

"Your friend has impeccable taste," Aubrey managed.

Lindsey beamed at him. They settled in to watch the rest of the show with their fingers entwined.

The curtain closed all too soon. As the electric chandelier brightened, Aubrey disentangled himself with no small amount of reluctance. Leaving Lindsey's side was the last thing in the world he wanted to do, but the hour was late, and Monday required an early rising. He refused to become a second Smith.

"I'm sorry," Aubrey said, pressing Lindsey's hand in his own. "But you know where to find me if you should want me again."

Lindsey smiled. "I do. And I certainly will."

Aubrey quieted the flutter in his chest with a cough.

The walk to the train station was cold and damp. Aubrey's burning cheeks kept the chill at bay. He scarcely noticed the temperature or anything else until he boarded the train and heard a familiar voice.

"Going my way?"

Aubrey gave a start. There stood Halloway again, in the entrance to the train car.

"Yes," Aubrey admitted. It'd be ludicrous to pretend otherwise.

"Splendid," said Halloway, and sat down across from him. The train jerked into motion. Halloway waited until the screeching whistles and clanging bells subsided, then asked, "I don't suppose I could convince you to model for me?"

"No," said Aubrey. "You couldn't."

Halloway shrugged. "Only asking."

"As you have before, with the same result."

"Yes," said Halloway, "but I assumed you refused me for reasons that wouldn't apply in light of what we've learned tonight."

"I'd prefer it if you didn't paint him, either."

Halloway's eyebrows almost touched his hairline. "No need to be territorial. I'd hoped we might become friendlier, considering our common ground."

"If this is blackmail," said Aubrey, "then it's clumsily done."

Halloway's jovial expression shut down like a portcullis over a castle gate. "Nothing of the kind."

He put his chin in his palm and turned to the window. An uncomfortable silence settled over the train car. Aubrey tapped his index finger against his knee.

"About tonight..." Aubrey began.

Halloway lifted his head and turned back to him.

"I'd prefer you didn't mention it to anyone," Aubrey finished.

Halloway waved him off. "Wouldn't dream of it."

"Thank you," said Aubrey. Then, "I'm sorry for what I said earlier. It was unfair of me."

"It certainly was," said Halloway, but he couldn't keep up his disapproving expression for long. His mouth quirked to one side in a half-smile. "Fortunately for you I'm a forgiving soul."

Aubrey smiled back.

☙

"Sir Geoffrey would see you in his study, sir," a footman said on the following afternoon.

Lindsey, who'd bent over *The English Mechanic and World of Science*, snapped upright. Few good things ever followed those words. On his best behaviour ever since his father pulled him from Eton, Lindsey hadn't heard the phrase in years.

Despite the short distance between the library and Sir Geoffrey's study, Lindsey found plenty of time to fret over what his father wanted. Sir Geoffrey's valet, Jonathan, met Lindsey at the study door. Lindsey stopped short of the threshold and waited to be announced.

Black walnut paneling covered the study walls from floor to ceiling. Three narrow Gothic windows dotted the north side. Apart from them, the study depended on gas for light. In Lindsey's childhood, it had been

90

whale oil. Lindsey didn't think an ocean's worth of whales could brighten the grim chamber.

Sir Geoffrey sat at his desk, an enormous affair of black walnut with a bas-relief reproduction of the family coat of arms carved into its front. A matching armchair stood before the desk at an angle, a hollow imitation of the throne Sir Geoffrey occupied. He seemed at ease in his fortress, his eyes cast down at the *Pall Mall Gazette*, a forgotten cup of tea by his left hand. At Jonathan's reappearance, he raised his eyes.

"Master Lindsey, sir," said Jonathan.

Sir Geoffrey gave the slightest of nods. Jonathan vanished down the corridor.

Unable to stall any further, Lindsey walked with silent tread to stand in front of his father's desk, and waited.

Sir Geoffrey took another minute or so to finish reading his article. Then he folded up his newspaper, set it aside, and deigned to look up at his son. "Sit down."

Lindsey perched on the edge of the seat, hesitated, then allowed his left elbow to settle on the small patch of upholstery on the chair's arm. No sooner had he done so than Sir Geoffrey stood and strode out from behind his desk to tower over his son.

"You haven't chaperoned your sister on a ride through Hyde Park in some time."

As far as scolding went, this seemed as though it would be mild. Inwardly, Lindsey relaxed a fraction. Outwardly, he maintained the posture of a cast-iron bar. "No, sir, I haven't."

Sir Geoffrey's right eyebrow twitched. Lindsey feared he'd come across as insolent and hurried to correct himself.

"If she requires chaperonage, I'm happy to oblige. She need only ask."

Still Sir Geoffrey said nothing. Lindsey restrained a nervous jitter in his left leg and tried again.

"In the future, she won't need to ask. I will offer."

Sir Geoffrey sighed. Whatever test he'd set, Lindsey had failed.

"Rowena is more than capable of asking for what she wants," Sir Geoffrey said in the tone of a man who'd been asked often enough. "Your negligence concerns me only insomuch as it represents a change in your habits. Rather than tending your sister, or your friends, or even your literature..."

Here Sir Geoffrey paused. The angle of his brows made plain his opinion of Lindsey's literature, as if Lindsey didn't already know.

"...you tend your factory."

Lindsey's heart stopped.

Whether Sir Geoffrey had heard it from his fellows at the club, or from friends at the theatre, or from the country house staff, Lindsey couldn't say. But nothing else could explain this meeting.

Sir Geoffrey knew about Aubrey.

Lindsey resolved not to panic. Panic would solve nothing. Sir Geoffrey had neither pity nor time for those who cracked under strain. Least of all his own son.

Sir Geoffrey continued. "I suppose you think me old-fashioned. But I am not so set in my ways as you might believe."

Lindsey's eyes widened. Surely his father didn't both know and approve.

Sir Geoffrey noted the change in his son's expression—Lindsey had been careless—and mirrored it. "I understand to derive one's income from property alone is passe. Income from investments and industry is the way of the future. But a gentleman doesn't dirty his hands with the day-to-day details of such business. He employs an agent to manage his affairs. You, being yet a youth, have none. I can recommend several worthy candidates for the post."

Lindsey took a half-second too long to respond. In his defence, his mind reeled with mingled relief and disappointment—his father didn't know, and so couldn't approve—and focused on ensuring none of it showed in his expression or posture.

When he felt prepared to address his father's proposal, he found it inspired dismay. An agent would become a middleman between him and Aubrey. An agent recommended by Sir Geoffrey would doubtless report to him behind Lindsey's back, with tales of the curious relationship between Lindsey and his lowly clerk. An agent would ruin everything.

But Lindsey had never in his life contradicted his father to his face.

A month ago, Lindsey would've acquiesced to his father's plan and swallowed his complaints. But a month ago, he'd have lost nothing of true value. Now, he'd lose Aubrey. He couldn't bear it—not with stoicism, which his father demanded above all else.

"Thank you, sir," Lindsey forced out, stalling for time. "I appreciate your concern."

Sir Geoffrey responded with an expectant look.

"But," Lindsey continued without any idea what would follow. Then in a burst of inspiration, he added, "I should endeavour to understand the business before I allow others to manage it on my behalf. It would be the simplest thing for someone to take advantage of my ignorance and ruin me. None of your candidates ever would, I'm sure, but if I don't learn to judge for myself now, I'll be at the mercy of others forever. When I've learned the business, I'll delegate. But first I must learn."

Sir Geoffrey remained silent. Lindsey's mouth went dry.

"With—" he managed, then cleared his throat. "With your approval, sir."

Sir Geoffrey continued to stare with an expression of what Lindsey thought might be surprise. He couldn't say for certain. He'd never seen his father surprised before. Then the left corner of Sir Geoffrey's moustache quirked up.

"Very well."

Lindsey caught his sigh of relief in his chest.

Sir Geoffrey strode around his desk and sat back in his chair. Lindsey relaxed a little in a shallow imitation of his father's posture.

"Your argument is compelling," said Sir Geoffrey. "When you're ready to employ an agent, come to me. I'll find someone trustworthy."

Lindsey thought he must be daydreaming. His father never relented so easily. Though Lindsey noticed how readily Sir Geoffrey agreed that Lindsey's ignorance bordered on vulnerability.

"Thank you, sir," Lindsey repeated, more sincere. He rose with a deferential nod and left the study.

☞

LINDSEY AWOKE TO the sound of someone calling his name. He opened his eyes and discovered Charles by his bedside, leaning over him.

Charles said something. Or rather, his lips moved, but Lindsey couldn't quite hear him.

"Speak up, Charles," said Lindsey.

A pained expression flicked across Charles's face. Perhaps he'd caught cold, and lost his voice. No, he was speaking again, and there were definitely sounds. Probably words. But jumbled, somehow. Lindsey couldn't understand them. He waited patiently for Charles to correct himself.

Charles repeated whatever phrase he'd uttered. This time, Lindsey caught the tail end of it.

"—is dead."

Lindsey bolted upright. "What? Who's dead?"

Charles grimaced and repeated himself a fourth time.

"Sir Geoffrey is dead."

CHAPTER TEN

LINDSEY STARED AT Charles. "Balderdash."

"I'm afraid not, sir."

Lindsey frowned. It wasn't like Charles to be contrary. "If this is your idea of a joke, Charles, it isn't funny. Now, what did you wake me for?"

A strange look came over Charles's face. Not quite sorrow—pity, perhaps. It disappeared, replaced by his customary calm. "I woke you to tell you Sir Geoffrey is dead, Sir Lindsey."

Lindsey began to think Charles might be serious. "And what makes you believe my father is no longer with us?"

"Jonathan found him so, sir, not a quarter of an hour ago. It seems he passed on in his sleep."

Impossible. Sir Geoffrey hadn't been the slightest bit ill last night. Lindsey was about to say so when Charles continued.

"Would you like to see him, sir?"

"Yes!" Lindsey got out of bed. "Yes, I would, by God."

That would put an end to Charles's nonsense once and for all. Lindsey would go to his father's chambers and find Sir Geoffrey sitting up in bed, wondering why the devil they'd barged into his room at such an hour.

Lindsey led the way down the hall, not at a run, but an efficient march. Charles hurried along behind.

Sir Geoffrey's bedroom door hung open. Jonathan stood at the bedside. Sir Geoffrey himself was asleep. Lindsey brusquely motioned Jonathan out of the way and approached his father.

"Sir."

In his peripheral vision, he saw Jonathan shoot a pointed look at Charles, who shook his head. Lindsey ignored them. They were both clearly delusional. Perhaps they'd dipped into the drinks cabinet. Sir Geoffrey would be livid when he heard of it.

"Sir," Lindsey repeated, louder, and reached for his father's hand.

It was cold, and refused to budge under his fingers.

Part of Lindsey's brain insisted the chill morning was at fault; the fire was out, the blankets thin, Sir Geoffrey's circulation poor. But another, smaller voice in the back of his mind grew louder by the second and threatened to break into a scream.

"Sir?" Lindsey fumbled with his father's wrist for a pulse.

Nothing.

Lindsey's grip tightened on the unyielding flesh. A hand settled on his shoulder.

"Come away, sir," said Charles.

Lindsey could've struck him for his impertinence. He resolved to so as soon as he felt like himself again.

For the moment, he allowed Charles to lead him from the room.

⌇

CHARLES SHEPHERDED LINDSEY back to his chambers, shaved him, dressed him, and ordered him a breakfast he barely noticed.

"I took the liberty of sending for a physician, sir," Charles said at some point between the dressing and the breakfast.

Lindsey could only nod his assent.

He had wild hopes when the physician arrived—perhaps Sir Geoffrey's affliction merely mimicked death, and he would recover—but they were swiftly dashed. The physician confirmed the terrible news and diagnosed the probable cause: a bleed on the brain. Sir Geoffrey had never awoken, had suffered little, his passing peaceful. Lindsey swallowed his protests and thanked the physician for his expertise.

All that remained was to inform the absent Rowena. Lindsey tried to compose the telegram on his own, but when his pen tore through his fourth attempt and gouged the leather top of his desk, he delegated the task to Charles. Charles performed it with admirable stoicism. After a gentle inquiry into whether or not Lindsey required his services further, and receiving a negative reply, Charles left Lindsey to his own devices.

Lindsey spent all of thirty seconds alone in his chambers before fleeing to the library. He pulled volumes from the shelves at random, desperate for distraction. None held his attention. The text of *Wuthering Heights* blurred before his eyes, panicking him until he realised his vision had failed not from a stroke, but from tears. He blinked them back and flung the book aside.

The library having failed him, he departed it with no clear idea of his next destination. A closed door yanked him from his daze. Upon opening it, he discovered his semiconscious steps had taken him to his father's study.

Lindsey entered the sepulchral chamber. It never occurred to him to turn up the gas lamps. He barely had the presence of mind to cross the room and collapse into the high-backed armchair in front of his father's desk.

He wasn't an idiot. He'd known the omnipresent spectre of mortality ever since the fateful winter afternoon when Sir Geoffrey entered the nursery for the first time since Rowena's birth to tell the children Mother wouldn't take tea with them today. Mother had to go away, but the place she'd gone was much nicer than here.

Lindsey, nearly seven then, couldn't imagine anywhere nicer than the nursery, except perhaps the Crystal Palace. He supposed Mother had gone there and asked when she would return.

Sir Geoffrey had seemed taken aback by the question and said, in a tone he probably hadn't meant to sound so gruff, that Mother wouldn't return. Ever.

Despite the turmoil in his tiny heart, Lindsey hadn't shed tears. He'd already shamed Mother into leaving him. He'd resolved not to do the same to his father.

Now that his father had left, regardless of his best efforts, he couldn't stem the tears streaming from his eyes.

He needed something to brace himself. He rose from the chair and ventured behind his father's desk to a small cabinet. Sir Geoffrey, with absolute trust in his staff, had never bothered to put his spirits under lock and key.

Lindsey poured a glass of brandy and sat down again, bringing the bottle with him. He meant to sip at it, but as he realised he'd spent his entire life in pursuit of his father's approval only to lose all chance of achieving it, he found himself draining the tumbler. He poured another, his hands shaking. Perhaps if he'd tried harder to mold himself into a more acceptable heir, Sir Geoffrey's nerves wouldn't have been so strained, and...

His shoulders heaved in a choked-off sob.

Lindsey forced his thoughts down another path. As he emptied his second glass, he conceived a terrible idea. By the time he'd gulped down the fourth, he lacked the faculties to talk himself out of it.

⁊

AROUND EIGHT O'CLOCK that night, Aubrey heard a shuffling stop and a thud on the landing outside his door.

"Warren?" a voice whispered. "Open up, will you?"

Aubrey rose from his desk. "Who's there?"

"Halloway. And your friend."

Aubrey frowned, confused, but opened the door regardless.

There stood Halloway. Leaning heavily upon him, cravat crumpled, eyes rimmed red, and reeking of brandy, was Lindsey.

"What the devil?" said Aubrey, standing back to admit them.

Halloway pulled Lindsey over the threshold. "Found him outside. Thought I'd best bring him in before Mrs Padwick noticed. I assume he's here for you? Unless Brown shares our proclivities."

"No, no," said Aubrey, adding, "Thank you."

"No trouble at all," said Halloway. "I'll just be going."

And he was gone. Aubrey closed the door and looked at Lindsey, who swayed like an elm in a breeze.

"Lindsey?"

Lindsey straightened up, squaring his shoulders and holding his chin high. "My father is dead."

"Oh." Aubrey cringed and tried again. "You have my sympathies."

The initial offense seemed to pass Lindsey by. "Your sympathies are the only ones that matter."

Aubrey, astonished, said nothing.

Lindsey waved his arm in a vague, sweeping gesture, twirling his wrist at the end of it. "You're the only one who understands what it's like. Being an orphan."

Aubrey didn't believe he was the only orphan in Lindsey's circle of acquaintance, but he had more pressing concerns. "How'd you get here?"

"Train," said Lindsey. Aubrey was about to argue the train didn't deposit its passengers on individual doorsteps when Lindsey added, "Hansom."

"You hired a cab?"

Lindsey blinked slowly and nodded slower still.

Aubrey felt torn between concern for Lindsey's well-being and admiration for his tenacity. "Where'd you get my address?"

"I'm your employer."

Aubrey awaited further explanation. Lindsey resumed peering blearily around the garret. Aubrey supposed it was all the answer he'd get from Lindsey's current state. And what a state it was. "You're drunk."

Lindsey barked out a laugh. "Should I be anything else?"

"Asleep," said Aubrey, thinking of the dreadful tasks awaiting the newly-minted orphan. Funeral arrangements, contacting relatives, settling questions of inheritance... No rest for the bereaved.

Lindsey stared at him. Aubrey interpreted the look as uncomprehending until Lindsey spoke, in a small, pathetic voice unlike his usual jovial tone. "Could I sleep here?"

His expression—raw, frail, lost—struck Aubrey marrow-deep, as if he looked not at a man, but a reflection of his own past, an abandoned child unable to grasp the hardships looming on the horizon.

Aubrey laid a hand on Lindsey's shoulder. "Of course."

Spidery fingers clutched the back of Aubrey's shirt, pulling the two men flush. Lindsey's jaw pressed into Aubrey's collarbone, his shuddering gasps hot in Aubrey's ear.

Aubrey, startled, had lifted his hands in self-defence. Now he lowered them, one coming to rest between Lindsey's shoulderblades, the other hesitating in mid-air before stroking the back of Lindsey's head. Lindsey relaxed against him at the touch, so Aubrey continued running his fingers through soft blond curls. They stood together, silent save for Lindsey's ragged sobs, for some time. At last, Lindsey pulled away, holding Aubrey at arm's length.

"To bed, then," said Aubrey.

Lindsey's chin dropped to his chest as he raised trembling fingers to fumble at his waistcoat buttons.

Aubrey caught Lindsey's hands in his own. "Let me."

Lindsey, his hands limp in Aubrey's hold, nodded.

Aubrey shucked off Lindsey's jacket, pulling long arms through stubborn sleeves with a gentle touch. He felt reluctant to step away even for the few seconds required to hang the article on a nail; Lindsey seemed near to collapse, either from drunken exhaustion or plain disinterest in remaining upright. Yet Lindsey stood firm as Aubrey untied his cravat, unbuttoned his waistcoat and shirt, unhooked his braces, and set all aside. Lindsey would need to wear them tomorrow. He'd brought no other clothes with him, and nothing of Aubrey's would fit—even if Aubrey had possessed more than one jacket.

Lindsey let Aubrey guide him to the bed with one hand on the small of his back, and sat down for Aubrey to untie his shoes. Aubrey hesitated before reaching for Lindsey's trouser buttons, but Lindsey didn't seem to notice the intrusion, save to stand again so Aubrey could remove them. As he stepped out of the cuffs, he steadied himself with a hand on Aubrey's shoulder. Aubrey noted the limb shook less than before.

Trousers were folded and set aside along with garters and socks. Soon Lindsey lay curled on his side, staring at the peeling wallpaper with unseeing eyes.

Aubrey pulled the blanket up over Lindsey's shoulders and turned away, resigned to sleeping at his desk. But something caught his wrist.

He looked down to find Lindsey's hand on his sleeve, and Lindsey's gaze more focused than it'd been all evening.

"Stay," Lindsey begged, his voice hoarse. "Please."

Only a monster could've refused. Aubrey nodded. Lindsey's fingers dropped their hold like a dead man's.

Keeping one hand on the bed, lest Lindsey think himself abandoned, Aubrey maneuvered around to slither under the blanket from the other side. The bed, barely wide enough for one and far too narrow for two, forced him to lie flush against Lindsey's back, nothing between them but the thin cotton of his own nightshirt. He had to admit the warmth of Lindsey's flesh provided welcome relief from the night's chill. He didn't want to admit he found it appealing for other reasons.

Lindsey rolled over and buried his face in Aubrey's collar. Aubrey drew the blanket up over Lindsey's shoulders again. His hand lingered on Lindsey's back, the muscles under it so tense they felt like bone. Aubrey rubbed his palm over them in slow circles. Lindsey relaxed under his ministrations. A trembling sigh escaped him.

"Go to sleep," Aubrey murmured.

He felt Lindsey nod against his shoulder, his breaths growing deep and steady. Aubrey followed him into slumber.

◦

LINDSEY AWOKE TO nausea and a headache the likes of which he hadn't known since Eton. He dragged the bedclothes over his head, but stopped halfway. Someone had replaced his linens with coarse wool. He forced his eyes open to regard the incongruity and found someone had replaced his entire room.

He lay naked on a narrow bed in a garret, hardly six by ten feet, smaller than a scullery. His clothes hung on a row of nails hammered over peeling yellow wallpaper. Overhead, bare beams sloped down forty-five degrees, forcing the ceiling to abut the top of the lone window. Outside, milky Earl Grey smog rolled past. The door at the far end of the room fit into its frame with a half-inch gap all around it. Dust motes stirred in the air, and Lindsey was utterly alone.

His first assumption—that he'd been imprisoned for public drunkenness—was disproved by the absence of bars on the window. Beyond that, he had no explanation for his present circumstance. From the wretched taste on his tongue he knew he'd been drinking. But why had he been drinking?

The moment his mind supplied the answer, he found himself dry-heaving over the edge of the bed.

His arms shook as he wrangled himself back into bed. He closed his eyes and pulled the threadbare blanket over his face. His father was dead. Lindsey himself lay naked and alone in a strange room, unable to recall how he'd arrived there, which he supposed should cause him more concern. Considering recent events, however, he couldn't bother to care about something so trivial.

"Lindsey?"

Lindsey whisked the blanket off his face and struggled to rise.

Aubrey stood by the door, one hand on the knob. He'd opened and shut it without so much as a squeak. "I'm sorry to wake you, but it's nearly ten, and I fear we'll both be missed if we delay much longer."

Lindsey nodded, then winced and grabbed his forehead as pain spiked behind his eyes. He heard Aubrey cross the room to pour something, and felt the mattress dip as Aubrey sat on the edge.

"Here. Drink this."

Opening his mouth for any purpose whatsoever was the last thing Lindsey wanted to do, but he let his eyes squint open and took the chipped mug from Aubrey. Tepid water helped clear the sour stench of last night's brandy. He pulled a face anyway.

Aubrey's hand settled onto Lindsey's shoulder, gentle as a butterfly alighting on a blossom. Lindsey leaned into the touch, and Aubrey rubbed his back in earnest.

"Where are we?" Lindsey asked.

Aubrey hesitated. "My room."

"In Manchester?" said Lindsey, as if Aubrey lived anywhere else.

"Yes." Aubrey appeared ashamed of it.

"Oh." Lindsey cast his eyes over the garret again in search of something, anything to compliment. His gaze slipped over the splintery floorboards and caught upon an area rug woven from cotton rags, which he almost called ingenious, but thought better of it, not wishing to condescend. The soapboxes stacked into shelves beside the bed contained a more promising prospect—periodicals in tidy piles.

"*The Engineer*," Lindsey read off the topmost volume. "Is that, er, good?"

Aubrey gave a pained smile. "It's all right."

Before Lindsey could atone for his solecism, Aubrey rose to retrieve his clothes and help him dress.

"You'll want this button looked at," Aubrey said as he did up Lindsey's shirt.

"Pardon?" said Lindsey, more concerned with staying upright than the details of his wardrobe.

"This button popped off, so I put it back on, only I didn't have any white thread, so I used black. Looks a bit off, but should hold until you're home. Your waistcoat'll cover it for now."

"You sewed my button?" Lindsey felt disproportionately touched by the gesture. He certainly couldn't sew any buttons. "How?"

"This morning." Aubrey's gaze remained on Lindsey's shirtfront. "While you slept."

"Thank you."

Aubrey coughed. "You're quite welcome."

Once dressed, Lindsey leaned against the wall, ducking his head to avoid the sloped ceiling. Aubrey went to his desk—which, it astonished Lindsey to realise, was an old door laid across more soapboxes—and retrieved a steaming hot roll from a wad of newsprint. He held it out to Lindsey, who recoiled.

Aubrey's jaw clenched, but his tone remained gentle. "I know it's not quite what you're used to..."

Lindsey, in the midst of waving off the roll, stopped abruptly. "What? No, no, it's not that, it's just—I don't think it'd stay down."

Aubrey appeared no less ashamed of his offering. He set it aside. "Promise me you'll eat when you get home."

"Of course," said Lindsey, wondering how he'd get home, and what Rowena would say when—

He jolted upright, banged his head on a rafter, and sat down hard on the bed with a heavy groan, letting his aching skull drop into his palms.

In an instant, Aubrey arrived to press a damp rag to his newest wound. "Are you all right?"

"No," said Lindsey, too far gone to lie. "My sister's on her way home. I have to meet her."

"You're in no condition to meet anyone."

"It's only a bump on the head."

"I didn't mean that."

Lindsey knew it, but he'd run out of words and settled for rubbing his knuckles against his forehead, willing Aubrey to understand. It seemed Aubrey did, leaning his head on Lindsey's shoulder and rubbing his back just as Lindsey wished. But it couldn't last.

"I've got to get to work," Aubrey said, his tone apologetic. "Halloway's on the first floor—"

Lindsey gave a start. Aubrey continued.

"—and we think it'd be best if you said you were with him. Portrait-sitting. It's a better explanation than..."

Aubrey trailed off. His hand had come up to scratch the back of his neck. Now he dropped it to his side, then shoved it into his trouser pocket, staring at the floor.

"I'm sorry," he blurted. "I can't do any better by you, and—"

"It's all right," Lindsey interjected, but Aubrey spoke over him.

"—you deserve better than this."

Lindsey blinked. "This is fine."

Aubrey said nothing.

Lindsey reached for him. Aubrey took the hint and leaned in to embrace him, cradling Lindsey's head by his collarbone.

"If there's anything you need..." Aubrey began.

"I'll be fine," Lindsey promised. And he would. He could be fine if Aubrey needed him to be.

Aubrey pressed a kiss to his ear.

CHAPTER ELEVEN

DINNER SEEMED NORMAL enough at first. Rowena took her usual place. Lindsey started to sit across from her, but her incredulous stare stopped him.

"What is it?" he asked.

Rowena continued staring. Lindsey suppressed the instinct to look over his shoulder to see if his father's ghost had materialised behind him. *Mark me.*

"Do you honestly expect him to show up to dinner?" Rowena said as if she'd read his mind. She pointed, not over Lindsey's shoulder, but at their father's empty seat.

Lindsey followed the motion, then returned to her for further explanation.

She sighed. "Sit down. No, not there—" as Lindsey moved to pull out the chair he stood behind, "—*there.* At the head, you imbec—" She bit off the insult.

It was Lindsey's turn to stare at her. "You cannot be serious."

"You're head of the family now," she said bitterly, as though Sir Geoffrey's death were his fault. "Start acting like it."

Lindsey could think of many things he'd rather do—self-immolate, for instance—but Rowena's visage had developed a murderous aspect. He shoved in the chair he'd selected for himself, strode to the head of the table, and hesitated.

"Oh for God's—!" Rowena began.

Lindsey threw himself into his father's chair.

"Happy?" he snarled.

"No," she shot back.

They exchanged glares, then turned their attention to the swiftly-cooling meal. Lindsey hardly tasted his portion. Rowena arranged hers into vague patterns, then tossed her napkin onto the table and left the room without so much as a goodnight.

Lindsey intended to retire to the library, but the slinking entrance of Belle halted his retreat. It seemed Jonathan had shooed her away from Sir Geoffrey's bedside, and she finally understood her master was gone forever. She curled up under the table at Lindsey's feet and expressed her misery in a low, steady whine. It carried throughout the house.

"Will someone shut that bitch up!?" Rowena shouted from the drawing room an hour or so into Belle's lament.

She fled to her chambers before Lindsey could grant her request. Just as well; he'd no idea how to grant it. He couldn't bring their father back. And Sir Geoffrey would've just shot the bitch to put her out of her misery. Lindsey didn't have the heart for it. Instead, he tempted the fretful beast with scraps of his own dinner. She had as much appetite for it as he did. So he patted her head, informed her she was a good girl regardless of her whines, and sat with her the rest of the night.

෨

ROWENA LEFT ALL the funeral arrangements to Lindsey, who rather wished she hadn't. He went with the standard set: a black walnut coffin lined with black silk, a hearse pulled by eight black horses wearing black-plumed bridles, a dozen mutes carrying staves wrapped in black crepe ribbons. Charles, Jonathan, Mr Hudson, and select footmen served as pallbearers. Lindsey followed alongside Clarence Rook, Miller, and Graves. Miller walked silent as the tomb. Graves veered towards melodrama, adorned with two black armbands, a black band on his top hat, black gloves, black handkerchiefs, black tie, and a jet-and-pewter tie pin shaped like a death's head. Clarence stood nearest Lindsey and gripped his arm when it seemed Lindsey's step might falter. With his support, Lindsey managed to keep his eyes dry as he laid his father to rest beside his mother.

Next came the will, read to the siblings by the elder Miller in their late father's study. Lindsey inherited the baronetcy, both houses, and the majority of the funds, none of it entailed. Lindsey supposed Sir Geoffrey had assumed there'd be time to see to it later. Rowena inherited a small independence. Not enough to set up her own household, but enough for her to stay in Lindsey's without draining his funds. She made no complaint.

She did, however, ask what Lindsey intended for the property. Lindsey shrugged. Realising his answer didn't satisfy her concerns, he raised his voice to say he was content to let everything remain as it was, though he did intend to rent additional property in Manchester.

"Manchester?" Rowena echoed incredulously.

"The mill profits should cover it," Lindsey assured her.

"What on earth will you do in Manchester?"

"Oversee the mill."

Rowena scoffed. "And nothing else, I'm sure."

Lindsey bit his tongue. He didn't wish to quarrel with her. Not now.

She continued without him. "Shall I manage your Manchester house as well?"

"Thought you preferred London."

"I do."

"Then you can have the town house, if you like."

"Oh?" She feigned surprise. "I'm permitted to keep it warm for you whilst you toil in your factory? Most generous of you, brother dear."

"No," said Lindsey. "I mean it's yours. I'll sign it over now, if you like."

Rowena paused her mockery, true astonishment on her face. "You're serious."

"As the grave," Lindsey replied thoughtlessly.

They stared at each other, then burst into laughter, much to the disturbance of Miller senior.

⌐

OVER THE NEXT few weeks, the London townhouse swarmed with women. Even the fog of grief couldn't obscure Rowena's ceaseless stream of well-wishers from Lindsey's notice. Officially she couldn't receive anyone, but dozens of tear-stained cards piled up on the silver tray in the foyer. Lady Pelham, a widow herself, made a respectable companion for her. She moved in shortly following the funeral.

One particular caller caught Lindsey's attention. A fortnight after his father's death, he met a plain-faced woman in a dark blue dress carrying a medical bag down the hall outside Rowena's chambers. She nodded to him as she passed, leaving a faint musk in her wake.

The musk grew stronger in Rowena's chambers. Rowena herself reclined on a plush settee with one hand pressed to her flushed forehead.

Lindsey cleared his throat, and she lifted her head, dropping her hand as if the limb were dead weight.

"Oh," she said in a tone which might have been disappointment. "It's you."

Lindsey, assuming his sister's grief matched his own, didn't take her impersonal greeting to heart. He inquired after her health. She replied she felt fine. He held out the latest issue of *Temple Bar*—his purpose in coming to her chambers. She instructed him to place it on an end table. He did so, and would've departed straight after, but he had one question left.

"Who was the woman in the blue dress?"

"Hmm?" said Rowena. "Oh—the midwife."

Lindsey gave a start. Rowena didn't seem to believe she'd uttered anything extraordinary. He coughed.

"You're not..." Lindsey trailed off, wishing he could phrase it more delicately. "...you're not 'in trouble,' are you?"

Now Rowena jolted. She blinked at him, wide-eyed, then threw her hand over her mouth to strangle what sounded like a laugh.

"No, no," she reassured him when she'd composed herself. "Merely a touch of hysteria."

Lindsey supposed that was a reasonable reaction to their loss. He wished her an expedient recovery and left.

On his way to his own chambers, he encountered a maid. He asked her to air out Rowena's chambers on account of the smell. To his astonishment, the girl blushed. Lindsey hurried to elaborate—he didn't intend to chide her for negligence, only he feared Miss Althorp was too distraught and distracted to request it herself. The maid blushed anew, her cheeks reaching untold shades of crimson, but she rushed off to obey with a squeak of, "Yes, sir!" before Lindsey could get any more out of her.

So the days passed in shades of muted gray. Lady Pelham's gentle smile provided solace to his sister, freeing Lindsey to seek comfort in his friends. Yet he didn't think Miller's pragmatism, Graves's irreverence, or even Clarence's companionship would alleviate his suffering. What he wanted most was to return to the narrow bed in the garret on the wrong side of Manchester and curl up next to his Aubrey in silence.

CHAPTER TWELVE

SIX MONTHS TO the day after Sir Geoffrey's death, Lindsey and Rowena sat together in the morning room. Rowena had turned it into a mourning room—a pun so weak Lindsey doubted he could take any pride in it even if his nerves weren't already strained.

Strained nerves aside, he thought he was coping remarkably well with his father's passing. He could concentrate enough to read again, though some old favourites felt frivolous now. He'd dined with Rook not two nights past, and if he'd been more maudlin than Rook would've liked, Rook, in his kindness, didn't mention it.

But Lindsey hadn't managed to meet with Aubrey. Men in mourning couldn't conduct business, and if their relationship were viewed as anything more than business, they'd be in considerable trouble. Thus, Lindsey couldn't visit the mill, nor could he invite Aubrey to either of his houses. He'd tried writing to him, but Rowena caught him in the act, and while she approved of his choice in mourning stationery, she couldn't condone the risk of putting his feelings for Aubrey in writing, and persuaded him Aubrey would be far safer if Lindsey refrained.

And so, Rowena aside, Lindsey led a lonely existence. She'd generously agreed to spend this particular morning with him and him alone. No conversation, of course, but Lindsey found it comforting to hear someone besides himself draw breath and turn pages. With the room so quiet, she had his immediate attention when she spoke.

"I thought perhaps we might reintroduce ourselves to society with a small dinner party."

Lindsey agreed. She presented the guest list: Lady Pelham, naturally; then Clarence and Emmeline Rook; Roderick Miller and his wife, Dolores;

and Lord Cyril Graves. Three gentlemen and three ladies made a perfectly balanced list. Yet Lindsey felt something missing.

"Is there room for Aubrey?" he asked.

Rowena arched an eyebrow. "Lindsey, darling, you cannot invite Mr Warren."

"Why not?"

She gave him a blank look. "He's a clerk."

"What does that matter?"

"Not at all, I'm sure. Will you invite the boiler-keeper, as well?"

"I believe you're referring to the stationary engineer, and no, I'm not on such familiar terms with him as with Aubrey."

"Thank God for that," Rowena murmured dryly.

"Oh, really now!"

"Lindsey," Rowena said in the same tone one might use to sooth a child's tantrum. "You are proposing to invite a clerk to a dinner party. He'll be out of place and utterly miserable. Who will he talk to?"

"Myself, for a start. And he's already met Graves. I'm certain our other guests would take well to him. I'd have no compunction confiding in Clarence, Emmeline's as quiet as any mouse you'd care to name—"

"I didn't realise I had the habit of naming vermin. Though you seem determined to befriend them."

Lindsey turned his back on her and strode away. Long steps brought him all too soon to the mantle. He faced it in defiant silence. Then he heaved a weighty sigh and looked to his sister. "I realise it's an imposition—"

"Do you?"

"Yes," he replied, though he understood her question had been rhetorical. "You planned dinner for six guests, and I've blustered in to demand a seventh. And for that, I'm sorry."

"But."

Lindsey acquiesced to her addition with a nod. "But I cannot host a celebration of all who've been kind to us in our time of need without inviting he who's been kindest of all."

Rowena sighed. "Lindsey..."

"That night—" Lindsey found his throat obstructed, cleared it with a cough, and continued. "The night our father passed, I couldn't bear to stay in his house."

"Yes, you went to your club."

"No, you assumed I went to my club. In actuality I spent the night at Aubrey's."

Lindsey derived some small glee from seeing his sister's careful mask drop in shock. She recovered quickly, but not quick enough to interrupt him.

"Contrary to your opinion of him," he continued, suppressing a wistful smile at the memory, "he didn't take advantage of me in the slightest. He took care of me. If not for him, no doubt I'd have made quite the scene anywhere else I cared to go in my intoxicated state—just the sort of scandal you've always feared."

"Good God." Rowena stared at him. "Where does he even live? I can't imagine he could afford anything but the meanest lodging house. Unless you're sponsoring him?"

Lindsey ignored the guilty twinge from her suggestion of sponsorship. "It doesn't matter where he lives! Without him, our family's reputation would be ruined! Imagine, dear sister—me, of all people, drunk as a sailor on a spree, staggering through the streets! Even my club would've refused me entry in that condition. But no, I went to Aubrey, who saw me through the night."

"No doubt he was well thanked for it."

"No doubt he deserves it, and more besides!"

He waited a long moment for her retort.

"Seven guests, then," she said.

Lindsey sagged in relief. "Thank you, Rowena."

"He'll be quite out of place, you understand. And there'll be no one for him to escort down to dinner."

"I'm sure he won't mind."

"And where should I send the invitation?"

Lindsey obligingly wrote down the address of Aubrey's lodging house.

❧

THE INVITATION, DELIVERED in a thick cream-coloured envelope, earned Aubrey a suspicious look from Mrs Padwick when she brought it up to him. Aubrey couldn't blame her. He never received personal letters, much less anything addressed in an unmistakably feminine hand. He perused its contents over his customary tinned supper.

Sir Lindsey Althorp and Miss Althorp
request the pleasure of Mr Warren's company
at Dinner on Wednesday, 18th of May
at eight o'clock

There followed the address of Lindsey's townhouse.

Panic filled Aubrey's mind with white fog, narrowing his perception until the insurmountable problem of the invitation engulfed his entire field of vision. Clearly, he had to refuse. He'd never attended a dinner party in his life. His presence would, at best, prove embarrassing. Doubtless Lindsey'd only invited him as a polite gesture. And while Aubrey appreciated it, he understood how ill-bred it would be to accept.

In the process of separating the RSVP card from the invitation, Aubrey dislodged a third paper—small, with ragged edges suggesting it'd been torn from something larger.

Looking forward to seeing you.

—L

A fluttering sensation bloomed beneath Aubrey's ribs. It didn't respond to his attempts to reason it away.

He'd neither seen nor heard from Lindsey these past six months. In his darker moments, he'd assumed they'd never meet again.

He ran his fingertips over the writing and around the ragged edge, imagining the hand that had inscribed the message and torn it free.

Refusal was no longer possible.

꩜

AT QUARTER TO eight on a Wednesday evening, Belgrave Square bustled with carriages bringing smart-dressed guests to dinners, parties, and sundry other entertainments.

It'd taken Aubrey the better part of the day to walk from his lodging house to Manchester Central, ride the train to St Pancras and Victoria Station, and walk to Belgravia. He kept a slow and steady pace, not wanting to work up a sweat and arrive dishevelled.

Even so, he felt out of place among society's elite. They strolled at ease in finery whilst he picked lint off his only jacket—a Sunday-best suit was superfluous for a man who crossed the street to avoid churches—and tried to behave as though he belonged. He felt as if, any moment now, some toff would recognise him as an impostor and have him removed by police.

In the midst of his efforts to talk himself out of his irrational concerns, one of the passing party-goers tapped his shoulder with an ebony cane.

"I say, boy," said the portly, middle-aged gentleman in top hat and tails. "Call us a cab."

As he spoke, he tossed a coin in Aubrey's general direction. It fell at his feet.

Aubrey looked down at it, then up at the gentleman. Having already passed from startled to indignant, he tempered his indignation into a veneer of cool indifference. "I beg your pardon?"

The gentleman stared at him.

Aubrey stared back.

The gentleman scoffed under his breath and turned away to find a more willing servant.

Aubrey made sure the gentleman wasn't watching, then stole another glance at the coin on the ground. It was a shilling. It could be his shilling, if he swallowed his pride and bent his knees for it.

He reminded himself he couldn't be late for Lindsey's dinner, and strode on to the appropriate address.

There stood an imposing edifice. Gleaming white granite steps led to a black door, taller than Aubrey by half, with a silver knocker shaped like a lion's head. Aubrey stepped up to the door and tapped it. The silver felt cold as the grave in his hand. He wondered if he ought've worn gloves; all the gentlemen in the street had pure white ones. How the devil they kept them clean remained a mystery. Aubrey suspected it had something to do with never lifting a finger for themselves. He shoved his bitterness aside, reminding himself he'd come at the behest of just such a gentleman.

"Yes?"

Aubrey, his eyes on gentlemen's gloves, hadn't heard the door open behind him. He spun around so quickly he almost fell down the steps. When he regained his balance, he faced a butler—mid-fifties, gaunt, with wiry gray sideburns and a suit superior to Aubrey's. The butler's dull, disinterested expression never changed as he waited for Aubrey's reply.

Aubrey swallowed. "This is Sir Lindsey Althorp's residence?"

"It is."

Aubrey considered pulling his invitation out from his jacket pocket, certain nothing less than material proof would convince anyone he belonged here, when the butler spoke again.

"You must be Mr Warren."

"I am." A blush flared in Aubrey's face, entirely uncalled-for in his opinion. He wasn't ashamed to be Aubrey Warren. Though he did wonder what'd given him away. Between his shabby wardrobe and social ineptitude, it seemed a toss-up. The butler gave no hint.

"Right this way, sir," he said, and stepped back to admit Aubrey into the house.

The foyer looked no less imposing than the exterior. A staircase rose from the centre, less grand than the one in Lindsey's country house, but far more impressive than the rickety back spiral Aubrey climbed every day.

Faint voices raised in mirth floated down from the upper floors. But the butler didn't lead Aubrey up to them. Instead, he took him down a corridor off to the side, where an unassuming door opened into a second stair. The back stair.

Aubrey had half a mind to refuse to go up it. If Lindsey didn't think him worthy to climb the same steps as the other guests, then he'd rather not attend at all. But before he could voice his opinion, a familiar form descended the stair.

"Mr Warren!" said Charles, an unmistakable expression of relief on his face. "You're just in time. Please, come with me. Thank you, Mr Hudson."

The butler—Mr Hudson—disappeared as silently as he'd arrived.

"Terribly sorry about all this subterfuge, sir," said Charles as he led a bewildered Aubrey up the stair.

"Quite all right," Aubrey replied automatically. He waited for Charles to elaborate further, but Charles said nothing as he blazed a winding trial up the stair and down dark halls to one particular door amongst a half-dozen identical ones.

"In here, sir," said Charles, holding it open for Aubrey.

It was a bedroom. Clearly Aubrey's reputation had preceded him.

"If you would remove your jacket, sir," Charles continued, doing nothing to change Aubrey's assessment of the situation.

"I beg your pardon?" said Aubrey, with less indignation than he'd shown the gentleman outside. Charles didn't so much as blink.

"I've another set aside for you," he said, holding up the article in question on a hanger. "One of Sir Lindsey's from his youth. It should fit with minor adjustments."

Aubrey tried to assuage his wounded pride. Even secondhand, the jacket was superior to his own, and a far better match for the other gentlemen's. It was irrational to feel insulted by the fact that Lindsey's cast-offs were above anything Aubrey owned. Aubrey removed his jacket.

When Charles produced a white waistcoat and tie, Aubrey reminded himself Lindsey's happiness would be worth it.

CHAPTER THIRTEEN

"Mr Aubrey Warren," said Mr Hudson from the drawing room threshold.

Aubrey stood beside him in the hall, resisting the temptation to peer around the corner like a spying child. At Mr Hudson's raised eyebrow, Aubrey squared his shoulders and entered the room.

Silence fell, and he froze under the sensation of a hundred eyes upon him. A closer examination revealed only eight people in the room, four ladies and four gentlemen, therefore merely sixteen eyes—which still felt like far too many for Aubrey.

The ladies sat in a circle of armchairs as delicate as their gowns. One woman, with bright blonde curls and aquiline features, bore a striking resemblance to Lindsey. Aubrey supposed she must be Miss Althorp.

The gentlemen stood on the other side of the room. Aubrey recognised Lord Cyril Graves from the theatre. Graves leaned with one hand on the closed piano lid in the far corner, next to two more gentlemen; one thick-set and mustachioed, the other lean, auburn-haired, and clean-shaven. Lindsey, who'd stood beside them when Aubrey first entered, swiftly crossed the room to take Aubrey's arm.

Aubrey's heart stopped at his first sight of Lindsey in six months. He searched his face for signs of strain. While faint shadows had developed under Lindsey's splendid blue eyes, he retained the familiar bounce in his step. His customary smile widened further when he reached Aubrey.

"You've made it!" Lindsey whispered, squeezing Aubrey's arm in delight. "Splendid!"

Aubrey hardly had the chance to smile in return before Lindsey whisked him over to the ladies. The first looked as pale and thin as Aubrey himself, in a dress as colourless as her mousy hair. She regarded him with wide, anxious eyes. The second appeared far livelier and more at ease in her surroundings, though she gave Aubrey a confused look. The third had the figure of a field hand but sat with aristocratic poise, and smiled as if sincerely glad to make his acquaintance. The last, Lindsey's sister, rose to greet him. She stood almost as tall as Lindsey, which would've seemed unusual for her sex had she not carried herself with more self-assurance than Aubrey had ever seen compacted into a single person—apart from Miss Brewster. Aubrey wondered what the latter would say about the company he found himself in.

"Miss Althorp, at your service," said Lindsey's sister, drawing Aubrey from his thoughts. While her brother's smile spread wide, hers just barely curled the corners of her lips. Without waiting for Aubrey's reply, she turned to Lindsey. "You've neglected your duties as host, darling."

Her tone sounded playful, and she smiled still, but Aubrey wouldn't have liked for her to address him so. Lindsey seemed used to it.

"A thousand apologies," he chuckled in return. "Rowena, this is Mr Warren. Lady Pelham—" the regal field hand, "—Mrs Miller—" the confused lady, "—Miss Rook—" the pale girl, "—Mr Warren."

Miss Althorp held out her hand. Lady Pelham did likewise. Aubrey hesitated between them before choosing his hostess, grasping her hand with a hurried how-do-you-do, then swiftly followed suit with Lady Pelham. This seemed satisfactory to both ladies, though Miss Rook still looked fearful and Mrs Miller bemused.

"If you'll excuse us," said Lindsey, saving Aubrey further embarrassment. He steered Aubrey back across the room to the gentlemen. "Graves, you remember Warren!"

Graves's gaze lingered on the too-long cuffs of Aubrey's jacket, and on his scuffed shoes, which no amount of polish could repair. Aubrey bit his tongue and returned the stare with a faint, cold smile. Graves cocked an eyebrow.

"I do," he admitted at last. Lindsey didn't seem to notice the chilly undertone.

"Miller, Rook," Lindsey continued, nodding to the mustachioed and auburn-haired gentlemen in turn. "This is Warren! I've told you about Warren, haven't I?"

"Often, and at length," said Rook. He looked down at Aubrey, not bothering to disguise the direction. "A pleasure to meet you at last."

"How do you do," said Miller.

Aubrey, suppressing panic at the thought of what Lindsey might've said about him—not out of malice, surely, but Lindsey's naïveté was as dangerous as it was charming—managed to respond appropriately to both men. Neither seemed to care.

"What were you saying about Braddon, Althorp?" said Rook. "Surely you don't rank her above Thackeray?"

Lindsey resumed the conversation Aubrey's arrival had interrupted. He held all the gentlemen's attention. Were it a physical object, he might've tossed it casually from hand to hand, so thoughtless and secure was his mastery over it.

But Aubrey's attention wandered. Anxiety heightened his senses. He caught a snatch of conversation from the other half of the room.

"—don't think I know any Warrens," said Mrs Miller. "Where did he come from?"

Her companions hurried to shush her, but Aubrey's ears already burned. He tried harder to focus on Lindsey's speech. Something about bosom friendship in the face of murder and betrayal. He hoped it was fiction. Knowing Lindsey, it probably was. Aubrey found it easier to concentrate on Lindsey's face rather than his words, for his face lit up, mercurial, flowing from expression to expression in his passion. Thus distracted, Aubrey didn't notice an approach from behind.

"Mr Warren?"

Aubrey pivoted, though unlike his manoeuvre on the doorstep, he kept his balance. He faced Miss Althorp and Miss Rook.

"Miss—" he began, then halted, unsure which to address first.

"Miss Rook would like a word," said Miss Althorp.

Without any further explanation, she joined her brother's conversation. Lindsey's literary opinions had been challenged by Graves, much to Rook and Miller's entertainment.

Aubrey turned to Miss Rook. As soon as they locked eyes, she dropped her gaze to the carpet.

"You're an engineer, Mr Warren?" She spoke as if she were afraid of the sound of her own voice.

"An amateur," Aubrey replied, striving to match her tone. He hoped Graves's argument would drown him out. Alas, Rook caught their conversation.

"Thought he was a clerk?" Rook said to Lindsey in a low voice.

Whatever Lindsey's response, Miss Rook jumped in before it.

"How exciting!" she said, a smile lighting her features. Her words remained quiet, but had gained vivacity, to Miss Althorp's apparent amusement. "Do you have an opinion on electricity?"

"No one wants to talk about that, Emmeline," said Rook, his cross tone loud enough for the whole room to hear.

"I do," Miss Althorp said just as loudly.

Aubrey found it difficult to believe Miss Althorp had genuine interest in electrical innovation, much less his opinion on it. He flicked his eyes back to Miss Rook, whose smile had waned. A bolt of clarity struck him—Miss Althorp supported her friend against Rook, who seemed to harbour an unaccountable hatred for electricity. Which left Aubrey caught between them. Delightful. He dared a glance at Lindsey, whose face bore an encouraging expression, and found the nerve to reply. "I've considered the benefits of converting a textile mill from steam to electric power."

Out of the corner of his eye, he caught Lindsey's surprised expression, and feared he'd overstepped his bounds.

"And?" Miss Rook prompted, distracting him from his concerns.

"It would give us a marked increase in efficiency," Aubrey continued, trying to ignore whatever Lindsey's face might do as he spoke. "However, the conversion process would have to be refined before we would abandon steam entirely."

"'We'?" Rook echoed with a disbelieving laugh, looking to at Lindsey.

Lindsey smiled and shrugged. "I trust Warren's judgement. He's the engineer, after all."

Rook scoffed. "And you're just the owner of the whole enterprise!"

"He's certainly taking more charge of it than you ever did," said Miller.

Rook glared at him, but Graves cut in before he could retort.

"If you don't like how he runs it, Rook, you should've kept a better hold on it."

Miller chuckled, as did Graves and Lindsey after him. Rook joined them a few seconds too late.

Miss Rook appeared pained. Miss Althorp took her arm and led her away to rejoin the ladies.

Aubrey turned to the other gentlemen and discovered Lindsey had approached him in the interim. He smiled, and Aubrey returned it.

"Forgive me," said Aubrey, his voice pitched below Graves and Miller's continued ribbing of Rook. "But is your friend Mr Rook any relation...?"

"He used to own our mill," Lindsey answered with a sideways glance in the oblivious Rook's direction.

Our mill. Aubrey braced himself against a warm rush of pride. "Until he sold it?"

Lindsey winced. "Wagered it, I'm afraid. Whist. My victory was pure luck. He never seemed to want it back. Which now I must confess myself most thankful for."

"He bet a *mill?*"

Lindsey coughed. "Yes, well, he usually wins. Besides, we were both rather foxed at the time. I daresay it wouldn't have happened otherwise."

Aubrey risked a glance at Rook, still conversing with the other gentlemen, and suppressed indignant rage at anyone being so irresponsible as to risk the livelihood of hundreds in a mere card-game. A touch on his arm brought him back to the present, and he looked up to meet Lindsey's expression of concern. Aubrey forced a smile.

"Hope you don't intend to do likewise. Wager the mill, I mean."

Lindsey laughed. "I should think not!"

Aubrey was relieved to hear it, and would've said so, but Lindsey's laugh had attracted attention. Rook in particular seemed suspicious of their conversation.

A bell rang in the hallway.

Aubrey looked to Lindsey for a clue to its significance, only to find him gone. He'd crossed the room to offer his arm to Lady Pelham, who graciously allowed him to lead her away.

All the other guests partnered up as if by instinct; Miss Althorp with Graves, Miller with Miss Rook, and Rook with Mrs Miller. Miss Rook spared a backwards glance and an apologetic smile as Miller steered her through the doorway and down the hall. Aubrey followed their sedate pace and reached the stair just in time to watch Lindsey and Lady Pelham vanish down it. Aubrey awaited his turn, descended alone, and entered the dining room.

If the drawing room was elegant, then the dining room was fantastic. Deep red wallpaper matched velvet curtains drawn over tall windows covering one long wall, and a gas chandelier glittered from the vaulted ceiling. The gold fixtures glowed like sunshine, and a dozen wall sconces burned, ready to take over if the artificial sun failed. Brilliant light reflected off a score of silver-covered dishes set out on the mahogany sideboard; off a trail of silver mirrors running down the centre of the table, with moss on either side to suggest a wild stream; and off the cutlery. Too much cutlery. Aubrey tried not to gawk at the place settings, though every horrified instinct bid him do so.

Three stacked white china plates, each slightly smaller than the last, sat in front of each chair. Atop them rested a napkin which at first appeared crumpled, but closer inspection revealed it'd been folded into a vague avian shape—possibly a swan. To the left lay two forks, one large, one small. To the right, a knife and two spoons. Above the plates, yet another fork and spoon. To the upper right, three wine glasses, two empty, one filled with water. To the upper left, a tiny, auxiliary plate hovered like a superfluous culinary moon, with a little blunt knife laid across it.

All told: three forks, three spoons, two knives, three wine glasses, four plates, and a napkin-bird, none of which Aubrey had any idea what to do with. He reminded himself gentlemen didn't panic, and strove to look as though he expected to encounter such place-settings at every meal.

By the time he'd recovered himself, all the other guests were seated. Aubrey took the only remaining chair, at the far end of the table. Miss Althorp sat to his immediate right at the foot. On his left sat Rook, who didn't appear any happier about the arrangement than Aubrey felt. To Rook's left, Mrs Miller, then Graves, and Lindsey at the table's head, as far from Aubrey as possible. Aubrey wondered if it was deliberate. On the opposite side of the table sat Lady Pelham, Miller, and Miss Rook, a much cheerier and less crowded side than Aubrey's.

The instant Aubrey sat down, the servants who'd stood sentinel around the room's perimeter slid into motion as fluidly as well-oiled clockwork. One stepped forward to fill Aubrey's wineglass.

"Thank you," Aubrey said as the man returned his glass to the table.

He heard a muffled gasp. Miss Rook, wide-eyed, put her fingertips over her mouth. Her brother, in Aubrey's peripheral vision, struggled to withhold a smirk. Graves stopped conversing with Lindsey, and both peered down at Aubrey's end of the table. The servant, meanwhile, had paused, his fingers stuck to the stem of Aubrey's wineglass.

Cold dread sank into Aubrey's gut. Not even five minutes into dinner, and he'd already embarrassed his host.

Then, Lindsey gave a slight nod. The servant let go of Aubrey's wineglass and retreated.

Aubrey swallowed his sigh of relief. Light chatter returned to the table, though Mrs Miller's eyes kept flicking to Aubrey whenever she thought he wasn't paying attention.

As the servants continued dispensing wine, guests removed their napkins from their plates. The ladies laid their napkins across their laps, as did most of the gentlemen, though Miller tucked a corner of his into his shirt collar. Aubrey followed the majority, arranging his napkin over his thighs just as another servant swooped in to place a steaming bowl on the plate where his napkin had been. Within the bowl, a circle of scallops floated in amber broth, green vegetable matter sprinkled liberally over it. Chopped leeks and carrots lurked beneath.

Soup. Aubrey could handle soup. He searched for a spoon. He found three. Glancing at Rook from under his lashes, he saw Rook select the roundest spoon, so he did the same.

Instinct told him to lean over the bowl to spare his borrowed clothes, but all the other guests sat upright as they ate, with no concern for their attire. So Aubrey straightened his spine and brought the spoon to his mouth.

It was divine.

Until that moment, he'd never realised food could literally taste rich. He'd experienced flavour before, and preferred some over others, though his pocketbook did more than his tongue to influence his eating habits. But this was something else entirely. Even the cold lunch he'd eaten at Lindsey's country house couldn't compare. The silky, savoury broth slipped down his throat. He choked back an unseemly sound and returned his spoon to the bowl for more.

"Is it to your liking, Mr Warren?"

Aubrey almost dropped his spoon. He looked to the speaker, Miss Althorp.

"The *consommé*, I mean," she continued. Aubrey couldn't tell if he imagined the teasing tone in her voice.

"Yes, quite," he said. Then, wary of the thin line between perfunctory and rude, he added, "It's delicious, thank you."

Miller gave Miss Althorp a look which seemed to question her sanity. Miss Althorp answered it with a serene smile, then turned away to continue her conversation with Miss Rook.

Aubrey gathered a second spoonful of soup—of *consommé*, he corrected himself. As he carefully consumed it, he listened in on the talk around the table. Graves had Lindsey's full attention discussing a new play. Lady Pelham caught was catching Mrs Miller up on the recent escapades of a mutual acquaintance. Rook appeared enthralled by the conversation between Miss Althorp and his sister, but Aubrey caught a glare from him out of the corner of his eye. A quick look, rectified quicker still, but enough to unnerve Aubrey and prevent him from taking a third spoonful. Instead, he listened to Graves and Lindsey, and, when he could get a word in edgewise, inquired how the latest show compared with the playwright's previous efforts, guessing the new play wasn't the first. His hunch proved correct. Graves went off on a tangent about the inevitable degradation of talent over time. Lindsey caught Aubrey's eye with an amused bite of his lip. Aubrey replied with a wry half-smile and returned to his soup—just as a strange hand reached over his shoulder and snatched it away.

Instinct told him to take up a fork and pin the hand to the table. But this was a dinner party, not a workhouse. Surely Lindsey hadn't invited him only to eat two spoonfuls of soup and go. There had to be a method to the madness. So he let the servant abscond with his soup and awaited a hint on what to do next.

The servant returned with a palm-sized slab of pink fish. Aubrey recognised it as salmon from the colour, though he'd never encountered it outside of advertisements. A line of pale green sauce was drizzled down its centre, with darker green specks sprinkled on top, and round, seed-filled slices of some green vegetable arranged around it.

After a subtle glance at what the other guests did, Aubrey picked up his smallest, shiniest fork and scooped out a bite-sized portion of salmon. As it touched his lips, he realised it was stone cold. He assumed there'd been some mistake between kitchen and table, but none of the other guests seemed perturbed by the temperature. Aubrey opened his mouth.

The salmon tasted so far removed from the tinned sardines he choked down every night, Aubrey couldn't believe they shared the name of fish. The flaky, sweet flesh paired deliciously with the warm, lemony, cream-rich sauce.

Wary of the servant's return, Aubrey took a second bite faster than he would've otherwise dared. The other guests talked around him. He had a creeping feeling his silence might be considered rude, perhaps shockingly so, but the food tasted so damned good. He managed to eliminate half the salmon before a servant whisked it away.

The next course appeared to be beef. Aubrey didn't often have the means to introduce beef to his diet. When he did, it was boiled or stewed. In his mind, beef had two forms: red and raw in the butcher's stall, or cooked brown and fit for eating.

This beef straddled the line.

Cut into thin strips, arranged with some kind of mushroom and a garlic-scented sauce, it boasted brown outsides and bright red innards. As Miss Althorp didn't send it back to the kitchen, Aubrey had to conclude this, too, was normal. Aubrey selected the outermost remaining fork, took up the knife in his other hand, and began to carve.

Blood welled up under the blade.

Aubrey stared as it beaded and spilled over onto the white china, leaving a pale crimson stain behind. Another wary look around the table showed his fellow guests remained undisturbed. They'd all begun consuming the victuals set before them—delicately, but with none of Aubrey's reluctance.

So the wealthy preferred their meat raw. Very well. Aubrey steeled his nerve and brought a bite to his mouth.

Flesh fell away into pure flavour. Chewing seemed unnecessary for such a tender morsel. It took considerable willpower to not gulp it down and immediately carve another.

Two more bites proceeded likewise. Aubrey realised he'd started hunching over his plate. He straightened and looked around. No one else seemed to have noticed—save Rook, who raised an eyebrow. Aubrey quickly looked away.

To prevent himself from wolfing down the beef, he turned his attention to the wine, left untouched since the servant poured it. Another glass of a slightly different shade had appeared in the meantime. His hand hovered between them, uncertain, until he decided on the more recent vintage. He supposed it tasted as it ought. Certainly better than gin. He returned to the beef. Rook continued to stare.

The next course came before Aubrey could polish off his beef. One whole, greasy little bird for each guest, doused in sweet-smelling sauce and accompanied by a multitude of multicoloured vegetables. Yet as much as Aubrey's tongue craved a taste, his stomach wanted none of it. He panicked as the other guests dug in, and looked to Lindsey.

Lindsey's plate was empty.

Aubrey stared in confusion, then caught sight of a servant behind Lindsey carrying off an uneaten bird.

So it was possible to refuse. Aubrey filed away the information for future reference and resigned himself to picking at the minuscule fowl. He sipped more wine as he did so. No one spoke to him—unsurprising, given he knew nothing of these people and had no gift for the art of conversation. He wondered what became of the untouched food. Perhaps the staff ate it. Aubrey let his eyes wander over to the servants standing by the sideboard. They didn't have the lean and hungry look of people surviving on the cast-offs of the upper crust. The look he'd seen in the mirror every morning until Mr Jennings had brought him on at the mill.

He felt no less full by the next course. As the servant brought him a plate, Aubrey cleared his throat uncertain of his script.

"No thank you," he said quietly, hoping it was enough.

The servant paused. Aubrey's heart leapt into his throat. Then the servant nodded and took the plate away.

Aubrey glanced around to see if anyone had noticed. No one. Not even Rook.

With no one paying him any attention, and nothing to occupy his hands beyond his wine glass, Aubrey's focus wandered back to Lindsey. Lindsey'd barely looked at him since the meal started, but he'd expected as much—Lindsey was hosting, after all, with seven guests to tend. At best, Aubrey could expect fourteen percent of Lindsey's attention. And Aubrey knew his company couldn't compare to regal Lady Pelham or ebullient Graves. Still, he couldn't banish the pang in his chest when Lindsey laughed at Rook's commentary. Nor could he keep from noticing how intently Lindsey listened to Miller's opinion on a new bill in Parliament.

He looked away from Lindsey. The other guests might be unfamiliar, but they caused him less pain.

"Are you quite well, Mr Warren?" said Miss Althorp.

Aubrey jerked to attention. "Yes, thank you."

Miss Althorp didn't look like she believed him, but to Aubrey's relief, she let the matter drop regardless.

The next course arrived—lemon ice in delicate-stemmed crystal bowls. Aubrey, whose guts had recovered somewhat, indulged in a few spoonfuls.

But despite its sweet flavour, the ice wasn't dessert. More roast fowl followed on a bed of watercress. Aubrey declined it. He declined the next course—asparagus—as well. Miss Althorp watched him, but said nothing, for which Aubrey felt most grateful.

The servants stepped forward again. Aubrey's stomach clenched in dread—surely dinner had concluded, surely the kitchen couldn't produce another course—then relaxed as they removed, rather than added, items. Plates, glasses, and silverware disappeared, and footmen came forth armed with silver knives and trays to scrape crumbs from the tablecloth. Aubrey tried to rein in his imagination, but couldn't help thinking of the knives as swords and the trays as shields. He calculated the cost of the silver used where he would've made do with his hand and an old newspaper. The other guests chattered on as if the table were cleaning itself.

Then, to Aubrey's horror, more food arrived. Peaches in green jelly, custard with apples and walnuts—dessert at last. He refused both and refrained from lifting his eyes to the heavens in exhausted thanks.

Dessert proceeded normally, as far as Aubrey could tell, until Miss Althorp caught Lady Pelham's eye. They stood in unison. Miss Rook and

Mrs Miller followed them. Lindsey leapt to his feet the moment all the women had stood. Aubrey scrambled to do the same. He managed to rise before Rook, which he counted as a victory even if he didn't know the purpose of the race.

The women filed out of the dining room, Miss Althorp in the lead. When they'd gone, Graves spoke.

"Go on, Warren!"

Aubrey started, then looked to Lindsey for confirmation. It seemed odd for the lowest-ranking man to lead the way.

But Lindsey couldn't meet Aubrey's look. He was preoccupied with narrowing his eyes at Graves.

"What are you about?" he said, his cold tone unlike anything Aubrey'd ever heard from his lips.

Graves's smile flickered. "Only joking, Althorp."

Lindsey maintained his disapproving look for an uncomfortable moment, then dropped it and sat down. The other gentlemen followed suit. This time Aubrey was dead last.

With all the gentlemen seated, a servant brought out a decanter of dark burgundy liquid and five crystal goblets to match. Having distributed these, and leaving the decanter with Lindsey, they departed. Lindsey poured a drink for each guests, starting with Graves and ending with Aubrey. He then proposed a toast—to good health, good friends, etc. Aubrey took a dutiful sip.

At the workhouse, overstretched elderly woman had put fussy children to sleep with a thimbleful of gin—watered down, more for economy's sake than to spare small stomachs. In later years, Aubrey'd encountered better stuff, but always served with the intention of making him more pliable and acquiescent to the wishes of the provider. They'd never encouraged him to savour its subtler flavours.

Lindsey's port was of similar quality. Aubrey tried to pace himself, but with nothing to add to the conversation, he had nothing to occupy his mouth but his drink. The first glass disappeared. Lindsey's offer to refill it was too cheerful and well-mannered for Aubrey to refuse. And to sit without drinking while the gentlemen around him drained their glasses felt like the height of boorish behaviour. So his second glass disappeared. Aubrey dreaded the offer of a third, though with two glasses in him, he had trouble remembering why it was so important he not have any more.

The quips around the table took the course of all conversation between Old Boys, in Aubrey's experience—a rapid descent into an incestuous, cannibalistic knot of references both literary and Classical until the English became as incomprehensible as the ancient Greek. Aubrey doubted he could've kept up with it sober. He began to wish he'd left with the ladies after all. Just as he considered making his excuses and departing alone, Lindsey cleared his throat.

"Perhaps it's time we rejoined the ladies," he said, rising from his seat.

Aubrey followed suit a bit too eagerly.

Matters didn't improve back in the drawing room. The ladies sat in the chairs they'd occupied prior to dinner. The gentlemen filed in to stand around them. Their conversation was light, frivolous, and beyond Aubrey's comprehension. He supposed he could've participated if he bothered to pay attention to its ebb and flow, but he was distracted.

A digestive tract accustomed to the spare and Spartan was ill-prepared for the dinner Aubrey'd devoured. The meal sat in his gut, heavy as a sack of stones. He felt like a corpse weighed down to sink in the Thames. Throwing port on top of it doomed him. If he opened his mouth to join the conversation, he knew he'd be sick.

"Best be going, then," said Miller as his wife stifled a theatrical yawn.

Aubrey watched the Millers say their goodbyes—yet still jolted in surprise when they stopped in front of him.

"So nice to meet you, Mr Warner," said Mrs Miller as her husband held out his hand.

Aubrey made the appropriate response without moving his jaw. He hoped they wouldn't take it personally. It was preferable to emptying his gullet on Miller's shoes.

Once they'd gone, led out by a footman who'd appeared as if by magic, Aubrey approached Lindsey.

"I should go," he said.

Lindsey seemed perturbed. "So soon?"

"I've work in the morning." Aubrey tried to keep the bitter tone from his voice as he wondered why Lindsey found his employment status so difficult to remember. "Thank you for dinner."

"You're very welcome," Lindsey replied, but Aubrey had already reached the drawing room door.

He met no servants until he entered the foyer. There, Mr Hudson materialised.

"My hat, please," said Aubrey. He didn't intend to sound imperious, but he couldn't gather enough air to explain himself properly.

Mr Hudson handed over the hat. Aubrey realised he'd forgotten to say goodnight to the other guests, to say nothing of his hostess, but he couldn't barge back into the drawing room with hat in hand, so he nodded his thanks to Mr Hudson and left.

The cold night air on his face would've perked him up were it not mixed with thick, choking smog. Aubrey's cough became a gag and he veered into the cleanest alley he'd ever seen to empty his aching stomach. He fell to his knees, barely missing the mess he'd made. Deep breaths brought more retching, until his hand on the white stone wall was the only thing keeping him upright.

"Sir?"

Aubrey couldn't turn around, couldn't even turn his head. He hadn't felt so sick since childhood. He could only kneel, helpless, at the mercy of whoever was approaching him from behind.

"Mr Warren?"

A hand fell on his shoulder. He flinched from it. The hand's owner bent down into Aubrey's line of sight. His vision swam until he recognised Charles.

"Are you all right?"

"Yes," Aubrey lied through his teeth.

Charles wasn't convinced. "Perhaps you'd better come back inside."

There were few things Aubrey felt less inclined to do. But unable to explain without dry-heaving, he hung his head. At least he'd kept his borrowed clothes clean. It occurred to him Lindsey probably wanted them returned. Doubtless that was why he'd sent Charles after him. And Charles could hardly strip him naked in the alley. Well, he could—Aubrey couldn't prevent him in his condition—but Charles didn't seem the type. Aubrey'd met the type years ago and had no desire to repeat the experience.

Regardless—Lindsey's clothes on Aubrey's body. Problem. Needed solving. Aubrey supposed he'd better go back in, if only to facilitate the exchange. He struggled to rise.

"There you go, sir," said Charles, catching Aubrey under the arms and pulling him up. He drew Aubrey's arm over one shoulder and steered him back down the alley.

CHAPTER FOURTEEN

AUBREY'S SUDDEN DEPARTURE distressed Lindsey, though he couldn't argue with his reasoning. Lindsey berated himself for not asking Rowena to hold the dinner on a Saturday, when Aubrey might've stayed the night. He sublimated his disappointment under his duties as host and the comfort of having provided Aubrey with a decent meal.

The other guests didn't stay much longer. Lady Pelham retired last, arm-in-arm with Rowena. When Lindsey stood alone in the drawing room, Charles appeared in the doorway.

"Mr Warren is in the blue guest room, sir," he said. Before Lindsey could express any elated surprise, Charles continued. "He's not well. I don't believe he requires a physician, but he's in no condition to return to Manchester."

Lindsey's delight disintegrated. He hurried off to the blue guest room. Upon arriving, he hesitated at the closed door. Opening it let a sliver of light from the hall into the otherwise dark chamber. It took a moment of searching to spy a miserable lump under the bedcovers. The sharp, sour scent of vomit wafted up from a chamber pot on the floor next to the bed. Lindsey wrinkled his nose, but approached regardless.

"Aubrey?"

The miserable lump shifted, revealing Aubrey's face. His already bone-white features had gone even paler, as if he'd suffered a vampyric attack. He squinted through bruised-blue eyelids, struggling to prop himself up on a trembling elbow. Lindsey laid a hand on his bare shoulder to stop him—the cold, clammy feel of Aubrey's skin causing him no small amount of concern—but Aubrey shook his head.

"Ought to be going," he croaked.

"Nonsense," said Lindsey. "You're in no fit state to travel. You'll sleep here."

Aubrey gave him a pleading look. "I'm really not up for much..."

Lindsey, upon realising what Aubrey thought he'd suggested, recoiled. "I only meant—that is to say—I would never—!"

But Aubrey turned away, screwing his eyes shut and clapping a hand over his mouth. His shoulders heaved twice, and the fit passed without further incident. Lindsey's hand moved from Aubrey's shoulder to his back, rubbing it as Aubrey had done for him half a year ago.

"Stay the night," Lindsey said. "Please believe I ask nothing more of you than that."

Aubrey didn't say anything.

"Would you prefer I go?" Lindsey asked.

Aubrey nodded.

In defiance of the impulse to wrap his Aubrey in a comforting embrace, Lindsey stepped away. "If you need anything, pull the cord by the bed. Don't hesitate to ask."

He had to strain his ears for it, but he caught Aubrey's faint thanks.

"You're welcome," he replied. "Goodnight."

It went against his every instinct as a host and a friend; nevertheless, he departed.

After instructing Charles to see to Aubrey's needs, Lindsey sought solace in the library. He arrived to find the door shut. As he reached to open it, voices within stopped him.

"—know better than to sneak out after dinner," Rowena scoffed.

"If Mr Warren so offends you," Lady Pelham replied, "why did you invite him?"

Lindsey would've turned and fled—the Althorp household had a long-standing rule against interrupting Rowena and her friends—but the mention of his Aubrey gave him pause. He glanced up and down the hall, then bent his ear to the keyhole.

"I intended to prove how unfit a companion he is for a man of Lindsey's station," said Rowena.

Had she plunged her ivory letter-opener between Lindsey's ribs, it would've pained him less.

Lady Pelham restored his hopes with her response. "If Lindsey truly cares for him, then—"

"—then society and the law should cast off their prejudices to the sound of glorious trumpets from above?" Rowena finished in her most sarcastic tone yet. "A notion as charming as it is unlikely."

Lady Pelham continued undaunted. "You're being rather hard on Mr Warren. It's only his first dinner. I myself was little better than a country rustic before you refined me."

"Before I ruined you, you mean."

Lindsey heard skirts rustling, and a soft sound very much like a pair of lips meeting in a kiss, before Lady Pelham replied, "Hardly."

Anything further escaped Lindsey's notice. He hurried away, his mind reeling.

The next morning, Lindsey rose at half-past eight, threw on his clothes without waiting for Charles, and returned to Aubrey's door by quarter-to-nine. He knocked, received no answer, knocked again, and opened the door.

Aubrey was gone.

Further investigation revealed he'd departed without leaving any message, had barely spoken to Charles on the way out, and had given no indication of his destination or if he intended to return.

Charles encountered considerable difficulty in convincing Lindsey to sit down to breakfast. Lindsey's brain churned, wondering why had Aubrey left. He'd got on well with the other guests before dinner, had displayed a respectable appetite throughout dinner itself—everything had seemed fine up to the point Aubrey became ill on his way out. Apart from Graves's little comment after the ladies' departure.

Once Lindsey remembered that little comment, everything else fell away.

Graves had offended his Aubrey. His Aubrey had left without saying goodbye. Surely these events were related. The more Lindsey thought on it, the tighter his jaw clenched.

Dealing with Graves required patience. Lindsey had none left. He called Charles to fetch a hansom and set out to confront Graves in the flesh.

Graves's rooms in Pont Street resembled an opium dream. Oriental rugs of incongruous shapes, sizes, and colours overlapped on the floor. The peacock-feather wallpaper disappeared behind rice paper screens painted with Nipponese women in floral robes. A blue-and-white china vase held a bouquet of fresh lilies. Gauzy, blood-orange curtains filtered what little sunlight escaped London's fog.

Graves himself reclined on a divan in a silk dressing gown patterned with gingko leaves, balancing an ivory cigarette-holder between two fingers.

"What a pleasant surprise!" said Graves, rising like Venus Anadyomene as Lindsey entered. "Come in, sit down. Sherry?"

"No, thank you," said Lindsey. He remained standing.

Graves, busy with the cut-crystal sherry bottle, took a moment to notice Lindsey's stance. "Are you feeling quite the thing, old boy?"

"What the devil were you on about last night?" Lindsey demanded.

"I'm afraid I don't—"

"Telling Aubrey to go off with the ladies. What the hell was that?"

Graves's half-lidded eyes flew wide. "Good Lord, man, it was only a joke. Surely a strapping working-class specimen like Mr Warren can take a few lumps."

Lindsey couldn't muster an appropriate response. Inappropriate responses, however, were abundant. He clenched his teeth to keep them at bay.

Unable to meet Lindsey's eyes, Graves busied himself pouring two glasses of sherry. He offered one to Lindsey. Lindsey refrained from knocking it out of his hand. Graves covered his evident concern with a shrug and set the spare glass down, sipping at his own.

"Why is this so important to you?" he asked once he'd swallowed.

"Because *he* is important to me!" said Lindsey. "I'd thought you of all people would understand."

A choking laugh interrupted Graves's next sip of sherry. "Me? Whatever gave you that impression?"

"Your companion at the theatre."

For an instant, Lindsey saw genuine alarm in Graves's eyes, but it was quickly masked.

"Oh, that!" Graves laughed again. "That was nothing, a night out on the town with an acquaintance."

"Do you massage all your acquaintances?"

Graves, in the midst of swallowing, coughed violently. "Massage?"

"Your hand on his neck," said Lindsey. "And his shoulders, and his waist, and—"

"Enough!" Graves put up a hand. "I cry you mercy."

Lindsey didn't feel merciful. "What is he?"

"A painter."

Lindsey glared, fed up with Graves's obfuscation. "And what is this painter to you?"

129

"Rather like what your clerk is to you, I expect. Though you'll note I don't bring my painter to dinner. I could, you know. Artists mix with all classes of society. But a clerk is another matter."

"I fail to see how."

"Then allow me to explain." Graves tossed his hair out of his eyes. "Halloway, as an artist, is a cultured individual capable of contributing to any conversation worth having. Warren, a clerk, stutters to a halt when invited to speak on anything more aesthetically complex than figures in a ledger. Halloway's knowledge of etiquette allows him to follow or break its rules as he pleases. Warren, meanwhile, flounders and drowns in the midst of a party he never should've attended in the first place. Unless you intended to humiliate him—in which case, I congratulate you on a job well done."

It was well Lindsey'd refused Graves's offer of a drink. If he'd had anything to hand, he would've thrown it in Graves's face. Some of this intent must've shown in Lindsey's expression, for Graves eyed him carefully before continuing.

"You think me cruel. If I am cruel, then you put de Sade to shame. After all, Warren is a perfect stranger to me. A snide comment from my lips means nothing to him. You, however, to whom he looks for guidance, abandoned him to wolves such as myself. The poor wretch hardly knew his left from his right, much less which fork to use. And you left him to starve in the wilderness without so much as a hinting cough."

Any protest on Lindsey's tongue died at the memory of the miserable lump Aubrey had become by the dinner's end.

Graves, ever vicious in debate, pressed on. "Scold me all you like. But if you truly want the best for him, you'd do well to understand he has his place, and we have ours, and ne'er the twain shall meet."

"There," said Lindsey, "I must disagree."

Graves shrugged again. "As you like. Have you finished that Proust yet?"

"Haven't found the time." Lindsey reached for his hat.

Graves stopped him with an outstretched hand. "Please, stay for breakfast. I can't bear to have you leave angry with me."

Lindsey, who'd already eaten, and needed to reflect on the disturbing ideas Graves had planted in his head, said nothing. Graves took the hint and rang for his valet to see Lindsey out.

"I wish you'd read Proust," Graves said as they waited.

"He bores me."

"Philistine. It takes nothing less than a kidnapping and an evil duke to keep your attention."

"Two evil dukes," Lindsey replied, smiling despite himself. "And a pirate."

∽

FRIDAY MORNING, TWO days after the disastrous dinner, a battering knock on Aubrey's door interrupted his efforts to knot his tie.

"One moment!" he called, fumbling for another half-second before giving up and leaving it loose around his neck as he leapt to answer the door.

His housekeeper stood in the hall, looking none too impressed with his dishevelled appearance.

"This came for you," she said, thrusting a cigar-box-sized package into his unready arms.

"Thank you," he managed.

Mrs Padwick wasn't appeased. "Postman knocked up Mr Brown with his rattle. Mr Jones, too. They've both complained."

"My apologies."

Mrs Padwick glared at him, then stormed back down the narrow stair. Aubrey closed his door as softly as possible.

The package felt heavier than it looked, wrapped in sharp-creased brown paper with twine tied in a neat little bow. While it bore the name "Mr Aubrey Warren" and his address, he found nothing indicating who'd sent it.

Wary of its contents, Aubrey set it down on his desk and slowly untied it. Beneath the brown paper and cushioning tissue lay a book. Its leather cover read, in gold-embossed type:

MANNERS AND TONE OF GOOD SOCIETY
BY A MEMBER OF THE ARISTOCRACY

Aubrey frowned at the mysterious volume. Careful not to crack its spine, he lifted it out of its wrappings and eased open the front cover. A folded piece of thick, cream-coloured parchment fluttered down onto his desk. He set the book aside for the moment and picked up the note. The paper had black borders, about a quarter-inch thick. The handwriting upon it flowed like vines climbing a trellis.

Dear Mr Warren,

I do hope you'll forgive the familiarity of this gift. It seemed to me you could make good use of it—far better than I ever could. As such, it is yours. Do call upon us again. Perhaps Tuesday at two o'clock would suit?

Your servant,

Miss Rowena Althorp

A factory whistle blew in the distance, startling Aubrey into action. He shoved the note into his trouser pocket and turned his attention back to the book. A cursory examination revealed someone had taken very light notes in pencil, starting with the Table of Contents. The chapter titled *Dinner Parties* was underlined, and a little star drawn next to its page number.

Aubrey supposed he should feel offended.

∽

"Post for you, Warren," Mr Jennings said through his open door as Aubrey entered the office. Smith, as usual, wasn't yet present. "Surprised it arrived before you did."

Aubrey wondered how Mr Jennings knew he'd received a package at home, then spied the two envelopes on his desk. He leaned into Mr Jennings's doorway to reply. "Won't happen again, sir."

"Not expecting any further deliveries?"

"No, sir—I mean, I'm not, but I've also no intention of arriving late again."

He meant to go on to acknowledge his other recent offenses—first when a grief-stricken Lindsey showed up on his doorstep in the middle of the night, and again just yesterday when the aftereffects of Miss Althorp's dinner party kept him from the office until the unthinkable hour of eleven—but Mr Jennings's blank stare stopped him.

"It's hardly quarter past seven," said Mr Jennings.

"Yes, sir, I realise—"

"No you most emphatically do not, Warren. It's a miracle I'm here this early, much less the post. If you consider this late, I shudder to think what 'on time' means in your mechanical mind."

Aubrey didn't quite know how to respond. "Sorry, sir," seemed his safest bet.

Mr Jennings shook his head and motioned for Aubrey to close the door.

Having done so, Aubrey returned to the letters on his desk. Both came in heavy envelopes. One bore a wax seal. He opened it first.

Dear Mr Warren,
Kindly do me the honour of receiving you Tuesday evening.

There followed an address in Grosvenor Square, and the signature: *Mr Clarence Rook.*

Aubrey, who knew he hadn't made a favourable impression on the man at dinner, frowned in confusion. He set the letter aside and opened the second envelope.

Dear Mr Warren,
We the undersigned invite you to an afternoon at the Catullus Club. Please find us at that address between noon and four on Tuesday.
Sincerely,
Lord Cyril Graves and Mr Roderick Miller, Esq.

As his eyes alighted on the name Catullus, Aubrey sat down hard behind his desk. He'd hoped never to visit the establishment again. Fate seemed determined to drag him back.

Including Miss Althorp's, all three invitations demanded his attention next Tuesday. Aubrey wished he could be surprised at people of means trying to schedule appointments during hours when working men would be... well, working. He'd need the whole day off for travel alone. As he approached Mr Jennings's office to request his reluctant holiday, he half-hoped he might be denied, and have an excuse to decline the invitations. But Mr Jennings failed him.

"It's about time you took a holiday, Warren," he said. "Take the train out to the country, get some fresh air. Perhaps you might even eat something. Godspeed."

Aubrey bit his tongue and returned to his books.

CHAPTER FIFTEEN

Tuesday found Aubrey standing in front of the Catullus Club's fashionable, yet discreet, edifice. With tremendous effort, he willed his reluctant legs to climb the marble steps, pass the doorman, and enter the foyer, where he encountered a porter behind an imposing black desk. His anxiety increased as he realised he faced the very same porter who'd presided over the club when Aubrey had left a decade ago, hoping to never return.

"Good morning," said Aubrey, praying the porter had forgotten his face.

"Good afternoon, sir." If the porter recognised him, he gave no sign of it. "May I ask what brings you to our establishment today?"

"Lord Cyril Graves and Mr Miller are expecting me."

"And who might I say has called for them?"

Aubrey had half a mind to say Ganymede, as toffs had encouraged him to in days of yore. He suspected he couldn't get away with it at his age. If his hosts expected to receive an impossibly-beautiful immortal youth, then they had an incredible disappointment coming. "Warren."

The porter rang a silver bell. A handsome footman rushed in. More than handsome—any artist would rejoice to have him for a model. The lad's cheeks bore a rosy blush, long lashes framed his wide grey eyes, his plump lips hung naturally parted, and one charming lock of his auburn hair refused to follow the rest and curled onto his forehead. His whole aspect projected Classical beauty, innocence with a coy edge. He couldn't be older than sixteen, seventeen at most. Aubrey's stomach turned.

"Mr Warren," said the porter, "is here to see Lord Cyril and Mr Miller."

The young footman ran off. The porter's cold gaze drifted back to Aubrey.

"Jem will return to direct you shortly, sir. In the meantime, may I take your hat?"

Aubrey surrendered it and settled in to wait. The foyer held a pair of leather-upholstered armchairs, but he preferred to stand as he flicked his eyes over the room, taking in the high ceiling and black marble floor. It hadn't changed a whit. He wished to God it had. He also wished for his hat back, if only to have something to occupy his hands, which threatened to fidget. He shoved them into his trouser pockets instead. In the left pocket he found the calling-card case Lindsey had given him, still empty. He rubbed his fingertips over the engraving. Minutes crawled by like hours. The porter ignored him all the while. Aubrey felt ready to give up on the whole enterprise and go home when handsome Jem reappeared.

"Right this way, sir!" he chirped.

Aubrey followed.

Jem led him down a winding trail through the club, down back halls and up servant's stairs—the stranger's path, of which Aubrey knew all the twists and turns. While secretive, the path brought Aubrey into sight of far more gentleman than he would've liked, thanks to doors left ajar; by accident or by design of the club's more exhibitionist members, Aubrey couldn't guess, and didn't want to know.

The rooms held more sofas and settees than chairs, and many chairs held multiple occupants. Most of the club's members had eyes only for each other and didn't pay Aubrey any attention, but one gentleman—snub-nosed, with salt-and-pepper muttonchops and another fair young footman on his lap—frowned a little as Aubrey passed by. Again, Aubrey wished for his hat back, though he knew covering his face with it would only attract more notice. He fixed his eyes on the back of Jem's head, lest he see more than he ought, and wondered how many laps Jem had sprawled on. If it at all compared to his own history at the club...

They arrived at a long hall on the second floor, filled with identical locking doors. Graves and Miller had reserved a private room. Aubrey's gut clenched.

Jem rapped his knuckles against a particular door to announce Aubrey. Upon receiving an affirmative response from within, he pushed the door open.

The far corner of the spacious chamber held a four-post bed large enough for three men. Aubrey tore his eyes away from the crushed-velvet curtains to focus on the room's occupants, who, to his relief, sat not on the bed but in two of four high-backed armchairs by the hearth. Both wore suits to put Aubrey's to shame, though Graves's cravat had crumpled, and Graves himself had flung one leg up over the arm of his chair.

Miller nodded to Jem, and the lad left the room. Graves gave Aubrey an appraising look. Aubrey stood his ground.

"You wanted to see me?" he said over the sound of the door closing, but not locking. He still had an avenue of escape.

"Please, sit," said Miller, making a broad gesture towards to the two empty chairs.

Aubrey would've preferred to stand, but he acquiesced and perched on the edge of the seat nearest the door. Neither gentleman offered him a drink from the cut-crystal bottle on the side table between their chairs, though Miller and Graves had a glass each—Miller's almost full, and Graves's half-empty.

Miller broke the awkward silence with a cough. "You must have some suspicion of why we've asked you here today."

"I don't, actually," said Aubrey.

"You astonish me, Mr Warren," said Graves, sounding not at all astonished. "Allow me to shed some light on the mystery. You were so charming at Miss Althorp's soiree, Roddy and I simply had to know more of you. We're positively afire with curiosity. Who are your people?"

Who were Aubrey's people, indeed. He'd wondered it often enough as a boy. By now, he'd reconciled with the question and resolved to let it remain unanswered. He'd no desire to divulge any of it to Graves's greedy ears.

Graves continued without him. "I don't believe I've met any other Warrens. At least, none of note."

"Then perhaps I'm the only noteworthy Warren."

Miller's bushy brows twitched. "Your father is in trade, I presume?"

"My father is dead."

"Congratulations." Graves toasted with his half-full glass. "I can only hope I might someday be so fortunate."

"My condolences," said Miller, with a sidelong glance at Graves. Aubrey acknowledged his condescension with a nod.

"Your mother, the same?" asked Graves.

Aubrey clenched his teeth and nodded again.

"Most unfortunate," said Miller. "Any siblings? Cousins?"

"I'm afraid not," said Aubrey. None he knew of, at any rate.

"Then," said Graves, "you are alone, Mr Warren?"

If Aubrey didn't feel alone before, he certainly did now. "Quite."

"So sad." Graves pursed his lips and shook his head, yet still didn't appear as distraught as he claimed. "You cut quite the mysterious figure. An orphan, no family... born where?"

Aubrey went very still.

Graves continued. "I only ask because—forgive me—I find myself somewhat confused. You live and work in Manchester, but your accent..."

Aubrey didn't dare breathe.

"You disguise it well," Graves went on. "My compliments to that. Nevertheless, it lacks the Northern burr. Truth told, it sounds like something of a muddle. If I had to guess, I'd say it originated near East London. Am I correct?"

Aubrey would've returned a very rude answer had Miller not interrupted.

"You mustn't believe we asked you here to discuss your origins, Mr Warren."

"No?" said Graves.

"No," said Miller, shooting Graves a disapproving look before returning to Aubrey. "It's Althorp we'd like to talk to you about."

Aubrey swallowed the instinct to flee. "Oh?"

Miller nodded gravely. "It's been said our Althorp is a flighty creature. I cannot in good conscience deny this. However, on the few occasions where his attentions become fixed, his devotion is absolute. His affection for his family and friends, par example, is unwavering. I've always supposed, should his interested ever include romance, the result would be the same."

"And now," said Graves, taking advantage of Miller's pause for breath, "it seems he's experiencing the throes of passion at last."

Aubrey's left eyebrow rose without his permission. "At last?"

Graves and Miller fixed him with identical blank looks.

Aubrey elaborated. "Surely he's expressed such an attraction before."

"Not to our knowledge," said Miller.

"And we'd certainly have knowledge of it," said Graves. "When Althorp's in a passion, the whole world knows it."

Aubrey didn't approve of Graves's tone.

Miller cleared his throat. "Althorp's failure to develop romantic interest before now isn't entirely his fault. Factors existed beyond his control."

"Such as?" asked Aubrey.

"Althorp went to Eton late," said Miller. "He'd had tutors at home after his mother's passing, but Sir Geoffrey—his father—was determined to keep him out of school as long as possible."

"Why?" asked Aubrey.

Miller scrutinised him. "You're aware of the reputation public schools have?"

Aubrey was aware, and fairly certain the same reputation applied to any institution housing boys of a certain age. Throw together a hundred-odd youths at the point in life when wild instinct bloomed, deny their association with maidens fair, and what else could result? He didn't have to imagine. He'd had first-hand confirmation at the workhouse, and from his former customers. More than a handful of the latter had used him to reenact a schoolboy's fledgling romance. Miller didn't need to know all that, so Aubrey simply nodded.

Miller, satisfied, went on. "It's a well-earned reputation, I can assure you. Old Sir Geoffrey had passed through the very same system as a boy. He knew what sort of things when on. And he knew his son. And he knew what anyone else who'd met the boy knew—that he was, and is, obviously and irrevocably inverted. But above all else, Sir Geoffrey knew the law. Schoolboys aren't often brought to trial, but boys grow to men, and not all men leave their passions behind at school. Sir Geoffrey thought it best not to expose his son to such influences in the first place, and intended to keep him out of school altogether. But you know Althorp—his booklust is insatiable. He was determined to be a scholar. When he was... thirteen? fourteen? fifteen, perhaps, Sir Geoffrey relented. And so, knowing I was already at Eton, Sir Geoffrey approached my father before the start of Althorp's first term, and charged me with the responsibility of seeing Althorp didn't fall victim to... 'youthful indiscretions', as he called them."

"Most tactful of him," said Graves.

Aubrey's mind reeled. "And how did Sir Geoffrey expect you to accomplish that?"

"Simply enough," said Miller. "I don't believe I flatter myself too much in saying I was a popular lad. Telling the other boys Althorp was under my protection sufficed to dissuade any would-be paramours."

"And Sir Lindsey himself?" said Aubrey.

"I distracted him with sport," Miller replied with a proud smile. "The physical exhaustion kept him from seeking other, less wholesome exercise. At first he despised my dragging him away from his books, but he was well-formed for cricket, and one comes to enjoy what one excels at. By the time I'd moved on to university, Althorp had an established reputation as the celibate sportsman. Companionable, yes, and more than willing to lend a hand up to underclassmen, but none dared do more than sigh wistfully from afar."

"And by Jove, how they sighed!" Graves broke in. "I can't imagine the self-control you exerted, Roddy."

"I'm afraid I don't follow," said Aubrey.

"If you could've seen him!" Graves leaned back in his chair, gazing fondly up into the middle distance. "Althorp as a boy—the absolute vision he presented—like a youthful Apollo! Verily glowing with the sun's own radiance!"

"A very pretty lad," Miller conceded. "Naturally, everyone fell over themselves to win his favour."

"To coax him into bed, more like," said Graves.

"Hush, you," said Miller before Aubrey could express the same sentiment with less tact. "And it wasn't self-control on my part, it was fear of what Sir Geoffrey would do if he found out. Not that he objected to the practice on an abstract level, you understand," he said to Aubrey. "It's only he didn't want his own son mixed up in it. Which is perfectly reasonable. Still, I'll admit there was some temptation."

"But you never succumbed." Graves wore an expression torn between admiration and disgust. "You altar-boy, you."

"But surely once you left..." Aubrey began.

Miller shook his head. "As I said, Althorp's reputation was secure."

"Which isn't to say nobody tried," Graves cut in. "Everyone tried. I tried! But he wouldn't have a one of us. Not even his fag, Evans." Graves sighed and shook his head. "Poor Evans would've licked his boots and more besides, but Althorp just patted him on the head and set him about fetching books from the library and keeping his cricket kit clean."

"And that was the end of it," said Miller. "Until the Labouchere Amendment passed."

"You're aware of the Amendment, are you not?" Graves asked Aubrey, his tone suggesting Aubrey wasn't the least bit aware.

Aubrey met Graves's sardonic smirk with a cold stare. "I am."

Graves raised his brows and returned to his drink.

Miller cleared his throat again. "Nobody took it seriously at first. We only realised what it meant after Cleveland Street. Sir Geoffrey understood the implications as soon as it passed, and pulled Althorp from Eton."

"What was that supposed to accomplish?" said Aubrey, failing to keep the indignant tone from his voice.

Graves shrugged. "Removing Althorp from temptation, to a location where his inevitable fall wouldn't be quite so public."

"Where the repercussions could be controlled," said Miller.

Neither one seemed inclined to elaborate further. Aubrey wondered if he'd gone mad. "And you all just went along with this?"

"Well, I'm hardly his father, am I?" said Miller. "It's not as if he lived in total isolation. We still wrote, visited, et cetera."

"And he had his grooms," Graves added with a lewd twist of his brows.

"What does that signify?" asked Aubrey.

Graves gave him a cool, quelling look. "You're not the jealous type, are you?"

Miller frowned thoughtfully, looking Aubrey up and down. "No. He's not."

Graves turned to Miller with a puzzled expression. Miller continued frowning.

Aubrey lifted his chin. "If you're implying inappropriate conduct between Sir Lindsey and his staff—"

"Implying!" cried Graves. "What's to imply? It's obvious! He wouldn't come to us asking after recommendations for discreet, handsome young men if he wasn't—"

"He didn't come to us," Miller interrupted him. "Miss Althorp did."

Graves flapped a dismissive hand. "Yes, yes, it's her household, she does the hiring; but she asked for those specifications on his behalf, surely."

"On his instruction?" asked Miller.

Graves's frown mirrored Miller's. "Of course! Why else would she? Unless..."

Both gentlemen turned to Aubrey. Graves leaned in.

"He must have! Hasn't he?"

Aubrey's jaw tightened. "It's not my place to say."

"Yes," said Graves, "but you'd know, wouldn't you?"

"Cyril," Miller said in a warning tone.

"What?" said Graves. "We're all friends here, aren't we? What's a little gossip between friends? Besides, this is pertinent! Do you mean to tell me Althorp hasn't fucked a single one of his—"

"No," said Aubrey, louder than he ought've.

Grave's eyes widened.

"No?" he echoed breathlessly.

"Let it go, Cyril," said Miller.

"Let it go! Good God, man, if this is true, then—" Graves whipped his head around to face Aubrey again, and laughed. "You lucky bastard!"

Aubrey forced out a syllable or two through gritted teeth, but it didn't deter Graves.

"All our years of pining, and you just fall into it!" he crowed. "You absolute dog! I don't know whether to shake your hand or slap your face!"

"Cyril!"

"Oh, come now, Roddy! Only think on it! How was he, then?"

This last, to Aubrey, was more than he could stand. He wrenched open his clenched jaw to tell Graves where he and his impertinent inquisition could go, but Miller's hand on Graves's arm forestalled him.

"That," said Miller, "is not what we called Mr Warren here to discuss, Cyril."

"Yes, but—!"

Miller talked over him in a tone that brooked no argument. "In fact, this revelation makes our intended topic even more important than we'd thought."

"And what topic was that?" snapped Aubrey.

"Althorp's heart," said Graves, wearing a disgruntled expression left over from Miller's interruption.

Aubrey stared at him. "Pardon?"

Miller folded his hands over one knee. "You are... involved... with Althorp, are you not?"

"For God's sake, Roddy!" huffed Graves. "As if it weren't obvious—"

"Yes," said Aubrey, if only to shut Graves up.

The look Graves gave him could've soured milk.

Miller nodded sagely. "As Althorp's friends, we feel a certain responsibility towards his well-being."

"Physical, psychological..." Graves twirled an idle hand. "Emotional..."

Aubrey wished they'd get to the point. "You believe I'm a threat to Sir Lindsey's well-being."

"Yes," said Graves, to Miller's evident dismay.

"Not a threat, precisely—" Miller began, but the damage was done.

"And how do you suppose I'd threaten him?" said Aubrey, working double to push down the snarl rising in his throat.

"You must understand," said Miller. "Althorp has led a sheltered life."

"Thanks in no small part to the actions of his friends," Aubrey countered.

To his surprise, neither gentleman argued the point. Miller went so far as to nod his agreement.

"A soul like Althorp's," said Graves, "needs coddling to preserve its pure-hearted nature. We should all hate to see him suffer any disappointment."

"Indeed, no, for then he might learn something, and what a horror that would be."

Both gentleman fixed him with shocked looks. Aubrey realised he'd spoken his last thought aloud. He swallowed.

"Forgive me, sirs," he said, rising from his seat. "I'm afraid I've overstepped my bounds."

"Oh no, nothing like!" said Graves in his least-sincere tone yet.

"However," Aubrey continued as if Graves hadn't spoken, "I assure you I've no intention of disappointing Sir Lindsey in any capacity. Does this satisfy you?"

"I suppose it must," Miller replied, exchanging a confused look with Graves.

"Excellent," said Aubrey.

He turned on his heel and left the room. If either gentleman called after him, he didn't hear it.

AUBREY COLLECTED HIS hat from the aloof porter and stormed out of the club. Rage fuelled him like coal in a furnace, stoking the boiler of his heart and driving the pistons of his legs to triple-speed. It wasn't so much the way Graves and Miller had spoken to him—he hated it, of course, and them, but he'd grown accustomed to such treatment from insecure twits clinging to the lowest rung of the upper classes. Nothing quite like kicking the man below you to make you feel taller. No, what blew the embers of his anger into roaring bursts of flame was their treatment of Lindsey. Lindsey, the kindest, gentlest soul Aubrey knew, incapable of duplicity. To learn the men Lindsey considered friends, and Lindsey's own family, had lied to him all his life, had caged him in his ancestral home like a dog in a kennel—

A shout caught Aubrey's attention, and he drew up short. More shouts and a horse's whinny helped him realise he'd almost marched in front of an omnibus. His emotions had clouded his vision just as surely as the perpetual London smog. He backed up to a lamppost and doffed his hat in apology, still seething.

The omnibus rolled away, wheels clattering on the cobbles. Aubrey continued leaning against the post, wrestling his temper into submission.

They'd lied to his Lindsey. All of them.

Yet, as he thought on it, he realised he'd done the very same since the day Lindsey walked into the mill.

The sobering realisation threw a pail of ash over his burning anger, smothering it in shame. The rest of his walk to Belgrave Square proceeded at a more sedate pace.

Having studied *Manners and Tone of Good Society* the night prior, he knew enough to avoid a second incident with Mr Hudson, though he still lacked a card to present. Mr Hudson took his breach of etiquette in stride and showed him in. Their twisting, turning path ended in a chamber almost identical to the drawing room, only with pale salmon walls instead of lemongrass, and no piano. Miss Althorp sat alone in one of three matching armchairs, a magazine lying open in her lap.

"Come in, Mr Warren," she said, without looking up, and before Mr Hudson could announce him.

Aubrey turned to Mr Hudson, but the butler was already halfway down the hall in the opposite direction, so Aubrey squared his shoulders and entered the room.

Miss Althorp folded her magazine—*Belgravia*—set it aside, and finally deigned to look up at him.

"Do have a seat," she said, flicking her wrist at the empty chairs.

Aubrey chose the seat nearest the door and thanked her for the privilege.

A smile pursed her lips. "May I offer you any refreshment?"

"No, thank you," said Aubrey, wondering where Lindsey was.

Miss Althorp, lacking extrasensory perception, didn't answer his unspoken inquiry. "Then to business: our dear Lindsey, and his best interests."

Aubrey resisted the urge to plant his forehead in his palms. "If I may be so bold as to interrupt, I believe I've already held this conversation with Sir Lindsey's friends."

"Have you?" said Miss Althorp coolly. "And what sort of conversation was it?"

"The sort where I'm told to bring no harm to Sir Lindsey, lest greater harm fall on my head."

Miss Althorp caught a fluttering laugh in her delicate fingers. In response to Aubrey's bewildered expression, she replied, "That wasn't the conversation I had in mind. I intended to congratulate you on the happiness you've brought Lindsey, and to express my hope that you'll continue to make him just as happy in the future."

Aubrey thought it was rather the same talk dressed up in different clothes, but kept that thought to himself. "I fear you overestimate me."

"No," said Miss Althorp, taking him by surprise. "I don't think I do."

Her gaze slipped away from his face. A faint line appeared between her brows, then vanished as she returned to him.

"Lindsey is not the most self-aware of men, but he is by far the most sincere. I feared when he finally realised his own proclivities, it would be through pinning all his hopes on someone unworthy of them, someone who might misuse his trust most cruelly. I confess when he first spoke of you, I held a great many suspicions towards your true motives. Having met you, however, I find you above suspicion."

Aubrey kept his sarcastic thanks to himself.

Miss Althorp continued. "From what I've observed—and I'm told I'm a very observant woman—you are nearly as attached to my brother as he is to you."

Aubrey jerked upright. He struggled to keep his tone casual as he asked, "What gave it away?"

Miss Althorp laughed again, tilting her head to one side. "Nothing you need worry about. You're quite discreet. If I hadn't sought out the evidence, I doubt I'd ever have noticed. But you do tend to follow him about the room with your eyes, and with a certain manner of anticipation. An eagerness to please, perhaps. I believe it would pain you greatly to see him suffer any discomfort."

Aubrey didn't reply, preoccupied with noting the behaviours she described and resolving to suppress them in the future.

"And there's also..." Miss Althorp paused, frowned for a moment, then continued. "A lack of artifice. One might feel tempted to attribute it to your upbringing, but again I flatter myself, this time in asserting I am not so prejudiced. After all, criminals exist amongst the lower classes, do they not? And they must have a talent for flattery and deceit. So it's clearly not impossible for one of low birth to possess such skills. But to return to my point—artifice—you lack it, utterly. And so you cannot possibly be toying with Lindsey's affections for personal gain."

Aubrey kept his jaw shut, unsure which of her insults to be offended by first. His reaction seemed to please Miss Althorp, who indulged in a close-lipped smile. She maintained it effortlessly as the seconds ticked past until Aubrey regained his composure and formed an appropriate response.

"You honour me, Miss Althorp, with your faith in my sincerity. I regret to report I cannot be so certain of your own."

Miss Althorp laughed yet again. Aubrey felt like a jester, in addition to a pet and an automaton.

"You wound me, Mr Warren," she replied. "I only hope to find the opportunity to prove myself to you in the future."

⌒

In Grosvenor Square, Aubrey found the Rook residence. The olive green paint on the door had chipped around the brass fixtures. Aubrey knocked. Several minutes later, the door swung inward, revealing a maid younger than Jem.

"Mr Warren?" she asked.

"Yes," said Aubrey, disturbed by how quickly word of his exploits has spread amongst the City's household staffs.

"Mr Rook is expecting you." Without further explanation, she turned and vanished into the dark foyer, leaving the door swinging open.

Aubrey, bewildered, stepped inside and closed the door. The maid had already climbed the unlit stair and turned a corner with no sign of stopping to wait for him. He trotted up after her and caught her up outside another closed door. The maid knocked twice, curtsied to Aubrey, and disappeared down the well-worn carpet of the hall before he heard the answering call, "Enter."

He opened the door to a gentleman's study. Barrister bookshelves lined the walls, a film of dust coating their glass fronts. Opposite the door stood a desk. Rook sat behind it, his elbows perched on its top and his chin balanced on his steepled fingers, facing Aubrey. What sunlight filtered through the fog to reach the narrow window became a shaft of light splitting the room in twain; Aubrey and the door on one side, Rook and the desk on the other. The study held no other furniture.

"Mr Warren," said Rook. "Come in."

With some reluctance, Aubrey shut the door and stepped forward into the shaft of light.

Rook let his hands fall to the arms of his chair and leaned back. "You must wonder why I've asked you here—"

"You wish to discuss Sir Lindsey."

Rook gave a start, then chuckled. "It seems I've underestimated you, Mr Warren. Yes, I wish to discuss our Lindsey. As of late, all he wishes to discuss is you. Hardly a gathering goes by without a word on Warren's diligence, his clever mind, his supreme underappreciated talents."

"I'm flattered to hear it," Aubrey forced out around the lump of panic in his throat. Rook made it sound as though Lindsey had taken out a public advertisement announcing their connection. "Though I'm sure it's undeserved."

"So modest. But I must say I'm baffled by one particular item. Lindsey claims you can sew."

Aubrey coughed. "It's a practical skill for a bachelor."

"Indeed. Particularly a confirmed bachelor."

Aubrey's heart stopped.

"But that's none of my concern," Rook continued. "No, what concerns me is the sewing. As you say, it's a useful talent for a man living alone, though I daresay most would hire the work out to their housekeeper or maid. However, as Lindsey informed us, you keep an economical household." A disconcerting smile appeared on his lips. "A very economical household. Lindsey considers it one of your virtues. But I must ask—if you've no mother, aunts, sisters, nor female cousins—no housemaid or tailor or seamstress in sight—how the devil did you learn to sew?"

Aubrey opened his mouth, scrambling for an explanation, but Rook beat him to it.

"My theory draws on trivia not typically available to men of my station. You see, workhouse children learn trade to earn their keep, or so I'm told. Shoe-repair is among them. This has the added benefit of teaching them to sew, which helps the girls catch husbands, and helps the boys survive sans brides."

"What a curious fact," said Aubrey.

"Allow me to put the question plainly: did you spend your tender years in a workhouse, Mr Warren?"

Aubrey, all his energies focused on not clenching his fists, wished to God he were a better liar.

"Mr Warren?"

"Yes!" Aubrey burst out. "Yes, I'm from the bloody workhouse! Are you satisfied?"

Rook's smile became a feral grin. "I'm afraid not. To my great distress, our dear Lindsey is a dreadful judge of character. He has a disquieting habit of befriending the wrong sort."

Aubrey felt Lindsey's friendship with Rook and the rest had already illustrated that point, but said nothing.

Rood continued. "It doesn't extend as far as one might fear—to my knowledge, he hasn't become inappropriate with his household staff.

146

However, I'm very much afraid no good friend of Lindsey could ever approve of the overt familiarity he's shown you."

Aubrey had no response that wouldn't prove Rook right, at least in vulgarity. He bit his tongue.

Rook went on. "While there exists some small merit in upward mobility, it's not enough to dispel the disgrace of any further contact between Lindsey and yourself. Still, you might yet surpass your origins by doing the right thing—the noble thing—and putting an end to whatever relationship exists. Immediately."

As much as Aubrey wanted to show Rook how a true workhouse brat would resolve their dispute, he restrained himself from a live demonstration. For better or worse, Lindsey cared for Rook. By venting his frustrations now, he'd only play into Rook's hands, and lose Lindsey in the bargain.

"I'm gratified," said Aubrey, "to know Sir Lindsey has such protective friends. And I'm flattered to hear you expect nobility from me. But there, I must disappoint you."

Rook's grin vanished. "Perhaps I haven't made myself clear—"

"On the contrary." Aubrey forced a smile. "Your request is as unmistakable as it is, regrettably, impossible for me to fulfil."

"There will be consequences for this."

"And I intend to face them. Was there anything else you wanted, sir?"

Judging by his expression, what Rook wanted was to plant his fist in Aubrey's jaw. Instead, he closed his eyes and inhaled slowly, nostrils flaring. When his eyes reopened, his smile had returned.

"I offer you my condolences, Mr Warren."

"I assure you, I won't need them."

Aubrey moved to open the door. Rook leapt up from the desk.

"Allow me," he said, his tone jovial once again.

He ushered Aubrey out of the study and into the hall. Aubrey's boot had just touched the first step of the stair when a third voice cried out.

"Mr Warren!"

Aubrey turned around and saw Miss Rook standing in the hall. Her petrified gaze flicked between him and her brother. Aubrey felt compelled to put her at ease.

"Miss Rook," he replied with a nod and a small but genuine smile.

Rook cleared his throat. "Mr Warren was just leaving, Emmeline."

"Oh, but he mustn't!"

Her outburst left both Aubrey and Rook at a loss. Rook recovered first.

"I beg your pardon?"

His voice had lost its well-oiled tones, leaving the hard edge of command barely hidden under the polite veneer of his actual words.

Miss Rook's shoulders twitched as if repressing a cringe. The sight reminded Aubrey of a child berated by an unreasonable workhouse foreman. He banked the anger welling up in his chest at the association. It wouldn't do to strike Rook.

"I have something to show Mr Warren," said Miss Rook. "It would take but a moment."

"Show Mr Warren?" scoffed Rook. "Surely he doesn't—"

"I'm equally sure," Aubrey said over him, "I've a moment to spare. What did you wish to show me, Miss Rook?"

Miss Rook cast a terrified glance at her brother, who grinned the toothy grin Aubrey'd seen quite enough of today.

"Yes," said Rook. "What did you wish to show him?"

Miss Rook seemed struck dumb. Then, with a sharp inhale, she gathered her courage and spoke. "A composition! On the piano-forte! I've written it for your birthday, Clarence, as a surprise, so you can't see or hear it until then, or it'll be ruined. But I do need someone to critique it—a gentleman, I've had plenty of ladies' opinions—and I believe Mr Warren has the most discerning ear."

Rook gaped at his sister. Aubrey gaped at his gaping. Miss Rook gave short gasps as if she'd run up a flight of stairs and wished to conceal it from her audience.

"What the deuce," said Rook, "does Mr Warren know about music?"

"More than you might think," said Aubrey. "I'd be delighted to judge your composition, Miss Rook."

"And who shall chaperon this little excursion? I don't intend to impugn Mr Warren's honour," Rook continued in a tone suggesting otherwise, "but I'll not have my sister gallivanting off alone with strange bachelors!"

Miss Rook bowed her head, shoulders hunched.

A sensible man would've stayed out of what was clearly just the latest battle in a lifelong war between siblings. Aubrey supposed he'd lost the right to call himself a sensible man the day he'd accepted Lindsey's overtures. "Forgive me, Miss Rook, but perhaps your maid might suffice?"

Miss Rook's demeanor brightened. She looked to her brother. Through grinding teeth, Rook replied in the affirmative. Without further ado, Miss Rook trotted down the stair. Aubrey followed her to a dim hallway papered in dark green, ending in a south-facing morning room.

The combined effect of the velvet couch, the silk curtains, the Arabesque rug, and the faux-ivy wallpaper, all in the same brilliant, popping shade of chartreuse, temporarily blinded Aubrey. When his vision adjusted, Miss Rook stood before him, beaming as brightly as the decor. Aubrey complimented her on its cheerful atmosphere, and she beamed brighter still.

Aubrey found the piano tucked away in a corner, buried in yards and yards of still more chartreuse. But look as he might, one thing eluded him.

"Should we not ring for the maid?" he asked.

Miss Rook bit her lip and looked at the carpet.

Aubrey took a half-step back towards the door. "If I've done anything to upset you, Miss—"

"It's nothing to do with you, really!" Miss Rook insisted, bringing her head up sharp. "It's just, it's nothing to do with the piano-forte, either."

Before Aubrey could inquire further, she marched to the piano, opened its bench, and pulled out a folio of sheet music.

"You're an engineer," she said, returning to hand him the folio. "An amateur, but an interested one?"

"Yes," he admitted, "but I don't understand..."

The folio fell open in his hands. He fumbled to keep from dropping the lot. As he did so, he spied a mathematical equation. He blinked at it and realised he held not a single note of music, but rows upon rows of sums and figures. Flicking through the pages, he saw others, interspersed with technical drawings—copied from *The Engineer*, yes, but well-copied, some with improvements. He looked up from the unexpected trove to lock eyes with Miss Rook, who was chewing her cuticles.

"Are these...?" he asked.

Miss Rook snatched her fingers from her mouth. "Mine, yes. I've kept real sheet music as well, to disguise it, but no one ever asks me to play except in jest. I'm hopeless at it. Ever since I was a girl."

"So you put the bench to better use," said Aubrey, unable to disguise his wonder. "Have you shown these to anyone else?"

"No, not a soul."

He almost asked why, then recalled how Rook delighted in playing the tyrant over the most trivial matters. If he ever discovered his sister's work...

"I'm indebted to you," Aubrey said instead. "For placing such trust in me. But... why me?"

She blinked. "You're an engineer."

"An amateur. There are other engineers. Better ones."

"None of them have ever attended one of Rowena's parties. If she approves of your association with her brother, surely you can be trusted with the darkest of secrets."

Aubrey dared not ask what she meant by "association". Looking at her puzzled face, he couldn't imagine she knew anything close to the truth. He relaxed with a weak chuckle. "I wouldn't go so far as to say she approves of me."

Miss Rook smiled. "When I first met Rowena, I came away certain she hated me. If you'd heard what she said of my complexion—but no matter. Regardless of any insult, not even a day later she sent me the prettiest little note, begging my presence at her house for tea the next day. And we've been the best of friends ever since. Believe me, Mr Warren, if she's bothered to speak to you at all beyond the minimum demands of propriety, you are in her favour. If she disliked you, you'd know it."

Aubrey absorbed this intelligence with a nod.

Miss Rook indicated the papers still in his hands. "As to the engineering..."

"What of it?" he said. She flinched, and he chastised himself before softening his tone. "What sort of input did you seek?"

"Anything," she begged. "You're the only scientific mind I've ever encountered. Please, don't spare my feelings. If there's any error, egregious or minor, I should like to know it."

A glance at the papers revealed none of the elementary mistakes he'd expect. "I see nothing of the sort. Your safety valve, in particular—"

Aubrey shuffled the papers to bring the illustration to the forefront. She stepped close enough to brush shoulders with him. He glanced at her, tamping down the instinct to spring away. But she, absorbed in the work, seemed totally unaware of their proximity. He couldn't think of a tactful way to bring it to her attention, so he focused on the illustration.

"It's perfect," he said, for it was. "Carbon paper couldn't make a better copy. How did you manage it?"

"Practice. What you hold in your hand isn't my first attempt. Or my second."

"Effort well spent," he assured her.

Miss Rook grinned in a manner far more pleasing than her brother. It vanished as her gaze shot past Aubrey's shoulder. Her expression flickered into fear before growing guarded and dark. She snatched the papers from his hands.

"Bessie," she said.

Aubrey turned in time to see the same maid who'd let him in curtsy on the threshold.

"Mr Rook said you needed me, Miss?"

150

Miss Rook held out the reassembled folio with a stiff arm. "Please return these to the bench, Bessie."

Bessie took the folio with a curious look at Aubrey. He smiled to put her at ease. She flinched as if struck and hurried back to the piano bench. It took her longer than he would've guessed possible to put the folio away, but she seemed determined to neither see nor hear anything else occurring in the room.

Aubrey returned to Miss Rook. "Perhaps I might take the liberty to write."

"To my brother, you mean," Miss Rook amended hastily, her panicked eyes fixed on Bessie. "I'm sure he'd be delighted. Though a note to Miss Althorp might serve you better."

A sideways glance made her meaning clear. If Aubrey wished to contact Miss Rook again, the Althorp household was the safest route. It seemed Miss Rook's intelligence extended beyond the realm of engineering.

Aubrey bowed and showed himself out.

⌒

AUBREY CONSIDERED TUESDAY a miserable loss. But Wednesday dawned with promise.

Ten or twelve hours toiling in silence seemed like paradise compared to his holiday. He went to work with relish, arriving at quarter to seven, and made good progress on all he'd missed the previous day. Nothing interrupted him until half-past nine.

"Morning, Warren!" Smith chirped as he crossed the threshold.

Aubrey lifted wary eyes from his ledger. "Good morning."

Smith hung up his hat and coat and went to his desk. Aubrey went back to ignoring him. Silence reigned for a blissful moment.

"Notice anything different today, Warren?"

Aubrey sighed heavily as he looked up at his coworker. The sight before him stopped his breath entirely.

Smith sat with his feet up on his desk, irreverent as ever—made moreso by the hat perched atop his head at a jaunty angle. Lindsey's hat.

Aubrey could only stare in horror.

Smith grinned and removed the hat, twirling it. "I ran out of ink yesterday, so I raided your desk. Hope you don't mind."

Aubrey forced an airy tone. "Not at all. I see you've found my spare hat."

"Bit nice for a spare, innit?"

Smith rose and made his way towards Aubrey's desk with languid steps, tossing the hat from hand to hand. Aubrey stood as well, holding out his hand for it. Smith glanced at the offered hand, snorted, then popped the hat back onto his head.

"Don't play coy with me, Warren. I know who it belongs to. And how you came by it."

The bottom dropped out of Aubrey's stomach. He let his hand fall with it. "Very well, I confess. I stole it."

Better a thief than a sodomite. His career would end either way, and he'd be imprisoned besides, but his Lindsey would be safe.

Smith clucked his tongue in disapproval. "The hat is Sir Lindsey's. And you fucked him to get it."

"Absurd."

"Logical conclusion," Smith countered. "All those late nights? Everyone knows what you're really up to."

"Repairing your mistakes," Aubrey replied through clenched teeth.

"No, you're a smart chap, you can fix those up like—" Smith snapped his fingers. "Besides, they're hardly as bad as all that."

"The truth would astonish you."

Smith's eyes narrowed. "You're a pansy, Warren. And a mary-ann. Everyone's known it from the moment they laid eyes on you. Workhouse brats can barely read; the idea that you could do sums strains the imagination. No, the only reason you're here is because certain persons—not to name names, but it rhymes with 'pennings'—can't restrain their primitive urges. If anything, it's me who pulls your dead weight. You were on your way out, you know, until Althorp decided he wanted a piece—"

Aubrey's fist connected with Smith's eye.

Smith reeled back with a yelp, one hand over his face. Aubrey stared, wondering for an absurd moment what'd happened, then realised his fist remained extended at arm's length in mid-air. He lowered it, his knuckles pulsing with pain. Smith continued expelling an uninspired stream of oaths. Every instinct in Aubrey's mind screamed for him to apologise and beg forgiveness. He clamped down on them and waited to see how Smith would react.

"Just goes to show you," Smith spat out at last. "You can take the boy out of the street, but you can't take the street out of—"

Aubrey lunged.

CHAPTER SIXTEEN

"WARREN!"

The shout came from the office doorway. Aubrey dropped his double-fisted grip on Smith's collar. Smith coughed violently.

"What the devil is going on?" Mr Jennings demanded, slamming the door behind him. "Explain yourselves!"

Aubrey opened his mouth, realised he had absolutely nothing to say in his defence, and shut it. This was the end. Twenty-four years of scrambling, scrabbling, and scraping for survival, gone up in smoke.

"He attacked me, sir!" Smith gasped. "Like a bloody animal!"

"Warren," said Mr Jennings. "My office. Now."

"Wouldn't do that if I were you, sir," said Smith. "Not safe to be alone with him, he's a mad—"

"Shut it, Smith," Mr Jennings snapped.

Aubrey retreated into Mr Jennings's office. Mr Jennings followed, closing the door after them.

"Sit," said Mr Jennings.

Aubrey obeyed.

Mr Jennings put his elbows up on his desk and folded his hands. "What happened?"

"I attacked Smith."

"For any particular reason?"

Aubrey hesitated. Mr Jennings already knew of Aubrey's proclivities, but it wasn't Aubrey's place to reveal Lindsey shared them.

Mr Jennings raised his brows. "This is most unlike you, Warren."

Aubrey thought perhaps Mr Jennings didn't know him so well as he thought, but said nothing. The silence stretched on until Mr Jennings conceded with a sigh.

"Do you know how Smith arrived at Rook Mill?"

Aubrey blinked, confused by the conversation's sudden turn. Mr Jennings, apparently taking the blink as an expression of interest, spoke on.

"When I was a boy, I had a... friend, named Jonathan. We grew quite close and remained so until his marriage. I myself was never the marrying kind, but there you have it. He moved to London to work as a reporter. He was dashed clever, always had been. I remained in Manchester to tend the mill. So we grew apart. Then—do you recall the epidemic of '66?"

"Before my time, sir," said Aubrey.

"Ah. Then you may count yourself fortunate. Cholera struck the East End. None so badly as previous years, but enough to carry off my Jonathan." Mr Jenning's throat seemed obstructed.

"I'm sorry, sir," said Aubrey, but Mr Jennings's waved him off.

"I might never have known it if it weren't for Jonathan's will. It named me guardian to his infant son. His widow was hardly situated to bring up the boy on her own. So I provided the necessary financial assistance for room and board, and to send the lad to school. The least I could do. I didn't have a hand in raising him personally—his mother wouldn't stand for that. I doubt she'd have accepted my money if she weren't in desperate straits. Regardless, years passed. I climbed the office ranks to become manager. By then the boy had grown enough to seek employment. I offered him a position here. He accepted. Thus, Jonathan Smith, junior, joined our ranks."

Aubrey, already listening closely, jumped to attention.

Mr Jennings nodded. "I hired Smith as a favour to his late father, as I afterwards hired you as a favour to myself."

Aubrey kept his face from falling. "I see."

"No, Warren, you never do. You're imagining favouritism as a result of our prior acquaintance. Were that the case, the entire mill would run on former telegraph boys. No, I hired you because even then you demonstrated a keen mind for maths and a sense of honesty the likes of which I haven't seen before or since. Do you know, you're the only one who never tried to blackmail me?"

Despite his best efforts, Aubrey's eyebrows rose a fraction of an inch.

Mr Jennings heaved another sigh. "I say tried. Most of them succeeded. All of them, in fact. But to the point—the favour to myself wasn't in hiring a boy I was over-fond of, but in hiring a man who would work diligently, efficiently, and without complaint. You've more than made up for Smith's failures. And frankly, you should never have needed to. I ought to have sacked him the first time he arrived at half-past noon and spent the day flicking pencil-shavings at his bin. Nostalgia has blinded me to his faults."

Privately, Aubrey agreed. Many times he'd tempered his self-righteous rage with fantasies of the day Mr Jennings would finally have enough of Smith's antics. But he'd never imagined it like this.

"So," Mr Jennings continued, "I shall remedy the oversight today. Return to your desk. I'll call Smith in, and dismiss him forevermore."

Aubrey nodded, but made no move to leave the office.

Mr Jennings raised an eyebrow. "You disagree, Warren?"

"It's only..." Aubrey swallowed. "He suspects."

"Suspects what, my dear boy?"

Aubrey smiled sadly. "That, for one."

Mr Jennings frowned in confusion, then realised his error. "Good Lord. Have I said that often?"

"Not in front of him, sir. But he suspects all the same." Aubrey cleared his throat. "He also suspects Sir Lindsey is similarly predisposed. And while his suspicions of you and I are baseless—at least, at present—his suspicions of Sir Lindsey and myself..."

"God's sake, Warren, surely you've not encouraged Sir Lindsey's attentions?"

Aubrey couldn't bear to watch Mr Jennings's wide-eyed shock turn to disappointment. He dropped his gaze. Still, he couldn't close his ears against Mr Jennings's long sigh.

"You've been discreet, I hope?" said Mr Jennings.

"I have, yes."

"But Sir Lindsey hasn't."

Aubrey said nothing, which said enough.

"Are you fond of him, Warren?" asked Mr Jennings.

Aubrey's head shot up at the question. He opened his mouth to respond, failed, closed it, swallowed, and tried again.

"I am, sir," he admitted. Then, though his sense of professionalism advised against it, he added, "Very fond indeed."

The corners of Mr Jennings's eyes crinkled. "Then I'm happy for you."

Aubrey blinked. Almost a decade had passed since Mr Jennings had spoken to him so openly. "Thank you, sir."

Mr Jennings smiled outright. "And as Smith hasn't any proof—"

155

"If I may, sir," Aubrey cut in. "I fear sacking him might provide an incentive to seek proof. Or to communicate suspicions to others better able to search it out."

Mr Jennings ruminated before replying, "What do you suggest?"

Aubrey rallied his courage to keep the note of defeat out of his voice. "Retain Smith. Sack me."

Mr Jennings shook his head. "Warren—"

"I attacked him, sir. Clearly I'm in the wrong."

"You were provoked."

"I oughtn't have taken the bait."

Mr Jennings rubbed his forehead, first with the fingertips of one hand, then letting his whole face fall into both palms. A full minute passed before he raised it again. "You're asking me to be rid of the best assistant I've ever had, for the benefit of the worst."

"If it ensures Lindsey and I are safe from Smith," said Aubrey, "then surely it's for our benefit as well."

Mr Jennings gave a half-smile. "Just 'Lindsey,' eh?"

Aubrey's face grew hot. He coughed. It didn't help.

Mr Jennings's smile flashed brighter, then disappeared. A battle waged across his face. Fondness warred with sorrow under a crumbling veneer of stoicism, told through minute contortions and tremors Aubrey found alarming to witness. Yet he drew no attention to it, lest he undermine Mr Jennings's efforts to wrench it all back under control. In the end, sentiment won out.

"I shall miss you, Aubrey."

Aubrey's eyes burned. He dispelled the lump in his throat with a quick swallow.

"And I, you," he replied, withholding the reflexive addition of *sir* to respond with, "Edward."

Mr Jennings coughed, but not before Aubrey caught sight of the tears welling in his eyes.

"Well," said Mr Jennings. "It's settled, then."

He rose and held out his hand. Aubrey shook it. Then, with a stiff nod, he turned his back on his benefactor and walked out.

Smith remained at his desk. Aubrey watched him in his peripheral vision, but didn't dare look at him directly, lest he succumb to the temptation to make Smith's right eyesocket match his swelling left.

To Aubrey's surprise, Smith seemed likewise determined to ignore him. Aubrey took advantage of it to gather his few personal effects from his desk. A shuffling sound interrupted him. He looked up to find Lindsey's hat on his desk, and Smith retreating to his own. Aubrey tucked the hat in with the rest of his belongings, retrieved his own hat from its peg, and left the office.

He strode like a self-regulating automaton down the eerily quiet Manchester streets. At mid-morning, well between factory breaks, most of the population remained hard at work indoors. The population who hadn't just been sacked. Unlike Aubrey.

A factory clock struck ten. Aubrey considered his next move.

Lindsey liked to keep abreast of developments at the mill, so by now Mr Jennings had probably dispatched Smith to telegram Lindsey with news of Aubrey's new employment status. Coming from Smith, the resulting telegram would no doubt vilify Aubrey. Not that Lindsey would ever believe such—at least, Aubrey hoped he would never. Regardless, the truth wasn't quite as Smith would tell it.

If Aubrey wanted to refute Smith's claims, he needed to act with haste. He steered his feet towards Manchester Central. Before he boarded his train, he sent a telegram of his own.

∽

"FOR GOD'S SAKE, what's happened?!"

Lindsey's cry stopped Aubrey dead on the threshold.

"Didn't you get my telegram?" Aubrey asked, one hand on the door jamb.

"I did," Lindsey said, but seemed far from soothed by it. He began pacing the length of the room, Aubrey's telegram clenched in one hand. "'On my way. Will explain everything.' What the devil am I supposed to make of that?"

Aubrey stepped into the room to shut the door behind him. "That I'm on my way, and will explain everything."

Lindsey whirled around to face him. "I dearly wish you would! Mr Jennings certainly didn't."

Aubrey pushed past his fear. "What did he say?"

"That you'd been sacked! Or, not in so many words, but—is it true?"

"Yes."

Lindsey gawked at him for two complete seconds before bursting out with, "Why?!"

"I had a row with Smith."

Lindsey's expression of mingled confusion and wrath smoothed out into confusion alone. "Smith who?"

"My coworker."

"The non-worker?"

Aubrey managed a weak smile. "That's the one. May I sit?"

"Yes. Yes, of course, here—" Lindsey rushed to pull up an armchair, then paused, staring at the object in Aubrey's hands. "Is that my hat?"

"Yes."

Aubrey attempted to hand it over, but Lindsey only looked more confused, so Aubrey motioned for him to sit and gave an abridged account of his morning's adventures. Even with the more offensive lines cut out, Lindsey was outraged out of his chair by the end of it.

"How dare he," Lindsey snarled as he resumed his pacing. "That ungrateful, ignorant—"

"—gentleman I no longer have to share an office with," Aubrey finished for him.

"He's the one who ought to be sacked!"

"And we're the ones who ought to be in prison."

Lindsey's enraged strides slowed to a halt. "Do you really think he would?"

"I'd rather not test him."

Lindsey looked to the floor, then to the chair he'd abandoned, and slunk back to throw himself into it. He put a hand over his eyes. After half a minute's silence, he broke out with a few well-chosen epithets for Smith, making use of a vocabulary Aubrey hadn't realised he possessed. Then he rubbed his hand over his face and let it drop.

"At least you're well rid of him,' he said.

Aubrey nodded along, but remained uneasy. "There's something else."

The words left his lips in a stammer, which caught more of Lindsey's attention than he would've liked, though he supposed it was as much as he needed. Still, he had trouble meeting Lindsey's curious expression.

"I've spoken with your friends," Aubrey began, "and I realise I haven't been as honest with you as I ought."

Lindsey, who'd smiled at the word "friends," cocked his head to one side. A lock of golden hair came loose and curled across his forehead in a most distracting manner.

Aubrey swallowed. "Through omission of detail, I've led you to believe I was born into the class I now occupy. This is a lie. My origins are lower. Much lower."

Lindsey lost his smile. Aubrey almost lost his nerve.

"My first memories are of a workhouse. We manufactured shoes. That's how I learnt sewing. After the workhouse, I found employment as a telegraph boy."

A wrinkle appeared in the space between Lindsey's brows. Aubrey's courage failed. His gaze dropped to the carpet.

"Doubtless you know the reputation that profession has acquired in recent years," he said to the Oriental pattern. "I'm ashamed to say it isn't entirely unearned."

Not a word of acknowledgement from Lindsey. Aubrey withheld a sigh.

"However, that experience provided the... connections which made it possible to find more respectable employment as a clerk in your mill."

Still, Lindsey said nothing. Aubrey lifted his eyes to the hearth, avoiding Lindsey's gaze.

"And now that I've revealed myself as a social climber of basest origins, you're well within your rights to throw me out. No doubt you're embarrassed to have ever associated with me. I assure you, I take no offense."

Aubrey waited for a response of any sort, but the silence stretched on. He dared to look up.

Lindsey appeared confused. "Why the deuce would I throw you out?"

Aubrey stared at him. "I've just confessed to wilful deception. To seducing you under false pretences. And more, besides."

"Yes, I understood as much. And quite frankly I don't see how it matters. Though it does explain a lot." A thoughtful look crossed Lindsey's features. "Is that why you were so uncomfortable at dinner?"

Aubrey felt nearly as uncomfortable now. Apparently some of this discomfort showed in his face, for Lindsey's mirrored it.

"Why didn't you say anything?" asked Lindsey.

"It's nothing," Aubrey replied quickly.

"It's certainly not nothing. It was ill-bred of me, and cruel, and—is there anything I can do to make it up to you?"

"You could do so this instant by dropping the subject."

Aubrey regretted his remark and the bitter tone in which he'd delivered it as soon as he saw Lindsey's shock become a forced, sad smile. Before he could recant, Lindsey spoke.

"If you'd prefer it, then by all means, I shall do so. But perhaps I might apologise in a more tangible fashion?"

"Such as?"

Lindsey leaned in to press his lips against Aubrey's. The kiss would've been chaste had Aubrey's mouth not opened eagerly at Lindsey's touch. Many moments passed before they broke away to breathe.

"I'm sorry for not telling you earlier," said Aubrey. "I fear pride is but one of my many vices."

Lindsey smiled. "Then you'll be happy to hear prejudice isn't one of mine."

Aubrey raised a confused eyebrow. Lindsey only grinned. Aubrey cast the comment aside and set himself to the task of removing Lindsey's cravat.

Some forty minutes later, when Aubrey went to retrieve the cravat from the library table, he found a brown paper package lying beneath it—addressed to *Mr Aubrey Warren*.

"What's that?" he asked.

"Oh," said Lindsey, breathless and distracted. "That. It's a gift. For you. To make up for the dinner."

Aubrey didn't ask why, though the question appeared on his face if not on his lips. "You didn't have to..."

"I know. But I wanted to. Still do, in fact. No sense mailing it now. Go on, open it."

Aubrey cast a wary look back at Lindsey, debauched and collapsed in his chair, his cheeks flushed and his gaze unfocused—enough of a sight to distract Aubrey from the gift until Lindsey waved him towards it.

The package, when lifted, felt heavier than expected. Aubrey untied the string less urgently than he'd untied Lindsey's trousers, and peeled back the brown paper more carefully than he'd peeled Lindsey's shirt from his shoulders. Beneath it all lay a book: *The Lives of the Engineers* by Samuel Smiles.

"The same chap who wrote that *Self-Help* book of yours," said Lindsey, who'd risen to peer over Aubrey's shoulder. "You seemed to like that one, and engineering, so I thought you might like this one, but—"

"I do," said Aubrey. "Like it, I mean. Thank you."

He turned to Lindsey as he spoke, hoping he could hear the sincerity in his tone, could read it in his face. Judging by Lindsey's shy smile, Aubrey thought he might. He pulled him down by the collar and kissed him to make sure of it.

HOURS LATER, ROWENA entered the library, fresh from a drive in the park with Lady Pelham.

"You've just missed Aubrey," said Lindsey.

"Oh?" Rowena flung herself onto the settee. "What a pity. I suppose he had urgent factory business? A bolt of cloth woven backward, or somesuch nonsense?"

She guessed near enough to the mark to give Lindsey pause, but a glance at her indifferent expression showed she was teasing.

"Something like that." Lindsey cleared his throat. "Actually, he's no longer employed at the mill."

"However did that come to pass?" said Rowena, tilting her head back to examine the towering bookshelves.

"Disagreement with a fellow clerk. He thought it best to seek his fortune elsewhere."

"And where else shall he seek it?"

"Who can say?" Lindsey replied, guilt gnawing at him as he realised he hadn't bothered to ask. He covered it with chatter. "It's not his first career change. He was a telegraph boy before he became a clerk, after all."

Rowena's head snapped down from the shelves and turned to face him. "A telegraph boy?"

Lindsey confirmed that was, in fact, precisely what he'd said.

Rowena continued staring at him. "Lindsey, you do know what telegraph boys are infamous for, yes?"

Lindsey shrugged. "Delivering telegrams?"

"Do you not recall the incident in Cleveland Street?"

"Some mix-up between the General Post Office and Prince Albert's men, wasn't it? Didn't seem terribly interesting."

Rowena stared at him harder.

Lindsey coloured under her scrutiny. "It's hardly relevant to me! I've no more connection to the post than any other sender or receiver of mail, and the Royal family are a bunch of bores. If I followed every scandal that cropped up, I wouldn't have time for anything else. It's a wonder you can keep up with it all."

"They're whores, Lindsey."

Lindsey blinked. "What?"

"The telegraph boys. They supplemented their wages with money from notable gentlemen in exchange for indecent acts. *That's* the scandal."

"Oh," said Lindsey. Then, "How do you know?"

"Because every so often I put down a magazine and pick up a newspaper. Something some people in this family could stand to do more often."

"But what do you care what a bunch of boys get up to?"

Rowena gawked at him. "What do I—? Oh, I don't know, Lindsey! It's not as though my own brother is at risk of suffering the same fate!"

Lindsey gaped right back. "You studied this for my sake?"

"Yes, you oaf!"

"Oh," Lindsey said again. He lapsed into thoughtful silence, then asked, "And what fate did they suffer?"

Rowena sighed. "A few of the boys served a short prison sentence. The man who ran the house went to prison as well—he's since fled to America. Lord Arthur Somerset, one of the gentlemen who hired the boys, has a warrant in his name and is tripping a merry path over the Continent to avoid arrest."

Lindsey considered the news. "Doesn't sound so bad."

Rowena kept looking at him as if he were stupid, a look he'd grown used to over the years, but had never liked. "He can never return to England."

"But he's not in prison," said Lindsey. "That's something, isn't it?"

"Hardly! He's been lucky, Lindsey. Extraordinarily lucky. And while you enjoy much the same felicity, there will come a day when it runs out."

"I'm not renting out telegraph boys."

"No, you're just committing indecent acts with a former telegraph boy. For free."

All Lindsey's good humour drained away.

"At least I hope it's free," Rowena added under her breath.

"You don't think Aubrey—" Lindsey began, his face white.

"—is a whore?" Rowena finished for him. "I'm sure I don't know."

"What must he think of me!" Lindsey cried.

Rowena balked. "What *he* must think of *you?*"

"Yes! I own the mill at which he worked! I paid him on some level, didn't I? What if he should think himself obligated to me!?"

"He is obligated to you."

"Not helpful, Rowena!"

"Actually, I believe you'll find I am." She rose from the settee. "And keep your voice down. Discreet and loyal as our staff may be, this is enough to set even the best of tongues wagging."

"Is that all you can think of? Reputation?"

"What else would you have me think of?"

"Aubrey, for one!"

"Mr Warren has proved himself more than capable of taking care of himself," said Rowena. "You, however, continually demonstrate a need for guidance."

"Then by all means," Lindsey snapped. "Guide me."

Rowena raised an eyebrow at his tone. Then her look softened. "Do you remember Uncle Theodore?"

A faint image formed in Lindsey's mind of a portrait in the ancestral hall of the country house. Blond hair, aquiline features, nothing to distinguish him from any other Althorp. "Hardly. He died well before we were born."

"Do you recall how?"

"He was a Navy man, wasn't he? Must've been scurvy or somesuch."

But Rowena shook her head. "Lieutenant Theodore Althorp served eight years in Her Majesty's Navy, until he was charged with sodomy. With witnesses, a guilty sentence was assured. He would hang. But before he could be court-martialed, the ship docked at some anonymous Pacific isle for provisions. He broke out of the brig and swam for shore. The soldiers on guard duty shot him before he reached it."

Lindsey's throat went dry as she recited her tale. "How do you know this?"

"I overheard Father telling Mother to account for his fears that you would suffer a similar demise. You were only five or so, but there was no one who reminded Father more of his dearly departed baby brother. He didn't want to see you come to the same end. And once I heard of it, neither did I. That's why I took interest in the Cleveland Street affair. That's why I hired only servants recommended by your similarly-inclined friends. And that's why I cannot, will not, approve of your friendship with Mr Warren."

"You don't know him!"

Rowena continued unfazed. "Your determination to socialise with him above all others attracts attention. And it takes very little attention to notice the two of you are closer than employee and employer should be. People will talk."

"Let them!"

Rowena snapped. "Why do you refuse to understand the danger you're in?!"

"What danger?" Lindsey demanded. "Who would use this information against me? What enemies do I have?"

"And Mr Warren? How many men has he had?"

"Don't—"

"How many men could he turn over to the police? How many men, encountering him in society, would see him as a snake, coiled, waiting to strike? How many would believe their only salvation is in striking first?"

Lindsey looked away, unable to meet his sister's blazing eyes. He swallowed hard. "I don't know."

❦

PERHAPS IT SEEMED suspicious for Lindsey to invite Aubrey to the Wiltshire house in the middle of the London season. But Lindsey preferred the privacy of the countryside for his intended conversation with Aubrey.

Lindsey spent a day opening the house up, airing out rooms, arranging matters with the staff, and generally stalling. By the end of it, he found himself rearranging the library furniture and, recognising the task brought him no closer to his goal, gave up procrastination.

He sent the letter to Aubrey. It would arrive in Manchester first thing tomorrow morning. Lindsey, not looking forward to a night of apprehension, returned to the library. Charles found him asleep with a book on his chest hours later, roused him, and encouraged him to go to bed. Once in bed, sleep proved beyond him.

Morning brought no relief. He had no appetite for the breakfast Charles served him, no opinion on the clothes Charles laid out for him, and no attention span for the newspaper Charles brought him. To his credit, Charles displayed no outward sign of vexation beyond a raised eyebrow. Lindsey barely registered it, or anything else, until—

"Mr Warren, sir," said Charles.

Lindsey leapt out of his chair, then froze. He'd had hours and hours to prepare for his meeting with Aubrey, yet, now Aubrey had arrived, he hadn't the faintest idea what to say or how to begin it. The silence stretched on, Lindsey all too aware of Aubrey's presence, just out of sight, awaiting his answer.

"Sir?" said Charles.

"Show him in," said Lindsey.

Charles disappeared from the threshold. Aubrey appeared seconds later. He smiled at Lindsey—one of those rare smiles where his effort to maintain a stiff upper lip failed to curtail the slow spread of joy across his face. Lindsey was loathe to dispel it. He tried to smile in return.

"Is everything all right?" Aubrey asked.

Lindsey looked into Aubrey's face, pale and sharp like broken porcelain, and mustered his words. "Since last we spoke, I have learned—I've attained new information regarding—"

Aubrey reached for his shoulder, but Lindsey stepped away. If interrupted, he couldn't guarantee he'd find it within himself to continue. He pulled at his collar and coughed.

"—about—telegraph boys," he forced out at last.

Aubrey's hand fell to his side as if dead. His ivory cheeks turned paler still. "And what have you learned?"

"It can involve a bit more than delivering telegrams," Lindsey admitted.

Aubrey didn't respond. Lindsey wished he'd say something, anything, to alleviate the tension between them, evident in Aubrey's hunched shoulders and Lindsey's hammering heart.

"Have you, then?" Lindsey asked.

"Have I what," said Aubrey, his tone flat. "Fucked other men?"

Lindsey choked. "Good God, Aubrey!"

"You already have your answer," Aubrey continued in the same flat tone. "I'm not diseased, if that's your worry. I was a careful whore."

"I don't give a damn for that!"

"You should. My caution's saved you that embarrassment at least."

"It's not embarrassment I'm concerned with!"

"Shame, then?" Aubrey sneered. "Or jealousy? You're enraged to know you're not the first to ravage me, is that it?"

"No!"

"Then it must be the money." Aubrey's voice grew more heated. "You're afraid I'm too expensive for your tastes."

"No, damn it!"

"Then what?" Aubrey bit off the words. "What've I done to deserve your ire?"

"Nothing!" Lindsey insisted, but Aubrey was past hearing him.

"I fucked men for money! What of it? We can't all be so lucky as you! Some of us are born in the bloody gutter and have to claw our way out! Would you have preferred I starved?"

"No!" Lindsey shouted.

Aubrey flinched. Whether the word itself broke through to him, or the volume, Lindsey couldn't say.

"Whatever you've done," Lindsey said, rushing to take advantage of Aubrey's temporary silence, "it doesn't matter!"

Aubrey watched him with wary eyes. "Then why ask?"

"I merely wish it to be understood that my position as your employer in no way obligates you to accept my advances."

Aubrey's lip curled. "You assumed I didn't understand this?"

"I feared—"

"—that my reciprocation was motivated by mercenary concerns?"

Lindsey paused. Aubrey'd never spoken to him in such a tone—quiet, yet sharp, with a breaking edge. Nor had he ever looked as he did now, lips tight, jaw clenched, his brow contracted to contain his temper.

Aubrey continued. "Did you believe me incapable of affection without money changing hands? I only hope I've exceeded expectations."

"No, never!" cried Lindsey. "That is to say—damn it, will you listen?"

"By all means," Aubrey hissed. "Speak on, *sir.*"

Lindsey closed his eyes and flexed his hands, the situation far too delicate to allow him to lose his temper.

"I've never doubted the sincerity of your affection," he said, each word slowly enunciated. "Not once have I feared you might make a fool of me."

He opened his eyes. Aubrey stood there, glowering, but listening.

Lindsey took a steadying breath. "Those nearest to me have warned me not to let myself be hurt by whatever may come to pass between you and I."

"Of course," Aubrey muttered.

"Please," Lindsey replied, his plaintive tone bordering on desperate. Most unbecoming in a gentleman. He winced.

Aubrey's glare remained, but his shoulders relaxed.

Lindsey continued. "I've never considered those warnings prudent or relevant. However, I've also been warned to take care for your sake. And those warnings, I should have heeded. As your former employer and social superior, any damage you could do to me by design is nothing compared to what I could do to you by pure accident. To what harm I fear I've already done."

"You'll find I appreciate your pity even less than I desire your disdain."

"You have neither! Can't you see that?"

"Apparently not," Aubrey snapped. "Though I'm sure you're eager to enlighten me."

Lindsey hesitated. "Would you prefer my silence?"

Aubrey studied him for a long moment, his expression softening. "No. Though I'd have you choose your words with more care."

A relieved smile twitched across Lindsey's lips before he returned to the grave discussion at hand. "I hope I've made clear to you how I hold you in the highest regard. My new understanding of your past employment hasn't changed this. It's only made me more aware of how my previous efforts to communicate my affection could be misconstrued as... as a payment, of sorts. Not that I doubt your intelligence!" He had to add that quickly; Aubrey's face had darkened again. "Indeed, you possess the most brilliant mind I've ever known. But I realise a man in your position might feel forced, as it were, to comply with my wishes, and I wouldn't force you for all the world."

Aubrey continued frowning, confused rather than enraged, yet he didn't speak.

Lindsey went on. "Perhaps you don't believe yourself worthy of defence, or perhaps you don't think yourself imperilled by me. I will defer to you on the latter point, but I cannot be moved on the former. You are a clever, steadfast, and...and frankly beautiful man, and I—"

It occurred to Lindsey that saying these precise words to this particular person at this exact moment might not be the wisest decision. This thought wasn't enough to stop him.

"—I love you."

CHAPTER SEVENTEEN

IT WASN'T THE first time Aubrey had heard that phrase. Dozens of men had muttered it into his ear as he lay under them, or gasped it into the air above his head as he knelt before them. It'd even tumbled from his own lips once.

Harry, a telegraph boy like Aubrey, had possessed a strong jaw, broad shoulders, and a coy smile. He and Aubrey had been frequent guests at the Catullus Club, brought up the back stair by a Post Office superior. Most nights they had worked the club separately. On occasion, a larger party of gentlemen had required a larger pool of telegraph boys to amuse them, and Harry and Aubrey were brought in together. Those nights, Aubrey had relished. Most of the toffs had thought Aubrey the beauty, but to Aubrey's eyes, Harry had outshone him by far.

It took had taken Aubrey months to gather his courage. Then, one cool September night, as they navigated the winding streets between the club and their own far less fashionable neighbourhoods, Aubrey grabbed Harry's wrist and tugged him into an alley. Even after a long night of paid work, Aubrey had a trembling, feverish kiss to spare for Harry's lips. He drew back fearful of Harry's reaction.

Harry rewarded his bravery with a handsome grin, then turned away. Aubrey watched, dumbfounded, as Harry moved to stride off into the night as if nothing had happened at all.

"I love you," Aubrey blurted out.

Harry spun to face him again.

Aubrey clapped a hand over his mouth. He hadn't meant to confess— had intended only to call Harry back to him and ask what would happen between them now—but there it was, hanging in the cold fog.

Harry laughed.

Aubrey forced a nervous chuckle and waited for Harry to explain the joke.

"You sound just like 'em," Harry said, still laughing.

"Like who?" Aubrey asked.

Harry snorted. "The toffs, who else?"

He cuffed Aubrey on the shoulder and went on his merry way down the alley.

Aubrey couldn't will his legs to follow. If he caught Harry up, he couldn't answer for what he might do. Hit him, perhaps—or worse, kiss him again.

As Harry disappeared into the fog, Aubrey departed in the opposite direction. In Hyde Park, it didn't take long to find another toff willing to give him a bed for a few hours.

Now, years later, in a warm, bright library miles away from the cold, dark alley he'd buried his heart in, Aubrey heard those words again. He knew he ought to respond, but his jaw hung useless, his tongue stilled.

Lindsey, meanwhile, seemed to realise what he'd said. He was moments away from understanding what a terrible mistake he'd made by assigning any non-monetary value to Aubrey's companionship. Every second ticking past brought them closer to the point when Lindsey would wake up from his fantasy and leave.

Stop him, every thought in Aubrey's mind screamed, but all he could do was stare. He watched Lindsey's expression shift from confusion to hurt, and still said nothing.

Lindsey's mouth opened. This was it. He'd ring for Charles to show Aubrey out, and Aubrey would lose him forever.

Aubrey leapt forward, grabbing Lindsey's cravat in one hand and clutching the back in Lindsey's skull in the other. He crushed their lips together in a violent parody of a kiss.

Lindsey didn't respond.

Aubrey let him go.

"What?" Lindsey gasped.

"Bad with words," Aubrey panted. "Can't—I can't say—"

His hands shook. Lindsey caught them and leaned in to press his forehead against Aubrey's.

"Try," he whispered, his smile far too kind. Aubrey wanted to bite it off—kiss it—slap it—he knew not what.

"I can't," he said, his voice breaking. He would've torn out his own throat for its betrayal if he could.

169

Realisation dawned on Lindsey's face. Horror bloomed in Aubrey's chest. Lindsey knew, then, knew he'd fallen in love with a heartless monster and his only recourse was to flee—

"It's all right."

It wasn't all right, it would never be—

"Aubrey."

Lindsey knew him for what he was and he was going to leave him and there was nothing Aubrey could do—

"Aubrey!"

Lindsey took Aubrey by the shoulders, his hold firm yet gentle, just enough to keep Aubrey from trembling. Aubrey couldn't recall when the tremors had spread from his hands to the whole of him.

"What's the matter?" Lindsey asked.

Aubrey couldn't speak. He leaned in to kiss Lindsey again. Lindsey pulled away.

"Please," Aubrey begged. "I can't say it. Just let me show—"

Lindsey gave him the same look one might give a trusted hound who'd begun frothing at the mouth. "You're not well."

Aubrey sagged. He didn't intend for more than his shoulders to slump, but suddenly everything slid sideways and Lindsey's grip became the only thing keeping him from tumbling to the floor.

Next he knew, he was on his back. A silhouetted figure came into view above him, immensely tall, with a golden halo.

"Aubrey?" it said in Lindsey's voice.

Aubrey squinted up at him, saw the ceiling, and realised he was lying on a couch.

Lindsey held out a glass tumbler of amber liquid. "Drink this."

Aubrey struggled to rise. Lindsey slipped an arm under his shoulders to help. Once up, Aubrey reached for the tumbler and noted with relief how his hand no longer trembled. He knocked back the drink in one swallow. It burned his throat, but he didn't cough, though his eyes watered. It did wonders for waking him up. His newfound awareness included an appreciation for Lindsey's handsome face so close to his own, though marred by a wrinkle of concern.

"Better?" Lindsey asked.

In reply, Aubrey lifted his hand to run his thumb over Lindsey's lower lip.

Lindsey frowned. "Perhaps I ought to call a physician."

"No, I'm—"

"You really aren't—"

"I heard you out," Aubrey said more forcefully than he'd intended. "Could you do me the same courtesy?"

Lindsey's jaw shut with a click. Aubrey put aside his guilt and gathered his courage along with his breath.

"I'm sorry," he began. "I cannot tell you what you've told me. Not in so many words. But I'd very much like to express my affection in other ways. With your permission."

Lindsey hesitated. Aubrey brushed his fingers over one sharp cheekbone and pulled Lindsey's face down to meet his.

The kiss started chaste. Then Lindsey's hand came around to comb through Aubrey's hair, and Aubrey's lips parted. All at once, Lindsey's resolve broke. He clambered onto the settee to straddle Aubrey's waist, one hand in Aubrey's locks while the other roamed his chest, endangering buttons. Aubrey heartily encouraged him.

When forced to part for breath, Lindsey sat back on his haunches, staring down at Aubrey with a mix of desire and concern. Aubrey panted beneath him, all too aware of the tightness in his trousers and the corresponding hardness trapped against Lindsey's thigh. Yet Lindsey made no move to resume their embrace.

"You understand?" Aubrey asked when the uncertainty grew too much to bear.

"Yes," Lindsey replied after another moment. "I believe I do."

Aubrey sighed in relief. Yet his anxieties remained. "If you don't want to—"

Lindsey quirked an eyebrow. "Do you?"

It took all of Aubrey's restraint to not roll his hips as he replied, "Desperately."

Lindsey grinned and leaned in to kiss him again.

⤚

So THAT WAS it. Lindsey knew Aubrey's wretched origins and loved him nonetheless. The legions of men who'd come before didn't matter. Nothing mattered, save Aubrey. Aubrey couldn't help admiring the notion.

He also couldn't help admiring the strength of Lindsey's arms as Lindsey pulled him upright and led him, laughing, to his bedroom. They fell onto the mattress in a heap, wrestling each other's clothes off until they were a pair of entangled nudes worthy of Halloway's art.

Aubrey pressed his lips to Lindsey's collarbone, tracing its curve to his shoulder and on down his arm. He reached those long, graceful fingers, took two in his mouth, and paid them such tribute with his tongue as to force Lindsey to muffle his moans in his pillow. But when Aubrey moved to straddle Lindsey's hips, Lindsey stopped him with a hand on his thigh.

"Would it be possible," Lindsey began, his words coming in a halting fashion. "That is to say, if you wouldn't mind..."

Aubrey raised an eyebrow as he waited for Lindsey to arrange his thoughts into complete sentences.

"Do you think," Lindsey managed at last, "perhaps we might try it the other way around?"

Aubrey frowned. "Pardon?"

Lindsey cleared his throat. "I mean, rather than myself into yourself, it might be yourself into myself?"

It took Aubrey a moment to untangle the logic. When he realised Lindsey's intent, he flinched. "You don't want that."

"Why not?"

"If this is your idea of—some effort at egalitarianism—of balancing the scales—"

"What?" said Lindsey. "No, of course not."

"Then why?"

Lindsey smiled coyly. "You seem to enjoy it well enough. Why shouldn't I?"

"I've had plenty of practice."

Aubrey intended to make his retort light-hearted, but the words carried a defensive edge. Lindsey seemed abashed. Aubrey swallowed his guilt and pressed his advantage.

"It's not terribly comfortable, the first time." Or the second or third, as far as Aubrey could recall.

"You doubt my courage?" said Lindsey.

"I doubt your understanding," said Aubrey, exasperated.

Lindsey gave him a considering look. "If the idea's truly distasteful to you, I'll not press the issue. But I wish you'd believe me when I say I'm in earnest to try. My faculties aren't so diminished that I cannot imagine the risk."

Aubrey hadn't meant to imply anything regarding Lindsey's intelligence. The idea of taking Lindsey as others had taken Aubrey in the past—that was distasteful, yes. But if the thing were done properly... Aubrey's pulse quickened, throbbing low in his groin. No, that notion wasn't distasteful at all. Quite the opposite.

Somewhat humbled, Aubrey replied, "If you're certain…"

"I am," said Lindsey.

Aubrey kissed him and left the bed to fetch the pomade.

As he returned, he instructed Lindsey to lie on his belly. Lindsey obeyed so willingly, Aubrey felt tempted to tell him to sit up and roll over. Instead, he positioned himself behind Lindsey, slathered his hand in ample lubrication, and pressed a finger in up to the first knuckle.

"Oh!" said Lindsey. "That's—"

"Too much?" said Aubrey. He'd halted at the very instant Lindsey exclaimed.

"No, no," Lindsey replied. "Not at all, it's… interesting."

"Shall I stop?"

"What? No, keep at it, I think I…"

Whatever Lindsey thought trailed off, lost forever as Aubrey resumed. His fingers delved deeper to graze a certain gland. Lindsey gasped. Aubrey couldn't help grinning.

"Good?" he asked.

"Yes, rather," Lindsey panted. "Is—ah—is this why you're so fond of—?"

"It's certainly a contributing factor," Aubrey admitted.

Slowly and surely, he worked Lindsey open, massaging that sensitive point until Lindsey rutted against the sheets and rocked back onto his fingers. Aubrey himself had a devil of a time resisting the urge to relieve his own tension by frotting against Lindsey's bare thigh.

"May I?" Aubrey asked, his voice hoarse.

"Yes," Lindsey hissed, following it up with a string of, "Please, please, *please*—" for good measure, cutting off with a groan as Aubrey's fingers withdrew.

Aubrey smeared a handful of pomade on his cock. It had stood at the ready for the past ten minutes, his instincts demanding he bury it in hot, quivering flesh. But his rational mind overruled his primitive urges. He braced one hand on Lindsey's shoulder and slowly guided himself inside. He had almost the whole head through the tight clench of Lindsey's hole before he felt Lindsey wince around him.

"Sorry!" Aubrey started to retreat, but Lindsey reached back to stop him.

"Go on," Lindsey gasped over his shoulder.

"I don't want to hurt you."

"You did warn me," Lindsey reminded him.

Still, Aubrey hesitated. Lindsey pushed back onto his cock.

Aubrey quickly pulled away, pinning Lindsey down with his free hand. "Don't do that!"

"Sorry," said Lindsey. "I just—give it another go, won't you?"

Aubrey sighed, massaging Lindsey's shoulder absent-mindedly as he thought the matter over. "You'll tell me if it pains you?"

"I believe I've already promised as much, yes."

Aubrey pressed into him once more. The head slipped entirely in. The ring of muscle clenched around his ridge, drawing an involuntary gasp from his throat. He jerked back just enough to feel it tug against his most sensitive nerves. The shock nearly cost him his balance.

Lindsey stiffened under him. Aubrey forgot his own pleasure and rubbed Lindsey's shoulder, leaning forward to press a kiss to the straining muscles of his back.

"Breathe," Aubrey said. "You're all right."

He could've used the reminder himself—the stimulation of such a tight sheath stole his breath away—but he waited until Lindsey's sharp inhale became a sigh before he dared move again. He sank halfway into Lindsey on the second push.

"How is it?" he asked, pausing as Lindsey shuddered beneath him.

"It's—" Lindsey gasped for air. Aubrey's heart leapt into his throat—if he'd hurt him, he'd never forgive himself—but Lindsey added, "Good, it's... very good. And yourself?"

Aubrey could only describe the feeling with an extended groan. Lindsey laughed.

Aubrey resumed the exercise, but Lindsey twitched beneath him so violently that Aubrey was almost unseated.

"Oh, God!" Lindsey cried. "There, that—could you do that again, please, it—"

Aubrey gave a gentle thrust. Lindsey clenched the sheets in white-knuckled fists, his ecstatic exclamations muffled in his mattress. Aubrey bit his lip to keep from laughing and sheathed himself to the hilt.

Lindsey squirmed under him with a wondrous gasp. Aubrey's arms, braced on either side of Lindsey's prone from, trembled with exertion. He relaxed them, bringing his chest flush with Lindsey's spine. He could feel Lindsey's breath reverberate in his own ribcage, could feel Lindsey's pulse pound through the flesh wrapped snug around his cock. He could've lain in such union for centuries, utterly at peace. Even so, it took conscious effort to keep the rutting instinct at bay.

"Are you...?" he whispered into Lindsey's ear.

"Fine," Lindsey replied hazily. "Better than fine."

Aubrey rolled his hips. Lindsey moaned into the pillow and pushed back against him. Yet still Aubrey gritted his teeth and held back. He knew all too well the damage an errant thrust could do.

But Lindsey pushed back again, more insistently, and Aubrey couldn't help snapping his hips forward to meet him. An exclamation in the affirmative from Lindsey, and Aubrey was off, his fingertips digging possessive marks into Lindsey's hipbones. He kept his movements shallow, though he couldn't check his speed. Lindsey responded with enthusiasm. They fell into a back-and-forth rhythm, a push and pull that wrung pleasure from every one of Aubrey's taut muscles. Lindsey lifted his hips from the mattress. Aubrey slipped a hand beneath him to tug his cock.

"More," Lindsey begged. "Please, I'm nearly—"

Aubrey dragged himself out until only the tip remained inside, then re-sheathed his cock in one quick shove. Lindsey gave an ecstatic cry. Repeating the motion caused Lindsey's command of language to devolve into murmured repetitions of Aubrey's name, his chant interrupted by arrhythmic gasps and half-stifled groans. It was all Aubrey could do to keep from spending at the sound.

Then, like the spring of an over-wound watch, Lindsey broke. His entire frame stiffened, clenching around Aubrey. His cock jerked in Aubrey's fist as he spent, calling Aubrey's name into his sheets until he collapsed, boneless, underneath him.

Aubrey kept up his pace throughout Lindsey's orgasm, slowing only when it ended. He couldn't keep his hips from rolling, his cock still raging hard, but he redirected his energies towards kissing Lindsey's shoulders and neck until Lindsey recovered enough to turn his head and attempt to meet his caresses.

"Have you...?" Lindsey asked.

Aubrey shook his head. "I can finish myself off."

"That's hardly fair." Lindsey wriggled his hips experimentally. A mischievous smile tugged at his lips when Aubrey bit off a moan in reply. Then he pulled himself up, Aubrey slipping out of him, and turned over to lie on his back, drawing his knees up.

Aubrey reached down between them to re-align his prick with Lindsey's hole, then pushed into Lindsey once more.

Now that they faced each other, Aubrey could watch the way Lindsey's lip caught between his teeth as he entered him and feel the warm rush of Lindsey's near-silent sigh. Lindsey encouraged him with hungry kisses and murmured reassurances, telling him he felt wonderfully, the fit just right, how Lindsey wanted him, wanted this. Aubrey pulled him down onto his cock, again and again, driving like a piston until Lindsey's voice in his ear, Lindsey's lips on his throat, Lindsey's hot flesh enveloping him, brought him to the brink. A whispered, "Yes," pushed him over the edge. He spent inside Lindsey in frantic thrusts, shuddering with a violence that would've broken him had Lindsey not wrapped his arms around him, holding him tight both outside and in.

Aubrey crumpled atop Lindsey, who caught him with a breathless laugh. Aubrey knew little else for many moments. When he regained focus, it was to Lindsey's lips on his cheek, and Lindsey's soft hands stroking his ribs.

Aubrey had done it. He'd taken his Lindsey, and neither of them were any worse for it. He felt worthy of a knighthood. Lindsey seemed to feel similarly, nuzzling at Aubrey's jaw.

"That wasn't so bad, was it?" Lindsey asked. His tone might've passed for irreverent, but Aubrey detected an undercurrent of concern.

Aubrey smiled and turned his head to catch Lindsey's lips in his own.

"No," he said when the kiss ended. "Not so bad at all."

⁓

THEY REMAINED IN bed for some time after, Lindsey reclining, Aubrey sitting up to look at him. One of Lindsey's arms lay behind his head. The other reached out to trail his fingers lazily over Aubrey's bare thigh.

"There's still the matter of your employment," Lindsey said, apropos of absolutely nothing.

Aubrey, lured into a sense of security by the gentle touches and murmured endearments immediately preceding the statement, balked.

"It's not right," Lindsey continued, frowning at the ceiling.

"Right or not," said Aubrey, "it's how things are."

"Then things are terrible." Lindsey rolled over to face him. "What will you do?"

"Clerk somewhere else. Mr Jennings will give me a good recommendation wherever I go. And an excuse for my dismissal that doesn't involve me punching a co-worker."

"But I thought you wanted to be an engineer?"

Aubrey swallowed hard, then forced a laugh. "Well, we can't all get what we want, can we?"

"Why not?"

Aubrey stared at him. "I should've thought it obvious."

"If it's a question of money—"

"Don't." Aubrey looked away.

"Don't what?" said Lindsey. "Help you? What would you have me do instead? Watch you suffer and do nothing to alleviate it?"

Aubrey didn't see why that would be so difficult. It came easily enough to everyone else. But such complaints were too petty to voice. "You might trust, having come this far on my own, I'm capable of continuing on in much the same fashion."

"Your capability has never been in question."

Aubrey, his gaze focused on his lap, couldn't see what expression accompanied Lindsey's proclamation, but its tone rang sincere. In the silence after it, Aubrey caught Lindsey's hand and brought it to his lips. Such a distraction had worked for him in the past. Not this time.

"If there's anything you need," Lindsey went on. "Anything I can do—"

"—I'll ask." Aubrey smiled through the lie. "All right?"

Lindsey's mouth twisted to one side, uncertain. "All right."

Aubrey attempted to kiss a smile back onto his face. It nearly worked.

CHAPTER EIGHTEEN

IN MANCHESTER THE next morning, Aubrey shaved, dressed, and opened the door to go out before he remembered he'd been sacked. He stared into the empty hallway with unseeing eyes. Then he shut the door and put his head in his hands to think the problem over.

He had the whole day to himself. No responsibilities, no appointments, no schedule of any kind.

And he hadn't the first idea what to do with it.

The day yawned before him, empty hour upon empty hour gaping into infinity. The thought of it made his stomach knot. His savings wouldn't last forever.

One short trip out to buy a newspaper later, he pored over the help-wanted advertisements. There weren't as many as he'd hoped. Still, he circled in pencil every business seeking a clerk. Tucking the paper under his arm, he ventured out into the city.

The first mill seemed promising. Its manager, Mr Dobson, listened attentively as Aubrey recounted his relevant work experience.

"What did you say your name was?" Mr Dobson asked when he'd finished. "Warren?"

"Yes, sir."

Mr Dobson frowned thoughtfully. "One moment."

Aubrey waited as Mr Dobson flipped through the documents on his desk. At length he produced a telegram and brought it close to his nose. His eyes flicked over the words. His frown deepened. He glanced back and forth between the telegram and Aubrey's face. Then he put the telegram down on his desk, his hand over the text.

"I'm sorry," he said. "I'm afraid the position's been filled."

Aubrey mirrored his frown, confused, but thanked him for his time all the same.

Similar scenes played out in every subsequent office Aubrey visited. One manager shut the door in his face the moment he said his name. Another was less careful than Mr Dobson in keeping his telegram's contents secret. The body of the message remained hidden, but Aubrey caught the sender's name. Block capitals spelt out SMITH.

Aubrey's eyes widened. He corrected his expression and returned his gaze to the manager's face in time to see a responsive flicker of fear in the man's eyes.

The contents of the telegram were easy enough for Aubrey to guess. He forced a smile and cut the interview short. No sense in wasting the manager's time, much less his own.

As he walked down the road away from the office, it took considerable effort to keep his chin up. Internally, his emotions volleyed between despair and rage. And yet, for all his anger, he knew he had no one to blame for his predicament but himself. Smith didn't need to stretch the truth to give any prospective employer more than enough reason not to want Aubrey in their office.

When Aubrey reached the next business on his list, he stared up at the door and found he couldn't muster the will to knock. He turned and started back for home. A hot packet of chips from a stall along the way improved his mood somewhat, but his mind remained overset by hopeless dread. Soon he wouldn't be able to afford food at all.

Aubrey trudged up the stairs to his garret well after seven. He made a game attempt at reading *The Engineer* as he finished off his chips, but couldn't focus. With a frustrated huff, he crumpled up the empty, greasy newsprint wrapper and chucked it into his wastepaper bin. Then he went to bed and lay staring up into the darkness.

Smith had destroyed all Aubrey's hopes of future employment in Manchester. Aubrey didn't want to leave the centre of the industrial revolution, the home of Mechanics' Institutes and engineering schools, and the rush and roar of iron and steam. But Manchester was hardly the only city in England.

London, for example. London had hundreds of offices and counting-houses and businesses who'd never heard of Smith, much less received his telegram.

It also had Lindsey.

❧

THE NEXT DAY, Aubrey boarded the train to London. The ride took up most of the morning. Aubrey spent it combing *The London Star* for potential leads. By the time he arrived at his destination, he had a list of offices to visit, sorted by neighbourhood and arranged in a loop through the city which would bring him back to the station by seven and home to Manchester by midnight. Before he visited any of them, he stopped at the Post Office to post a letter.

As he'd supposed, no one in London had heard of Smith. They'd also never heard of Mr Jennings or Rook Mill. Despite this handicap, Aubrey made some favourable impressions. He felt much better about his prospects than he had the previous evening, and relaxed enough to nap on the train back to Manchester.

When he returned to his garret, he found a letter shoved under the considerable crack between the bottom of the door and the threshold. He picked it up with a smile, which widened as he opened the envelope and saw it was exactly what he'd hoped—a reply to the letter he'd sent Lindsey that morning.

The day after, he made another trip to London, reading the same paper and making a similar list. But the labyrinthine route he planned didn't return him to the train station. Instead, after walking the city from noon to dusk, he turned towards Belgrave Square and landed on Lindsey's doorstep.

Mr Hudson raised an eyebrow at his appearance—the mud, soot, and smog hadn't been kind to his only suit—but led him into the library, regardless. There, Lindsey sat reading a fat leather-bound volume. When he saw who stood in the doorway, he broke into a grin and leapt out of his chair.

"Aubrey!"

Relief washed over Aubrey as he returned Lindsey's grin. He'd felt conflicted about inviting himself over Lindsey's house. He hated to be presumptuous. Yet it gnawed at him to spend so much time in London and none of it seeing Lindsey. The letter he'd received in reply, while affirmative, retained the perfunctory tone required to give the impression that their relationship remained businesslike. As such, Aubrey couldn't quite convince himself his presence was truly welcome.

Now, however, with Lindsey pulling him into a strong embrace, Aubrey had to admit he might be wanted.

Aubrey leaned into Lindsey's shoulder, enjoying the warmth of his body, the secure hold of his arms across his back, and the gentle nudge of his chin against the top of Aubrey's head. Lindsey loosened his grip to brush his fingers through Aubrey's hair. Aubrey tilted his face up for a kiss, which Lindsey provided with enthusiasm.

"Did you have any luck?" Lindsey asked when he broke it off. "Are you hungry at all? Thirsty?"

"Tired," said Aubrey, but he did so with a smile. "You?"

"Oh, fine as ever," said Lindsey. "Please, sit—"

Aubrey found himself ushered into a plush armchair with a glass of brandy by his elbow.

"Really," Aubrey began, "you don't have to—"

"Nonsense," said Lindsey, dragging his own chair close to Aubrey's. "Now, tell me everything."

He put a hand over Aubrey's, thumb rubbing across his knuckles. Aubrey turned his palm up to squeeze Lindsey's in return, and told all. Lindsey's hand clenched his as he described what Smith had done to his reputation in Manchester, but relaxed as he moved on to his greater success in London. Just as he finished, Charles arrived and announced dinner was ready.

"Dinner?" said Aubrey, after Lindsey sent Charles on his way.

"Dinner," Lindsey confirmed with a smile. It waned when Aubrey didn't return it. "Is that not amenable to you?"

Aubrey, recalling his last dinner at Lindsey's house, hesitated. "Won't your sister mind?"

"She's visiting Lady Pelham in Yorkshire. There's no one here tonight but us."

And the servants, Aubrey didn't say.

But when he followed Lindsey to the dining room, the only servant there was Charles. The table was set far more simply than at the dinner party, with fewer courses and more familiar fare. Lindsey watched Aubrey carefully as the latter took his first spoonful of soup.

"Is it...?" Lindsey began after Aubrey swallowed.

Aubrey smiled. "It's delicious. Thank you."

Lindsey relaxed and dug into his own bowl with a fascinating combination of relish and decorum.

"What were you reading when I came in?" asked Aubrey.

Lindsey swallowed. "Poe. *Tales of the Grotesque and Arabesque*. Are you familiar with him?"

Aubrey hated to disappoint Lindsey with his ignorance, but he couldn't pretend to know what he didn't. "What sort of stories does he write?"

Far from looking disappointed, Lindsey perked up. "Promise you'll stop me if I bore you."

Aubrey nodded, and Lindsey launched into a passionate explanation lasting through dessert. He had his dessert spoon in hand, and had used it to poke at his sorbet no fewer than three times, but hadn't brought any of it to his mouth—he kept pulling it away to throw his arms out wide in broad, emphatic gestures. Aubrey held back a fond smile at the sight.

"Doyle owes Poe a greater debt than he realises," Lindsey concluded. "No matter what Holmes would say on the matter."

Aubrey supposed he ought to read it for himself, and said as much. Lindsey, who'd finally managed to sneak in a mouthful of sorbet, gulped it down to grin at him.

"What have you been reading?" Lindsey asked.

"Nothing so fantastical as Poe," said Aubrey. "Just *The Engineer*."

Lindsey shrugged. "I'm interested." When Aubrey continued to hesitate, he added, "You've listened to me prattle on about Poe for the better part of two hours."

But Aubrey, glimpsing the clock on the wall behind Lindsey, shook his head. "I ought to return to Manchester."

Lindsey's face fell. "What? Why?"

"Because that's where I live."

"Well, yes, but—it seems dashed inconvenient for you to travel all the way back there, just to return to London in the morning."

Privately, Aubrey agreed. Aloud, he said, "What else can I do?"

Lindsey stared at him. "Stay here, of course."

The offer lifted Aubrey's heart to new heights. He swallowed hard to put it back in its place. "I don't want to impose."

"It's hardly an imposition if I invite you."

"After I've already invited myself over for dinner."

Lindsey scoffed. "That's not—dash it, surely you know you're welcome here at any hour?"

Aubrey didn't, actually. Such a notion hadn't entered into his wildest fantasies. He knew he ought to respond with gratitude, but shock trapped the words in his throat.

When Aubrey failed to reply, Lindsey added, "I'm happy to host you for as long as you remain in London. Perpetually, if need be. It'd be my pleasure."

Aubrey coughed. "Not perpetually. Just until I find employment. And a place of my own. Shouldn't take more than a week."

"It could take a decade for all I care," Lindsey said with a laugh. It died when he saw Aubrey's face at the thought of remaining unemployed for so long.

"A week," Aubrey insisted.

Lindsey's smile returned, weaker than before. "As you wish."

Aubrey mirrored it more sincerely. "Thank you."

They retired to the library after dinner. Lindsey happily handed his book over to Aubrey and selected another from the well-stocked shelves. Aubrey settled on one end of a long sofa. Lindsey stretched out on the remainder of it, the back of his head coming to rest on Aubrey's thigh. Aubrey cast a bemused look down at him. It took Lindsey a moment to catch it.

"This all right?" he asked, peering up from his book with wide eyes, all the more ridiculous for being upside-down.

Aubrey bit back a laugh and nodded. Lindsey gave him a concerned frown in return.

"Are you sure?" he said, starting to sit up. "Do you need more room?"

But Aubrey put a hand on his forehead and gently pushed him back down. Lindsey acquiesced, his head rubbing against Aubrey's thigh as he resettled. Aubrey kept his hand on Lindsey's curls and trailed his fingers through them as he read.

Aubrey hadn't read fiction since he'd been a boy in the workhouse, piecing together scraps of improving penny literature donated to the Sunday schoolhouse years before. Poe proved leagues above anything churned out by the authors of *Jessica's First Prayer* and *Froggy's Little Brother*. Yet even the tension of *The Fall of the House of Usher* couldn't keep Aubrey awake after the day—the week—he'd had. His eyes burned with exhaustion. He'd just made up his mind to soldier on without complaint when his half-stifled yawn caught Lindsey's attention.

"Sorry," Aubrey said in response to Lindsey's quirked eyebrow. "It's not the book, it's—"

"—staying up past eleven after rising at five to tramp all over London on foot?" Lindsey ventured a self-deprecating smile.

Aubrey blinked at him, chuckled, then bowed his head in defeat.

Lindsey shut his own book, plucked Poe from Aubrey's hands, and marked the page with a red ribbon from the library table drawer. Then he tugged the weary Aubrey up from the sofa, put an arm around his waist, and led him down the hall to bed.

The soft, warm bed began lulling Aubrey to sleep as soon as he crawled between its sheets. He stayed awake just long enough to feel Lindsey's lean limbs curl around him. Then he was out.

He awoke the next morning with his cheek on Lindsey's breastbone. He lifted his head from the steady rise and fall of Lindsey's chest to gaze upon his sleeping face. The temptation of his parted lips proved too much for Aubrey. He crawled up to kiss them. Lindsey, half-waking, gave a hum of pleasure. Aubrey pulled away to watch his blue eyes flutter open.

"Good morning," said Aubrey, unable to suppress a self-satisfied grin.

Lindsey echoed the sentiment and leaned in for another kiss. Aubrey happily complied, rearranging his hips to line up with Lindsey's. As he'd suspected, Lindsey's prick stood as ready as his own. They'd both gone to bed naked, which made it easy for Aubrey to frot their cocks together between their bellies. He grinned wickedly down at Lindsey as the latter's throat bobbed in a swallow of eager anticipation. Then Aubrey rolled his hips. Lindsey arched his back and spent in short order. Aubrey's crisis followed close behind.

An hour or so after a more drawn-out encore, Aubrey rose, washed, and dressed to hunt for work again. Lindsey, still abed and watching throughout, persuaded him to stay just long enough to gulp down a hot cup of tea and a biscuit. He couldn't, however, persuade him to come back to bed, or to take a holiday from his quest.

Even after rising late and leaving Lindsey's house later still, waking up in London rather than Manchester gave Aubrey an early start on his search for employment. He covered more ground than the two preceding days, following up on the more promising offices he'd visited on his first trip into the city.

When he returned to Belgrave Square that evening, Lindsey awaited him with a ready smile, a hot meal, and hours of fascinating conversation interspersed with quiet leisure. That night, Aubrey slept better than ever before, no doubt aided by the sweet release that came with clenching Lindsey's cock between his own slick thighs.

The rest of the week fell into the same routine; Aubrey woke in Lindsey's bed, marched all over London, and returned to Lindsey in the evening. Throughout the day, the thought of Lindsey kept his chin up and a smile on his lips. He could happily spend forever like this—provided he found employment soon.

Saturday arrived. Aubrey rose at half-past six and began to dress. A low grumble from Lindsey stopped him.

"Where're you going?" Lindsey mumbled, rubbing a hand over his eyes.

Aubrey, who'd bent to put on stockings, abandoned the effort with one off and one on. "To look for work."

"On a Saturday?" Lindsey sat up and blinked at him. "Who'll be hiring on a Saturday?"

"Plenty of people, or so I'm hoping. Most offices should be open for half the day."

"Good God," Lindsey groaned.

Aubrey bristled. "We can't all afford to live on five days' pay."

"No, I know, it's just—it doesn't seem fair."

"It isn't. And yet, here we are."

Lindsey sighed. "You'll be back in the afternoon, then? We could attend the theatre tonight. Or the opera."

Aubrey preferred the theatre, but a more pressing concern pushed itself to the forefront of his mind. "I haven't anything to wear."

"Borrow something of mine. Or if you return early enough, have a tailor come 'round and take your measurements. It wouldn't be ready for another few days, but you'd have it by next Saturday, and then we could..." He trailed off at the look on Aubrey's face.

"I should probably find work before I buy a new suit," said Aubrey.

Lindsey frowned in confusion. "I meant I would buy it for you."

Aubrey had suspected as much. His eyes flicked over to his only jacket, hanging off the back of one of Lindsey's chairs. Its battered, dusty elbows and frayed cuffs looked even more worn in the midst of all Lindsey's luxuries. Aubrey couldn't deny it needed replacing. A new suit might even better his employment prospects. Yet the thought of Lindsey spending so much tied Aubrey's guts into knots. Knowing Lindsey was rich as any Rothschild did nothing to ease Aubrey's conscience. The money might be meaningless to Lindsey, but it meant everything to Aubrey.

Rather than voicing any of his actual concerns, Aubrey replied, "I had a notion we might visit the Crystal Palace. They've got an electrical exhibition on."

Lindsey would likely be terribly bored, but Aubrey wouldn't need a new suit to attend.

To Aubrey's surprise, Lindsey didn't seem at all bored by the prospect. On the contrary, his face lit up as if it, too, were powered by electricity. He announced his delight at Aubrey's suggestion and shrugged on a dressing gown to cross the room and give Aubrey a celebratory kiss. Aubrey found himself smiling in return as Lindsey ran a hand through his hair and on down his cheek.

～

THE OFFICES OPEN on Saturday weren't as promising as Aubrey hoped, but the prospect of an electric afternoon with Lindsey did much to soothe the pangs of chronic unemployment. He returned to the Althorp residence at quarter to three. The moment he stepped into the library, Lindsey tossed aside *Varney the Vampire* and took up Aubrey's arm in its place, pulling him out of the house to a waiting hansom.

Travelling from Belgrave Square to Sydenham by hansom cab couldn't be called a fiscally responsible decision by any stretch of the imagination, but the sight at the journey's end drove all question of cost from Aubrey's mind. The Crystal Palace's magnificent glass walls glowed from within, banishing the fog with clean electric light. He approached its entrance, Lindsey beside him, stepped over the threshold, and stumbled to a halt, struck dumb by the overwhelming display of scientific progress.

Every engineering firm in England, and several foreign, was exhibiting their newest, most advanced electric innovations. Aubrey's eyes skipped from the passenger lift to the travelling crane to the wall of incandescent lamps. The glow intensified as the whirring hum of electric power surged through the air around him. He stood gawking for far longer than a reasonable man ought.

"Are you all right?" said Lindsey, a note of amusement in his voice.

"Fine," Aubrey replied, a half-second too late. Then he remembered to blink, and to turn and look at the person he'd spoken to.

Lindsey gazed down at him with a dimpled half-smile. The soft crinkling around his eyes suggested far more warmth than the electric lights had to offer. Aubrey felt his cheeks heat up with it. He stuttered a little as he began his explanation of the exhibition. No matter how many half-formed words tumbled from Aubrey's lips, Lindsey's affectionate look never wavered. Aubrey hoped the affection he felt in return showed in his own expression.

"If we could only see the motor transformers!" Aubrey said some hours later, having just finished his short lecture on the electric tramway for Lindsey's benefit. They'd meandered through most of the exhibition by this point. The sunlight filtering down through the Palace's glass walls had developed an orange glow.

"Motor transformers?" Lindsey echoed. He walked beside Aubrey with his hands clasped behind his back. Aubrey imitated his pose, lest the urge to take Lindsey's arm overwhelm his better judgement. Not that the crowd swarming around them seemed to pay them any particular mind, but still.

"They power the whole exhibition," Aubrey replied, daring to bring an arm up to gesture broadly at their surroundings, then quickly replacing it behind his back, safe from temptation. "Ten of them, forty kilowatts output apiece, hidden away underneath the Palace. I only know of it from *The Engineer.*"

"And the public is prohibited from gazing upon this marvel of engineering?"

"Not prohibited, precisely, but I don't believe permission is easy to come by."

Lindsey nodded thoughtfully and looked off into the distance. Aubrey's attention returned to the tram. Thoughts of fantastical future transportation distracted him for many minutes. When he came back to himself, Lindsey had disappeared.

Lindsey's name sprang to his lips. He only just managed to prevent himself from calling out. Panic proved harder to suppress. Nevermind that Lindsey was a grown man, permitted to leave if he wished, and more than capable of looking after himself.

Aubrey swallowed his fears and cast his eyes over the crowd in a slow, methodical search. Lindsey stood head and shoulders above most men. He couldn't stay hidden for long. Most likely he'd wandered off out of boredom. Aubrey couldn't blame him. No one could be expected to listen to his engineering chatter indefinitely. The real surprise lay in how Lindsey had tolerated it up 'til now.

"There you are!"

Aubrey whirled around to see Lindsey approaching him with a surly engineer in tow. Lindsey waved merrily at Aubrey, who found himself grinning in reply.

"Right where I left you!" said Lindsey as he drew up beside Aubrey. "Mr Warren, this is Mr Gowrie. Mr Gowrie, Mr Warren."

"How do you do," said Mr Gowrie tonelessly.

"Mr Gowrie has agreed to show us the motor transformers," said Lindsey.

Aubrey, preoccupied with shaking Mr Gowrie's hand, jerked his head up to regard Lindsey, who looked very pleased with himself.

"That's—!" Aubrey choked down his instinctive oath of surprise—and his desire to embrace Lindsey along with it—and looked back to Mr Gowrie. "Dashed good of you, sir!"

Mr Gowrie's mustache didn't so much as twitch. "If you'll follow me, gentlemen."

As Mr Gowrie turned away, Lindsey bent his head towards Aubrey's and spoke in a low tone.

"Do let me apologise for running off without explanation. I wanted it to be a surprise."

Aubrey squeezed his arm in gratitude. He didn't dare open his mouth, lest he say something to attract the crowd's attention. He wondered what Lindsey had done to obtain permission to see the transformers. Title and fortune probably had something to do with it. He felt a twinge of frustration, but the promise of engineering spectacle quieted it, leaving him with a vague sense of guilt, which he found easier to dismiss.

They followed Mr Gowrie down an electrically-lit staircase to a subterranean corridor. As they walked, Lindsey looked around with a puzzled expression.

"Rather warmer than I expected," he said. "Drier, too."

Before Mr Gowrie could do more than inhale, Aubrey spoke.

"Fire insurance requires each transformer be housed in its own separate brick enclosure. So they've repurposed the archways supporting the Palace's heating system. Thus—" He waved his arm up at the brickwork. "—warm and dry."

Mr Gowrie raised an eyebrow. Aubrey would've explained himself, but Lindsey stepped in.

"Mr Warren," he said with a look of tremendous pride, "is an engineer."

"Aspiring," Aubrey rushed to correct him.

Mr Gowrie glanced between them. "Indeed."

Aubrey turned his attention to the transformers. True to *The Engineer*'s promise, ten massive machines hummed in perfect harmony. The sight prompted a corresponding hum in Aubrey's chest. He imagined what a similar system could accomplish if installed at Rook Mill.

"How do they...?" Lindsey began.

Mr Gowrie opened his mouth to explain. Aubrey beat him to it. A torrent of words—mentions of high-tension currents, field magnets, volts, poles, and circuits among them—poured from his mouth. When it closed some minutes later, Aubrey found both Lindsey and Mr Gowrie staring at him. He coloured.

"At least," he coughed, "I presume that's how it works. Mr Gowrie can no doubt correct me."

But Mr Gowrie merely raised his formidable eyebrow again. "Are you certain you're an *aspiring* engineer?"

"Quite," said Aubrey.

Lindsey grinned. "Could you elaborate on the difference between watts and volts?"

Aubrey was only too happy to explain.

Back in Belgrave Square after the Palace closed for the night, Aubrey did his best to show his appreciation for the afternoon's indulgence. The way Lindsey's cock jumped in Aubrey's hand, as if current ran through it, accompanied by electrified gasps from Lindsey's throat, assured Aubrey his message of gratitude was well-received.

&

"WHEN CAN YOU start?" said an office manager the following Monday.

Aubrey blinked, stunned. He hadn't dared hope to hear those four words so soon. He recovered in time to agree to seven o'clock on Wednesday morning. The manager, Mr Lawson, shook his hand on it. Aubrey left the office with a step so light he feared he'd float away.

Mr Lawson's office handled bookkeeping for a shipping firm. The work, even further removed from engineering than Rook Mill, wouldn't be glamorous, but the promised pay was almost double what Aubrey had earned previously. He could afford to rent his own room in London, perhaps even multiple rooms, and still put away something towards retirement. Hell, after six months or so he could buy a new suit to wear to the theatre with Lindsey. He quick-stepped towards Belgrave Square to give Lindsey the good news.

"Wonderful!" Lindsey cried, once Aubrey told him. He kissed Aubrey in celebration and seemed intent on celebrating further, but Aubrey forced himself to pull away.

"I must return to Manchester," he said. "Pack up, give notice to Mrs Padwick, that sort of thing."

"Do you need any help?"

Aubrey tried to picture Lindsey in his garret, carrying a soapbox of *The Engineer* back-issues down the rickety stair, and choked back laughter. "No, but thank you."

189

Lindsey looked a little disappointed, so Aubrey kissed him again and promised to return the following evening.

On the train back to Manchester, Aubrey's mind wandered miles away and ahead to his future in London with Lindsey. He walked dazed and distracted from Manchester Central to his lodging house, up the stairs to his room—the room he'd soon leave behind, and good riddance.

However, before he could leave, he had to confront the pile of mail shoved under the door in his absence. On top of *The Engineer*'s latest issue lay a letter postmarked two days past. Aubrey opened it with a worried frown.

Dear Mr Warren,

Splendid news! I have spoken with our chief engineer, Mr Cartwright, and he has a position available for you as a coal passer. It is difficult work, and not quite what you are used to, but I have no doubt you will turn it to your advantage and rise up to become a proper engineer in no time. Do write back with your decision as soon as possible.

Best regards,

Mr Edward Jennings

P.S. Don't worry about Mr Smith. I have the matter well in hand.

Aubrey sat down hard on the edge of his bed and stared at the letter. The paper crumpled in his clenched hands.

CHAPTER NINETEEN

DESPITE SPENDING MOST of the night and all the next morning's train ride considering the problem, Aubrey had come no closer to a solution by the time he reached Lindsey's doorstep. He found Lindsey at breakfast, surprised at his early arrival, but delighted to see him. Aubrey sat beside Lindsey as he was bid and made a valiant effort at returning Lindsey's joyful expression, but could do little more than push his bacon around his plate.

"Is there anything else you'd prefer?" Lindsey asked.

Aubrey jerked to attention. "No, sorry, it's—I haven't any appetite."

"Everything all right?" said Lindsey, frowning. A handsome frown, but the sight cause a pang in Aubrey's chest regardless.

"Fine," Aubrey hurried to reassure him.

Lindsey hesitated, then spoke again. "Forgive me, it isn't that I don't believe you, it's just..."

"...you don't believe me?" A wistful smile tugged the corners of Aubrey's mouth.

Lindsey mirrored his expression. "If there's anything I can do..."

"I'll ask," said Aubrey, the lie coming to his lips even easier the second time.

Lindsey's forced smile did nothing to alleviate Aubrey's guilt. Aubrey sighed and set down his fork.

"I received a letter from Mr Jennings," he said. Lindsey's eyebrows rose against his reluctance to explain further, so he added, "He's offered me a job as a coal-passer."

"Excellent!" said Lindsey. "What's a coal-passer?"

"The person responsible for keeping the engine fed."

"Ah," said Lindsey. "And this... distresses you?"

"I have to refuse," said Aubrey. "A coal-passer doesn't earn near so much as a clerk. And I can't return to Manchester. Not when I've everything waiting for me in London."

Lindsey nodded along, but his brows remained knitted. Aubrey returned to his plate. He poked a few morsels, then dared another glance at Lindsey, whose expression hadn't changed.

"What?" said Aubrey.

"You don't seem entirely at peace with that decision."

Aubrey, unused to being so transparent, hurriedly dropped his gaze and replied to the table rather than to Lindsey. "It doesn't matter. I'm moving to London. I've a new job. A good job. I'd be an idiot to turn it down to shovel coal."

The room fell silent, save for the tines of Aubrey's fork scraping his plate as he stabbed at his eggs.

"Is it because coal-passing has more to do with engineering than clerking?" Lindsey asked.

Aubrey brought his head up sharp to regard Lindsey, whose confused frown had given way to concern.

"It does," Aubrey admitted. "But that's irrelevant."

"But if you'd prefer it—"

"—then I'm an ass, and deserve to starve in the gutter, which is where I'll end up if I—" Aubrey swallowed. "Besides, if I return to Rook Mill, I become your employee again."

"I could sell it back to Clarence."

Aubrey blinked. "What?"

"Clarence Rook," said Lindsey. "If I return the mill to him, then you'd be his employee, not mine."

Aubrey stared at him, unable to comprehend the notion of a massive property transfer for no other purpose than his personal comfort. "Mr Rook would slash wages back to where they were when you acquired the mill. And he'd sack me again in the bargain."

Lindsey appeared shocked. "Why would he do that?"

In lieu of explaining exactly what Lindsey's dearest friend had imparted to Aubrey during their meeting, Aubrey replied, "Because I've a habit of violence towards my fellow staff."

"Only under duress."

Aubrey shook his head. "This clerking job—it's the only one I've ever earned. Every other position I've held has resulted from personal connections. My—" Aubrey scrambled for the correct word. "—friendship with Mr Jennings convinced him to hire me on as an office boy, and before that—the Post Office didn't hire me for my brains."

"Then they were fools," Lindsey replied with conviction. "You're brilliant."

Aubrey's instinctive protest stuck in his throat.

Lindsey spoke on. "Let's pretend your friendship with certain individuals provided an advantage in seeking employment. What good would this advantage have done if you hadn't proved yourself worthy of the positions you held? Would Smith have done half as well in your place?"

"Smith still has the job I was sacked from. I'd say he's done better."

Lindsey, who'd opened his mouth to continue, choked off whatever he'd intended to say.

Aubrey supposed he ought to feel victorious. He'd made his point and silenced his opponent. By the rules of logical debate, he'd won. Yet all he felt was a growing, gaping void in his chest. His soul threatened to sink into it.

Lindsey's grimace became a sad smile. "Your mind's made up, then. Clerking over coal-passing."

"Yes, but—" Aubrey stopped himself.

"But what?"

"Nothing. It's not rational."

"To the devil with rational," said Lindsey. "What is it?"

Aubrey forced the words out in a rush. "Clerking in London would be a step away from engineering. Likely forever. If I start as a coal-passer, I could learn on the job and advance to fireman, second engineer, engineer—"

"So become a coal-passer."

"At what cost?" said Aubrey. "It wouldn't be fair to Mr Lawson. I've promised to start first thing on Wednesday."

"What do you owe him? Write an apologetic letter and wash your hands of it."

"It wouldn't be fair to you!" Aubrey blurted.

Lindsey sat back and stared at him. "What?"

"If I return to Manchester, it's farther from you—and we've already planned that I'd move to London so we might be—" Aubrey cleared his throat and looked down at his plate, stabbing his eggs again. "It's not fair to you to have me run off, not after you've been so obliging. Putting up with my nonsense."

"What nonsense?"

"This," Aubrey didn't say. Instead, he replied, "You wanted to go to the theatre, and I dragged you all over the electrical exhibition."

"I suggested we attend the theatre," said Lindsey, enunciating each word with careful patience. "You suggested we visit the Palace. I agreed, and had a wonderful time. We both did. That's not nonsense. You listen to my prattling about Poe and Braddon and Doyle and heaven knows what else. You overlook my blunders—"

Aubrey lifted his head. "What blunders?"

Lindsey half-smiled. "I asked you if you rode horses."

"That's—" Aubrey coughed. "Anyone could make that mistake."

Lindsey's sheepish smile broadened. "I gave you a calling-card case."

Aubrey, who hadn't realised Lindsey had recognised his error, flushed scarlet. "And I cherish it!"

"You do?" Lindsey sounded genuinely surprised.

Aubrey thrust a determined hand into his jacket pocket and produced the object in question. Silver flashed in the morning sunlight. Lindsey stared at it. Then a tentative grin appeared on his face, and he closed his hands over both the case and Aubrey's palm.

"My point," he said softly, gazing into Aubrey's eyes, "is I'm delighted to see you happy. And stricken to see you miserable. Engineering—if you could've seen your face at the exhibition!—it makes you so—" He shook his head. "I can't bear to watch you throw that away. You shouldn't let anyone stop you from striving for what you want most. Least of all me."

Aubrey's reply—that Lindsey was what he wanted most—stilled on his tongue at Lindsey's tone. It sounded as though Lindsey knew precisely how it felt to be kept from his most heartfelt desires. What could prevent one of England's richest, handsomest bachelors from having everything he wanted, Aubrey couldn't fathom. He thought back on what Miller and Graves had told him of Lindsey's school days. That must be what Lindsey meant; his father keeping him from school, and his friends shielding him from romantic developments.

Then Aubrey recalled why Graves and Miller had wanted to speak with him in the first place. Why Rook and Miss Althorp had done the same. Every person in Lindsey's life wanted Aubrey out of it. And Lindsey wanted—

Aubrey.

Lindsey wanted Aubrey most of all.

The revelation swept over Aubrey, flooding his mind with panic.

"Are you all right?" Lindsey asked.

Aubrey didn't trust himself to speak. He stood and closed the short distance to Lindsey's chair. Lindsey looked up at him, his stunning blue eyes wide in confusion. Aubrey closed his own and swooped down to press a ferocious kiss on Lindsey's parted lips. Lindsey returned it with equal passion. When the awkward position grew too much to bear, Aubrey pulled back to rest his forehead against Lindsey's.

"I suppose I'll be an engineer," said Aubrey, still not daring to open his eyes.

Lindsey kissed him again. "A brilliant one."

Aubrey laughed and nuzzled Lindsey's throat.

Dear Miss Rook,

I write to thank you for showing me your compositions for the piano, and to inform you of a recent change in my own circumstance which may interest you. I am no longer a clerk. I am now on my way to becoming an engineer by profession. The position is less intellectual and more physically rigorous, but I have already learned much in my first week of employment and look forward to expanding the breadth of my knowledge as time goes on.

Regarding The Engineer—if you have no subscription of your own, perhaps the copies I have already acquired might be of some use to you? Forgive me if this is an impertinence; I am not well studied in the ways of society.

Your servant,

Aubrey Warren

Dear Mr Warren,

I am delighted to hear of your promotion! Your offering of The Engineer is far from impertinent, it is most generous of you and I am thankful for it. My father, God rest his soul, had a subscription when I was a child. I used to steal away the issues before he could send them on to Clarence at Oxford. I'm not sure what Clarence did with the ones that made their way to him. He didn't bring any home with him when he left university. He cancelled father's subscription as soon as father died, much to my private distress. I was able to save a few issues from his purge. 7th of July 1871 is a particular favourite of mine.

To our purpose: I cannot have The Engineer delivered to my house for reasons we have already discussed, but Rowena's address ought to be safe enough. I may read it in

195

her library. She very kindly does not consider this rude of me, for she is often reading herself when I arrive for morning calls. We pass the time v. quietly this way. Forgive me, such news must bore you terribly. Please tell me everything you have learned in your new position. Life is very dull for me otherwise.

Your friend,
Emmeline Rook

❧

Dear Miss Rook,

As promised, here are the last eight months of The Engineer, *with a short note for company. I regret I cannot write more. I no longer have a desk at work, and light is in short supply at home. I fear a description of my day-to-day would put you (or anyone) straight off to sleep. However, I have learned that our own steam engine is rated at 35 horsepower, will stand a cold water pressure of 135 pounds without displaying weakness, and can carry up to 85 pounds of pressure. Our chief engineer is Mr Cartwright, and he has been more patient with me than I deserve. For the most part, my duties consist of watching the gauges, and adding water and fuel as needed. Our mechanical stoker means I shovel less coal than might be supposed, but still more coal than any clerk shovelled before. Apart from that, what I learn comes from eavesdropping on Mr Cartwright's commands to engineers more senior than myself. I do hope you will forgive me for that.*

Your servant,
Aubrey Warren

❧

Dear Mr Warren,

Thank you, thank you, thank you ever so much for your gift! I'm afraid I quite bored Rowena, imploring her to look over my shoulder at the reports of the Electrical Exhibition (which I am sorely vexed to have missed!) or Edison's latest patent. Did you by any chance catch the note on page 87 of 29 January of this year regarding what occurs when simple table salt is mixed with whitewash? It is an old experiment, I know, but the limited view I have had of the world until now makes it quite new to me. I would dearly like to try it for myself, but I dare not perform any such experiments in my own house for reasons we have already discussed.

Forgive my naïveté in being jealous of your position. I should love to shovel coal into a great thrumming engine, fuelling the fires of industry! But I trust the reality of your situation is none so exciting as my imagination makes it. Still, I beg you will continue to tell me all that occurs. You are a coal-passer. Who must you surpass to become chief engineer?

Your friend,
Emmeline Rook

⁓

Dear Miss Rook,

You're very welcome. You're already making far better use of them than I ever did. I would perform the salt and whitewash experiment myself and report the results back to you, but I fear my landlady would not be well pleased.

In the interest of giving a full and complete account of the engineering done at the factory, I will attempt a sketch of my co-workers. The second engineer of the day shift is Mr Hepworth. He is nearer to forty than thirty, I believe, with almost twenty years of engineering study under his belt. I shall not be able to surpass him for some time. I fear he may resent any attempts on my part to do so. But he has no objection to my work as a coal-passer. Mr Cartwright likewise continues to find my progress acceptable. There is also a day fireman, Mr Barr. I do not have much opportunity to socialise with them on the job, but they all seem like good fellows.

Your servant,
Aubrey Warren

⁓

Dear Mr Warren,

Rowena has been so gracious and kind and allowed me to perform the salt and whitewash experiment in her house. I'm afraid we put off the cook and housekeeper in the process, but Rowena concurs that it is a small price to pay for the progress of scientific understanding. The Engineer recommends mixing three parts quicklime to one of common salt. The result is a wash hard as adamantine and impossible to remove. We had anticipated this result, and thought ourselves well prepared by applying the mixture to the back of an old magazine cover (NOT The Engineer!!!) with a worn-out watercolour brush, but the chemical reaction was complete before the brush made it from pail to paper, and the end result of our experiment is a lump of what might pass for enamel stuck on the end of a brush handle. The sable hairs are completely obscured, with no hope of extrication. Rowena said she was glad she had not sacrificed a new brush to the rites of Science. I was eager to repeat the experiment and affirm our conclusions, but I fear Rowena was quite bored by the prospect, and so it shall have to wait. *Truth told, I would much rather be experimenting with magnets and glass tubing and copper wires, but those are harder to procure.*

Returning to The Engineer, I have reached the 12 February issue of this year and find myself in agony at not having attended Mr Tesla's lecture before the Institution of Electrical Engineers. I should have dearly loved to see the incredible phosphorescent glow produced by the passage of high-frequency volts through Mr Tesla's very body! Imagine, to be in his position! To feel such power coursing in one's own mortal frame! What a thrill it must be!

Rowena does not seem enthused about my proposal of repeating Mr Tesla's experiment in her home. She is, however, warming to the notion of accompanying me to the Crystal Palace. The Palace is very old news to you and the rest of the engineering world, I'm sure. Still, I cannot help but want to see it for myself. Rowena thinks it unlikely that we should be permitted to view the motor transformers underneath the floor of the Palace, but I should like to try. Surely it couldn't hurt to ask permission? Failing that, I should like to ride the electric passenger lift.

Your FRIEND,
Emmeline Rook

༄

Dear Miss Rook,

My congratulations on the success of your experiment in chemistry, and my condolences and commiserations with your agonies regarding Mr Tesla's lecture. I myself was lucky enough to visit the Crystal Palace. I hope you may do the same. It is a truly inspiring sight. If you do manage to convince Miss Althorp to accompany you, I do hope you will write back and tell me your opinion of all you have seen. Particularly of the motor transformers, if you can get a look at them. They are most impressive.

The mill continues on much the same day after day. Do not take that as a complaint! I much prefer watching the gauges to filling the ledgers. I've learned far more on the job as a coal-passer in a month than I ever did in all my years as a clerk.

Forgive the brevity of this letter. Light is in short supply here at the end of the work day. I hope it finds you well.

Your friend,
Aubrey Warren

༄

FOG ROLLED OVER the cobblestones of the Rook Mill yard, the sun little more than a faint sliver on the eastern horizon. The mill itself, empty of

198

workers, loomed over the chill morning in silence. Aubrey waited by the boiler shed for the chief engineer, as he'd done every day these past two months.

The chief engineer, Mr Cartwright, arrived at quarter to seven. He nodded good-morning to Aubrey, who returned the gesture. The second engineer, Mr Hepworth, would soon follow, and together the three men could start the mighty mechanism and bring power to the mill—like Prometheus granting fire, as Lindsey put it.

In the meantime, Aubrey and Mr Cartwright waited in companionable silence. Unable to converse during the twelve hours a day the engine ran, Mr Cartwright seemed to have fallen out of the habit of conversation altogether, speaking only when necessary to impart technical information—which suited Aubrey fine.

The clock tower struck seven. Hepworth didn't appear. Instead, a thin, grubby boy ran up with a letter clenched in his fist.

"Cartwright?" he said.

Mr Cartwright handed over a penny for the letter. The boy scampered off.

Whatever the letter's contents, they didn't sit well with Mr Cartwright, whose cheeks drained of colour as he read. He folded the letter up and turned to Aubrey.

"Think you can handle the engine yourself?" he asked. "At least until Hepworth comes along."

Aubrey confirmed he could. Mr Cartwright thanked him and took off as near to running as respectability allowed.

Aubrey continued waiting for Hepworth. At half-past seven, he could delay no longer. He started the engine.

It took some fiddling, as he was alone and had to run between stations to check gauges, turn cranks, and pull levers, but he managed. The engine came alive, roaring with "the fires of industry," as Miss Rook would have it. Aubrey stood back to monitor its progress.

At eight o'clock, a figure approached. Aubrey couldn't determine its identity through the perpetual fog, soot, and lint. He thought it might be Miss Brewster come to discuss union duties now that he'd become a proper member of the workforce, but as the figure stepped closer, he recognised it as Smith.

Before Smith opened his mouth, Aubrey spoke, pitching his voice above the engine's clamour.

"What do you want?"

"Mr Gardener wants a word," Smith replied, his face pinched up in disgust at his proximity to the greasy machine.

He had to repeat himself twice, unused to speaking over the engine. The unlikelihood of his message made it even harder for Aubrey to understand. Mr Gardener was the foreman of the weaving room. Aubrey couldn't recall ever exchanging a word with him. He only recognised the name thanks to his former payroll duties.

"Tell him to come out here," Aubrey directed, jabbing a finger down at the cobblestones beneath his feet.

Smith shook his head.

"I can't leave the boiler," said Aubrey. "There's no one else to watch it."

"I'll watch it," said Smith.

Aubrey gawked at him. "You?"

Smith bristled. "Can't be that hard. You manage all right."

Aubrey would've liked to demonstrate exactly how hard it was, but he doubted even the steel plates of the boiler could break through Smith's thick skull.

"Fine," Aubrey said, pointing to the gauges. "Watch these. If any of them go above this level—" he tapped the appropriate spot on each, "—run and fetch me. Otherwise, stay here, and don't touch anything."

"Who died and made you king of the boiler?" said Smith. But before Aubrey could respond, he rolled his eyes and added, "Fine. As you wish."

Aubrey reluctantly turned to go.

"Quick step, mind!" Smith called after him. "Gardener's not a patient fellow!"

CHAPTER TWENTY

Mr Gardener had no idea what Aubrey was talking about.

"Who are you, again?" he shouted. They'd met in the stairwell outside the weave room, but a closed door did little to muffle the cacophony of the machines.

"Warren," Aubrey shouted back. "Coal-passer."

"Thought you were a clerk."

"I was, but—"

"Weren't you sacked?"

"No, I—"

"So a disgraced clerk thinks he can come up here and waste my time?" Mr Gardener stood shorter than Aubrey—a small miracle—but the puckered frown under his walrus moustache indicated a sizeable temper.

Aubrey withheld any sign of his own impatience. "Mr Smith said you wished to speak to me."

"Oh, Smith said that? How convenient, him having such a commonplace name as Smith."

"Mr Gardener—" Aubrey began.

But Mr Gardener had already turned away to yank open the weave room door. With a final glare at Aubrey, he passed through and slammed it shut.

There was nothing for it but to return to the yard. Aubrey descended the stairs in haste, fuelled by his annoyance with Smith. As he departed the mill and strode across the yard, he readied a fiery sermon against stupid schoolboy pranks and the idiots who pulled them.

But when he reached the boiler shed, he found no one to hear it. Smith had gone.

Aubrey could've kicked the boiler in frustration. He settled for checking the gauges. All read normal. None of their needles had moved so much as a millimetre since he'd left them. He watched them a minute or so longer. They remained still.

Too still.

The boiler, the furnace, and the engines all generated constant vibrations along with steam power. The omnipresent thrum should've rattled the needles. Furthermore, it'd taken Aubrey at least a quarter hour to run into the mill, speak with Mr Gardener, and run back. In that time, the furnace should've consumed fuel, the boiler should've consumed water, and both gauges should've dropped. Yet they hadn't. They'd remained fixed at the point where Aubrey had seen them last. Where they'd been when he'd left Smith alone with the machinery.

Aubrey expelled a stream of every oath he'd ever heard, from workhouse to whorehouse to mill yard and back again.

Of course Smith would interpret his instructions literally. Anything to avoid the labour of watching the gauges. Much easier to prevent the needles from moving in the first place.

Unfortunately, this left Aubrey with no way of knowing the actual pressure in the boiler. If he kept it running, he'd do so blind, every passing second ticking closer to a potential explosion. The only safe option was to shut it down.

If Smith hadn't broken those mechanisms as well.

Which, of course, he had.

Every lever had disappeared, most unscrewed, some snapped off. The toolbox Aubrey turned to for wrenches or pliers or anything to replace the levers had also vanished. As had the knobs and dials. The boiler, furnace, and engine roared on beyond Aubrey's control.

Horrific headlines flashed through Aubrey's mind. The Atlas Works explosion of 1858. The catastrophe at Billinge in 1865. Thick metal panels torn like wet tissue, careening through brick walls with enough force to decapitate a man and send his head flying a hundred yards off in the opposite direction. Stories he'd pored over in *The Engineer*, stories he'd seen as mere illustrative case studies, were now all too applicable to his present reality. Everyone within a thousand yards of Rook Mill was in mortal peril.

Aubrey sprinted back towards the mill. With every stride he racked his brain for a plan. He could run onto the mill floor and shout for everyone to leave. "BOILER EXPLOSION!" at top volume would probably do the trick. However, a panicked rush at the exits could kill and maim as many as the explosion itself.

He vaulted up the stairwell two steps at a time. In the midst of one such leap, he realised he didn't need everyone to know the details of the imminent danger, necessarily. He just needed them to leave in a quiet and orderly fashion.

And for that, he knew exactly where to go.

"You again?" Mr Gardener shouted over the clatter of the machines as Aubrey entered.

Aubrey ignored him and strode down the line of workers to tap one woman on the shoulder. Miss Brewster turned around with a scowl. It softened into a raised eyebrow as she recognised him. Aubrey jerked his head towards the door. She followed him into the stairwell despite Mr Gardener's protests.

"Good morning, Mr Warren," she said when they could hear each other.

"Have you planned for a strike?" he replied.

For the first time in their acquaintance, he'd surprised her, rather than the reverse. She gave him a long, wary look. "I have."

"Good," he said, surprising her again. "It needs to happen now. Stop work and walk out. Everyone. Can you manage it?"

She crossed her arms. "That depends. If we walk out now, can you guarantee Sir Lindsey will agree to our terms?"

"If you don't walk out now, I can guarantee you're at risk of being blown to pieces."

Miss Brewster's eyes widened. "Is that a threat, Mr Warren?"

"No, I—" Aubrey shook his head. "Something's wrong with the boiler. Mr Cartwright's gone. I can't fix it alone."

"And it's going to explode," she concluded in a detached deadpan, as if she couldn't quite believe it herself. "And take all of us with it."

"Unless we get everyone out of range."

"Without causing a panic." Miss Brewster nodded. "I believe I take your meaning, Mr Warren."

"Can you do it?"

"I can." She squared her shoulders. "And I shall."

Without another word, she turned on her heel and re-entered the weave room. She strode straight to the nearest girl and put a hand on her shoulder. When the girl met her gaze, Miss Brewster raised her fist and made a sign across it. The girl's expression changed from curiosity to

203

resolve. She stepped away from her machine, put a hand on the shoulder of the girl next to her, and made the same sign as Miss Brewster. And so on down the line. Miss Brewster, meanwhile, galvanised the next row of girls.

Mr Gardener's face turned a spectacular shade of scarlet as he shouted at his radical workforce. He caught sight of Aubrey in the doorway and, pointing an accusatory finger, attempted to rush at him, but the women's march towards the exit impeded his progress. Aubrey escaped down the stairwell.

Word travelled between floors much faster than Aubrey had expected. By the time he reached the yard, the entire weave room had followed, and a few men from other stations as well. The crowd swelled as he stood helpless, wondering how best to herd them outside the mill complex entirely. Before he could gather the courage to address them, one girl clambered atop the shoulders of another, and, through shouts and arm gestures, told the crowd their goal lay outside the mill bounds. The workforce flowed towards the gate, most men marching, some boys skipping along with their fists in the air, and the women with their heads held high.

Unfortunately, their route ran between Aubrey and the boiler shed. He'd given up hope of cutting through their ranks and was plotting an alternate route around the back of the mill when a voice behind him called, "Warren!"

Aubrey turned to find Mr Jennings rapidly approaching. His mouth moved, but the crowd's murmurs had grown to rival the rumble of machinery, muffling all speech. Only when Mr Jennings's stood in front of him could he understand him.

"What the devil's going on?" Mr Jennings demanded.

"It's a walk-out, sir," said Aubrey.

"I can bloody well see that!"

In all the time Aubrey had known Mr Jennings, he'd never seen him angry. Sad, frustrated, resigned, yes—enraged, no. But the Mr Jennings who confronted him at present had a throbbing purple brow, and Aubrey had to suppress an instinctive backwards step.

"The boiler is going to explode," said Aubrey, leaning in lest one of the crowd overhear him. If they started a panic, all Miss Brewster's careful organisation would be for nought.

"What!" cried Mr Jennings.

"Please, sir." Aubrey held up his hands in supplication. "Walk out with everyone else. I swear I'll have a satisfactory explanation after—"

204

"A satisfactory explanation for a boiler explosion!?"

One of the passing workers whipped his head around to give Mr Jennings a second glance. He may have intended to stop, but the crowd pushed him along.

Aubrey motioned for Mr Jennings to keep his voice down. "Edward, please!"

That got him Mr Jennings's full attention. Aubrey didn't waste a second of it.

"Miss Brewster and I are trying to get everyone to safety. Please, go with them—for supervision or solidarity, it doesn't matter. Just please get yourself and Smith out of range!"

Mr Jennings frowned. "Smith?"

"Yes. Isn't he with you?"

"He hasn't deigned to grace us with his presence today, no."

Aubrey stared at him. "What?"

"I said he's not here, boy, so you needn't worry about him. Or me, either. I'll walk with you."

Aubrey was only half-listening. "No, no, I must—see to the boiler—"

"Aubrey!"

The ill-considered shout had no effect. Aubrey had already run off. Mr Jennings's voice was replaced by the drone of the crowd and the distant clatter of unattended machines. These, too, fell off as Aubrey drew closer to the boiler shed. Mechanical clanging and a high, persistent hiss filled his ears. He came around the corner and stumbled to a halt. In front of the boiler, prybar in hand, his back to Aubrey, stood Smith.

"What're you doing?" Aubrey shouted over the industrial noise.

Smith whirled around. Seeing Aubrey, he snarled. "What your mother ought've done when she realised what she'd whelped!"

Aubrey forced his fists to unclench. "That trick's not going to work twice."

"Sod off!"

Aubrey gave up trying to pry any useful information from Smith. He cast his eyes over the machines. Apart from some scratches and dents, the situation didn't seem much changed from how he'd left it. Which meant pressure had continued building in the boiler all the while. The impending explosion would be colossal.

Smith hit the boiler with his prybar.

Aubrey threw his arms up over his face, but the boiler merely squealed in protest. Smith brought the prybar back for another blow. Aubrey hastened to interrupt him.

"Whatever you're trying to do, it's not working."

"It should've gone off by now! I don't know what's—" Smith seemed to recall who he was speaking to and rounded on Aubrey with a violent expression. "Oh, you think you're so clever! Just 'cause you shovel coal, doesn't make you an engineer!"

"More of an engineer than you," Aubrey said, stepping forward.

Smith lifted his prybar high over his head. "Come any closer, and I'll—"

What Smith intended, Aubrey never found out. The cuff of Smith's jacket, held aloft, caught on the shafting of the mechanical stoker. Before Aubrey could even think to shout a warning, the mechanism yanked the jacket up, and Smith with it. The prybar fell to the cobblestones, its clanging impact overwhelmed by Smith's screams and his bones snapping as the rotating shaft forced his body to wrap around it.

Aubrey rushed to the machine's controls to stop the horror—but the knobs had disappeared, the levers broken off. Smith's sabotage had been thorough, if ignorant. He'd left Aubrey with no way to shut down the stoker.

Smith's ear-splitting shrieks resolved into words. "Help me! For God's sake, save me!"

Aubrey snatched up the prybar and thrust it into the stoker's open maw. Teeth designed to devour coal screeched against steel. The stoker shuddered to a halt.

Smith's screams became wheezing sobs. "Please, please..."

The stoker trembled with unspent energy. Pressure was building, Aubrey knew, regardless of what the gauges read. He had no time to think of that. He needed something to tear the stoker open and pull Smith out.

"The toolkit!" he shouted up at Smith. "Where?"

Smith could only sob.

Aubrey spun in a futile circle, searching for anything Smith had left untouched. Each passing second felt like hours. In desperation, he dropped to the ground and peered under the machines. There, in the oil and soot, lay a forgotten wrench.

He grabbed it and launched himself at the stoker. Every nut he tried had rusted stuck, every bolt stripped, and every failed attempt rattled the machine, tearing more screams from Smith.

Aubrey backed off, forcing himself to abandon his panic and consider the whole. The boiler couldn't stop until the furnace stopped. The furnace couldn't stop until the stoker stopped. The stoker couldn't stop whatsoever. And all the while, fire burned, steam built up, pressure rose.

Pressure needed to fall.

He ran to the boiler. Smith had wired all the safety valves shut. Aubrey reached to untie one and snatched back burned fingers. The wires, glowing hot, had melted together. Untying them was now beyond Aubrey's power.

So Aubrey tightened his grip on the wrench and swung.

The first blow glanced off the valve. The second struck true, taking the valve off with it.

Steam spewed forth in a concentrate jet, billowing into scalding clouds. It'd just begun to sting Aubrey's flesh when, with a deafening bang, the boiler ripped open from the valve outward. The explosion flung Aubrey across the mill yard. Steam engulfed his airborne form, the agony unlike anything he'd felt in his short, painful life. His own screams joined Smith's.

When he struck the cobblestones some hundred yards distant, he was silent.

CHAPTER TWENTY-ONE

TERRIBLE BOILER EXPLOSION AT MANCHESTER. — A most violent boiler explosion took place at Rook's cotton mill this morning, killing one and injuring several others.

Mr Jonathan SMITH, Jr, aged 26, clerk, was caught up in the machinery and killed outright by the explosion. Mr Aubrey WARREN, aged 24, coal-passer, was thrown no fewer than one hundred yards and badly scalded. He was removed to Withington Hospital, where he now lies in a precarious state. Three other mill employees are likewise injured: Miss Maud WILSON, aged 20, piecer, slight burns; Miss Mary MARSHALL, aged 16, piecer, twisted ankle in flight from mill; Mr Thomas WHITE, aged 42, mule-spinner, cut by glass from broken window. Further injury to humanity was spared by the curious coincidence of a union walk-out occurring at the very moment of the explosion. Considerable damage to property also resulted from the incident, as the boiler itself is rent in twain, with fully half of the wreckage being forced across the mill yard and crashing through the back wall of the mill, crushing textile machinery on three floors. The noise of this calamity carried no less than two miles.

A formal investigation is ongoing.

⁓

THE SAME MORNING, Lindsey organised the library of his new house in Chorlton-cum-Hardy, just outside of Manchester. As he straightened the books on the gleaming mahogany shelves, he heard a distant boom of what he assumed to be thunder. He looked out the window, perceived no rainclouds, shrugged, and returned to his happy task.

Lindsey had acquired the house when Aubrey accepted Mr Jennings's offer to become a coal-passer. Rowena arrived soon after, staying in one of the guest rooms whilst she helped Lindsey arrange the house to his liking. Graves rendered assistance via correspondence, offering up hints from *The House Beautiful*. Lindsey deferred to them on most points, but ignored all outside suggestions regarding the south-east guest room. He'd earmarked it for Aubrey; it had sober slate blue walls; a black walnut desk, shelves, and wash-stand; and a modern metal bed frame large enough for two. A few of the adventure novels Aubrey had mentioned enjoying as a boy adorned the shelves. Lindsey had left the rest for Aubrey to fill as he wished.

All that remained was to invite Aubrey to see it for himself. Lindsey had just begun composing the letter when he received a telegram from Mr Jennings.

Not thirty seconds after, Lindsey hurtled down the stairs towards the front door, shouting for Rowena as he ran.

The ensuing argument would've become the stuff of legend, had anyone besides Charles overheard it.

"You cannot go!" Rowena insisted for the third time.

Lindsey paced the foyer like a caged tiger. "You ask me to know the one I love is lying in agony—alone, in hospital, with no friend to comfort him—and do nothing?"

He punctuated each point by stabbing his finger at the front door. He would've passed through it long ago had Charles not bodily barred the way. Charles remained there now, calm yet firm, bearing silent witness to their dispute. Lindsey considered himself above coming to blows with his valet, but gave serious thought to relaxing his moral code.

"You will damn him and yourself!" Rowena shot back. "In society's eyes there's no reason for you to take any personal interest in the matter. No other mill owner would give half a damn if one of their engineers got himself blown up."

"Got himself—!?" Lindsey rounded on her.

"Nevertheless," she said over him. "You must feign indifference. It's the only way to keep him safe."

"For God's sake, Rowena, he's dying!"

"Then let him die in peace."

Lindsey gaped at her. She pressed on.

"If you go to him now, and he should survive, you will condemn him to two years hard labour in Newgate. To say nothing of what would befall yourself. You must wait."

"For what?" Lindsey roared. "For the law to change? For him to perish? For you to develop a single scrap of human empathy? Horns will sound,

209

and the devil will triumph over the might of Heaven, before you ever show anything so precious, so mortal, as compassion!"

Rowena's face went white with rage. He expected her to shout something just as horrible back at him, but when her jaw unclenched to speak, her voice was low and cold.

"Go, then. Go and be hanged, for all I care."

Lindsey realised her eyes glistened with tears.

Before he could apologise, she fled up the stair. A door slammed after her.

Lindsey stared stupidly at the path she'd taken, then turned to Charles, whose stoic expression hadn't changed.

"That..." Lindsey struggled for words. "...that wasn't very well done on my part, was it?"

"I wouldn't presume to say, sir," Charles replied.

Lindsey, too drained by anger to muster any annoyance at Charles's response, blinked at him, then climbed the stair. Charles didn't follow.

A brief investigation proved Rowena hadn't locked herself in her guest chambers, as Lindsey'd first assumed, but in his own bedroom. He knocked on the door. No one answered.

"Rowena?"

Her skirts rustled, reassuring him she was, in fact, alive.

"Rowena, I'm sorry. I've been an ass. I didn't mean it. Please come out. You were right. I need you."

She said nothing.

"Please," he begged.

He waited two hours in vain.

Rowena didn't come down to dinner. Charles brought a tray up to the locked door and left it with a few words regarding the temperature of the meal over time. Lindsey, sitting alone in his new dining room, ate nothing. Charles was a competent chef, provided the party was small, but Lindsey had no appetite.

Night crept over Manchester. Rowena remained in Lindsey's room. Lindsey endeavoured to wait up for her and made it to one o'clock before the day's stress caught up to him. He crept to Aubrey's room. There he drifted off into an uneasy sleep, jolting awake again and again, his brain afire with what-ifs and if-onlys.

By dawn, Lindsey would've charitably described himself as a wreck. Charles came to his door at nine, but he'd already awakened hours earlier.

"Any word from hospital?" he asked over Charles's greeting.

"None, sir," said Charles, laying out Lindsey's clothes. "From hospital or mill."

Lindsey felt ready to crawl back under the sheets until he realised, in order to retrieve his clothes, Charles must've gone into his bedroom. Which meant it'd been unlocked. Which meant Rowena—

Lindsey dressed in a waistcoat-rumpling rush and ran downstairs to find Rowena finishing her breakfast in the dining room. She raised her eyes to him.

"Good morning," she said, after a long silence.

"Rowena, I'm sorry."

"Yes, I recall you saying something to that effect last night. Do sit down, your bacon's getting cold."

Lacking the energy to do otherwise, Lindsey sat down. He managed a few mouthfuls. Then anxiety cramped his insides and reduced him to pushing his food around his plate in a haze. Rowena watched him carefully, saying nothing. Their grim repast was mercifully interrupted by Charles arriving with a telegram.

Lindsey snatched it from Charles's fingers. "From hospital?"

"From Mr Rook, sir," said Charles.

Lindsey knew it already, having read it through twice before Charles spoke.

Mr Clarence Rook

Sir Lindsey Althorp

My condolences for your troubles. Come to me at your convenience and I will do my best to distract you.

Lindsey dropped the telegram, letting his face fall into his hands. When he lifted his head, Rowena had the telegram.

"But this is ideal," she said.

"I fail to see how," said Lindsey.

"It gives you the perfect excuse to leave Manchester."

Lindsey shot upright. "Leave Manchester! Now? Aubrey—"

"It will remove you from the temptation to rush to his bedside. And, if you succumb to temptation regardless, we'll have a few hours' warning of it."

Lindsey stared at her. "Remove me from temptation. You've picked up where Father left off, haven't you? First Eton, now Manchester. Is there nowhere we might keep little Lindsey out of trouble? Perhaps you'd better dispense with the formalities and put me under lock and key once and for all."

"There's no call for melodrama," said Rowena.

"I'm astonished you haven't put a leash and collar on me," Lindsey continued. "'If found, please return to Rowena.'"

"Stop it."

"'But in the meantime, don't let him near the other boys, he's an incorrigible sodom—'"

"Stop it!"

Rowena stood up from the table. Lindsey cut his speech short.

"If you can't take this seriously—" she began.

"I am," said Lindsey. "I will. I'm trying. I'm sorry."

She glared at him, then sat.

Lindsey swallowed hard. "I'll return to London on one condition: you visit Aubrey in my stead."

Rowena's glare became a stare.

Lindsey hurried to explain his reasoning. "It's perfectly appropriate for you to see him. Angel of the house, angel of mercy, and all that. You can pretend to care, and I can pretend not to."

His throat closed. He feared he'd lost her with that final strike against her character, but when she replied, her tone sounded as kind as he'd ever heard it.

"I'll have to visit the other victims as well," she said. "Wouldn't do to show favouritism."

Lindsey held his breath.

She sighed. "Send me a telegram from London, and I'll go to Withington Hospital."

And so he went.

⁂

"YOU LOOK DREADFUL," Clarence said after the parlour maid had shown Lindsey up to the study.

Lindsey smiled weakly. Clarence rewarded him by draping an arm across his shoulders and leading him to a chair.

The train ride from Manchester to London had been a waking nightmare. Lindsey had spent it staring out the window, fantasising about jumping up to yank the emergency stop and demand a return to Manchester, to Withington Hospital, to Aubrey. He'd made himself sick imagining Aubrey's face—his clever, handsome face—twisted in pain, his body wracked with wounds. Perhaps even now Aubrey drew his last rattling breath to cry out for Lindsey, his fingers grasping for a phantom hand.

Clarence poured Lindsey a glass of whisky. Lindsey managed a thankful nod as he took it. He drained it in silence. Clarence let him. He neglected to refill Lindsey's glass, instead standing over Lindsey, leaning back against his bookshelves and holding his own glass with no apparent intention of drinking its contents.

"Terrible business," said Clarence. "Do allow me to offer my condolences. What can I do to ease your burden?"

Lindsey would've told him not to trouble himself, that his friendship was comfort enough, but grief made him sluggish.

Clarence continued without his input. "I'd be happy to take the mill off your hands."

Lindsey blinked at Clarence, then at his empty glass, then at Clarence again. Surely he'd misheard. "Pardon?"

"The expense of paying off the injured parties and shutting it down is an unjust imposition on you. Let me take care of it."

"That's—" Lindsey struggled for words. "—dashed good of you to offer, but I couldn't possibly—"

Clarence shook his head. "I should've done it long ago. Ought to have bought it back the week you won it from me."

"Steady on!" Lindsey bolted upright. "How could I possibly hold you to that debt? What gentleman would? I'd have given it back gladly then, but now—now, it's impossible. I couldn't ask you to take over a broken enterprise."

"Lindsey," Clarence chuckled. "You haven't the heart to do what needs to be done."

Lindsey supposed Clarence meant it as a compliment. He waved it away. "What needs to be done is reconstruction."

Clarence's indulgent smile faltered. "What?"

"I intend to rebuild," said Lindsey. "Lord knows I can afford to. It'd be unfair to the workers to do otherwise. Best get things back to normal as soon as possible, no matter the cost."

Clarence appeared at a loss. "There'll be an inquest."

"Inquest be damned," Lindsey snapped, surprising himself. "I'll weather it."

An inquest was nothing to the agony Aubrey faced. The thought of Aubrey's pain made Lindsey wish his glass full again, and simultaneously glad it was empty.

"You seem awfully attached to the mill," said Clarence. "I can't imagine why. It's not as though you depend upon it."

Lindsey considered telling the truth. He didn't mind playing fast and loose with his own reputation, but he wouldn't be risking his alone; he'd endanger Aubrey, as well.

But Clarence was his dearest friend, the subject of his first tender fantasies, the guardian of his schoolboy days. Surely Clarence, of all people, could be trusted with their secret.

As Lindsey mulled over his dilemma, he noticed Clarence studying him.

"Perhaps," Clarence said when they locked eyes, "there's more to this than a mere mill."

Lindsey perked up. If Clarence had already guessed the truth, it'd make Lindsey's confession far easier.

"Perhaps," Clarence continued, "it's something to do with a certain clerk-turned-engineer you invited to dinner."

Lindsey didn't approve of Clarence's tone. "And if it does?"

Clarence shrugged. "Then it's no concern of mine. A man's home is his castle, and his bed is his own business."

It ought've felt reassuring to hear Clarence say so, but Lindsey found he couldn't relax. "Then why mention it?"

"Because it's beginning to have repercussions outside the bedroom." Clarence set his full glass down on his desk. "*Par exemple*, your refusal to relinquish the mill. But I think I can persuade you yet. Let's strike a bargain. You give me the mill, and I give you my sister's hand in marriage."

"Why should I want that?" asked Lindsey.

"Because," Clarence said with an air of quotation, "it is a truth universally acknowledged, that a man in possession of a need to deflect society's suspicions, must be in want of a wife."

Lindsey wondered if Clarence had put something besides whisky in his glass.

"More plainly put," Clarence continued, "society looks less askance at a man's friends if the man in question is wed to a woman."

"Society has yet to look askance at me."

"Yet," Clarence echoed.

Lindsey frowned. "I appreciate your concern, but—"

"Then you mistake me. If you don't marry my sister and return the mill to me, I will give society reason to look askance at you and your clerk."

Had Lindsey not been seated, he would've staggered. As matters stood, he gripped the arm of his chair in one hand, while the other clenched dangerously tight around his empty glass. He meant to ask a question, but his voice had plummeted along with his hopes, turning it into a pathetic monotone. "Why."

"I'm in need of funds," said Clarence, lacking the decency to look abashed.

"You can't be desperate enough to sell off your own sister. Surely your uncle will settle your debts."

"I fear you underestimate my debts. My father made a similar error. When he left the mill to me, he cut off my allowance from the family trust. I can't touch a penny until my twenty-fifth year. He supposed the mill's profits would support me until then. Alas, no. So I endeavoured to be rid of it, assuming my uncle, as executor of the will, would reinstate my allowance in its place. I put up the mill against your infinite fortune, and lost. But I, too, erred. According to my uncle, if I can't be trusted with a mill, I can't be trusted with anything. Thus, until I come into my rightful inheritance, my only hope lies in recovering the mill. Getting rid of my sister and her drain upon the household is a bonus to me, and a favour to you."

Lindsey stared at the man he'd called his friend. A man who might've been more than that, if he'd felt so inclined.

Lindsey's sense of decency, dignity, and justice demanded he refuse Clarence's terms. But decency, dignity, and justice were immaterial. Aubrey, lying broken and alone in Withington Hospital, was all too material. He'd endured enough already. Lindsey couldn't risk any further harm to him, should he survive.

It was only a marriage, after all. Just a little matrimony. Probably wouldn't even hurt. And besides, the mill was worthless without Aubrey.

Lindsey withheld a sigh. "When should I propose?"

"Now will do."

Lindsey gawked at Clarence. "Now?"

"Why not?" asked Clarence. Lindsey could think of a hundred thousand reasons, but before he could voice them, Clarence continued. "She's downstairs. I can arrange for the maid to be out of the way. You'll have perfect privacy."

"And if she should refuse me?" Lindsey asked.

Clarence's expression grew darker than any Lindsey had yet seen upon his face. "She had better not."

CHAPTER TWENTY-TWO

WITHINGTON HOSPITAL HAD grown out of the Chorlton Union Workhouse in Nell Lane, Withington. Later, Aubrey would reflect with bitter irony upon the circumstances that led him from one workhouse to another.

At the time of his arrival, however, he concentrated on not screaming. He succeeded in his brief moments of consciousness between fainting fits on the way to hospital. But his resolve had worn thin by the time he arrived, and he felt very thankful for the chloroform in the operating theatre. When he next awoke, he was but one patient in a long row of beds.

His wounds caused him excruciating pain, but pain he could endure. The true torment came from the burning itch crawling under his bandages. He writhed in a futile effort to escape it. If hospital staff hadn't belted his limbs to the bed frame, he'd have clawed his skin off. Or what remained of it, anyway.

Once they'd tied him down, he'd had nothing to forestall his madness but counting the seconds until his next dose of morphine. After a half-dozen doses, he lost count.

At some point between doses, he heard a voice. He ignored it as he'd come to ignore all hospital sounds—the cries and moans of his fellow patients, the chatter of the staff, and his own fever-induced auditory hallucinations. The cacophony rose and fell around him. But the voice didn't abate. With nothing better to distract him, he supposed he might as well listen to it.

"—hope you appreciate the sacrifice, Mr Warren," it concluded in a brisk tone.

Aubrey gathered what few wits remained to him and concentrated on opening his eyes.

The speaker was an angel.

No, that was ludicrous. It'd take more than a mere brain fever to sway his rational mind into believing in angels. He'd given up hope of angelic intervention long ago, when yet another one of his workhouse playmates died crying out for a mother she'd never known. A sparrow couldn't fall without God watching, but He seemed blind to impoverished children.

Still, angel or no, the figure above him sat tall and elegant, with a golden halo.

Hope thrilled through Aubrey's chest. "Lindsey?"

"No," said the figure, "though I can see how one might become confused."

Disappointment sobered him, and he realised the voice belonged to a woman. A woman with a striking resemblance to Lindsey.

"Good morning, Miss Althorp," Aubrey tried to say, but the words tangled up somewhere between his throat and his tongue. Only a creaking whine escaped him.

Miss Althorp cocked her head to one side. "I'd ask if I could do anything for you, but I doubt I'd receive an intelligible reply."

Aubrey said nothing, his mind afire with questions. Why had she come here? What did she want from him? Where was Lindsey? Doubtless Lindsey had more pressing concerns—like preventing the entire mill complex from collapsing, assuming it hadn't done so already. Whatever his business, it had kept him from Aubrey's bedside. If he'd ever intended to visit at all. Aubrey supposed it was stupid to hope for such. In the midst of berating himself, he realised Miss Althorp had continued speaking.

"I'm told you enjoy engineering periodicals," she said. "I brought some along, though you don't seem in any condition to read them."

So she'd come to taunt him. How sweet.

"Shall I read aloud, then?"

Aubrey blinked in surprise.

Miss Althorp took it as consent. She picked up a magazine from beyond Aubrey's field of vision and began declaiming.

"'We suppose that everybody having worked on the plan laid down in our issue of the 16th of April, has succeeded in drawing that mysterious spark out of the inert matter under his hands—'"

Aubrey instantly recognised the editorial style of *The English Mechanic and World of Science*.

"'—we say mysterious spark advisedly, for who can tell but what the essence of the life principle be not involved in that strange and vivid manifestation?'"

His attention wavered somewhere between frictional electricity and Leyden jars, but he appreciated the distraction from his sorry state. He drifted off entirely when she began reciting the Ellershausen process for refining iron.

When next he woke to the prick of a needle in his arm, Miss Althorp had gone. She had left a stack of magazines in her place.

♋

Miss Rook, it would give me great pleasure to make you my bride.

Lindsey left Clarence's study in a rage. As his swift strides carried him through the hall to the top of the stair, he banked the smouldering coals of his temper. He couldn't imagine any woman accepting a marriage proposal delivered in a furious shout.

Miss Rook, would you be so kind as to become my wife?

Cold feet couldn't prevent him from descending the staircase, however slowly. As he sank down, step by step, he ran through his proposal again and again, trying to make it pleasing to his ear in form, if not in content.

My dear Miss Rook, your brother is a monstrous ass and my continued liberty depends on shackling myself to you, and you to me, regardless of our individual wishes. Shall we wed?

By the time he alighted on the ground floor, he was angry again. His white knuckles clenched the banister as he closed his eyes and took a deep, steadying breath. It wasn't Miss Rook's fault her brother was a lying, cheating, conniving wretch intent on ruining Lindsey's life. She was Rowena's friend. If he had to marry, a familiar face was preferable. And besides, she...

Lindsey attempted to recall any of Miss Rook's finer qualities, and realised he knew none. Rowena thought her a worthy companion, though due to her own merits or Lindsey's insistence upon maintaining his friendship with Clarence, he couldn't say.

No matter. His own feelings on the occasion were irrelevant. It must be done. It would be done. Even if he would've preferred to refuse Clarence's offer and go to prison, he wouldn't let Aubrey suffer the same fate.

Besides, Miss Rook... could play the piano?

Lindsey sighed, straightened his cravat, and marched to the morning room. The door hung wide open. He paused on the threshold.

218

The morning room remained just as Lindsey remembered it—furiously chartreuse. As Clarence promised, its sole occupant was his sister, her hands full of embroidery. She seemed unaware of his arrival.

Lindsey gazed upon his unfortunate bride-to-be. Even in her own element, away from the crush of society, she appeared small. Her thin, pursed lips and narrowed eyes expressed grave concern, far more than needlework required. She'd pulled back her pale brown hair into a severe bun, to which a lilac ribbon added no levity. The bright chartreuse of the room made her look doubly washed-out.

Seconds ticked past. Lindsey gave up postponing the inevitable and announced himself.

Miss Rook's head shot up. Her grey eyes widened. Lindsey hurried to beg her pardon. She forced out a staccato greeting as she rose and set her embroidery aside with trembling hands. He made a small bow. She curtsied in return.

"Forgive the intrusion," said Lindsey. "May I enter?"

She nodded with an ineptly-disguised look of confusion.

Lindsey stepped into the room, hesitated, then crossed the carpet to stand before her. How to begin? He recalled the proposals he'd read in his novels. Few of those conditions applied to his current predicament, but he found some parallels.

"If I might have your hand," he said.

She gave it, her expression growing still more confused.

Lindsey dropped to one knee.

"Oh!" cried Miss Rook.

"Miss Rook," said Lindsey. It was more difficult than he'd expected to keep his eyes on her face; they seemed to want to fall to the floor. With his attention focused on maintaining eye contact, it was almost impossible to remember the speech he'd prepared. "It—it would be an honour—would you—"

He swallowed. Miss Rook blinked at him. He tried again.

"Would you do me the honour of becoming my bride?" Not quite as elegant as he'd hoped, but it did the trick.

Miss Rook gasped. Her grip on his hand tightened. Yet she said nothing.

"Miss Rook?" Lindsey asked.

"I..." she began, her pale cheeks blotched with blush. "That is to say... Do you truly wish...?"

"Yes," Lindsey lied.

As soon as he did, he regretted it. A lie was an inauspicious beginning to any marriage. Even one of convenience.

Miss Rook didn't notice his discomfort, overwhelmed by her own. "But, Mr Althorp—!"

"Lindsey," he corrected gently.

"Of course," she hurried to add. "Forgive me—Sir Lindsey—"

That wasn't at all what Lindsey had meant, but the poor girl looked so upset already, he didn't dare correct her again. She continued regardless.

"—it's only—I hadn't supposed you were the marrying kind!"

Lindsey balked. "I beg your pardon?"

She clapped her free hand over her mouth, mortified, and mumbled through it. "I said I hadn't supposed you were the marrying kind, sir."

"Whatever do you mean by that?" Lindsey asked, though he had a creeping feeling he knew exactly what she meant, and she wasn't the only person in his circle of acquaintance to hold that opinion.

Miss Rook made a fist of her hand, allowing more of her voice to slip out around it. "Forgive me, please, I must have misunderstood..."

"Misunderstood what, Miss Rook?" Lindsey said softly. Her voice sounded so small, he feared to speak any louder, lest he overpower her entirely.

Despite his efforts, she looked thoroughly miserable as she replied, "I'd assumed you and Mr Warren had... an understanding, of a sort. At least, he seems to hold you in high regard, and you... and Rowena said... and my brother... but no, it cannot be, for you couldn't be so cruel as to offer me marriage when your heart belonged to another, could you, Sir Lindsey? Though I fear it must come as a crushing blow to Mr Warren."

Were it not for Miss Rook's convulsive grip, Lindsey would've sunk to the floor.

"Sir Lindsey?" she asked, as he bowed his head.

"Forgive me," said Lindsey, blinking away the burn of unshed tears. "The last few days..."

"The factory," she murmured. Louder, she added, "Please, accept my condolences. Such a terrible accident. But so few casualties—a miracle, surely?"

A miracle. Lindsey caught a bitter laugh in his throat, lest it escape and become an anguished howl. "Yes. All spared, apart from Mr Smith and Mr Warren."

A cry of anguish tore through the air. To Lindsey's astonishment, it didn't issue from his own mouth. He lifted his head and saw Miss Rook's face mirror his distress.

"Mr Warren!?" she echoed. "It can't be!"

"You didn't know?" Lindsey asked.

She shook her head with violence and snatched her hand away to cover her face.

Lindsey leapt to his feet. He raised his hands to her shoulders in an instinctive gesture of comfort, but a sudden awareness of propriety stopped him short. His arms hung in mid-air, uncertain and useless. "I'm sorry, I thought you knew—"

She pulled her face from her hands, saw him looming over her, and shrank away. "No, I'm sorry, I should have—"

Lindsey lowered his arms and stepped back. "We're both sorry, then. Equals at last." A lame smile twitched at his lips.

Miss Rook tried to return it, and failed. "Mr Warren—is he—?"

Lindsey swallowed hard. "He's tended by excellent surgeons, and has my sister to comfort him. That's all we can do for now. Please sit down."

This last he added because Miss Rook had turned very pale. She allowed him to guide her to the least uncomfortable-looking armchair in the room and perched on the edge of its seat, her eyes downcast.

When she spoke again, her voice wavered with uncertainty. "How is it that while your friend lies wounded, you come to ask for my hand in marriage?"

Lindsey had underestimated her. He wasn't prepared for questions. Particularly not questions with awkward, painful answers. Before he could craft a suitable lie—and wonder how many lies he'd have to tell to secure this engagement, and how many he'd need to tell in the coming years to keep the resulting marriage from dissolving—she continued.

"Forgive me, Sir Lindsey," she begged, still not meeting his gaze. "It's not my place to question. I'm happy to accept your offer. I couldn't dream of a better prospect."

She looked up at last with a valiant attempt at a smile. A heart of stone couldn't lie to such a face. Lindsey stood no chance.

"Miss Rook," he said, "before you accept, I would have you know the whole. My heart—I hold Mr Warren—I cannot offer you what I've already given to him. I cannot be a husband to you in every way I ought. But I would offer you friendship, and a loving sister, and every comfort you ask. I wouldn't impose upon you in any way. Indeed, I daresay I'd impose on

221

you far less than most husbands." He failed to withhold a rueful smile. "In exchange, I'd ask you to keep our secret."

Miss Rook stared at him. "Then, you and Mr Warren are...?"

"As you've guessed," said Lindsey. "Though I'd prefer it not be so widely known."

"Of course. Hence your offer."

She didn't seem enthused. Lindsey couldn't blame her.

"I wouldn't make such an offer indiscriminately," he assured her. "You are my dear sister's friend, and your brother is... well."

Miss Rook bit her cuticles. Then she put down her hand and lifted her chin. Her shoulders twitched, almost straightening before falling back into their customary slump, but her chin remained up. "Sir Lindsey, before I accept, I would have you know the whole."

Lindsey blinked. What possible secrets such a shrinking female might have, he couldn't fathom.

She didn't wait for him. "First, Mr Warren and I are well acquainted. We've corresponded through your sister these past months. I trust our continued friendship is... is acceptable?"

Lindsey, still stumbling over the revelation, took a moment to realise she sought his consent. "Yes, yes of course."

Miss Rook let out a tiny sigh of relief. "Thank you. Secondly, though my brother is, as you say, a dear friend to you..." She faltered again. Her eyes flicked over the room, seeking escape, perhaps, or courage. Courage she found, and continued. "He has not been so to me."

Yesterday, Lindsey would've never believed Clarence capable of cruelty towards anyone, much less his own sister. Today, it seemed obvious. It enraged Lindsey to think any brother—even Clarence—could harm such a gentle sister as Miss Rook. He expressed his anger in a quick clench of his fist. Miss Rook saw the motion before he could repress it. Her eyes widened. He relaxed his hand as rapidly as possible. He might fail as a husband in every other aspect, but by God, he'd be a better protector than her brother. She, lacking insight into his private resolve, rose to put distance between them.

"If we're to be wed," she said, keeping an anxious eye on his hands, "I will have nothing more to do with him. I will not receive him in our home. I will not be a guest at his mercy. If you must keep up your acquaintance with him, then I ask you not speak of it to me. I will not hear of him."

"Done," said Lindsey.

Her gaze returned to his face. "What?"

"As far as I'm concerned, he's dead to me the moment you accept." If not before.

"Oh. Thank you." She seemed on the verge of saying more, but held back.

"Is there anything else?" Lindsey asked, thinking perhaps she required gentle prompting.

"Yes," Miss Rook worked out at last. Then silence.

If her first condition revealed a clandestine friendship with a bachelor of high character but low birth, and her second condition demanded the exile of her only brother, Lindsey couldn't imagine what her third condition might be. He hoped their marriage wouldn't be an endless parade of skeletons from closets. His nerves wouldn't stand it. Though at least he'd never be bored.

"Third..." She drew in a great breath and burst out, "I'm to be permitted to study engineering!"

Lindsey stared at her. "What?"

Miss Rook seemed to fear she'd reached the end of her potential *fiancé*'s patience. She repeated her request at a much lower volume, with the addendum, "If the notion doesn't offend you, Sir Lindsey."

"Not at all," Lindsey forced out, preoccupied with the question of how the deuce a nice young lady like Miss Rook got mixed up in engineering. His own interest in the subject had been minimal-to-nonexistent until... Oh. "Is that how you came to correspond with Mr Warren?"

Miss Rook nodded meekly.

Lindsey smiled. "Then it seems I'll have an engineer for a wife."

She chanced a smile in return. It didn't last. "My brother—"

"Has no objection to the match," said Lindsey, which was enough of the truth for now. He held out his hand.

Miss Rook took it. "Thank you, Sir Lindsey."

"Just Lindsey."

Her second smile prevailed. "Then you may call me Emmeline."

CHAPTER TWENTY-THREE

To Sir Lindsey Althorp,

TAKE NOTICE that by virtue of the provisions of the Boiler Explosions Act, 1882, 45 and 46 Vict., c. 22, we hereby require you to attend personally before us at the Rook Mill offices on Monday the 13th day of June at one of the clock in the afternoon, for the purpose of being examined upon oath upon the following matters, that is to say, the causes and circumstances attending the explosion of a Boiler which occurred at Rook Mill the morning of Wednesday the 8th day of June.

AND TAKE NOTICE that we also require you then and there to produce all books, papers or documents, which may be in your possession, or under your control, containing any information relative to the matters aforesaid.

AND WE FURTHER GIVE YOU NOTICE that under Section 7 of the said Act the Court may order the costs and expenses of this Formal Investigation, or any part thereof, to be paid by you, or any person summoned before us.

Given under our hands this 10th day of June.

Mr Gordon & Mr Lawrence

NOTE. — Any person neglecting or refusing to attend as required by this Summons will incur a penalty not exceeding Ten Pounds.

࿐

LINDSEY DIDN'T KNOW what he was doing.

Rowena would say this was true regardless of what occupied him, but it was especially true today. This wasn't a dinner party or a night out at the theatre. This was an inquest. An investigation called to order more expediently than most, because one man had died, and another—but Lindsey tried not to dwell on Aubrey's fate. Rowena assured him Aubrey was "stable" and "comfortable." Lindsey had to trust she spoke true.

In the meantime, the law compelled him to return to the scene of the explosion.

He arrived at the mill offices promptly at quarter to one. The offices, situated across the yard from the boiler shed, and sheltered by the mill itself, had escaped the explosion with no more damage than shattered windows. There, Lindsey found the Court.

A Court appointed by the Board of Trade had no judge, jury, or bailiff. It did, however, have a barrister. Mr Gordon had twenty-three years of experience in his field, and his partner Mr Lawrence was an equally-experienced engineer. The two of them comprised the entire Court.

Mr Gordon was short and thin, his face overpowered by an enormous bottle-brush moustache. Very little impressed him. Lindsey certainly didn't.

Mr Gordon interrogated Lindsey with the assumption that he'd arranged the explosion for insurance purposes. Lindsey resented the implication. However, he couldn't give the true reason he'd never endanger the mill without condemning Aubrey along with himself, so he kept his answers perfunctory. Yes, he was satisfied with the mill's profits. No, he wasn't in urgent need of funds. He had no gambling debts, no expensive habits, no financial strain of any kind. His sister wasn't shopping him out of house and home.

Mr Lawrence, taller and rounder than Mr Gordon, listened with his arms crossed over his ample bosom and a bored look on his black-bearded face. He had no further questions for Lindsey. However, both he and Mr Gordon expressed a preference that Lindsey not leave Manchester and, if that proved impossible, they'd prefer he remained on English soil.

Lindsey readily agreed. He made one request in return—that they permit him to witness the rest of the investigation.

Mr Gordon and Mr Lawrence exchanged speaking glances.

"I see no reason not to grant it," said Mr Lawrence.

Mr Gordon conceded.

⟡

AFTER LINDSEY'S INTERVIEW came the interrogations of every workaday soul present at the mill during the explosion. The questions filled the hours between Monday afternoon and Thursday morning. Overall, the workers' testimonies indicated the mill's closure would cause great displeasure. To paraphrase one Miss Mary Brandon, aged six-and-twenty, it was among the few mills where one needn't suffer unseemly advances from one's superiors to secure one's pay. (Her actual testimony expressed this fact in far more colourful terms.) Most of the female workforce agreed. They also agreed that, while the motions of the walk-out were premeditated, the actual date and time came as a surprise. The male population denied all knowledge of the walk-out and claimed to have simply followed the crowd. While many had heard of Mr Smith and Mr Warren, none knew either gentleman particularly well.

Lindsey, to his shame, didn't know any of his workers particularly well, either. He didn't recognise anyone until Miss Sarah Brewster. She gave no sign she recognised him in return. Mr Gordon gave her no chance to.

"Miss Brewster," he said as she took her seat in the centre of the office, with the three men looking down at her. "Please describe the events of the day in question, to the best of your ability."

Miss Brewster took an impatient breath. "I arrived at the mill when my shift started and worked as normal. About a quarter-hour into it, Mr Warren taps me on the shoulder and begs a word."

"Was it usual," asked Mr Gordon, "for Mr Warren to ask to speak to you?"

"No, sir. Most times he avoided me."

"Then why did he seek you out?"

"I was getting to that." She flashed a sarcastic half-smile. "He takes me to the stairwell and tells me the boiler's about to go sky-high, and could I please get my girls to leave in a quiet and orderly fashion."

Mr Gordon leaned forward. "Mr Warren knew the boiler was about to explode?"

Miss Brewster shrugged. "He's an engineer, isn't he?"

"He is a coal-passer."

"Still works with the engine. I figured he knew best, so I tapped my girls on the shoulder and we walked out."

"You went on strike."

"That's what I told 'em, yes, on account of when you tell folks the boiler's ready to blow, they tend to rush the exits and crush each other something awful."

"You'd trained these women to be ready to walk out at a moment's notice?"

226

"Best to be prepared," said Miss Brewster.

"You've attempted to organise a workers' union in the past," said Mr Gordon.

Miss Brewster shrugged again.

"In fact," Mr Gordon continued, "you and Mr Warren planned the explosion as a deliberate anarchist attack on the mill!"

"I say!" cried Lindsey.

Mr Gordon and Mr Lawrence ignored Lindsey's outburst, both focused on Miss Brewster's reaction. She blinked at them.

"Well?" said Mr Gordon. "It's true, isn't it?"

"No," said Miss Brewster. "It isn't."

"You expect me to believe you're incapable of such an act?"

"Don't expect you to believe it, no," said Miss Brewster. "But it's true regardless. I'm for workers' rights, not anarchy. And Mr Warren is for neither."

Lindsey didn't agree with her last remark, but could hardly say so aloud. He settled for a disapproving frown. Miss Brewster ignored it.

⌒

THE INQUEST CALLED in Mr Jennings on Thursday afternoon.

Where was Mr Jennings on the morning of the explosion? In his office—that is, until the walk-out, at which point he exited the office and held a short conversation with Mr Warren, who feared the boiler might explode. Mr Warren departed, and the boiler exploded shortly thereafter. Mr Jennings hadn't seen Mr Smith at all. But, as Mr Jennings explained, that wasn't unusual, as Mr Smith had practised terrible work habits for years prior to the explosion. The Court returned to the question of Mr Warren.

"Mr Warren is on record here as a 'day coal-passer'," said Mr Gordon, flipping through the payroll records. "However, earlier records refer to him as a senior clerk...?"

Mr Jennings coughed. "He and Mr Smith had a disagreement. I was forced to demote him."

Mr Gordon raised his brows and lowered his spectacles. "What sort of disagreement?"

Lindsey didn't move, didn't dare breathe, lest he reveal all through some nervous tic.

Mr Jennings coughed again. "I believe Mr Smith made some disparaging remarks regarding Mr Warren's parentage."

"And how did Mr Warren take these remarks? Badly, would you say?"

"If forced to, yes."

"Badly enough to seek revenge?"

"Certainly not!" Mr Jennings spluttered on before Mr Gordon could continue his interrogation. "Sir, I realise you're not acquainted with the young man in question, but I can assure you a thousand times over that Mr Warren is nothing if not steadfast, trustworthy, and devoted to his work above all else! He'd never allow anything so petty as *revenge* to—"

"So devoted to his work," Mr Gordon interrupted, "that he might murder his rival to regain his lost position?"

But Mr Jennings shook his head vehemently. "Not in the least! He far preferred engineering to clerking. It was always his ambition."

Mr Gordon lowered one eyebrow and raised the other to new heights. "Was it?"

"Yes! That's why I particularly asked Mr Cartwright to make room for him among the boiler-keepers!"

"Quite an extraordinary effort to make on behalf of a man who'd already caused trouble."

Mr Jennings puffed out his chest at the affront. "I assure you, sir, that was an isolated incident occurring under extraordinary circumstances. Aside from that, Mr Warren is—was—an exceptional clerk."

⊙

THE COURT NEXT called the chief engineer, Mr Cartwright. Mr Lawrence had at him first. Lindsey couldn't follow the technical details of their rapid-fire interview, but he thought the gist might be that the boiler was properly inspected and in good repair right up to the morning of the explosion. Judging by the look on Mr Lawrence's face, this wasn't how most investigations ran. Still, he surrendered his witness to Mr Gordon.

"How do you explain the gauges?" Mr Gordon demanded. "All their needles stopped at a point indicating optimal conditions. Coincidence?"

Mr Cartwright shook his head. "All I can say is they weren't so when I left."

"About that—you say you left at seven o'clock? For what purpose?"

"I had a letter telling me my sister was dying."

"My condolences," said Lindsey. Both Mr Gordon and Mr Lawrence glared at him for speaking out of turn.

"Save 'em," said Mr Cartwright. "She wasn't even ill. Didn't know what I was on about when I turned up on her doorstep in Liverpool."

"May the Court see this letter?" said Mr Gordon.

Mr Cartwright produced the article in question. Mr Gordon examined it with rigor, but found no fault in its veracity.

"With all due respect for your fraternal devotion," said Mr Gordon as he returned the letter, "the Court has learned by your own testimony that the second engineer, Mr Hepworth, didn't appear for work that morning, and therefore the Court must ask—what possessed you to leave the mill in the hands of a mere coal-passer?"

"I wouldn't call Mr Warren 'mere' anything," said Mr Cartwright. Lindsey privately agreed.

"How would you describe him, then?" asked Mr Gordon.

While Mr Cartwright was more taciturn than Mr Jennings on the subject of Aubrey, he had much the same testimony. Yes, Mr Warren was clever enough to have done it, and yes, he could be said to have had a motive, but Mr Cartwright didn't believe Mr Warren capable of such an act. In Mr Cartwright's words, Mr Warren had too much respect for himself, the mill, and engineering to sully it with murder.

⁓

THE NEXT LOGICAL step was to summon the second engineer, Mr Hepworth, and discover why he'd taken an unexpected holiday the morning of the explosion. Unfortunately for the Court, Mr Hepworth was nowhere to be found.

Whilst the Court searched for him, a telegram arrived from Withington Hospital. Mr Warren was awake, aware, and well enough for a short interview.

The Court lost no time in travelling to Withington Hospital.

CHAPTER TWENTY-FOUR

LINDSEY SPENT THE journey to Withington with his heart in his throat, unable to look Mr Gordon or Mr Lawrence in the eye. He stared out the train window, seeing nothing until the hospital loomed into view.

Withington Hospital's architecture seemed welcoming enough, designed around an open yard for patients' exercise. Fresh air flowed through the wards. Sunshine reflected off the glazed brick walls and the nurses' starched white uniforms. Yet Lindsey felt only dread. The friendliest, most scientifically-advanced hospital in England remained a hospital. He could wish for no better place for Aubrey to receive treatment, but he still wished his Aubrey wasn't in hospital at all.

Aubrey's ward held thirty or so patients in two rows of beds. The wall between each bed opened up into a window, beneath which stood a waist-high cabinet. A long table ran down the centre of the ward. Nurses retrieved medicine and bandages from its drawers. All nodded politely to the Court. Lindsey, busy searching the ward for any sign of Aubrey, barely met their eyes.

Less than a minute after they entered the ward—which felt like an hour to Lindsey—a surgeon approached the Court and shook hands with Mr Gordon and Mr Lawrence. He tried to do the same with Lindsey, but Lindsey took no notice of him. He'd spotted a familiar pair of worn boots under the foot of a particular bed. It took considerable self-control to keep him from leaping over the table to reach them.

"Sir Lindsey?" said Mr Gordon.

Lindsey whipped his head around to reply. "Yes?"

"We're ready to proceed, if you are."

Lindsey forced a nod.

The surgeon led them to the bed and began explaining Aubrey's condition to the Court. Lindsey heard none of it, his attention arrested by the sight of Aubrey himself.

Aubrey lay strapped to the bed, his limbs belted down to its four corners. A hundred needle-pricks had bruised the crook of his left elbow to a violent shade of purple; his right arm had a splint. Thick bandages covered the right half of his face. The left half looked as white as the linen surrounding it. His cheek had hollowed. His cracked lips parted for shallow, intermittent breaths. His eye, sunken in its socket, rolled back and forth with only the barest sliver visible beneath its heavy lid.

After his initial glance, Lindsey turned away. He couldn't bring himself to look again, lest his emotions bring him to his knees by Aubrey's side, where he belonged.

Mr Gordon, having no such weakness, sat on the cabinet beside Aubrey's bed. "Can you hear me, Mr Warren?"

An abbreviated hiss came in reply, almost inaudible under the omnipresent hospital murmur. Belatedly, Lindsey realised it was as much of a "yes" as Aubrey could manage.

Mr Gordon continued. "I represent a Court appointed by the Board of Trade to investigate the explosion at Rook Mill. Will you answer my questions truthfully and in good faith, under penalty of perjury?"

Another hiss from Aubrey. Lindsey wanted to scream.

"Good," said Mr Gordon. "Now—can you tell me what happened the day of the incident? From the beginning."

Lindsey stuffed his hands into his trouser pockets to keep from throttling Mr Gordon. *From the beginning.* When his Aubrey could hardly breathe, much less recite an in-depth account of what'd likely been the most painful day of his life.

A thin whisper flowed from Aubrey's lips. Mr Gordon bent close to catch it, taking notes all the while.

Lindsey stared at the vaulted ceiling and tried not to wish he could trade places with Mr Gordon. He wouldn't take notes—he'd take Aubrey's hand, cradling the pain-clenched knuckles. He'd tell Aubrey he needn't exert himself so, that Lindsey trusted in his innocence, that he could rest. He'd tell him about the new house in Chorlton-cum-Hardy and the room set aside for him. He'd lift Aubrey out of bed and carry him there himself.

When Mr Gordon finished, Mr Lawrence stepped in and inquired about the boiler's state prior to the explosion. Aubrey gasped out his answers. Half an hour later, Mr Lawrence stood, apparently satisfied with Aubrey's testimony.

The surgeon turned to Lindsey. "Do you have any further questions for Mr Warren?"

Lindsey stared at him, then shook his head, dropping his gaze to the floor.

꙳

THE INVESTIGATION STAGNATED. Lindsey, awaiting word from the Court, paced his Chorlton-cum-Hardy house. Rowena left his side for an afternoon to attend to business in London. Lindsey thought of returning to Aubrey in her absence, but he remembered her warnings. Furthermore, Charles seemed under strict orders from her to keep Lindsey away from Withington. No matter where in the house Lindsey went, Charles manifested between him and any outdoor egress. Lindsey felt both relieved and surprised when Rowena returned in the evening with Emmeline in tow.

Emmeline looked much happier than she had in London, though the faint circles under her eyes told Lindsey she, too, feared for Aubrey. She expressed her hopes for his recovery upon her arrival. Lindsey accepted them as graciously as he could.

"Have you seen him?" she pressed on. Something of Lindsey's pain must've shown in his face, for she added, "Forgive me, I don't mean to pry—"

"It's all right." Lindsey forced a smile. "Yes, I have."

"How is he?"

"He's... alive."

Emmeline's hopeful expression wavered. Lindsey hurried to bolster it.

"I'm sure a visit from yourself would do much for his spirits. Rowena's seen him already; she must've told you."

"I did," said Rowena, taking Emmeline's arm. "He's doing quite well, given the circumstances. Do cheer up, dearest. Why don't you sit down in the parlour? I'll join you in just a moment. Charles will look after you in the meantime."

Emmeline smiled weakly and followed Charles out of the foyer. Rowena turned to Lindsey.

"I apologise for not giving advanced notice of our guest," she said, and continued over Lindsey's assurances that he didn't mind whatsoever. "Her life in London has become an absolute nightmare. I don't know what's provoked Clarence, but he's in a devil of a mood. I thought it best if she stayed with me. It won't attract any notice—she's about to become my sister, after all. You don't mind, do you?"

Lindsey, having already told her as much, and distracted by his guilt at provoking Clarence into doing God-knew-what to Emmeline, took a moment to muster an appropriate reply. Rowena accepted it with a nod and swept off to tend to her guest.

The next morning dawned dull and grey. The miserable weather threatened to drag down the dispositions of everyone under Lindsey's roof. Rather than allow that to happen, Rowena proposed they spend their day exploring Manchester.

"I'm told it offers a wealth of scientific interest to the intelligent tourist," she informed Lindsey with a sidelong glance at Emmeline.

Emmeline took to Manchester as if born to the shriek of a factory whistle and the clang of steel-on-steel. Lindsey supposed this explained how she and Aubrey got along so well. He wished he could share her enthusiasm for the city—and indeed, the way her face lit up when she caught sight of the billowing chimneys brought a smile to his own lips—but he could only think of how Aubrey, too, would've enjoyed this outing. He resolved to repeat the adventure when Aubrey left hospital.

"Don't you agree, Lindsey?"

"Eh?" Lindsey glanced down to meet inquiring looks from his *fiancée* and sister; Emmeline confused, Rowena sardonic.

"I... I was just asking," Emmeline said after a prompting eyebrow from Rowena, "if you also thought the mill's architecture had a certain, er, beauty to it?"

Lindsey looked up to find they'd wandered into the yard of an unfamiliar factory. The glazing bars in the windows had the perfect delicacy of spiderwebs. He mentioned it. Emmeline seemed relieved.

Upon their return to Chorlton-cum-Hardy, Charles handed Lindsey a telegram from the Court.

HEPWORTH IN CUSTODY. QUESTIONING AT NINE TOMORROW. WILL NOT WAIT FOR YOU.

⌑

"FOR THE RECORD: your name?"

"Tim Hepworth."

"Occupation?"

"Second engineer."

"Where were you at the time of the explosion?"

Hepworth gave the Court a blank look. Lindsey didn't tap his foot on the floor, despite his nerves. Hepworth didn't appear much younger than forty. Certainly too old to think silence could save him from the consequences of his actions.

Mr Gordon consulted his paperwork. "According to the testimony of your superiors, you should've been tending the boiler."

"Yes, sir."

"And were you?"

"No, sir."

"And why not?"

Hepworth kept mum.

Mr Gordon adjusted his spectacles. "Need I remind you, Mr Hepworth, your questioning is part of an official investigation to determine the cause of a boiler explosion that has already killed one man and may well claim the life of another before the day is out?"

Lindsey flinched.

Hepworth had gone pale. "You needn't remind me, sir."

"Then tell me," said Mr Gordon. "Where were you at the time of the explosion?"

Hepworth mumbled something unintelligible.

"Speak up, Mr Hepworth!"

"I was at the bloody races," Hepworth snapped.

Lindsey gaped at him. "What the devil were you doing at the races?"

A glare from Mr Gordon was not unlike the glare of an Etonian tutor with cane in hand. Lindsey didn't shrink from it physically, but he thought his soul might.

"With all due respect, Sir Lindsey," said Mr Gordon, his tone implying very little respect indeed, "you're here under the condition that you do not interfere with the proceedings. If you cannot control yourself, I must ask you to leave."

"My apologies," Lindsey assured him. "It won't happen again."

Mr Gordon narrowed his eyes, then returned to Hepworth. "What were you doing at the races?"

"It's not like I make a habit of it," muttered Hepworth.

"All the more reason to question your presence there," said Mr Gordon. "Now answer me."

Hepworth forced a sigh of annoyance even Lindsey could see through. "Because I'd come into a small sum and thought I deserved a holiday to celebrate it. Figured Mr Cartwright and Warren could get on without me for a day."

"Apparently they couldn't," said Mr Gordon, "for on the very day you abandoned them, the boiler exploded."

Hepworth winced.

Mr Gordon continued. "When you say you 'came into a small sum,' what exactly do you mean?"

A bead of sweat appeared on Hepworth's temple. Lindsey watched it trickle down the side of his face to drip off his jaw in total silence.

"Mr Hepworth—" Mr Gordon began.

"Smith gave me five pounds," Hepworth blurted.

Mr Gordon blinked. "I beg your pardon?"

"He gave me five pounds to skip work and said there'd be another five in it for me if I kept mum about the how and why."

Mr Gordon opened his mouth to question further, but Hepworth's tongue ran on like a mad bull.

"He said it was a lark, he was playing a trick on Warren, and I thought, good, take the new man down a peg—you should've seen how chummy Mr Cartwright and Warren were, Warren'd hardly been there a month— but I never thought Smith meant to blow anyone up! Honest!"

Hepworth's panicked eyes flicked between Lindsey and Mr Gordon. Lindsey, with years of practice speaking to his father, kept his face blank even as his mind blazed with the horrific truth. The explosion was no accident. Aubrey was the victim of a deliberate, premeditated attack.

Mr Gordon had no such thoughts to distract him from his relentless pursuit of the truth. "Did you help Mr Smith sabotage the boiler?"

"No!" said Hepworth. "I just didn't show up to work, that's all!"

"You taught Mr Smith how the boiler functioned, then?"

"No!"

"You told him where he might go to attain such knowledge?"

"If I told him anything, I told him to go to hell!" Hepworth cried. "I'd tell him so now, if he weren't already there!"

Lindsey, harbouring many of the same sentiments, excused himself from the Court for a breath of fresh air.

Once Lindsey reentered the office, he discovered Mr Gordon and Mr Lawrence busy tearing it apart for proof that Smith had the mechanical knowledge required to sabotage the boiler. They'd gone over his desk already and turned up nothing. The Court recalled Mr Jennings, who could offer no insight except to say Smith's desk was such a mess that papers had been known to slip out of drawers and fall down into the gap between the drawers and the interior wall of the desk. Thus, Mr Lawrence was persuaded to disassemble it. Among the ensuing wreckage, the Court found a single hand-drawn diagram.

"Thomas Cowburn's safety valve!" Mr Lawrence panted with exertion as he showed Lindsey the paper. "And copied out of *The Engineer*, I'll bet my hat on it."

Lindsey could make little sense of the drawing under his nose, but he nodded anyway, which satisfied Mr Lawrence.

In fact, the Court felt altogether satisfied Smith possessed both the motive and the means to sabotage the boiler. Likely Smith hadn't intended to off himself in his revenge against Mr Warren, but, as Mr Lawrence put it, "What goes around, comes around." The Court adjourned to write up its report on the incident for the Board of Trade, and bid Lindsey *adieu*.

⁂

LINDSEY LEAPT OUT of a hansom and trotted up the steps of the Chorlton-cum-Hardy house. Charles barely managed to open the door in time.

"Where's my sister?" Lindsey demanded.

"In the library, sir," replied Charles. He might've said more, but Lindsey hurried off.

"Rowena!" he called out as he flung open the library door, and halted. "Oh. Miss—Emmeline."

Emmeline sat on the floor by the hearth, a variety of magazines fanned out around her. Rowena stood with one hand on her chin, frowning down at them. Emmeline looked up at Lindsey's entrance; Rowena didn't.

Lindsey recalled the iron rule of the Althorp household—never interrupt Rowena with her friends—and mixed an apology into his greeting. Emmeline would've stood to reply, but Rowena stopped her with an outstretched hand, lest she disturb the papers. Emmeline did her able best to curtsy from the floor.

"We're selecting reading material for Mr Warren," Rowena replied to Lindsey's unspoken question, still not looking at him. "Emmeline's brought her sheet music."

Lindsey gave Rowena a puzzled look, though she didn't turn to regard it. Emmeline, however, noticed. She caught his attention with a little wave and held up a sheaf of handwritten pages for his perusal. Lindsey, still confused, took them and discovered they were engineering notes. Sheet music, indeed. He laughed.

"I know little of music," he confessed as he returned the papers to her, "but your compositions seem brilliant to me."

Emmeline blushed and mumbled her thanks to the carpet.

"Should I bring *The Engineer* again?" asked Rowena. "He seemed to enjoy it when I last—Emmeline, darling, what on earth is the matter?"

Emmeline's face had drained of colour. She flipped through her engineering notes in a panic.

"Emmeline?" asked Lindsey.

"Cowburn's safety valve is missing!" she cried.

Lindsey and Rowena exchanged a bewildered look.

"I beg your pardon?" said Rowena.

Emmeline flinched. "The design I copied out of *The Engineer*—it's not here!"

"You just gave it to Lindsey," Rowena explained patiently.

"No, she didn't," said Lindsey.

Rowena gave Lindsey a look indicating severe displeasure with his decision to contradict her.

Lindsey elaborated. "She gave me her engineering notes, but the illustration wasn't among them."

This explanation mollified Rowena. She turned a comforting smile on Emmeline. "Then you must have left it at home."

Emmeline didn't return her smile. "But I can't have! That is, if I have, then it's not in my piano-bench either, for I'm sure I left nothing behind, and—"

"Emmeline," Rowena gently interrupted, but Emmeline couldn't be stopped.

"—so I must've dropped it, which means it's out there for anyone to find, and if Clarence finds it—!"

Her grim prediction ended abruptly, its conclusion too terrible to voice. Her hand flew to her mouth as she cast a fearful glance at Lindsey and Rowena.

"Then we'll take the very next train to London," said Rowena, "and find it without delay."

Lindsey, meanwhile, tried to quiet the disturbing hunch in the back of his mind. He found he couldn't. "When did you last see the drawing? Are you certain it only went missing today?"

Emmeline's eyes widened farther than Lindsey had supposed possible. Rowena glared at him. He couldn't blame her. There was all her effort to calm Emmeline down, wasted.

"Forgive me," he added. "My questions are idle and unhelpful. I'm happy to accompany you home to distract Clarence from your aims."

"Would you?" said Emmeline.

The look she directed up at him contained more hopeful gratitude than Lindsey could bear. He forced a smile and ignored Rowena's look of suspicion.

CHAPTER TWENTY-FIVE

"Do you suppose Charles minds?" Emmeline asked on the ride from Lindsey's house to Manchester Central.

"Minds what, dearest?" Rowena replied without taking her eyes off the scenery.

"Having to hail a cab just as he's finished sending one away," said Emmeline.

Lindsey's stomach twisted with guilt.

"Charles knows what side his bread is buttered on," said Rowena.

Emmeline blushed and fixed her gaze on the approaching city.

They caught the train almost as it departed. The nearer it drew to London, the more Emmeline fidgeted with her gloves. Lindsey knew from experience how unnecessary movement annoyed Rowena, but Rowena said nothing of it. The journey continued in silence.

When the cab from Victoria Station pulled up to the Rook residence, Emmeline turned pale. Lindsey knew he ought to say something—comfort her, somehow—but his mind was miles away in Withington Hospital. The best he could manage was a brave smile as he handed her out of the cab. Emmeline mirrored it weakly. Rowena patted her arm. Lindsey went on ahead to the door.

"Sir Lindsey to see Mr Rook," he said to the parlour maid.

The maid peered around him to give the ladies an inquiring look, then directed the same up at him.

"Miss Rook has come to retrieve her sheet music," he added.

The maid didn't appear to believe him. "Mr Rook is at his club, sir."

"Then," said Lindsey, "I'll leave Miss Rook and Miss Althorp in your capable hands while I go meet him."

The maid curtsied.

This time, Lindsey caught the cab before it rattled off to its next fare.

⟡

BOTH CLARENCE AND Lindsey belonged to the same club in Pall Mall. Lindsey himself had sponsored Clarence for membership, a gesture he now bitterly regretted. He had half a mind to withdraw his own membership and seek fraternity somewhere else. Anywhere else, provided it was far from Clarence.

Lindsey asked for Clarence at the door. A footman directed him upstairs to the smoke-filled billiard room. There he found Clarence engaged in the activities one might expect.

"Lindsey!" Clarence cried with a grin upon spotting him, then bent forward to line up a neat shot with his cue.

"I'd like a word," said Lindsey.

"I suppose I have time for just the one." Clarence made the shot and handed the cue off to a fellow member, who handed over five shillings and took his place in the game.

"Another wager?" Lindsey asked as Clarence led him to an empty reading room down the hall.

"Do you intend to preach at me?" Clarence countered, shutting the door behind them. "I'm afraid you don't have the moral high ground, considering your proclivities."

Lindsey chose to ignore that remark. "The inquest is complete."

"Oh? Congratulations."

"They believe the boiler was sabotaged."

"Indeed."

"By Mr Smith, a clerk with no apparent knowledge of engineering."

"How enterprising of him."

"They found a drawing of a safety valve in his desk."

"Fascinating," Clarence deadpanned.

Lindsey blinked. He'd felt sure his last point would garner more of a reaction. He tried again. "Your sister is an engineer."

Clarence raised an eyebrow. "Is she, now?"

"Yes, and you damned well know she is, because you're the one who stole her safety valve diagram and planted it in Smith's desk!"

Clarence stared at him, then smiled. "Oh, well done."

"Is that all you have to say for yourself?" Lindsey demanded.

"What's left to say?" Clarence turned away to select an armchair. He found one to his liking, sat down, and leaned back.

Lindsey watched him in disbelief. "Why?"

"Isn't it obvious? I wanted the mill, and I wanted Mr Warren out of the way. There are my two birds, and the explosion, my single stone. I'd hoped to quietly remove him from your life—"

"What the devil is 'quiet' about blowing him up!?"

Clarence ignored Lindsey's outburst. "Had Smith succeeded, as he assured me he would, neither he nor Mr Warren would've been caught in the explosion. I intended to have Mr Warren, inexperienced engineer, take the fall for a tragic accident."

"But why?" Lindsey repeated. "Why would you do this?"

"I've told you already. I required funds. I needed to eject my spinster sister from my household and reclaim the mill. Unfortunately, and much to my surprise, you grew rapidly attached to the latter. It took some investigation to discover why, but once I had the confidence of my former employee—"

"Smith," Lindsey supplied, recalling the fight between that miserable wretch and his proud Aubrey.

"Precisely. He made the matter perfectly clear. From there I started to plan. I had to convince you the mill and its brooding little clerk—"

"Don't," said Lindsey.

Clarence checked himself at Lindsey's tone, and continued. "—weren't what you wanted. I spoke to Mr Warren directly and advised him his continued pursuit of you wouldn't end well."

Lindsey let out a hysterical laugh. "*His* pursuit of *me?*"

"Regardless, I made it clear he'd be happier elsewhere. He declined to heed my warning. My hand was forced. I turned to my sister's immodest hobby for the solution."

Lindsey stared, aghast, at the man he'd called his friend.

"You think me cruel," said Clarence.

"Oh, I think far worse than that!"

"Then you do me a disservice," Clarence continued as though Lindsey's hands weren't shaking with rage. "I did warn Mr Warren, after all. I gave him ample opportunity to remove himself from your company. Alas, he refused to see reason. He has only himself to blame for what he suffers now."

"No," said Lindsey. "I believe both myself and the law will blame you."

241

"You may blame me all you like, though I'd rather you didn't. As for the law, I doubt that will ever enter into it. In order for the law to blame me, you must tell them what transpired here. And you really can't afford to, Lindsey. If you turn me in for conspiracy to murder, I must confess my motive, and I'm afraid my motive doesn't reflect well on you. Or on Mr Warren, for that matter."

Lindsey's blood, boiling with righteous fury, ran suddenly cold.

Clarence grinned.

Lindsey refrained from slapping the grin off his traitorous face. "If you'd but asked me for the money, any sum you named, I'd have gladly surrendered it!"

"And be indebted to my dearest friend as well as my creditors? I think not."

"Yet my position as your 'dearest friend' didn't dissuade you from murdering—"

"It's hardly murder yet," said Clarence. Lindsey protested that Smith was very much deceased, but Clarence spoke over him. "Your precious clerk may not be so handsome as he once was, but he lives. For now."

"I warned you," Lindsey growled, "not to speak so lightly of him."

"And I warned you," Clarence replied, "that I could speak very lightly of your affair to very interested ears."

They exchanged glares. Lindsey's hot blood couldn't match Clarence's cold indifference.

"The mill for my sister and my silence," Clarence said when Lindsey looked away. "It's a fair price."

There was nothing fair about it, but Lindsey departed the club without further argument.

⁓

THE RETURN RIDE to Grosvenor Square didn't take long. Certainly not long enough for Lindsey to think of a plan.

When he arrived on the Rook doorstep, the bewildered parlour maid peered around him as if his narrow frame could hide Clarence from view.

"Mr Rook still at the club, sir?" she asked.

Lindsey nodded. She let him into the house and directed him to the morning room. He found Rowena and Emmeline methodically disassembling it. At his entrance, Emmeline bolted upright from the sewing basket she'd been rooting through.

"Clarence?" she asked, her voice shrill with fear.

"At his club," Lindsey assured her.

Emmeline sighed with relief and sank into a chair, then jumped up to flip over its cushion in search of her missing diagram.

Rowena, meanwhile, fixed Lindsey with a curious look. "Why haven't you remained with him?"

The truth stuck in Lindsey's throat. He knew he should tell Emmeline her search would prove fruitless. But Rowena's suspicious gaze stilled his tongue.

Rowena had never questioned his sudden engagement to Emmeline. On the contrary, she'd congratulated his cunning. For the first time in his life, she'd assumed he'd acted with intelligence. Lindsey, exhausted with fear for Aubrey's survival and reeling from Clarence's partial confession, hadn't possessed the energy to disabuse her of the notion. To do so now would be, at best, awkward. At worst... He had no desire to bring a fresh hailstorm of rage down on Emmeline's head. To say nothing of what the revelation of her brother's murderous plot would do to her nerves. Coming clean with Rowena would have to wait.

"Perhaps it'd be best if none of us were here when Clarence returns," he said.

Emmeline paused in her search, turning to give him a look of horror.

Lindsey, knowing how well-placed her fear was, added, "It may in fact be better for none of us to be in London at all."

Emmeline sat down again, hard.

Rowena, rather than replying to Lindsey's announcement, looked to Emmeline. "York is lovely this time of year. Particularly the Pelham estate. It's been ages since we've seen Charity."

"On such short notice?" asked Emmeline. "Wouldn't she mind?"

"Not in the least," said Rowena. "She'll be grateful for the company. How long do you need to pack?"

"No more than half an hour," said Emmeline. She glanced nervously at Lindsey. "If we have that long?"

"I'll make sure you do," he promised.

Her expression of relief twisted the knife in his ribs. "Will you accompany us?"

Rowena raised an eyebrow. "Thought I'd advise him to do so, I think it far more likely he'd prefer to remain in Manchester."

Lindsey didn't need to tell her she was right.

CHAPTER TWENTY-SIX

"YOU'RE GOING HOME today, Mr Warren," the nurse announced cheerfully as she changed Aubrey's bandages. "Isn't that nice?"

With morphine flowing through his veins, Aubrey could hardly recall where home was. But the nurse seemed so happy about his impending departure, Aubrey didn't wish to ruin her good mood, so he mumbled, "Yes," in return.

She beamed at him. "Your friend should be arriving shortly."

Aubrey frowned, ignoring the prickling pain under his bandages. His first impulse was to tell her he didn't have any friends. Then, slowly yet steadily, faces trickled into his mind from his memories. He struggled to match those faces up with the names of people who'd visited him in hospital. Miss Althorp had. He felt sure of it, thanks to the periodicals she'd left behind as proof. But he didn't think anyone could mistake her for his friend. Nor would she, as an unmarried woman of means, make an appropriate escort for a low-born bachelor, inverted invalid or no. Miss Rook was his friend, but again, an unwed lady, and he wasn't quite sure if he remembered her accompanying Miss Althorp, or if he'd imagined it. Everything had blurred together since the explosion.

He had a dim recollection of Lindsey's golden curls contrasted against the dark ceiling. But it was only a flash, and an impossible one. Lindsey wouldn't be so foolish as to come see him here. And yet, when he considered the word "friend" and all its implications, Lindsey's smile came foremost to mind. If he had a friend in this world, it was Lindsey. So it must've been Lindsey the nurse meant.

The thought of Lindsey typically inspired fond emotions. But the thought of Lindsey coming here, now, to risk his liberty for a glimpse of Aubrey's ruined body—that thought inspired only panic. Aubrey struggled

244

against the anodyne in his veins for a solution, and found one. He would leave hospital before Lindsey arrived.

The nurse, finished with his dressings and trusting in the morphine to keep him still, departed. Aubrey counted her steps as she went. When the last one echoed away, he sat up, balancing on his good elbow and ignoring the flash of agony rippling across his wounds.

The staff had removed his restraints some time ago—chronology had become difficult to reckon, though he thought it'd been a week, perhaps. At first, a nurse had come by once a day to get him up and walking down the ward. He'd needed two nurses to support him then, but he'd since graduated to a weary, self-reliant shuffle.

Now, he swung his legs over the edge of the bed and braced himself to stand.

"What're you about?"

Aubrey stopped, swallowed, and looked guiltily up.

The nurse had returned with something folded in her arms. "Eager to be off, are we?"

Aubrey looked at the floor.

"Well, it wouldn't do to wander out-of-doors in a nightgown, now would it? Here." She set the folded articles down on the bed beside him.

Aubrey glanced over and, with a jolt, recognised his own clothes. The trousers and stockings he'd worn upon his arrival; the drawers, shirt, waistcoat, and jacket provided by an unknown hand. He wondered what'd become of the waistcoat he'd worn the day of the explosion. More particularly, he wondered what'd become of the contents of its pockets. He hadn't seen the calling-card case Lindsey'd given him since that day.

"Where—" he started to ask, then stopped. The unintelligible croaking of his throat wasn't worth the pain it caused in his face.

"Yes," the nurse said patiently. "These are for you to wear."

Aubrey gave up.

He let the nurse put the clothes on him—modesty was a luxury he could ill-afford after untold weeks in hospital—and thanked her. Talking grew easier the more he exercised his right to speech. Walking didn't. His initial attempt to rise made his head swim, and startled the nurse besides. In the end, he made it to a chair three steps from the bed. There the nurse left him, telling him to be of good cheer and to wait for his friend to arrive.

Aubrey did wait, at first. He passed the time searching his pockets for the calling-card case. He'd just concluded he was foolish to think nobody had made off with such a valuable piece when he felt something cold and hard in his trouser pocket. Pulling it out into the light, he beheld a tarnished, battered, half-melted lump of silver, barely recognisable as what it'd once been. He put it away again, more determined than ever to escape before the gentle soul who'd given it to him stumbled in. Standing proved an unsteady and uncertain prospect, but he lurched up anyway.

"Where're you going?"

A man's voice. Aubrey planted his good hand on the back of his chair, locked his quaking knees, and looked up.

Halloway stood at the foot of his bed.

Aubrey stared, at a loss to understand Halloway's presence. His own actions, however, he could explain. "I've got clothes on."

"Yes, you certainly have," said Halloway. "Very forward-thinking of you. Here, let me give you a hand—"

Halloway stepped forward just as Aubrey's legs failed. He fell against Halloway, who didn't even stumble.

"That's right," said Halloway. "Lean on me, that's the ticket."

"What're you doing...?" Aubrey asked, the "here" getting lost along the way.

Halloway gave him a strange look. "Miss Althorp didn't tell you?"

Aubrey started to say no, then thought back over his time in hospital. It was entirely possible Miss Althorp had told him something and he'd been too distracted to remember. "I'm not sure."

Halloway's confusion turned to pity. He put on half a smile to disguise it, but Aubrey saw through him. Aubrey tried not to resent him for it.

Halloway cast a considering look down the ward—full of patients and staff, but none paying them any particular attention—and leaned in to speak more softly. "I'm taking you to Sir Lindsey's house." Then he shrugged. "Or anywhere else, if you'd rather."

Aubrey considered this new information, his thoughts coming in vague waves between the throbbing in his skull. He needed money, clothes, and employment—even if his behaviour during the boiler explosion hadn't cost him his job, the mill itself had blown to pieces, which didn't bode well for his career—and, though he felt loathe to admit it, some food and a soft bed wouldn't go amiss, either.

What he wanted, however, was Lindsey. So he nodded.

Halloway half-carried him out to the street. He left Aubrey leaning against a lamp-post while he hailed a cab. One arrived in short order.

Aubrey expected the cab to take them to the train station. He braced for a long, lurching ride. Instead, the driver steered his horse down a suburban lane in the opposite direction. Aubrey turned to Halloway, who seemed unperturbed.

"Thought we were going to Lindsey's," said Aubrey.

"Yes," said Halloway. "Sir Lindsey's house in Chorlton-cum-Hardy."

Aubrey stared at him, then closed his eyes and leaned back in his seat. He didn't have the strength to ask when Lindsey had moved house, or why. Belatedly, he realised he'd forgotten to add a "Sir" in front of Lindsey's name. Halloway tactfully didn't mention it.

The cab pulled up in a neighbourhood of spacious homes and green gardens. Charles, waiting at the base of the front steps, rushed to help Aubrey out of the cab. Aubrey would've preferred to pretend he didn't require assistance, but the ride had done nothing to help his pounding head and trembling legs. He made sure to thank Charles and Halloway both as they brought him up the steps. Charles opened the door, Aubrey limped through on Halloway's shoulder, and—

There, in the foyer, stood Lindsey.

He had a hollow look to his cheek, and disquieting circles under his eyes, but his face—astonished wonder melting into relief and joy—was like sunshine to Aubrey, who'd known only darkness for so long.

Lindsey stepped forward, reaching for him.

Aubrey pushed off of Halloway with a burst of strength. New bolts of pain shot through his arm and ribs. He didn't care.

Lindsey caught him, held him up, held him close, held him tight. Aubrey buried his face in Lindsey's collar. His scent, warm, masculine, familiar, filled Aubrey's lungs until his heart felt ready to burst with sheer relief. Lindsey's hand brushed through Aubrey's hair.

"Welcome home," Lindsey whispered, and pressed a kiss to his ear.

Aubrey said nothing. He didn't trust himself to speak. He clung to Lindsey until his good arm shook. He heard voices behind him—Halloway making arrangements with Charles. Then Lindsey pulled back, and it took all Aubrey's strength to keep from collapsing.

Lindsey caught him again, a concerned frown flickering across his face. "Charles, help me get him upstairs."

Stairs were the last thing Aubrey wanted to surmount at the moment, but he kept silent and acquiesced to Lindsey and Charles supporting him. His legs burned before they'd made it even halfway up, but he refused to complain. Then they reached the landing, and a hallway, and a door, and he found himself in a clean, quiet bedroom. A single-occupancy bedroom. A vision of heaven after six weeks in an open hospital ward.

Aubrey looked over the bed, the bookshelves, the desk, the hearth, and the washstand—with a mirror above it. In the mirror stood a man with his arm in a sling, half his face swathed in linen, the other half covered in scraggly black bristles in stark contrast to skin as pale as the bandages.

It took too long for Aubrey to recognise himself. When he did, a wave of shame washed over him. His bedraggled, ghastly reflection looked all the worse beside such a strong and handsome figure as Lindsey.

Lindsey didn't seem to notice. He sent Charles off to attend to something else, then sat Aubrey down in an armchair by the window.

"Would you like anything?" he asked, keeping hold of Aubrey's good hand. "Tea? Something to eat? Anything at all?"

"A razor," said Aubrey.

Lindsey gave him a blank stare. Aubrey gestured at his unkempt face.

"Ah," said Lindsey. "Yes, of course."

He retrieved the basin from the washstand, along with soap, brush, and razor. He didn't bring a mirror. Aubrey, too tired to question it, watched Lindsey whip up a lather. Then Lindsey moved to bring the lathered brush to Aubrey's jaw, but hesitated.

"Is this all right?" he asked.

Aubrey's pride said no, but his exhaustion said yes. He nodded.

Lindsey brushed on the lather, skirting the edges of the bandages, then took up the razor. The scrape of the blade echoed in the otherwise silent room. Lindsey performed his task with meticulous care, his brow furrowed in concentration. It paid off; Aubrey didn't feel a single nick. When he'd finished, Lindsey gently washed away the remaining lather and ran a thumb over Aubrey's smooth cheek.

"Better?" he asked.

Aubrey nodded again. He smiled, too, for good measure, and felt a corresponding pinch under his bandages. "Thanks."

Lindsey smiled in return and pressed a quick kiss to his lips. "Anything else I can do for you?"

Aubrey tried to think of what he might need, but the pounding in his head precluded all thought.

Lindsey's face took on a look of concern. "Are you all right?"

"Fine," Aubrey responded automatically. When it became apparent Lindsey didn't believe him, he added, "Just tired, is all."

This, Lindsey understood. He suggested the bed. Aubrey spent a little too long considering the fine linen cases over fat pillows; the thick blue coverlet; the width and breadth of the frame; the depth of the mattress; the whole of it in its own room and not in a long row of groaning, miserable invalids, before he agreed that yes, God yes, he could use some rest. Lindsey took his assertion in good humour.

Aubrey started to remove his jacket, hindered by the splint on his arm. Lindsey swooped in to pluck the jacket from his shoulders and likewise made quick work of Aubrey's waistcoat, shirt, shoes, and trousers, and, guiding Aubrey to the bed, helped him into it. Aubrey's eyes shut the moment his head met the pillow.

When next Aubrey woke, he was burning all over. The pinpricks of a thousand needles manifested wherever flesh made contact with anything but air. He bit back a groan. Something cool and damp pressed against his forehead. It stung as much as it soothed. He flinched.

"Sorry," said Lindsey's voice.

Aubrey forced his eyes open and beheld Lindsey's face above him. He tried to say Lindsey's name, but couldn't gather enough breath. He tried to reach for him, to pull that handsome face closer to his own, but his fingers refused to rise more than an inch above the mattress.

Lindsey caught Aubrey's hand in his own and kissed his knuckles. Aubrey let him; his hands ached less than the rest of him. Then Lindsey rearranged the damp cloth on his forehead, which had soaked up Aubrey's fever until it felt lukewarm. Still, Aubrey appreciated the gesture. Though he wished everything else in the world weren't made of pain, it was a comfort to have his Lindsey beside him at last.

"Lindsey," said Aubrey. His eyes slipped shut. He didn't think he could open them again. His hand clawed at the sheets, searching for Lindsey's.

Lindsey found him and clasped his hand between both of his own. "It's all right. I'm here."

"Stay with me," Aubrey begged, and hated himself for it, hated the fear he couldn't push down.

"I will," said Lindsey, and the fear receded, just a little.

The pain, however, did not.

CHAPTER TWENTY-SEVEN

AUBREY DIDN'T DRIFT off to sleep again. His body wouldn't let him. The ache in his skin down to his bones tightened as if wound by a winch. His fever gave way to chills, then built back up to boiling. Cold sweats coated his skin in slime. He couldn't breathe for coughing; his nose ran unchecked. His guts cramped up—this, combined with the room spinning every time he moved his head or his eyes, left him heaving into a basin beside the bed until he brought up the stringy remains of what little water he'd managed to swallow, and bile after that.

Throughout it, Lindsey never left him.

Aubrey knew it was selfish to want this, knew it was unfair to ask Lindsey to hold vigil over him, yet he couldn't loosen his vise-like grip on Lindsey's hand, or bring himself to tell Lindsey to go.

He didn't want to die, but if he must, he wanted Lindsey holding him when he went.

As the sun set, his heart sped up. His chest pulsed with pain. Certain this was the end, he refused to say as much aloud, unwilling to cry mercy when he knew none would come. Instead he rolled onto his side, towards Lindsey, and curled up as best he could, pulling Lindsey's hand to his aching ribs and stuttering heart. Lindsey put an arm around his shoulders. His touch burned Aubrey's back. Aubrey gritted his teeth, determined to die with dignity.

Yet, despite Aubrey's fears, the stabbing pain in his heart began to fade away, leaving him gasping in its wake, his cracked ribs grinding together with every panicked breath. Perhaps the worst was over, and from hereon out he might recover. No sooner had the thought occurred than a spike of agony pierced his breastbone, knocking the wind out of him. Again he screwed his eyes shut and waited for the end. Again it was denied him.

The cycle of mortal fear interspersed with flashes of calm continued until dawn. Far from bringing relief, the sunrise creeping in between the curtains struck Aubrey like cigarettes stubbed out in his eyes.

In the midst of this, Lindsey tried to persuade Aubrey to eat breakfast. Sips of weak tea went well enough. But the first bite of toast didn't go halfway down Aubrey's gullet before his aching guts contracted and brought it all up again.

Aubrey hoped that was the end of it. He hoped in vain. Like clockwork, the chime of every quarter-hour saw him bent in half over a basin. His efforts produced nothing but acid and bile.

Still, Lindsey stayed.

Lindsey propped him up, brushed his sweaty hair off his steaming brow, wiped effluvia from his mouth, rubbed his back, held his hand, murmured reassurances—and Aubrey couldn't so much as thank him.

"You don't have to," Aubrey managed to gasp sometime in the afternoon.

"Don't have to what?" Lindsey asked.

"Do this." Aubrey's burning eyelids fell shut as he spoke. "All this."

Lindsey's fingers trailed across his forehead. "Nevermind that. Get some rest."

Aubrey, too exhausted to protest further, obeyed.

༄

AT DAWN ON the second day, Lindsey left Aubrey's bedside for a moment—only a moment—to compose a telegram to his sister. He would've liked to send for the family physician as well, but he'd have a devil of a time explaining Aubrey's presence in his house. He could already hear Rowena's scolding in his mind—reminding him, quite correctly, of the danger he'd put Aubrey in by telling anyone he was there.

It took perhaps five minutes for Lindsey to write the message. He spent every second fearing Aubrey would pass on without him there to forestall it. When he'd finished, he handed the telegram off to Charles and hurried back to Aubrey's bedside.

Aubrey lay twisted on his side, grinding his teeth in his sleep. Lindsey searched for a pulse in his thin wrist. After a terrifying half-second wherein it seemed Aubrey had no pulse at all, Lindsey found its frantic flutter. He laid a hand on Aubrey's burning forehead and settled in to wait.

Charles returned. Rowena's answer didn't.

"I'm sure she'll send word as soon as she hears of it, sir," said Charles. "In the meantime, perhaps you might catch some sleep of your own."

Lindsey gave him the wild-eyed look of a man who hadn't slept in two days and had no intention of starting now.

"Very well, sir," said Charles, and departed to tend to the household.

Lindsey watched Aubrey's fretful slumber, marking each rise and fall of his bandaged chest. His own eyes burned with exhaustion, yet he didn't dare close them, lest he miss the moment his Aubrey needed him most. The shadows in the room grew long and dark.

Charles reappeared in the doorway. "Lord Graves to see you, sir."

Lindsey, who'd lifted his head expecting further encouragement to sleep or eat, balked. "The devil does he want?"

"If pressed to imagine, sir, I'd suspect he wishes to express his condolences for your recent difficulties."

Lindsey considered the issue, then released Aubrey's hand with reluctance, and stood.

"Look after him," he instructed Charles, gesturing to Aubrey's sleeping form as he forced himself to walk away. "See that he wants for nothing."

Charles nodded. Lindsey spared another glance at Aubrey's sleeping face—jaw clenched, brow furrowed in pain—and left the room.

The Chorlton-cum-Hardy library was none so grand as that in London or Wiltshire. Still, it held all Lindsey's favourites, and served well enough for conducting business. Lindsey walked in to find Graves standing on the tips of his toes to examine the upper shelves. A paper-wrapped bouquet of lilies lay on the library table. Graves, intent on his snooping, didn't notice Lindsey's entrance. Lindsey shut the door behind himself.

"Oh!" said Graves, jumping to attention. "There you are."

Lindsey knew the protocol for this situation; it had been drilled into him through twenty-odd years of society life, but he found he could muster no greeting for his guest. He stared at Graves, then at the flowers, then Graves.

"For the invalid," said Graves, flapping a hand at the bouquet.

Lindsey felt fairly certain lilies were a funereal flower, but knew better than to argue with Graves. "Why are you here?"

"Why shouldn't I be?" laughed Graves. "To express my condolences, of course, and my sincere wishes for—"

"No," said Lindsey, "I meant—why would you? You don't care for Aubrey."

"Aubrey?"

"Warren," Lindsey growled.

"Oh, him." Graves tossed his hair out of his eyes. "Yes, well, I do recall some less-than-diplomatic words concerning his attendance at dinner—"

Lindsey, who'd watched Aubrey endure more pain than he'd imagined any man could bear, didn't have enough restraint left to keep his hands from clenching into fists.

Graves's eyes followed the motion. "—and I'd like to apologise."

In all the years Lindsey had known Graves, he'd never once heard him drop his sardonic tone. Nor had he ever seen Graves's mouth in a thin line, neither smirk nor pout. With astonishment bordering on horror, Lindsey realised Graves was being sincere. Before Lindsey could respond in kind, Graves, who never could stand silence, filled the air with chatter.

"Whatever my personal feelings on your choice of paramour, it is nevertheless your choice and not mine. As your friend, I respect it. And no matter Mr Warren's origins or intentions, I confess myself more than a little offended that you suppose me so unfeeling as to not wish him well. Or indeed, wish the same for any poor creature who suffered so. When I imagine my poor Halloway so afflicted—!"

Graves broke off, turning away to press the back of his hand against his forehead.

Sincere Graves was unnerving. Theatrical Graves was familiar. Lindsey relaxed. "Thank you."

Graves dropped his hand to give Lindsey a coy smile—no doubt pleased with his own newfound empathy.

"Halloway told me," he said with a note of pride for his artist. "Tongues have wagged in Mr Warren's absence from the lodging-house. Fortunately none but Halloway and myself realise where he's gone."

"I trust I may depend upon your discretion."

"Of course!" Graves waved a dismissive hand. "How fares the invalid?"

The situation called for polite fiction. Lindsey opened his mouth to recite it.

"Poorly," he said instead. Too drained to stop himself, he added, "No, worse. He's dreadful. He's dying."

Fear gripped Lindsey's soul anew as he spoke the last two words. Judging from Graves's expression, he felt similar.

"Oh." Graves swallowed hard. "I'm very sorry to hear it."

Lindsey, preoccupied with mashing the heels of his hands into his own eyes, hardly heard him.

Something tickled Lindsey's knuckles. He lowered his hands and found Graves flapping a handkerchief at his face. He jerked back, then hesitantly plucked the handkerchief from Graves's fingers and buried his face in it.

"Thank you," he mumbled through the silk.

"You're quite welcome," Graves replied with a note of uncertainty.

Lindsey took a moment to compose himself. Not only did he despise his inability to protect the one he loved—the mere idea of Aubrey's suffering was innately unbearable. In a just world, such a goodly heart would be spared all agonies. Lindsey wished Rowena would reply to his telegram. He wished he knew what to do without her.

Graves coughed. Lindsey lifted his head from his handkerchief. Graves regarded the ceiling, his hands clasped behind his back.

"Graves!" Lindsey cried, feeling as though he saw his friend properly for the first time.

Graves jumped, bringing his head down sharp to look at Lindsey. "Yes?"

"You're an invert!"

Graves stared at him. "Well-spotted."

"No, I mean—" Lindsey struggled against his fatigue to find the appropriate phrasing. "You must know people. Discreet people. Who would you send for if Halloway were ill?"

The thought of Halloway falling ill made Graves's eyebrows shoot up in alarm and temporarily robbed him of speech. Then he straightened his shoulders and rose to the challenge. "Dr Pilkington. Good chap. One of our sort. Keeps his mouth shut and his medicine chest open."

Lindsey's mind stumbled at "our sort." He hadn't supposed men like himself or Graves went into medicine. Though, now that he considered it, it seemed the most natural thing in the world. Inverts were gentlemen, artists, engineers, and clerks. Why shouldn't they be physicians?

"I'm afraid I don't have his card with me," Graves continued. "But I assure you, he's quite discreet. I can tell Charles where to send the telegram, if you'd like."

"Thank you," Lindsey said a third time.

Graves patted his shoulder, a fluttering gesture that felt more like dusting than comfort. "Think nothing of it."

☙

ESCAPING STEAM SHRIEKED in Aubrey's ears. Billowing clouds filled his vision. Blind and deaf, he stumbled through the dense fog covering the mill yard. He knew there were other people in the fog, people depending upon him, but he could neither see nor hear them. The air hung hot and heavy with precipitation. The thick fog dragged at his ankles, making every step a slow, agonising struggle. Beads of boiling sweat poured from his skin. The shriek pitched louder, higher. He had to go on, had to reach the boiler before—

"Aubrey?"

A hand clasped his shoulder. He wrenched out of its grip, shaking himself awake.

He found himself in bed, far from the mill. Dawn had broken while he'd slept. It burned his eyes. His sheets were damp with sweat. Everywhere skin met linen, he felt spiders crawling. Underneath it all, the bone-deep ache thrummed on.

Lindsey leaned over him, looking concerned. He gently brushed Aubrey's hair back from his clammy forehead. "I'm sorry to wake you. The doctor's here."

"What doctor?" Aubrey croaked. He couldn't afford a doctor. Outside of Withington, he'd never seen one in his life.

"Dr Pilkington," said Lindsey. "It's all right, you can trust him. Graves vouched."

Aubrey didn't consider Graves's endorsement particularly reassuring, but between his raw throat and pounding head, he wasn't in any position to argue.

Lindsey left his side to open the door. Through it came a man in his mid-forties with a sober suit and a well-waxed moustache.

"Good morning, Mr Warren," said the stranger.

Aubrey tensed. The stranger paused his approach and smiled kindly at him.

"Good morning," Aubrey ventured.

"Dr Pilkington, at your service," the stranger continued. "Your friend Sir Lindsey asked me to look in on you."

Aubrey remained wary. "Friend" was an ambiguous term. It told nothing of how much Dr Pilkington knew, or what excuse Lindsey had given him.

Lindsey hovered in the doorway. "Pardon me—ought I to stay or go?"

Dr Pilkington glanced over his shoulder at him. "That's entirely up to Mr Warren."

Both men turned to Aubrey, which did nothing to ease his nerves. He didn't want Lindsey to leave. But he'd taken up so much of Lindsey's time already, far more than he deserved. A doctor's examination would be humiliating enough without Lindsey watching. But without Lindsey, the humiliation would be compounded by terror.

"He can stay," Aubrey said.

Lindsey shut the door and returned to Aubrey's bedside, across from Dr Pilkington. He gave Aubrey a brave smile.

Aubrey would've returned it, but felt too exhausted for even that small effort. He turned back to Dr Pilkington, who'd produced a stethoscope in the meantime, and sat rubbing the round end vigorously against his palm. Seeing he had Aubrey's attention, he held it aloft.

"May I?" he asked.

Aubrey nodded.

Dr Pilkington pulled the bedclothes aside, undid the top three buttons of Aubrey's pyjamas, and pressed the stethoscope gently yet firmly to Aubrey's breastbone. Though warmed by friction, the remaining temperature difference set off the fever burn in Aubrey's skin. Aubrey held back a hiss of pain.

"Breathe normally," said Dr Pilkington.

Aubrey endeavoured to follow instruction without voicing his agonies. It wasn't pretty, but he managed. All the while, he felt Lindsey's presence beside him. He didn't dare look in his direction, lest he encounter pity. He trained his eyes on the ceiling instead.

Something brushed his wrist. He glanced down to see Lindsey's hand on the bedspread, palm-up, next to his own.

Aubrey grasped it tight and looked back up at the ceiling.

Dr Pilkington moved the stethoscope slightly to the left, listening intently, his eyes on his silver pocketwatch. He put both watch and stethoscope away a moment later.

"A little fast," he said, pulling the bedclothes back to rights with a well-practised motion. "But otherwise quite normal. How do you feel?"

Aubrey, who felt anything but normal, answered, "Fine."

Lindsey let out a quiet sigh.

Dr Pilkington raised his brows. "I can't help you unless you're honest with me."

Aubrey said nothing. When it became apparent his reply wasn't coming, Dr Pilkington continued on his own.

"Sir Lindsey tells me you've been ill for three days since your release from Withington Hospital. You've suffered steam burns on your face, right side, and right arm. The arm is also fractured, as are three of your ribs. Am I correct in assuming hospital staff administered morphine for your pains?"

Aubrey supposed he could afford to admit that particular truth, and muttered, "Yes."

"And have you taken any morphine since your discharge?"

"No."

"Any laudanum?"

"Yes."

"How much?"

Aubrey looked to Lindsey for the answer. Lindsey provided it.

Dr Pilkington's moustache twitched in a wistful smile. "I believe I understand the nature of your complaint, Mr Warren."

"And?" said Lindsey.

Dr Pilkington set his medical bag on the edge of the bed and began rifling through its contents. "Morphine withdrawal."

"I'm not an opium eater," Aubrey protested.

"I never suggested you were," said Dr Pilkington. "However, the dosage you received at Withington created a dependence. Lacking morphine, your body reacted violently—purging, tremors, nervous excitement, et cetera. All of which I can assure you is perfectly normal and unlikely to result in your death. Had Sir Lindsey given you more laudanum, you might've suffered nothing worse than a bad headache. As it stands, you're in the midst of withdrawals. Unpleasant, but not lethal." He withdrew a long, slender needle from his bag, alongside a bottle. "More morphine will put you to rights."

As the word "morphine" left Dr Pilkington's lips, dread seized Aubrey's brain. He'd seen what became of opium's thralls. Plenty of his workhouse companions were inmates as a result of their guardians' dependence on the stuff. He reckoned just as many had gone on to follow in those guardians' footsteps. He couldn't fault them for it. True escape from the circumstances they'd been born to was nigh-on impossible. The best most could hope for was the illusion of escape—and opium, cheaper per ounce than gin, seemed a bargain. Until its procurement took priority over rent, and food, and sundry other debts, and any attempt to stop the slide into disgrace brought on the agonies Aubrey now knew so well. "There but for the grace of God go I," as the workhouse chaplain used to say. In another life, Aubrey could easily see himself falling prey to opium's charms. But not in this life.

"No," said Aubrey.

Dr Pilkington paused, his needle over the bottle. "Pardon?"

"I don't need it." Aubrey's lips trembled with the lie, but he refused to complete the morality campaigners' cliché. Already an orphaned workhouse brat seduced into depravity by rich men's coin, all he needed was opium, and the newspapers would have their next salacious exposé: *The Maiden Tribute of Modern Gomorrah.*

Dr Pilkington raised an eyebrow at Lindsey.

"Aubrey, please—" Lindsey began.

"You said this wouldn't kill me," Aubrey said to Dr Pilkington. "What happens if I refuse your morphine?"

Dr Pilkington put the needle down. "Your withdrawal symptoms will continue. Most cases peak after two or three days. According to Sir Lindsey's timeline, you're past the worst of it, though you still have a few days of discomfort ahead. More morphine would—"

"—make an opium eater of me," Aubrey concluded.

"—would ease your withdrawals," Dr Pilkington finished with patient disregard for Aubrey's interruption. "Morphine is the only effective anodyne for your wounds. You need it to recover. Gradually reducing the dose as your condition improves will eliminate your dependency without causing further withdrawal symptoms, leaving you no more a morphinomaniac than Sir Lindsey or myself."

Aubrey stared the doctor down. Dr Pilkington remained unmoved. Pain flared in Aubrey's cracked ribs with every breath. His skull throbbed. His eyes burned.

"All right," Aubrey mumbled.

"Good man," said Dr Pilkington.

The needle entered the bottle. Aubrey turned to the ceiling. A prick of his arm plunged chemical relief into his bloodstream, forcing him to relax. As if from a great distance, he felt himself falling, slowly and softly, like a feather in infinite descent. His head lolled on the pillow, bringing Lindsey into his field of vision. He knew he ought to be ashamed of himself, but couldn't remember why. He waited for Lindsey to scold him.

Lindsey simply squeezed his hand.

CHAPTER TWENTY-EIGHT

AUBREY SPENT THE first few days revelling in his ability to rest. Thanks to Dr Pilkington's prescription, Aubrey could sleep and eat again, though his appetite wasn't quite as robust as Lindsey or the doctor wished. By the fifth day of lying about waiting for his strength to return, he'd had enough of convalescence.

With the veil of pain lifted, Aubrey took stock of his new circumstance. It did nothing to stop his feelings of uselessness and sloth. Luxury surrounded him, and heaps of it. High ceilings towered above his head, William Morris paper covered the walls, and the Persian carpet on the floor supported all the modern comforts money could buy.

Aubrey's morphine-addled mind stuck on the desk in his sickroom. Leather-topped, drawers upon drawers, black walnut polished to a gleam—a far cry from the old door balanced on soapboxes in Aubrey's garret. The thought of touching it filled him with anxiety. The press of a pen would dents its leather; a careless closing of a drawer would scuff its polish. He stared at it for upwards of an hour, wondering how to use it without ruining it, then gave it up for lost and resolved never to try.

When he recovered enough to leave his bed, he discovered the wardrobe. More than large enough to sleep in if one so desired, it held an army outfitter's worth of clothes. Shirts, waistcoats, trousers, jackets, and three suits; a grey and a navy suitable for an office or strolling about town by day, and one black evening suit that wouldn't look out of place beside Lindsey's at the theatre. Aubrey assumed it was overflow from Lindsey's wardrobe. Then he saw the trouser-legs were much too short, as were the shirtsleeves, and he realised it all fit his own small frame. Lindsey must've taken the measurements from the clothes Halloway had brought from the lodging house. Aubrey tried to estimate the cost of the lot. When the figures climbed higher than his life's savings, he gave up.

And yet, Lindsey insisted the desk, the wardrobe, and everything else were Aubrey's to do with as he wished. Aubrey couldn't begin to wrap his head around the notion.

Doctor's orders forbade sharing a bed—Aubrey would've told Lindsey to hang doctor's orders and stay with him, if he didn't fear Lindsey's own health would fail after restless nights with an invalid—but no such restriction applied to the daylight hours. Aubrey spent most of those sleeping. Morphine left his mind good for little else.

Yet Lindsey, who Aubrey supposed must've felt bored to tears, stayed beside him. When Aubrey's arms trembled, his grip too weak to hold a spoon or cup, Lindsey steadied his hands with his own. When Dr Pilkington thought his patient recovered enough for light exercise, Lindsey walked Aubrey up and down the hall. And when Aubrey felt too tired to walk, yet too awake for sleep, Lindsey read to him. But no fiction, no matter how beautifully declaimed, could drown out the nagging voice in the back of Aubrey's mind, calling him useless, saying he trespassed on Lindsey's kindness, and wasn't pulling his weight. Lindsey himself didn't seem to care.

Aubrey's wounds remained bandaged. Dr Pilkington had changed the dressings on the day he began Aubrey's treatment, but he couldn't be expected to do so indefinitely. He had a host of aristocratic, hypochondriac inverts to tend, or so Aubrey inferred from his more diplomatic explanations.

Still, it came as a shock to Aubrey when, on an otherwise peaceful afternoon, Lindsey reached for the bandages on his arm.

"What're you doing?" Aubrey demanded, flinching from him.

Lindsey withdrew his hand, looking confused. "Changing your dressings."

"No you're not."

Lindsey sat back, a frown creasing his brow. "Someone has to. You needn't be afraid, Dr Pilkington taught me how. I promise I'll stop if it hurts."

"No, that's not—" Aubrey bit off his protest. The decreased morphine dosage, while it soothed his pains and prevented a relapse into withdrawals, left him far too muddle-headed and irritable for his liking. "I'll do it myself."

A sorrowful look flashed across Lindsey's face. "Aubrey…"

"I can manage."

"Yes," said Lindsey, "but you don't have to."

Aubrey braced to scramble away if Lindsey tried to touch his bandages again. But Lindsey made no further attempt. He sat quiet, his expression sombre. Aubrey thought it resembled pity. He couldn't stand it, not from anyone, and particularly not Lindsey. He'd say anything to stop Lindsey from looking at him like that.

"I don't want you to see—" Aubrey began, then gave up and made a careless gesture at his own face.

Lindsey's pitying look intensified. "I don't mind—"

"I do," said Aubrey, sharper than he intended.

Lindsey rubbed his hand over his face, letting it linger on his mouth as he rolled his eyes to the ceiling, then dropped it with a sigh.

"Charles could do it," he said, but Aubrey shook his head, so he added, "Or I could hire a nurse. I'm sure Dr Pilkington could recommend one."

"For how much?"

Lindsey blinked at him. "What does that signify?"

"Everything. Dr Pilkington's services alone must've cost—"

"You don't have to worry about that," said Lindsey, staring at him as if he'd started speaking in tongues.

"Yes, I do!" Aubrey insisted. "You don't understand—I've only so much saved up, I can't afford—"

"And I can," said Lindsey. "It's all right, you don't have to afford anything, I'll—"

"No!"

Lindsey balked.

Aubrey unclenched his fists. "I'm sorry. I don't mean to be ungrateful, you've been very kind, but I can't accept all this. It's too much."

"It's too much to ensure you're comfortable?"

"This isn't comfort, this is—" Aubrey struggled against the morphine to remember the word he wanted. "—luxury."

Lindsey's eyebrows rose. "Luxury?"

"Yes." Aubrey cast about the room for an example. "The hearth fire's burned for almost a week."

Lindsey craned his neck to regard the fixture in question. "Is it too warm?"

"No, that's not what I—" Aubrey shook his head and tried again. "What're you paying for coal?"

Lindsey turned back to him. "Haven't the foggiest. Charles sees to it."

Aubrey knew what it would've cost to keep a fire going in his garret, but he wasn't there now, and Lindsey wouldn't understand the price. He tried another approach.

"This dressing gown, then." Aubrey picked at the sleeve where it hung slack from his wounded shoulder.

"Don't you like it?" asked Lindsey.

As a point of fact, Aubrey liked it very much. He'd never worn silk before. He'd only touched it whilst disrobing richer men. When he'd awoken a few scant days ago and found himself wrapped up in it, he could hardly believe he wasn't dreaming. The soft blue paisley fabric, so smooth it felt almost liquid, shifted deliciously over his skin with his every move. Yet he couldn't help thinking the touch of his flesh soiled it. That such low, filthy skin as his shouldn't be swathed in such decadence.

"It's not about whether or not I like it," said Aubrey. "It's about the price. It must've cost at least—"

"—a trifle," said Lindsey. "Hardly worth mentioning."

"—more than I make in a bloody year," Aubrey snarled.

Lindsey drew back, his eyes wide.

Aubrey felt a stab of remorse. "I'm sorry, it's just... I'm not even employed anymore. I'm just lying here, taking and taking, and the cost keeps adding up and I can feel it towering over me and—" He forced himself to breathe. "I haven't earned it. I haven't earned any of this."

"Who said you had to earn anything?" asked Lindsey. When it became apparent Aubrey didn't see fit to dignify the question with a response, Lindsey continued. "You're recovering from a terrible illness, after surviving a boiler explosion and saving God knows how many people in the process, and all that after—"

"Please," Aubrey begged, his eyes screwed shut against Lindsey's list. "Stop."

Lindsey fell silent. Then, in a softer and more uncertain voice, he added, "What would you have me do instead?"

His tone twisted a knife into Aubrey's conscience. Aubrey kept his eyes closed, knowing the sight of Lindsey's face would break his resolve. "I need you to keep an account of the cost of my care. I'll repay every penny."

"I don't expect you to repay me," said Lindsey, affronted.

"I do." Aubrey opened his eyes to gaze into Lindsey's. "That is, I expect myself to be the sort of man who repays his debts. I was born into charity. I can't accept any more of it."

To Aubrey's surprise, Lindsey appeared wounded. "You think this is charity?"

Aubrey preferred Lindsey's pitying look to the hurt expression he now wore. "No, no, that's not what I—"

Lindsey's expression softened. "It's all right. You shouldn't worry about any of this. You're not well."

"That's no excuse!"

"Aubrey," said Lindsey, halfway between exasperated and amused. "When people are ill, they *rest*."

Aubrey let out a mirthless bark of laughter. "Rest! Nobody rests! They clench their jaws and soldier on. They go to work and let the fires of industry sweat the fever from their brows. They scrape and stumble and get up and go on, because if they don't—" Aubrey's breath failed him; he coughed to gather more of it. "—they don't eat. Their children starve. They can't pay their rent. The whole family is tossed into the street. If they swallow their pride and go to the workhouse, their spouse and children are ripped from their arms to waste away in dark corners and die alone. So they work. They work until they drop, and every penny left pays for their funeral, lest the corpse end up on a dissection table!"

Lindsey stared at him.

Aubrey turned away, unable to bear Lindsey's scrutiny. His fists clenched the bedsheets, worrying the linen between his knuckles. Broken ribs creaked as his chest heaved with exertion. He waited for Lindsey to tell him he was exaggerating—things couldn't possibly be so dire outside these walls, where the common rabble lived and died and no one gave a damn.

"I'm sorry," said Lindsey.

Aubrey cringed. "No, I'm sorry. You couldn't have known. It's not like I've been forthcoming on the subject."

Lindsey's hand slipped over his own. Aubrey turned his palm upward to grasp it tight.

"Regardless of how things may have been," Lindsey ventured, "they needn't be so any longer. You can rest now."

Aubrey wanted to believe him. But— "I'll not be a kept man."

"And I've no intention of keeping you. At least, not in that sense. Certainly not against your will. But... can a man not support his friend in a time of need? You'd do the same for me. You've done it already. So please," said Lindsey, his voice breaking, "let me look after you. Just for now. Until you're well again."

Aubrey's heart wrenched at the thought of Lindsey in his place. He'd give anything to prevent Lindsey's pain. Even now, it took tremendous effort to deny him. And yet. "If you'll let me change my own dressings."

Lindsey's pleading expression turned to defeat. "Very well."

Aubrey squeezed his hand. Lindsey continued to look miserable. Shortly after, Lindsey departed Aubrey's sickroom, leaving behind clean linen bandages.

Aubrey had yet to see the damage the explosion had done to his body. His injuries felt stiff, which he attributed to his wrappings. As he unwound the dressings on his arm, he saw the skin itself had tightened its hold on the flesh beneath.

He let the bandages fall away and stared at the swirling pink crust on the far edge of his arm, from bicep to wrist, and a patch on the back of his hand. Prodding it caused a queer prickling sensation, burning for several moments afterwards.

Aubrey recalled how Lindsey had kissed the same flesh long ago, before the accident. He couldn't imagine Lindsey doing the same to the rough and broken skin he now wore.

He pushed those thoughts aside and re-dressed his burns, pulling the bandages taught as if firmer dressings would fix it. He repeated the process with the hideous scars over his ribs. Then he threw his dressing gown over the wash-stand mirror and re-wrapped his face blind.

⟲

THE NEXT DAY, Lindsey tread carefully around Aubrey, speaking in low tones, keeping his inquiries as short as possible, and answering Aubrey's own with slow nods.

Aubrey's conscience helpfully informed him this was all his fault for being an ingrate. He didn't bother arguing with it. He kept his mind busy thinking how best to atone for his behaviour, and reward Lindsey's considerable effort and kindness. At length, he fell back on the oldest solution he knew. When next Lindsey came to fluff his pillows, Aubrey caught him by the cravat and pulled him down for a kiss.

It took Lindsey a moment to reciprocate. When he did, his lips moved hesitantly, not matching Aubrey's eager ministrations. Aubrey felt sure he could've coaxed Lindsey into more, but it pained him to hold himself up for so long. He let Lindsey go and collapsed onto his pillows.

Lindsey looked at him curiously. "Are you all right?"

"Fine," Aubrey lied. "Just missed you, is all."

Lindsey smiled—though his eyebrows stayed at a confused angle—and gave a careless shrug. "Well, here I am."

Aubrey worked to keep the desperation off his own face. Evidently he didn't succeed, for Lindsey developed a look of grave concern and laid the back of his hand against Aubrey's forehead.

"I'm fine," Aubrey insisted. "Don't you want to kiss me?"

Lindsey turned his temperature-gauge around to stroke Aubrey's hair. "Of course I do."

"Then why—" Aubrey broke off, hating the pitch his voice had developed. It sounded too much like a plea.

Lindsey frowned. "I don't want to hurt you."

"You won't," Aubrey assured him. "You can't. You could never. Please."

He hadn't intended to speak that last word aloud, but there it was.

Lindsey hesitated. Then, to Aubrey's relief, he closed his eyes and leaned in.

The second kiss was far more successful. When Aubrey's aching ribs forced him to break away for air, he kept nuzzling along Lindsey's jaw.

"I'm sorry," Aubrey mumbled when his lips reached Lindsey's ear.

"What for?" Lindsey whispered.

"For being an ass," Aubrey said aloud.

Lindsey drew back to kiss his forehead. "You're nothing of the sort."

Aubrey gazed up at him, weighing the consequences of the notion growing in his mind. "I want to tell you something."

Lindsey ran his thumb over Aubrey's unbandaged cheek. "What is it?"

"I don't know." Aubrey ignored Lindsey's confused head-tilt and blundered on. "That is, I wish I could say everything, but I don't know where to begin. I've told you some of my history, but... not so much as I ought. Not as much as you've told me of yours, freely. I'd like to balance the scales."

Lindsey sat back, his hand trailing from Aubrey's face to his palm, which he clasped tight. "It's not a contest."

Aubrey chuckled weakly. "I'm aware. Is there anything you'd like to know?"

"Yes," Lindsey admitted after a tense pause.

"Ask me," Aubrey begged. "Please. I'm tired of keeping secrets."

Lindsey bit his lip. Aubrey noted the concern furrowing his brow and the sympathy in his eyes. He'd hate to see it turn to disgust and contempt, and yet—he'd no wish to keep anything from him.

At last, Lindsey spoke. "You said you were born in a workhouse. May I ask where?"

"Homerton Workhouse. In Clifton Road. East London." As he spoke, Aubrey watched Lindsey's face. Concern remained, but sympathy dominated. Lindsey didn't seem to think any less of him as a result of this revelation.

"And your parents?" asked Lindsey.

"From Whitechapel, most likely. Father dead before I was born, mother dead soon after. I don't know their names. The warden assigned mine at random." Aubrey kept his tone neutral, but Lindsey winced nonetheless.

"How did you get from the workhouse to the Post Office?" Lindsey asked. As Aubrey paled, Lindsey added, "You needn't speak of it if you don't wish to."

Aubrey shook his head. "I made a promise, and I intend to keep it." Though he did cast his eyes away from Lindsey's face as he pondered where to begin.

"All us workhouse children attended a Sunday school. The chaplain, Mr Newell, took a liking to me. Paternal, I suppose. I was quiet, and listened well enough to parrot back his sermons. So he favoured me. The only person who ever had, at that point. It inspired loyalty in me. I became a little Biblical scholar. I intended to follow him into the church. Didn't put much stock in the divinity of it—the Almighty seemed indifferent to my lot, so I felt indifference in return. Mr Newell, however, was kind to me, so I went wherever he led, with all my childish affection.

"But there was another affection in me, too. Brotherly friendship, I thought. I didn't have a better word for it. I'm sure you know the feeling."

Lindsey chuckled. A return smile flitted across Aubrey's lips, but he kept his eyes downcast.

"I'd had the physical side of it with some of my workhouse fellows, but it didn't last, and it didn't satisfy. I thought I'd found the solution in Mr Newell. I'd have done anything for him. That's why I worked so hard at my lessons. Desperate to please him, to be the sort of boy he could love—"

Aubrey broke off, blinking hard, and cleared his throat.

"But as I said, my lessons were Biblical. Only a matter of time before I stumbled across passages that made it very clear what I wanted was unacceptable. The church would never have me. A better boy would've humbled himself into something more tolerable. Instead, learning the Lord looked on me not with indifference but with hatred, my indifference changed to hatred as well. I turned from Mr Newell, certain he'd do the same to me if he knew my monstrous truth. To his credit, he kept reaching out, but I couldn't bear the disappointment I'd become, and—" Aubrey laughed. "—I actually hid in a cupboard once to avoid him."

Lindsey didn't laugh along. Aubrey resumed his tale in a more sober tone.

"The workhouse turned me out at fifteen, same as all the lads. Mr Newell offered to find me respectable work. I ought've refused. I didn't deserve his kindness after how I'd shunned him. But I accepted, because the alternative was life on the street for as long as it took for me to end up in the workhouse again. So I became a telegraph boy. It seemed normal enough at first. I took a fancy to my superior. He reciprocated, and we..." Aubrey coughed. "You can imagine the rest. It went on for a month or so before he made a business proposition. I was sick of starving and hungry for affection, and his suggestion sounded like it'd solve both problems, so I agreed. He'd send me to this house or that hotel, I'd get on my knees or belly, and I'd walk away with more money than I'd make in six months delivering telegrams. Easy money. I became... good at my job, to put it politely. My superior started sending me to gentlemen's clubs and the like. That's where I met—"

Aubrey stopped short. His conscience protested what he was about to reveal, but he'd promised Lindsey the truth.

"—Mr Jennings. He became a regular customer, though he could hardly afford it. I suppose he liked my face. Everyone did. Or used to, anyway. Then the law changed. I thought I'd better get out of the business before I ended up in Newgate. I mentioned it to Mr Jennings as a courtesy, to give him notice to find someone else. He surprised me with a job offer. I had to take a clerking examination and start as an office boy for nothing, but those were still better terms than I could've hoped for. And the rest is history. Very boring history."

He waited for Lindsey to reply. The room remained silent. Aubrey looked up to find Lindsey staring at him.

"I like your face," said Lindsey.

Aubrey stared back. "You can't know that. You haven't seen it since..."

Lindsey brushed Aubrey's hair away from his bandages. "I don't mind."

Aubrey couldn't muster the energy to argue the point. "Is there anything else you wanted to know?"

Lindsey gave him a long, considering look. Aubrey braced himself for whatever question Lindsey might pose.

"Why engineering?" Lindsey asked.

Aubrey choked, coughed, and finally unleashed the peals of laughter bubbling up from his burnt lungs. Lindsey gave him a very odd look. Aubrey couldn't blame him.

"Sorry," Aubrey gasped out when his ill-timed humour subsided. "Expected a harder question."

Lindsey appeared much relieved. "You don't mind, then?"

"Not at all." Aubrey leaned back into his pillows. "Mr Newell let me accompany him to improving lectures. One was by an engineer with a life story like the ones in the book you gave me. Started with nothing, built up everything. I supposed Mr Newell meant to teach me a lesson about the virtues of labour and perseverance. Instead, I learned the possibility of wresting some control over Creation back from the Almighty. Engineering would allow me to remake my circumstances into what I needed them to be." He gave a wistful half-smile. "Bit arrogant on my part. Certainly sacrilegious."

"Hardly," said Lindsey. His hand found its way into Aubrey's hair again. Aubrey leaned into the contact. His eyes fell shut.

"Was there anything else?" Aubrey asked, finding it difficult to ward off sleep without a task to complete.

"Nothing that can't wait," said Lindsey.

"I'm awake," Aubrey insisted.

"I know."

Aubrey squinted his eyes open just enough to see the fond smile playing on Lindsey's lips. He mirrored it as he drifted off, though only half of it showed through his bandages.

෴

AUBREY REGAINED CONSCIOUSNESS to the sound of shifting parchment. He rolled his head across his pillow and beheld Lindsey seated at his bedside with a writing desk perched in his lap. Papers spread out over the desk, the arms of Lindsey's chair, and across the bed, newspapers and magazines mingling with telegrams and letters. Aubrey watched him work for a minute or so before Lindsey glanced up.

"Sorry," Lindsey whispered with a sheepish smile as he caught Aubrey's eye. He reached out to sweep up the papers, but Aubrey stopped him with a shake of his head.

"I don't mind," Aubrey mumbled, sitting up. Lindsey swooped in to put an arm under his shoulders and ease him into a more comfortable position, adding another pillow for good measure. Aubrey thanked him and asked, "What're you working on?"

Lindsey shrugged as he sat down again. "Nothing particularly pressing. Writing to Graves about *The Strand.*"

"No bills?"

"No." Lindsey seemed confused by the possibility. "Halloway sends his regards—through Graves—and wonders if he might have the privilege of retrieving your personal effects from the lodging house, should you want them."

Aubrey froze.

Lindsey looked up from the letter. "Aubrey?"

Aubrey bit his lip, weighing his options. "There are some things I'd feel more comfortable knowing the exact whereabouts of. If it's not too much trouble."

"Of course." A concerned wrinkle appeared between Lindsey's brows. "Is something the matter?"

"No, it's just—" Aubrey'd spent twenty-four years keeping everything about himself close to the vest. Talking openly, even with Lindsey, still didn't feel natural to him. "My savings."

Lindsey raised an eyebrow. "Savings?"

"Under my mattress." A hot flush rose in Aubrey's cheeks. "Fifty pounds, two shillings, and four pence. That's all."

Fifty pounds, two shillings, and four pence he'd skipped meals and worked years on end without a holiday to scrape together. He felt ridiculous mentioning it to Lindsey, to whom such a sum meant nothing.

And yet, Lindsey replied with quiet affirmation, as if it were the most natural thing in the world. Aubrey watched his pen move across the paper, noting the sum in large, looping letters.

"Was there anything else?" Lindsey asked, looking up. Aubrey searched his face for mockery, but found no trace of it in Lindsey's eyes.

"My clothes," said Aubrey, adding, "I know they're not much, but they're mine, and—I'd like them."

A faint frown appeared at the corners of Lindsey's mouth, but he nodded and wrote it down all the same.

"The ones you've given me are fine," Aubrey went on, his eyes on Lindsey's pen rather than his face. "Better than fine, but—"

Lindsey laid down his pen and took Aubrey's hand. "It's all right. I don't mind."

Aubrey desperately wanted to believe him. Seeing his gentle smile and feeling Lindsey's hand close over his own, Aubrey thought he might be able to.

"Thank you," said Aubrey.

Lindsey released Aubrey's hand and returned to his writing. "What about your books? And your magazines?"

"Most of the latter are with Miss Rook. But yes, I'd like my books as well." All three of them. It seemed preposterous compared to Lindsey's library, hundreds of volumes spread across three houses.

Lindsey listed out Aubrey's books—all the titles memorised. It took Aubrey a moment to read them upside-down, but when he saw they were there, he couldn't help smiling.

"That's all, I think," said Aubrey when Lindsey's pen stopped.

Lindsey nodded again, but his brow furrowed. "Forgive me if this is an impertinent question, but... why do you have fifty pounds in your mattress?"

Aubrey reminded himself Lindsey had a very different upbringing. "I didn't want to go back to the workhouse."

Lindsey's eyes widened. "Was that likely?"

"If I survived long enough, yes."

Lindsey stared.

"I have no family," Aubrey elaborated, keeping his voice flat to deter Lindsey's pity. "I'm not inclined towards the fairer sex. I'll never have a wife or children. If I live past a working age, there's no one who'll take me in. So I've got to look after myself for as long as I can, and failing that, I need the means to pay someone else to do it. Because if I can't..." He swallowed hard, dropping his gaze. "I was born in a workhouse. I know what happens if you start your life there, and I've seen what happens at the end. I'd rather die at forty in the street than—"

He broke off, his breath coming ragged. His hands had formed fists without his notice. He tried to flatten them, but his trembling fingers refused.

Lindsey's hands covered his own. Aubrey breathed a little easier, though his arms still shook.

"That's why I saved," Aubrey said, working hard to keep his voice steady, and pleased to find it sounded stronger than he felt. "Either I'd make enough to live out my final years comfortably, or I'd drop in harness."

And now, with the mill gone and his face in shambles, he didn't know what he'd do.

Lindsey rubbed his hands in a soothing gesture. "I'm—"

"Please," said Aubrey. "I know you mean well, and I'm grateful for it, but for the love of God, please don't say you're sorry."

Lindsey said nothing. Aubrey lifted his head to meet his gaze. Lindsey looked nearly as tired and broken-down as Aubrey felt. Before Aubrey could do anything to alleviate this, Lindsey lifted a hand to Aubrey's cheek and leaned in to kiss him.

Aubrey opened his lips for him, relieved to be back on familiar ground.

ᗧ

"YOU DON'T NEED these anymore," said Dr Pilkington.

Aubrey followed his open-handed gesture, encompassing Aubrey himself from head to hip. "Beg pardon?"

"The dressings," said Dr Pilkington, returning his stethoscope to his bag. "I can remove them now if you'd like."

"No, thank you."

Dr Pilkington raised an eyebrow. Aubrey pretended he could neither see the gesture nor intuit its meaning.

It'd taken some time, but Aubrey had convinced Lindsey he could handle a visit from Dr Pilkington alone. As such, Lindsey was waiting elsewhere in the house whilst Dr Pilkington stared Aubrey down in the sickroom. Aubrey resisted the urge to clutch his dressing gown tighter around his shoulders.

Dr Pilkington sighed and shook his head. He left Aubrey with a tip of his hat and a reminder of how to reach him if need be. The door closed behind him.

Aubrey let the collar of his dressing gown slip from between his clenched fingers. It fell open, revealing his bandaged chest. He'd wanted to tear the wrappings off as soon as he'd awoken in Withington Hospital. Now that he had permission, he found himself paralysed.

Having sat on the edge of his bed for the last quarter-hour, he willed his jellied legs to stand. Gravity pulled the smooth silk off his shoulders to pool on the bedspread. He stared down at himself for another minute or so. Then, with a long, low breath through pursed lips, he stripped the linen off his chest.

Tossing the bandages aside, he arched his back and stretched. Deep breaths ached less now—little more than a twinge. He'd changed his bandages before, but hadn't yet acclimated to the ticklish brush of air on his new skin. Likewise, his eyes still slid away from the grotesque scars plastered across his chest.

He peeled the bandages from his arm. This, too, repelled his gaze, but he forced himself to stare at it, flexing the tendons under the unyielding scars, willing himself to understand that this was his flesh now.

His chest and arm freed, only his face remained.

Aubrey approached the mirror over the wash-stand. His reflection looked better than when he'd arrived. His cheek had become, if not fuller, then less hollow, and the dark circles under his eyes had faded to a paler blue. He kept his gaze on his face, staring himself down, ignoring the burns on his arm and chest. Then, not breaking eye contact with his reflection, he reached for the linen wrapped around his skull.

CHAPTER TWENTY-NINE

AUBREY PEELED THE bandages off—would've torn them off, pain be damned, if he hadn't feared what lay underneath—and stared at his new reflection.

Red and white swirled in a raised crust on Aubrey's face, reaching from his jawline to his temple, as far forward as the corner of his mouth and as far back as his ear. It looked as if someone had attacked one of Madame Tussaud's waxworks with a blowlamp. His ear was half gone, melted by scalding steam. Luck alone had saved his eye.

It occurred to Aubrey nobody could accuse him of being merely a pretty face now.

He laughed, bitter and helpless. Only half his face grinned. The face that had garnered such acclaim at the Catullus Club, that had secured his employment at Rook Mill, that had captivated Lindsey—that face had gone, replaced by a stiff, scarred mask. Aubrey had nothing left but his wits and industry. He couldn't imagine it'd be enough.

Good God, what would Lindsey say?

The thought drove any hint of a smile from Aubrey's lips. All Lindsey's work to keep him alive, and not even a handsome face for his troubles. Even Aubrey, with his grim sense of humour, couldn't laugh at the realisation this would mean the end of their dalliance. It'd be ludicrous to expect Lindsey to carry on with the hideous creature he'd become. Perhaps Lindsey would be kind in his parting, but it'd be a parting nonetheless.

Aubrey stopped trying to plan for a future with his new face. Without Lindsey, it hardly seemed worthwhile.

Someone knocked at the door. "Aubrey?"

273

Lindsey's voice. Aubrey suppressed the instinct to lock the door, to stall for time, to delay the moment when Lindsey would gaze upon what all his pains had wrought. Better to get it over with as quickly as possible.

Aubrey drew in a deep breath and turned away from the mirror. "Come in."

The door opened to reveal Lindsey, tall, golden, handsome as a Hellenic hero, with a hopeful smile on his lips. To his credit, his smile didn't disappear as he caught sight of Aubrey's ruined face. His eyes, however, flew wide, flicking over Aubrey's scars to linger on the hideous half of his face. Aubrey couldn't blame him. It was a staggering sight.

Lindsey's eyes met Aubrey's again. His smile broadened, as if to make up for his initial shocked silence. Aubrey tried not to resent the effort.

"How are you feeling?" Lindsey asked.

"Fine." It took everything Aubrey had to muster the lie. "I'm fine. Everything's fine."

Lindsey stepped up to catch Aubrey's scarred hand and bring it to his lips. Aubrey let him. But when Lindsey leaned in to kiss his cheek, Aubrey flinched.

The troubled look crossing Lindsey's face felt like more than enough punishment to Aubrey. A pained smile replaced it. Aubrey didn't know which was worse. Lindsey opened his mouth—probably to apologise, though he'd done nothing wrong; the fault was all Aubrey's. Aubrey hurried to cut him off.

"Here." Aubrey tilted his head, turning the scarred portion towards Lindsey.

Lindsey reached for him. Aubrey braced himself, determined not to let his courage fail twice.

In his peripheral vision, Aubrey saw Lindsey's fingers touch his scar, but felt nothing save a vague pressure, as if Lindsey caressed him through thick folds of cotton.

Lindsey traced his scars down to his jaw. "Does it hurt?"

As if summoned by suggestion, pain bloomed from the point of contact. Aubrey hissed involuntarily through his teeth.

Lindsey snatched his hand away. "I'm sorry."

"No, I—" Aubrey forced a smile, and could feel how lopsided it must look. "It's fine."

The lie was no more believable a second time—Lindsey's expression made that plain. Aubrey tried to smile wider, but his already-tight scars wouldn't budge. Lindsey winced for him. Aubrey turned the burned half of his face away.

"Whose face is not worth sunburning," said Lindsey.

Aubrey managed not to flinch, though he felt as if Lindsey'd struck him. Still, his pride wouldn't go down without a fight. "Pardon?"

Lindsey coloured. "Oh. It's Shakespeare. *Henry V.*"

Aubrey, feeling ignorant as well as ugly, let his gaze drop to the floor.

"In my own words, then," Lindsey continued, "I think it looks a bit dashing."

Aubrey raised his head and found a bashful smile on Lindsey's lips.

Lindsey brought his hand up to Aubrey's unscathed cheek. Aubrey leaned into the gentle touch, willing it to firmness, then caught Lindsey's hand in his own and kissed its palm.

Aubrey dared another look at Lindsey, whose expression had lost some of its sorrow. Lindsey stepped closer, tilted Aubrey's chin up, and soundly kissed him. He broke it off sooner than Aubrey would've liked, but since he did so to clutch Aubrey in a tighter embrace, Aubrey couldn't complain overmuch.

"I'm sorry," Lindsey whispered into his ear.

"Don't," said Aubrey. "Just—"

He pulled back, took Lindsey's face in both hands, and claimed his mouth with his own.

Lindsey responded with enough enthusiasm to push Aubrey back towards the bed. He stopped only to kiss Aubrey's cheek, jaw, and on down his throat. His hands travelled further still. Aubrey's breath caught as Lindsey's fingertips trailed over the scars on his chest.

"Am I hurting you?" Lindsey asked, his hands suspended over Aubrey's skin.

Aubrey shook his head in vehement denial and grabbed Lindsey's waist to pull him in for another kiss.

Lindsey's hand alighted on Aubrey's inner thigh, tracing the outline of his swelling prick through his drawers. He cupped it gently, running his thumb down its length.

"May I?" Lindsey whispered.

Aubrey nodded and watched, amazed, as Lindsey smoothly knelt before him.

Lindsey kissed his way down the trail from Aubrey's navel to his groin. He dipped his head lower, his lips grazing Aubrey's cock through the thin cotton.

Aubrey compulsively grabbed the bed frame in one hand, bracing the other against the mattress behind him. He focused what little mental acumen remained to him on keeping his hips still.

Lindsey, with no regard for Aubrey's efforts, kept at it. He mouthed Aubrey to full hardness and continued until a damp stain appeared on his drawers. Then, mercifully, he released Aubrey's prick from its cotton prison. A glance up from beneath his lashes, a ghost of a smirk, then he wrapped his lips around the head of Aubrey's cock.

Soft, slick, warm, wet—a multitude of marvellous sensations enveloped his most sensitive flesh. Aubrey threw his head back, knees trembling. His gasps grew frantic as Lindsey took more of him into his mouth, running his thumbs over the crest of Aubrey's hipbones. When Lindsey bobbed his head—a subtle motion, like small waves lapping the hull of a ship— Aubrey bit his lip to keep from crying out.

Before Aubrey knew what he was doing, he'd removed his hand from the bed frame to clutch Lindsey's head. He pulled it back just as fast, to settle on Lindsey's shoulder, but Lindsey looked up, calmly took Aubrey by the wrist, and re-placed his hand on his head.

"I can't—" Aubrey began as his fingers clenched in Lindsey's locks. "I'm going to—"

Lindsey pulled away just long enough to reply, "I don't mind," with an encouraging smile. Then he returned to his task. His tongue swirled over the head of Aubrey's cock, under his foreskin—

—and and Aubrey couldn't hold back. His hips bucked. He feared for Lindsey's throat, but Lindsey tightened his grip on his thighs and held him in check as he spent.

Wracked with pleasure, Aubrey knew nothing beyond Lindsey's relentless ministrations, licking and sucking throughout his crisis, until he'd drained every drop of vitality from his wretched frame. Aubrey's knees buckled.

Lindsey caught him and laid him on the bed, then stretched out beside him, one arm thrown over his chest, the other hand tangling in his hair.

Aubrey wanted to reciprocate, but the exhaustion he'd kept at bay caught up with him. He drifted off, even as he returned the kiss Lindsey pressed to his lips.

He came around in roughly the same position, with the bedclothes pulled up over his shoulders. Lindsey lay atop them, running his fingers through Aubrey's hair and gazing wistfully at his ruined face.

"Am I not hideous?" Aubrey asked.

Lindsey gave him a look suggesting he believed Aubrey'd gone mad. "You're alive. That's more than I'd dared hope."

It wasn't what Aubrey'd asked, but Lindsey pulled him close and held him tight, as one might hold something precious that'd nearly been destroyed, and Aubrey supposed that was answer enough.

∽

His Aubrey lived.

Lindsey gazed down at Aubrey—no longer sleeping, merely resting—and blinked back tears of sheer relief at seeing him breathe without wincing, shift without flinching, move without cringing in pain. He felt something within himself relax, like a taut clock-spring unwinding in his chest. His Aubrey was safe and warm at home in his arms.

Aubrey rolled his head onto Lindsey's shoulder. Lindsey focused on the comfort of contact and not on the question Aubrey'd just asked. *Am I not hideous?* As if something so insignificant as scars could make him any less brilliant in Lindsey's eyes. His brave, bold Aubrey. Who more than deserved a rest after all the world had put him through. Lindsey thought he could use one himself.

Of course, "rest" wasn't in Aubrey's vocabulary. Much to Lindsey's lazy chagrin, Aubrey sat up. Lindsey grumbled vaguely and pawed at his shoulder to get him back down. Aubrey smiled and stroked his arm in return—paying particular attention to the inside of his forearm, just below his wrist, where thin, soft skin shivered with sensitivity—but remained upright.

"What now?" Aubrey asked.

"Dinner, if you're hungry," Lindsey offered.

Aubrey blinked at him, then laughed. It sounded finer than any symphony to Lindsey's ears. He rose to put his arm around Aubrey's shoulders—already narrow, now almost skeletal, though they'd filled out some since Lindsey'd brought him home.

Aubrey hummed in contentment, but still asked, "I meant, what will you do with the mill?"

Leave it to his practical Aubrey to bring them down to earth. Lindsey swallowed. "I'm afraid it's not up to me."

"Why not? The inquest concluded you weren't at fault. They can't take it away from you."

"I gave it back to Clarence."

Aubrey frowned. "Rook? Why?"

Lindsey wished he'd thought to offer Aubrey a dose of laudanum before the conversation began. The stress would do his nerves no good. "It's nothing you need trouble yourself—"

"It bloody well is! What's he done to you?"

Lindsey paused. Aubrey seemed all too ready to believe the worst of a man he'd met but once. Clarence's confession arose in Lindsey's mind. A terrible suspicion formed with it. "What's he done to *you?*"

Aubrey paled. "Nothing."

The suspicion grew darker. "What did he say?"

"He's your friend—"

"Not anymore, he's not," said Lindsey. "Not after what he's done to us and to Emmeline."

"Emmeline?"

Lindsey froze like a hare who'd wandered into the path of a hound. "Miss Rook, I mean."

Aubrey's frown twisted in confusion. "Since when do you call her...?"

"We're engaged," Lindsey blurted.

Aubrey stared at him.

"I meant to tell you," Lindsey rushed to explain. "That is, I'd hoped to wait until you were more fully recovered—didn't wish to burden you—"

Aubrey continued staring.

"I don't love her!" Lindsey declared. "That is to say, I like her, certainly, but—it's not what it seems!"

"What is it, then?" Aubrey asked.

Lindsey'd intended to tell a truncated version of the truth. The fear and uncertainty in Aubrey's eyes demanded better of him.

The full truth took Lindsey two hours to tell. It involved some hesitation, much looking at the ceiling, and more worrying of bedsheets between his fingers. On the rare occasions when Lindsey could bring himself to look Aubrey in the eye, he found Aubrey's fear replaced by quiet rage. Still, he spoke on to the end.

At his story's close, silence fell like sleet, forming an icy prison to chill Lindsey to his core. Then, a point of warmth; Aubrey's hand closing tight over his own, banishing the cold.

"Miss Rook is a remarkable woman," said Aubrey. "I wish every happiness for you both."

The appropriate response was thanks. But something in Aubrey's tone left Lindsey confused. "That sounds... final."

"It is," said Aubrey. Before Lindsey could protest, he continued. "Marrying her to appease Rook only works if we stop producing blackmail material for him to use against you."

Lindsey felt the chill return. "No."

"He won't be satisfied with a ruined mill and a rich in-law. He'll keep coming back. He'll have more demands, he'll gamble you out of house and home—"

"I don't care."

"I do." Aubrey smiled, weak and lopsided. "That's why I have to leave."

"But none of this is worth anything if I lose you!"

Aubrey seemed surprised by this, but stood firm. "I'm sorry."

"No, wait—" There was a solution, there had to be, there must— "Give me time. Until you're well, at least. I'll find a way out of this. If I don't..."

"You'll let me go?"

"I'll see you comfortably settled. Then I'll go."

Aubrey didn't reply for some time. When he did, he spoke with determination. "Until then, you'll not be planning alone."

⟋

DESPITE THE THREAT of Rook looming over their heads, the following week contained some of the happiest days Aubrey had ever known. He spent most of them in the library with Lindsey. They passed the time reading, separately or aloud. The content mattered little. Lindsey's company and the sound of his voice gave Aubrey comfort; those mellifluous tones flowed with the words of Doyle or Dickens or whoever had captured Lindsey's fancy on a particular day.

When Aubrey tired of literature, he explored the library. In a table drawer, he found a chess set, its ivory and ebony pieces meticulously carved. He held them up to admire the craftsmanship, which drew Lindsey's attention from *The Trail of the Serpent*.

"Do you play?" asked Lindsey.

"No," said Aubrey. "But I'd like to learn."

Lindsey's dismay turned to delight.

Aubrey feared Lindsey would coddle him, but quickly found he'd underestimated him. Lindsey's explanations were thorough; his demonstrations brutal. Aubrey grinned over Lindsey's apologies for thrashing him in their first match.

"Don't bother," said Aubrey. "I relish the challenge."

By the end of the week, Aubrey had won three matches, and Lindsey couldn't have looked prouder of the monster he'd created.

Between books and magazines and chess, they continued asking and answering any questions occurring to either of them about the other. Thus, Lindsey learned how the workhouse forced its children into uniforms marking them out as charity cases whenever they ventured outside its walls; Aubrey learned of public school discipline through caning regardless of the offence. (The latter gave Aubrey a better understanding of some toffs' tastes he'd indulged as a telegraph boy.) Aubrey told Lindsey of the annual Sunday school treat—a picnic in the country, the only spot of green they saw all year—and Lindsey told Aubrey of Rowena's attempt to reenact the legend of William Tell with her first archery set.

At regular intervals throughout the days, Charles dropped in to announce meals, bring tea, or deliver the post as it arrived. One of these deliveries included a letter on familiar stationery.

"It's from Rowena," Lindsey announced as he tore it open. A few seconds' perusal later, he added, "She proposes a visit from her and Emmeline. Emmeline is particularly anxious to see you well."

"Then my reality may disappoint her," Aubrey replied, but he did so with a smile.

CHAPTER THIRTY

MISS ALTHORP AND Miss Rook intended to arrive on Monday morning. Aubrey spent Saturday night in fitful slumber. Miss Rook may have appreciated his past correspondence, and Miss Althorp may have visited him in hospital, but neither had spoken to him since his release. Or seen the resulting scars. His concern increased the following day as he listened for the sounds of hansom wheels in the street, high-heeled boots on the doorstep, and voices in the foyer.

"Are you all right?" Lindsey asked him several times.

"Fine," Aubrey repeated, tugging the collar of his new suit.

He'd spent the morning avoiding mirrors. He didn't want that vision of horror in his mind's eye when he met the ladies. Apart from Charles and Lindsey, Aubrey'd seen no one since he'd removed his bandages, and no one had seen him. Lindsey had taken it well—extraordinarily well, and Aubrey could never adequately express his gratitude. Charles seemed indifferent, as per usual. (*Good morning, sir. I see you've blown half your face off. Dinner at seven? Very good, sir.*) Aubrey didn't dare hope Miss Althorp and Miss Rook would be so forgiving of his hideous visage.

Charles announcement from the library threshold startled Aubrey out of his anxious catatonia. Lindsey leapt from his chair, tossing *The Strand* aside as he left to greet their guests. Aubrey intended to follow, but found his legs wouldn't obey his order to stand. He sat rooted to the sofa, his hands fisted on his knees.

The library door remained ajar after Lindsey's departure. Voices floated in from down the hall. Voices belonging to Aubrey's friends, people who'd come for the express purpose of seeing him. He reminded himself of this twice before he could force himself upright to walk out of the library and down to the foyer.

At the foot of the grand stair stood Lindsey, Miss Althorp, and Miss Rook. Lindsey held Miss Rook's hands. Miss Althorp gazed upon them with fond patience. Aubrey cleared his throat, stepping out of the doorway's shadow and into the room.

Miss Rook's face, which had smile at Lindsey, dropped into an expression of pure horror. Her wide eyes flew straight to Aubrey's scars.

"Oh, Mr Warren!" she cried in perfect anguish.

Aubrey winced. "It's not as bad as it looks." In response to her shocked silence, he added, "I mean, it doesn't pain me at all. There's no denying it looks dreadful."

"Nonsense," said Miss Althorp, who'd done little more than raise an eyebrow at his appearance. "It looks... distinguished. Don't you agree, Emmeline?"

Miss Rook seemed very near tears.

"Shall we retire to the parlour?" Lindsey suggested, putting a gentle hand on her shoulder.

"Actually," said Aubrey. "I might retire entirely."

He stepped towards the staircase, but stopped at the incredulous stares of everyone in the foyer.

"Are you all right?" Lindsey asked.

"Fine," said Aubrey. "Just tired, is all."

Tired of being gawked at, tired of the pity and disgust in his friends' eyes, tired of wearing such a face as the explosion had given him. He forced a smile—half a smile, the best he could manage with half a face—and turned towards the stair.

"Mr Warren—wait!"

It was the loudest noise he'd ever heard from Miss Rook. Aubrey whirled around and saw, by the expressions Lindsey and Miss Althorp gave her, the same held true for them. But Miss Rook only had eyes for Aubrey's ruined face. She stepped forward.

"Please," she said. "It was terribly rude of me. I'm sorry to have offended you."

"No," Aubrey rushed to reply. "Miss Rook, I'm the one who's given offence. I should never have forced you to gaze upon—"

He intended to gesture at his scars, but never got the chance. Miss Rook shook her head vehemently.

"The sight of your face doesn't offend me! It's just I never expected—that is to say—I knew the explosion was terrible, but I never imagined—forgive me—how much you had suffered from it. It's the thought of the pain you've endured that frightens me. Not the sight of your face. Please, stay. I'm so happy to see you. Forgive me."

Aubrey stared at the tears brimming in her eyes and swallowed away the corresponding lump in his throat. "There's nothing to forgive."

"Excellent," said Miss Althorp, startling them both. "Now that's settled, may we please move on to the parlour?"

Lindsey gave her a sharp look.

"Of course," said Aubrey. He held out his good arm for Miss Rook. She accepted it with an expression of tremendous relief.

The parlour looked more like the reading room of a gentlemen's club than a proper sitting room. Aubrey supposed it lacked a feminine touch. Neither of the ladies seemed to mind. Miss Rook eagerly sat beside Aubrey. Miss Althorp took longer to settle, her eyes roaming over the bookshelves until she gave them a nod of aloof approval.

Charles had brought in the tea things while everyone was in the foyer. As Lindsey doled out refreshment, Miss Althorp took command of the conversation. She sat with her back to the grandfather clock and occupied the party with idle chatter for precisely fifteen minutes. When the last second ticked off, she turned to her brother.

"Have you been out at all in the last month?"

Lindsey neglected to answer her. He appeared to be pretending he hadn't heard her inquiry, which was absurd, since she sat all of three feet away from him.

"He hasn't," Aubrey answered for him. "I've tried to encourage him, but he won't budge."

"Really, Lindsey," said Miss Althorp. "I understand you're tending to an invalid, but if you keep this up, you'll become one yourself."

"Told you," said Aubrey, unable to suppress a wry smile at the face Lindsey pulled.

"To say nothing of how you must be boring poor Mr Warren half to death," Miss Althorp continued.

Aubrey wouldn't have gone that far, but he had no chance to refute her claim; she barrelled on without him.

"Why don't you show me the neighbourhood shops? We can let our engineers catch each other up on all their scientific nonsense in peace, without our ignorance distracting them."

Lindsey gave her a suspicious look, then turned to Aubrey with solemn concern. "Will you be all right?"

"Probably," said Aubrey. "I doubt conversing with Miss Rook will injure me overmuch."

"That's not what I meant," Lindsey began. Aubrey quieted him with a gentle pat on the arm.

"I know," said Aubrey. "I'll be fine, don't worry. Go on and see the world for me. Bring back news of fresh air and sunshine."

He'd meant his final words in jest, but Lindsey's expression suggested they'd struck a little close to home.

Miss Althorp decided the matter by rising from her seat. Lindsey gave Aubrey a parting embrace—it startled Aubrey to have Lindsey display their affection so openly, but the ladies didn't seem to mind—then followed her out. They were gone for all of three seconds when Miss Rook spoke.

"Have you had the opportunity to consider the possibility of powering textile mills with electricity?"

Aubrey grinned in return and obliged her with upwards of an hour's worth of technical speculation. It'd been too long since he'd spoken with someone who understood the matter. Lindsey was always a willing audience, but most of Aubrey's engineering talk flew over his head. Miss Rook, in contrast, had the light of comprehension in her eyes, a sight Aubrey sorely missed.

"I only wish Clarence would consider it in his mill renovations," she sighed.

Aubrey grimaced. "I think he's a little preoccupied with blowing it up."

"What?" said Miss Rook, aghast.

"Lindsey didn't tell you?" asked Aubrey, though the answer was writ plain on her features.

"Tell me what? What's happened? What has Clarence done?"

Aubrey hated to distress her further, but she had a right to know her brother was a murderer. Particularly if such knowledge prevented her from falling back into his clutches. "Mr Rook arranged the boiler explosion through a third party. He stole your valve diagram to frame his pawn and bragged to Lindsey afterwards. He thought it would help him recover his losses from Lindsey. And he was right."

"But surely Lindsey won't accept this!" Miss Rook cried.

"He hasn't a choice. If he doesn't, Mr Rook will tell everyone about... him and I."

Miss Rook stared at him. "He's blackmailing you."

"Yes."

"After trying to kill you."

"Also yes."

Miss Rook's wide eyes, formerly locked with Aubrey's, dropped to the floor. Her pose resembled a plant which had never seen the sun. "I suppose I ought to be surprised."

"Are you?"

Miss Rook bit her lip. "No. I'm relieved. Now I have proof of what a beast he is." She hastened to add, "That's rather selfish, isn't it? I'm sorry."

"You've nothing to be sorry for," said Aubrey.

She gave him a sad half-smile. "It's very kind of you to say so, but you needn't pretend. I know I'm a selfish little fool."

Aubrey stared at her.

"You're nothing of the sort," he forced out around the lump of indignation in his throat, but Miss Rook paid it no heed.

"Oh, but I am," she insisted. "Sitting indoors all day, contributing nothing to the household, no feminine talents, no marriage prospects, a constant annoyance to my brother, perpetual drain on the family funds. A most unnatural female. I'm quite monstrous in my own way. Perhaps if I'd been a better sister, Clarence wouldn't... And his plan couldn't have succeeded without my stupid engineering fancies."

"Poppycock," said Aubrey.

Miss Rook hung her head.

Aubrey tried again. "Miss Rook, please—will you look at me?"

Too late, he realised what an imposition his request was in light of his repulsive features. Miss Rook raised her eyes, but kept her head bowed. Aubrey supposed that would suffice.

"I know you don't believe me. But I beg you to listen. None of this is your fault. No sane or just person would consider you responsible. I'm sure Miss Althorp would tell you the same. I can only hope someday you realise it's true. Regarding your brother's villainy, you are blameless. Utterly blameless."

Miss Rook couldn't look him in the eye, but she whispered, "Thank you."

Aubrey had expected further resistance or a plea to change the subject. Gratitude flummoxed him.

"Think nothing of it," he stammered. "I'm sorry to have distressed you, Miss Rook."

"Oh, please—!" She lifted her head, her face shining with tears. "Please, call me Emmeline. It's absurd to go on like that after all this."

"Of course," said Aubrey as if he understood. "Miss—Emmeline."

She smiled through her tears.

❧

SHOPPING IN CHORLTON-CUM-Hardy didn't have the variety of London, but Lindsey and Rowena found a bookshop to suit their purposes. Lindsey roamed the shelves in search of something to bring home to Aubrey. Rowena found a copy of *Carmilla*—her fourth, by Lindsey's count—and seemed satisfied.

"What do you think?" Lindsey asked her as she approached him with her completed purchase. "*Experimental Engineering and Manual for Testing,* or *Decorative Electricity, with a Chapter on Fire Risks?*"

Rowena cast her skeptical gaze over the technical manuals. "Surely he's had enough of that by now?"

Lindsey looked down at the books in his hands, reconsidering.

"Emmeline, on the other hand..." Rowena added.

Lindsey glanced up at her. "Do you think she'd...?"

"It's about time you gave her a betrothal present. Jewellery is traditional, but frankly I think she'd appreciate electricity more."

So Lindsey left the shop with both books wrapped up in brown paper.

They returned to the house to find Aubrey and Emmeline right where they'd left them, though Emmeline's eyes looked a little red. Rowena called Emmeline away to go over her purchases. Lindsey had just time enough to sit beside Aubrey on the sofa, throw an arm around his shoulders, and ask how he fared, when Rowena came storming back in.

"I'm persuaded you have something to tell me, Lindsey?"

Her tone had a forced lightness to it, like lace cuffs on a tiger. Over Rowena's shoulder, what little Lindsey could see of Emmeline appeared fearful. He attempted to bring this to Rowena's attention via a hinting cough and significant glance, but nothing could sway her from her course.

"You know of it, Mr Warren?" she asked, turning her ferocious focus on Aubrey. "Perhaps you can enlighten me as to what role Clarence Rook played in the mill explosion."

Lindsey, in the midst of protesting her assault on the convalescent, choked.

"I'm sorry," Emmeline whispered. "I thought she knew."

"It's all right, Emmeline," said Aubrey.

"Yes, you were quite right to tell me," said Rowena, her unflinching gaze fixed upon Lindsey. "Particularly considering no one else had."

A year ago, Lindsey would've stammered an apology and begged her forgiveness. A year ago, his father had lived and had controlled his every move. A year ago, Aubrey had been a total stranger and Clarence a trusted friend.

"Clarence has already forced me to dance to his tune," Lindsey said, his voice low and cold. "I saw no reason to add another piper to the mix."

"This again?" Rowena scoffed. "It's not a question of control, Lindsey, it's—"

"It's my own damned mess!" said Lindsey. "I made it, and I'll be the one to fix it!"

Aubrey put a hand on his arm. Lindsey looked at him, but Aubrey's eyes were on Emmeline. Lindsey followed his gaze and found her no less terrified than when the conversation had begun. Indeed, she seemed a great deal more. A wave of remorse washed over him.

"Forgive me, Emmeline," he said. "I didn't mean to shout. I'm not angry with you, I swear."

"No one is," Rowena added, glancing back at her friend before returning to her brother. "However, with you, Lindsey, I confess myself more than a little vexed. It's all very well for you to speak of cleaning up your own mess. If it affected you, and you alone, I would commend your sense of personal responsibility. But this isn't just between you and Clarence. It's between Clarence and Emmeline, Clarence and Mr Warren, Clarence and myself—Clarence and the world entire, it seems! What would befall us if the course you've plotted should fail?"

Lindsey swallowed. "I take your point."

Rowena looked as though she had a great deal more to say on the matter, but reigned herself in. "Have you called on Miller?"

"Miller?" echoed Lindsey.

Rowena maintained her patient tone. "Your schoolfriend, Roderick Miller."

"What about him?"

This broke her calm facade. "Oh, for God's—! He's a barrister, Lindsey!"

"Oh," said Lindsey. Then, "Oh, I see!"

"I'm afraid I don't," said Aubrey, glancing between the pair of them.

"You think there might be some legal recourse against my brother?" said Emmeline.

Rowena favoured her with a brilliant smile. "Precisely."

CHAPTER THIRTY-ONE

LINDSEY DEPARTED FOR London the next morning. Aubrey tried to remove the anxious crease from his brow before he left, but for all his nuzzling caresses, the best Lindsey could muster in return was a weak smile and a peck on the lips.

Miller held the post of associate partner at the firm of Roberts and Schaw. A spotty office boy brought Lindsey up to Miller's office—smaller than the office Miller would've had at his father's bank, but he seemed contented. Its oak door matched the oak bookshelves lining the walls, and the pair of chestnut leather chairs. Miller directed Lindsey to one as he entered, then sent the boy off for tea and closed the door behind him.

"Now," Miller said with a friendly smile as he sat at his desk. "What sort of trouble is it?"

From Miller's demeanour, it was plain he had no knowledge of the thorny labyrinth of problems Lindsey'd become entangled in. Lindsey gave a look of intense interest to the bare bit of wall between the top of the window and the ceiling.

"Althorp?" said Miller.

Lindsey swallowed and met his gaze. "I'm being blackmailed."

Miller leaned back in his chair, and sighed. "I'm sorry to hear it."

"I don't suppose there's anything you could...?"

"I'd need more details," said Miller. "Do you know who's blackmailing you?"

"Yes."

"And?"

Lindsey dropped his gaze to the arm of his chair and drummed his fingers upon it.

"Althorp, I can't help you if you don't—"

"Clarence," Lindsey forced out through clenched teeth.

"What?"

"Clarence Rook."

Miller said nothing. Lindsey dared a glance up and saw his eyes had gone wide.

"Good Lord," Miller murmured. Aloud, he added, "What the deuce is he holding over your head?"

Lindsey chewed his lip as he considered how much to reveal. Just a few months ago, he would've gladly told all. But then, his dearest schoolfriend hadn't yet shown his true colours. Lindsey found he couldn't trust as he once had.

"He claims," Lindsey said, pronouncing each word with care, "Mr Warren and myself have engaged in lewd and indecent acts."

Miller didn't seem quite as surprised as Lindsey might've hoped. "What is he demanding?"

"He wants me to return the mill. And marry his sister. And fund his future fancies indefinitely."

Miller sighed again. Lindsey waited for his advice. It didn't come.

"Well?" Lindsey said, when he could no longer stand the silence. "What should I do?"

"Pay him," said Miller.

Lindsey gaped at him. "That's all you have to say?"

Miller picked up a pen from his desk and fiddled with it. "It's really all you can do."

"Aren't you going to ask if there's any truth to his allegations?"

Miller gave him an exasperated look. "I think we both know the answer to that."

Lindsey stared at him a moment longer, then threw a hand over his eyes. "Damn it, does everybody know!?"

"You could be a little more discreet," said Miller.

Lindsey groaned.

"As it stands," Miller continued, "you'd have a devil of a time convincing a jury Rook's claims are false."

"So we'd go to prison regardless," said Lindsey.

"I'm afraid so."

Lindsey rubbed his hands over his face, sighed, then found the strength to lift his head. "And when he demands more than I have?"

Miller didn't reply.

Lindsey looked at the man who'd been the boy with all the answers at Eton. He wanted to shake him by the shoulders, slap him, anything to make him cough up the solution to Lindsey's problem. Hell, a response of any kind! Lindsey deserved that, at least. He opened his mouth to demand it.

Someone knocked.

"Tea, sir," squeaked the office boy from the other side of the door.

Miller jerked upright. "Come in."

The boy entered with the tea-tray balanced on one arm. He set it down on the desk between Lindsey and Miller, never lifting his eyes. Lindsey fumed in silence. Miller blithely studied the ceiling.

"Will that be all, sir?" asked the boy.

Miller grunted and waved in dismissal. The boy departed. Silence fell in his wake.

The teapot steamed. Miller made no move to pour it. Lindsey watched the cloud curling from the spout and waited. After a long, agonising minute, Miller sighed again and stood. Lindsey followed his lead with a confused frown.

"There is one more thing," said Miller as he made his way to the door. He paused with his hand on the knob.

"Yes?" said Lindsey.

Miller swallowed and met Lindsey's curious gaze with one as grave and imposing as the tall shelves of law volumes looming around them. "It might be best if you didn't call upon me again."

Lindsey stared at him. Miller looked away and opened the door.

Lindsey, unable to force a protest past the lump in his throat, left without a word.

⁊

AFTER LINDSEY'S DEPARTURE, Aubrey stayed abed until Charles knocked to announce breakfast.

Downstairs in the breakfast room, Aubrey met Emmeline and Miss Althorp. Emmeline greeted him warmly. Miss Althorp, evidently not a morning person, managed a dignified nod over her steaming coffee.

"Rowena and I are going for a drive after breakfast," said Emmeline, brimming with excitement. "Will you accompany us?"

Aubrey coughed. "I'm afraid I've an errand of my own. But thank you for the invitation."

Miss Althorp glanced up from her coffee with a look of repressed suspicion. "What sort of errand?"

"Surveying the damage at Rook Mill," said Aubrey.

"Clarence never allowed me to visit the mill," Emmeline said wistfully. "I should dearly like to see it. May we join you?"

Miss Althorp didn't seem enchanted by the notion.

"I'd be delighted," said Aubrey, "but I'm afraid Miss Althorp would be terribly bored."

Emmeline turned a puzzled look on Miss Althorp, who quickly changed her expression of dread into indulgence.

"If it were possible, I should love to go," said Miss Althorp, doing a much better job of feigning enthusiasm than Aubrey would've. He supposed she'd had more practice. "However, it wouldn't be appropriate for my brother's *fiancée* to gallivant about town in a bachelor's company."

Emmeline's face fell, giving Aubrey a twinge of regret.

Miss Althorp smiled on. "I did have a notion to visit the Crystal Palace when we returned to London. That is, assuming such entertainment would interest you, Emmeline."

"Very much so," said Emmeline, though her confused frown remained. "Perhaps Aubrey and Lindsey might join us then?"

"Of course," said Aubrey. "You must see the motor transformers, after all."

The smile returned to Emmeline's face.

Having finished breakfast, the ladies retired to dress for their ride. Aubrey picked at his eggs for another quarter-hour, his guts clenched in anxiety. When he gave up and left the table, he found Miss Althorp in the foyer, pulling on her riding gloves, a crop under her arm.

"I do hope you'll forgive any offence I may have caused," she said. "But it seemed you wished to make this pilgrimage alone."

Aubrey blinked in surprise, discomfited by her powers of intuition. "I—thank you. You're quite an astute observer, Miss Althorp."

A coy smile curled her lips. "Aren't I just?"

With that, she swept from the room, leaving Aubrey to his journey.

Aubrey had intended to walk to the mill. He lasted a half-mile before exhaustion forced him to admit defeat and hail a hansom. The driver who stopped for him seemed skeptical. His eyes caught on Aubrey's ruined face as he looked him over. Aubrey pushed his bitterness down with his best half-smile. The driver relaxed, and Aubrey directed him to the mill. At the ride's end, he paid the driver with Lindsey's money, made note of the exact amount in his memorandum-book, and turned to regard the wreckage of Rook Mill.

Having experienced the explosion first-hand and read newspaper reports after the fact, he'd expected the worst. But the mill complex was no longer the boiling conflagration of his nightmares. All was calm, all was quiet. The yard, once bustling with the rumble of machines and the cacophony of humanity, now held only the echoes of the industry. A factory of ghosts, made no less ghastly by the gaping three-storey hole in the side of the mill.

Sweat broke out on Aubrey's brow as his eyes slid away from the sight. He turned from the wreckage and looked at the offices—undamaged, just as Lindsey'd promised. He walked towards them on unsteady legs, stumbling around patches of broken paving stones, and collapsed against the wall. He leaned on the cold bricks and drew in shaking breaths. Keeping his eyes downcast, not daring to look up, lest he find another reminder of the disaster, he told himself this was nonsense. The danger had passed. The boiler was destroyed, and Smith—

"Mr Warren?"

Aubrey's head shot up, his eyes wide and wild.

Miss Brewster raised her hands and took a step back. "Are you all right?"

Aubrey blinked at her. Same sober blue dress, same flat cap pulled down over her dark hair, same severe expression—save a mournful curve to her lip. At least she had escaped the disaster unscathed.

"Fine," he gasped. He pushed off the wall, locked his knees, and managed to stay upright. "I'm—I'm all right. Thank you for asking. You look well. What brings you here?"

Miss Brewster lowered her hands. Her eyes flicked over the burns on his face. He gritted his teeth against her scrutiny.

"I'm seeking news of what's to become of the mill," she said, looking him in the eye again. "Three months since the explosion, more'n two since they declared it sabotage, and not a bit of work's gone into repairing it. Checked back every week, I have, and nothing. You wouldn't happen to know anything about it, would you?"

The words were just as Aubrey expected, but they lacked the customary bite. Something in her tone didn't sound quite like her. Aubrey realised it was concern. For the mill, he assumed. Concern for himself was laughably unlikely. He mulled over how much he could safely reveal to her. "I've heard rumours."

She cocked an eyebrow. "What sort of rumours?"

"Sir Lindsey intends to return the mill to Mr Rook."

Miss Brewster stared at him. "Well, I must say I'm disappointed, Mr Warren. Not in you, of course. But I thought Sir Lindsey was more invested in the welfare of his workers. A little boiler explosion shouldn't scare him off."

Aubrey failed to stifle his bark of laughter. "A little explosion!?"

Her expression softened. "Relatively speaking. Only one man lost? It's unheard of. He ought to be celebrating. And rebuilding."

"I'm sure he would, but—"

"—but for all his bluster, he's a typical boss. Terribly sorry, his hands are tied, nothing to be done. I know the type."

Aubrey had a hundred defences against the slander of Lindsey's character. He could voice none of them. Instead, he replied, "I'll have a word with him."

Miss Brewster gave him a sharp look. "You're in contact with him?"

Aubrey could've slapped himself for his stupidity. He hastened to cover it. "I'll arrange a meeting."

"He'll meet with you, you think?"

"He'd better." Aubrey clenched his jaw and gestured at his scars.

Miss Brewster gave him a considering look. Aubrey waited in perfect anxiety to see if his bluff would succeed.

At last, she nodded. "I trust I can depend on you to accurately represent our interests."

Aubrey withheld a sigh of relief. "You can."

He supposed their conversation over, but Miss Brewster didn't leave. For the first time in their years of acquaintance, she appeared uncertain.

"I'm sorry," she said.

Aubrey gawked at her. "Whatever for?"

The look she directed at his ruined face spoke far louder and more succinctly than words ever could have. She added, "For not taking you out of range with the rest of us."

Aubrey shook his head. "Miss Brewster, I had every opportunity to go with you. My decision to stay is my own responsibility. If anything, it's I who should apologise for putting everyone at risk. If I hadn't antagonised Smith—"

"—he wouldn't've blown you up?" she scoffed. Aubrey hardly had time to nod before she rolled her eyes at him. "What could you have done to justify his trying to murder you and everyone else in the mill? If that's how Smith liked to resolve disputes, it was only a matter of time until he killed someone. Or tried to. You'll note he didn't succeed, and d'you know why? Because of you. We owe you our lives, Mr Warren—and don't you dare shrug that off! You could've run off to save your own skin. But you ran upstairs to get us out, then back to the boiler to do what you could to put off the inevitable. All my girls escaped death thanks to your warning."

Aubrey had difficulty absorbing the thesis of her speech. Still, as her words washed over him, her tone regained its familiar determination, and her hands found their customary position on her hips. Aubrey thought that just as comforting, if not moreso. A half-smile appeared on his lips. "You'd have done the same in my place."

"Naturally," said Miss Brewster. "Don't think I'm unduly flattering m'self if I say so."

She stuck out her hand for him to shake, and once he'd taken it, went off to continue her inspection of the premises.

Aubrey entered the offices alone.

CHAPTER THIRTY-TWO

THE SIGHT OF Smith's desk disassembled and piled into a corner gave Aubrey pause. His own desk appeared untouched. The door to Mr Jennings's office remained shut. Aubrey knocked.

"Yes?" came Mr Jennings's voice.

"It's Warren, sir. May I come in?"

The resulting silence turned Aubrey's stomach. Then a chair scraped against the floor and the door swung open.

"By Jove!" Mr Jennings cried with open delight. "Aubrey—!"

The rest of his intended speech dissolved as he glimpsed the right side of Aubrey's face. For one long, terrible second, he stared. Then his gaze flicked over to Aubrey's left eye and fixed upon it. A tight smile replaced his lost enthusiasm.

"Come in," he said, standing aside to allow Aubrey entrance.

Aubrey mustered an expression of thanks and took the proffered seat.

"How have you been?" asked Mr Jennings.

Though the question was doubtless intended for Aubrey, Mr Jennings directed it at the wall behind Aubrey's head. It seemed Mr Jennings couldn't bear to look at Aubrey's new face. Which was just as well—Aubrey could hardly bear to be looked at.

"Better than I was," said Aubrey. "And yourself?"

"Oh, fine, fine," Mr Jennings replied in the least-convincing tone Aubrey'd ever heard from him. His eyes flicked to the window, then down over his desk.

"And the mill?" Aubrey asked when Mr Jennings failed to say more.

"Much as you left it. Ownership has passed from Sir Lindsey to Mr Rook. Mr Rook is awaiting funds to repair the premises. Where he intends to acquire these funds, I don't know. My estimation of the cost is imposing to say the least."

Aubrey had an inkling of where Rook hoped to find the necessary funding.

"At any rate—" Mr Jennings shot a nervous look at the door behind Aubrey. "—Mr Rook himself is due to arrive shortly. Was there anything else you needed?"

The question Aubrey'd come to ask stuck in his throat. He coughed to force it out. "How did the valve diagram end up in Smith's desk?"

Mr Jennings went pale.

This development told Aubrey nothing he didn't already know. Emmeline hadn't missed her diagram until after the explosion.

If everything had gone according to Rook's plan, Smith would've fled the mill before the explosion. Having never officially reported for work, nothing could have tied him to the scene of the crime. With the blame falling upon Aubrey, likely deceased, no one would have suspected Smith.

However, Smith was dead on the scene, and questions arose. The inquest would've delved too deep for Rook's liking—unless they believed Smith had acted alone. To believe he had acted alone, they needed to believe him capable. What better to convince them than a hand-drawn illustration demonstrating knowledge of engineering?

But Rook couldn't have planted it himself. He'd have needed someone who belonged in the office. Someone who'd already been cleared by the inquest. Someone who'd proved himself a company man.

Someone like Mr Jennings.

Though it didn't come as a shock, it still pained Aubrey to have his worst suspicions confirmed. He stood to leave.

"Wait!" cried Mr Jennings. "My dear boy, please—"

"What?" Aubrey clenched the brim of his hat to keep from jamming it onto his head and stalking out regardless of Mr Jennings's protests. "What do you have to say to me?"

Mr Jennings shrank from him. Aubrey wished he could know this was due to the fury evident on his face, and not the hideous burn that swept across it.

"I had nothing to do with the explosion," said Mr Jennings. "Mr Rook only approached me afterwards. He made threats—I'm a weak man, you know as much already—blackmail—"

Aubrey tried to muster sympathy, but the best he could manage was a wellspring of pity that brackened into bitterness.

"—Smith was already dead," Mr Jennings continued, "and I thought—I thought you—"

Mr Jennings choked up. Aubrey, who'd found it difficult to meet Mr Jennings's gaze as he stumbled over his confession, looked up to find tears in Mr Jennings's eyes.

Mr Jennings found his voice. "I'm very much relieved to see you well, Aubrey."

Aubrey desperately wanted to feel the same relief. Yet it eluded him. "Did Smith... will there be a funeral?"

His inquiry did nothing to lift Mr Jennings's spirits. "Some weeks back, yes."

"Oh." There wasn't any love lost between Aubrey and Smith, but having been instrumental in Smith's death, Aubrey'd thought attending his burial was the least he could do.

"It was a quiet affair," Mr Jennings added, as much to himself as to Aubrey. "Or at least, that's how I arranged it. Mrs Smith didn't permit my attendance. I had a devil of a time convincing her to let me pay for it. Lord knows she couldn't afford to put him in anything but the meanest—" He inhaled sharply, and continued. "Regardless, it seems she holds me responsible for her son's death. I can't blame her. I feel much the same."

He fell silent, staring off into the distance and blinking hard. All the rage that had swelled in Aubrey's heart caved in on itself. Sympathy surged in to fill the void.

"I'm sorry," said Aubrey. Then, because that paltry set of syllables felt so woefully inadequate, he added, "God, Edward, I'm sorry for everything, I should've—"

Mr Jennings's eyes flew wide at something over Aubrey's shoulder.

"Well, this is interesting," said a voice behind Aubrey.

A chill went up Aubrey's spine. He whirled around. In the office doorway stood Rook.

Rook seemed just as surprised to see Aubrey. Like Miss Brewster and Mr Jennings, his gaze lingered on Aubrey's scars. Unlike Miss Brewster and Mr Jennings, he didn't bother to disguise his disgust. His curled lip pulled into a condescending smile as he finally deigned to look Aubrey in the eye. As if to himself, he mused aloud, "Whatever do you think you're doing here, Mr Warren?"

"Leaving." Aubrey stepped towards the door, but halted when it became apparent Rook had no intention of moving aside to let him pass.

"Really?" said Rook. "It looks quite like something else. Rekindling an old romance, perhaps. What would Lindsey say?"

Mr Jennings gave a startled cough. Rook smiled wider. Aubrey ignored them both.

"He'd say nothing," Aubrey replied, "because he knows better than to lend credence to the lies dripping from your forked tongue."

Rook's eyes widened, though his smile remained. "You tread upon thin ice, Mr Warren."

"As do you," said Aubrey. "Permit me to leave before I do something we'd both regret."

Rook raised an eyebrow and stepped back with an exaggerated sweep of his arm. "By all means."

Though it pained Aubrey to leave Mr Jennings to face Rook alone, he departed with no more than a tip of his hat and a sympathetic look. Mr Jennings returned the gesture with a grim nod.

"Now, Mr Jennings," said Rook, the echoes chasing Aubrey down the hall. "About the cost of the repairs..."

⟳

LATER THE SAME afternoon, Lindsey returned to Chorlton-cum-Hardy, bypassing his sister in the library and heading straight upstairs. He knew of but one cure for his misery. He wanted his Aubrey.

Aubrey he found hunched over the desk, his forehead clenched in one hand. As Lindsey shut the door, Aubrey whirled around.

"Tell me you have good news," Aubrey begged.

Aubrey's face, full of desperation and pain, proved more than Lindsey could bear. He lowered his gaze and shook his head, tossing his coat over the bedpost. It slid down and flopped onto the floor. Lindsey stared at it, unable to muster the will to put it to rights. His limbs felt heavy as iron, his joints stiff with rust. He willed his legs to carry him to sit on the edge of the bed. There he let his head fall into his palms and his shoulders slump under the burden of Miller's betrayal.

Lindsey supposed he ought to feel angry at Miller, but instead had plunged into the gulf of mournful despair that gaped in his chest and threatened to swallow him whole.

He heard the scrape of a chair, followed by approaching footsteps, and felt Aubrey's hand alight on his shoulder. Lindsey wanted to lift his head and greet him, but swallowing the lump in his throat without letting a sob escape took most of his concentration. Then Aubrey's weight sank onto the mattress beside him, Aubrey's arms wrapped around his shoulders, and Aubrey's lips pressed against his ear. Those same lips parted for speech, and—

Someone knocked on the door.

Aubrey bolted up from the bed.

"Lindsey?" Rowena called from the hallway. "May I come in?"

Lindsey looked to Aubrey, who stood well away from him now, his hands shoved deep in his pockets, then turned to the door. He worked to keep the annoyance out of his voice as he replied, "Yes."

Rowena entered, glancing at Aubrey before directing her full attention towards Lindsey. "I do hope you'll forgive the intrusion, but I couldn't bear the suspense another minute. Did you speak with Miller?"

"Yes," said Lindsey. "He'd prefer I no longer associate with him publicly."

Rowena blanched. Lindsey braced himself.

"Well," she said. "Perhaps Miller would also prefer the true cause of his wife's barren womb didn't become public."

"Rowena!" said Lindsey.

"Or perhaps how he chose to spend their Venice honeymoon? And in whose company?"

"You leave him be!"

Rowena sniffed. "I merely suggest we remind Miller what true, stalwart friends we've been to him over the years."

"Then we'd be no better than Clarence," said Lindsey. "Besides, it's not as though I have any legal recourse. If I charge Clarence with blackmail, I must explain the source of said blackmail. The best we can hope is that he'll end up imprisoned alongside us."

Rowena considered this. "Perhaps removing our funds from his father's bank will suffice."

Lindsey dropped his forehead into his hands with a groan.

"My funds, at least," said Rowena, unmoved. "I'm not comfortable with such a weak-willed bloodline overseeing my fortune."

"Rowena, please—" Lindsey's voice broke.

"Miss Althorp," Aubrey said in the same instant with greater volume.

Rowena looked sharply at him as though startled to find him present, much less speaking. They locked eyes for a long moment. Then, with a sigh, Rowena returned her gaze to Lindsey.

"You'll join us for dinner, I hope?" She glanced at Aubrey to indicate his inclusion in the invitation. "Emmeline and I are returning to London in the morning."

Lindsey nodded. Rowena left without another word, much to his relief.

Aubrey remained standing as he watched her depart. Once she'd gone, he approached the bed again. Lindsey held out a hand for him. Aubrey clasped it close.

"I'm sorry," Aubrey said as he sat down beside Lindsey. "About Miller."

Lindsey grimaced. "Hardly your fault. No sense dwelling on it."

Aubrey leaned his head on Lindsey's shoulder. Lindsey, grateful for the grounding weight, settled his own head atop Aubrey's.

"How was the mill?" Lindsey asked.

"Better than I expected," said Aubrey. "Rook shouldn't have much difficulty rebuilding. Mr Jennings was there. And Miss Brewster. She's anxious to see her girls back at work. I told her the mill would revert to Rook's control. She didn't like that."

"She and I are of a like mind," Lindsey muttered.

Aubrey squeezed his hand. "I promised her I'd discuss it with you."

"She knows?" Lindsey asked, uneasy.

"Not about us. I said you'd be obliged to meet with me on account of my face. Or what's left of it."

Lindsey gave that face a look of grave concern.

Aubrey's unblemished cheek blushed. "You're not to blame for it, any idiot knows that, but I had to think of something to cover for..." He made a quick gesture between Lindsey and himself. "She believed me, anyway, which is the point. Now I just need to tell her I've failed."

"How so?"

Aubrey gave him a hopeless half-smile. "She wants me to convince you to keep the mill. Which is impossible, but I can't very well tell her why."

Lindsey lapsed into thoughtful silence, regarding how Aubrey's fingers interlaced with his own. "Perhaps it isn't impossible."

"With all due respect to Miss Brewster, I'm loathe to trust any more people with our secret."

"No, I mean, perhaps I could keep the mill after all. I could speak with Clarence, renegotiate our terms—"

Aubrey shook his head. "As soon as he sees you want it, it'll become more precious to him than life itself. No price you name will be high enough. He'll get more satisfaction from holding it over your head than he could ever get from your money."

Lindsey stared in horror. "You don't know him."

"Do you?" The low, level tone of Aubrey's inquiry didn't match the fire in his eyes.

Lindsey met them as well as he could. "I thought I did."

Aubrey's expression softened. Lindsey didn't catch more than a glimpse of it. It was easier to look down at his shoes.

"I thought I knew him, because he knew me so. Better than my father, my sister, my friends... better than anyone. Until you."

Aubrey rubbed his back. Lindsey craned his neck up towards the ceiling, blinking fiercely.

"I told him everything. From the moment we met. You have to understand, at Eton he was..." Lindsey's throat burned. He swallowed the turmoil rising in his chest. "Beautiful. The most perfect being I'd ever seen outside of a painting. Before that I could only feast my eyes on the Hercules in my book of Greek heroes; after I met him, it never sufficed. I didn't believe he was real when I first saw him. Then he approached and actually spoke to me. I was so astonished I could hardly reply. I blubbered a few words—something idiotic, I'm sure. But he didn't scoff like my father or roll his eyes like Rowena. Even Miller had such a paternalistic air— infuriating in retrospect—but Clarence had none of that. He spoke to me, and when I replied, he listened. It was intoxicating, to have someone listen. I poured out my soul to him. I'd have done it for anyone who asked, but for him—if every word had been a knot of thorns, and had torn me to pieces as I spoke, I'd have happily declaimed the whole *Iliad* if he'd wished to hear it."

The burning behind his eyes grew unbearable. He dropped his head nearly to his knees to run both hands over his face. They clenched to fists on his brow. "I was so stupid—"

"You were a child."

"I told him I loved him, for God's sake! And when he mistook it for— no, he knew, the bastard, he knew what I meant—"

"Lindsey—"

"Can you believe it, I was grateful to him! Grateful! For the acceptance of that—that loathsome—"

Lindsey didn't remember standing up. He only realised he'd done so when Aubrey rose to meet him. Still, he spoke on.

"I was a fool. I'm still a fool. If I hadn't been so quick to trust him, we'd never have found ourselves in this mess."

Aubrey looked up at him with grave, soulful eyes. Then he reached up to wrap one arm around Lindsey. The other hand cradled the back of Lindsey's head. Lindsey needed no further prompting to bury his face in Aubrey's collar. Aubrey clutched him tight, a stronger hold than his frail frame belied, and one Lindsey couldn't begin to express his gratitude for.

"You're right," he mumbled instead. "I don't know him." He screwed his eyes shut and choked on the lump in his throat. "I don't know him at all."

⁕

ONE COLD GREY morning after Rowena and Emmeline had returned to London, Aubrey awoke alone, save for a Lindsey-shaped pocket in the bedsheets.

Aubrey rose, dressed, and wandered downstairs to the breakfast room. Lindsey wasn't there, either. Charles had begun clearing away cold eggs and sausage.

"I'll make some fresh for you, sir," he assured Aubrey as the latter entered the room.

Aubrey looked at the nearly-full dishes in Charles's hands. "These seem fine to me."

Perhaps it was Aubrey's imagination, but for an instant, he thought he saw Charles's eyes widen.

"As you wish, sir." Charles returned the plates to the sideboard. "Though I assure you it'd be no trouble."

"Seems a waste is all," said Aubrey.

Charles's shoulder twitched as if he'd almost shrugged, but he made no comment beyond, "Of course, sir," and reminded Aubrey if he should have need of him, he only had to pull the bell-rope by the door.

Left to his own devices, Aubrey felt enough at ease to stick his sausages on a fork and reheat them over the hearth's smoldering coals. Even lukewarm, they tasted rich and hearty. Aubrey polished them off, then stacked the dirty plates into neat towers on the sideboard and brushed the crumbs off the table into a wastebasket. He spent another minute wondering if he should pull the bell-rope to inform Charles of this development, or if Charles, busy with other work, oughtn't be interrupted. Electing not to disturb him, Aubrey left the room.

The halls remained quiet. Even the ambient sounds of industry were absent. The only noise came from the deep, dignified tick of the grandfather clock in the foyer. It struck half-past eleven. The chime made Aubrey jump. He stared at the clock face, considering the empty hours ahead. He knew he should seek employment, but with every Manchester paper carrying news of the Rook Mill explosion, and his name with it, he'd have to return to London for work, or go elsewhere. Birmingham, perhaps—which seemed a bit much for a spontaneous day trip. If his excursion to Rook Mill had proved anything, his legs wouldn't carry him to Manchester Central, much less out of the city. He resigned himself to wandering the house.

The dining room, parlour, and bedrooms were all empty. The library contained Lindsey.

Lindsey sat at the massive mahogany desk under the bay window, his back to the door. Papers were spread out all around him, with books stacked by his elbow.

Aubrey entered with a fond smile. The door closing behind him alerted Lindsey, whose look of curiosity changed to delight as he recognised Aubrey.

"Looking for me?" Lindsey asked.

"No, but pleasantly surprised to find you." Aubrey put his hands on Lindsey's shoulders and rested his chin atop Lindsey's head. "What're you working on?"

"Correspondence." Lindsey hastily shoved aside a hardbound copy of *Wormwood: A Drama in Paris*. "There's some for you, too."

"Oh?" Aubrey swallowed his panic. Few people knew he was staying with Lindsey. If anyone else had found out...

Lindsey retrieved the letter in question and held it out to Aubrey with a smile.

Aubrey recognised the cream-coloured stationery and relaxed a fraction. But only a fraction. Miss Althorp, while familiar, remained a terrifying prospect. He took the already-opened envelope and realised it was addressed to Lindsey rather than himself.

"Rowena is planning a dinner party," Lindsey explained as Aubrey read over the letter within. "For you."

Aubrey, having concluded as much from the letter's text, tried to will away the lump of dread in his stomach.

"She wants our opinion on the proposed guest list," Lindsey continued, oblivious.

Aubrey had just reached that part of the letter. Miss Althorp intended to invite Lindsey and himself, along with Emmeline, Lady Pelham, Graves, and Halloway. As fond as Aubrey felt towards Emmeline, and as friendly as he was with Halloway, he had to admit the presence of Lady Pelham and Graves gave him pause.

"That's... very kind of her," Aubrey said. "But I'm afraid I don't understand."

"Parties are how Rowena shows affection," said Lindsey. "She wants to celebrate your recovery."

Aubrey refrained from asking what Miss Althorp had intended to show him at her previous dinner party. "My face is hardly suited for an evening out."

Lindsey's smile fell into a stony expression. He stood to face Aubrey with one hand on his shoulder. The other came up under Aubrey's chin and tilted it towards the sunlight.

"Your face," said Lindsey, "is a mark of ingenuity and survival. Only a fool would shy from it."

Aubrey would've scoffed, but Lindsey bent to kiss him, and being held in warm arms and accepting Lindsey's caresses proved a more comfortable and comforting course of action.

"Besides," Lindsey added as they parted, "Emmeline and Halloway are very much looking forward to seeing you again."

Aubrey sighed, leaning into Lindsey's shoulder. "All right."

Lindsey rubbed his back. An answering smile came to Aubrey's lips. If nothing else, he'd have Lindsey beside him. Such support gave Aubrey courage enough to confront an army. By comparison, a little dinner party was nothing.

CHAPTER THIRTY-THREE

"Aubrey!"

The cry sprang from Emmeline's throat the moment Aubrey's foot crossed the threshold of the London house parlour. Aubrey froze in the doorway. He had just enough time to take in the crowd—Miss Althorp beside Lady Pelham on a chaise, Graves in an armchair, Halloway standing beside him with one hand on the chair's back—then Emmeline rushed to meet him in a flurry of chartreuse silk.

"It's so wonderful to see you!" She took his hands and peered earnestly into his face. "How have you been? Better, I hope?"

"Much better," said Aubrey, his shoulders relaxing from their startled posture. "And you—?"

"Oh, I'm quite well!" said Emmeline. "Wonderfully, tremendously well, now that you're here!"

"Good evening, Lindsey," said Miss Althorp from her seat, lifting her chin as though it would help her see over Emmeline's shoulder.

Emmeline glanced back at her, then turned to Aubrey and looked up at Lindsey behind him. She blushed.

"And—and it's wonderful to see you as well!" she said, adding, "Lindsey," in an uncertain tone.

Lindsey laughed, laying a hand on Aubrey's shoulder. "May we come in?"

"Yes—" Emmeline dropped Aubrey's hands and scuttled backward. "—yes, of course, how stupid of me—"

"Not in the least," said Aubrey, smiling at her.

She hesitated before returning it, but seemed sincere when she did.

Lindsey's hand descended to Aubrey's waist. Aubrey allowed Lindsey to guide him into the room. Lindsey settled him into an armchair by the fire. Another chair sat close by. Lindsey pulled it even closer, but continued standing.

"Warm enough?" he asked, his hand on Aubrey's shoulder.

"Yes," said Aubrey.

"Not too warm?"

"No, no." Aubrey smiled despite himself. He caught Lindsey's wrist and pulled him towards the empty chair. "For heaven's sake, sit down."

Lindsey obeyed, perching on the edge of the seat and leaning towards Aubrey. Aubrey released his wrist and held his hand instead. Lindsey sat back and breathed easier.

Aubrey glanced around the room, intent on finding Emmeline, and inadvertently locked eyes with Graves. Graves quickly looked at the ceiling, then to the vase of fresh-cut flowers by the window, then towards Halloway—but Halloway had abandoned him to approach Aubrey's chair.

Aubrey tensed. Halloway's eyes alighted on his scars. He opened his mouth to speak. Aubrey beat him to it.

"Does this—" Aubrey gestured to his ruined face. "—mean you'll finally give up asking to paint my portrait?"

He felt Lindsey flinch beside him. The ladies' conversation came to a sudden hush. Graves's eyes widened.

Halloway raised his eyebrows. "If you insist. Though I can't promise I'll give up hoping you'll change your mind. It'd make a striking piece."

Aubrey meant to say thanks. Instead he replied, "You don't have to humour me."

"I've never humoured anyone in my life," said Halloway. "You have impeccable bone structure. It'll take more than burns to rid you of it."

Aubrey's lips twitched. Then he laughed outright. "You win."

Halloway's confused look changed to wonder. "You'll let me paint you?"

"Have you read that Proust yet, Lindsey?" Graves asked a little too loudly.

Lindsey squeezed Aubrey's hand before answering Graves. Halloway rolled his eyes and returned to his patron. Aubrey allowed himself to relax.

"Aubrey?"

Aubrey brought his head up sharp to regard Emmeline standing by, her hands twisted in her skirts.

"Emmeline!" he replied. "Please, sit down. Is there a chair—?"

He started to rise. The motion alerted Lindsey, who jumped out of his seat as if bitten by a cobra. Lindsey offered Emmeline his chair, and, when this only made her more uncomfortable, he pulled over another. Emmeline alternated between apologising and thanking him throughout.

"It's no trouble, really," Lindsey assured her. "All settled, then?"

Aubrey nodded. Lindsey hovered for a moment longer before returning to Graves, who huffed with impatience, but took up the thread of their discussion regardless. Emmeline watched them, her shoulders hunched. Aubrey cast about for something to put her at ease.

"You look... very bright," he said, not having the least idea how to compliment a woman.

She gave a start and turned to him with a smile. "Thank you! It's all Rowena's doing. She took me to her dressmaker—she always has the most fashionable dresses, I'm sure you've noticed—and said I might have one in any colour I chose, so—" She dropped her eyes to her chartreuse gown and smoothed out the wrinkles her nerves had made in it.

"It's very nice," said Aubrey, and meant it. Anything that distracted Emmeline from her troubles was nothing short of marvellous.

Emmeline beamed at him, her expression as bright as her dress. "Have you heard about Willans and Robinson's high-speed engines?"

They passed the next quarter-hour in happy technical discussion, so absorbed that the dinner bell had to be rung twice for their benefit.

The other guests paired off much like they had at Aubrey's first dinner party, but in different configurations: Graves arm-in-arm with Halloway, and Miss Althorp with Lady Pelham, leaving Lindsey, Aubrey, and Emmeline to figure out the rest themselves.

Lindsey turned to Aubrey and seemed about to speak. Before he could, Aubrey caught his eye and flicked his gaze significantly in Emmeline's direction. Lindsey frowned. Aubrey cleared his throat. Lindsey conceded.

"Emmeline," said Lindsey, "may I take you down to dinner?"

He held out his arm for her. She stared at it, then turned to Aubrey.

"I don't wish to intrude..." she began.

"You'd be doing nothing of the sort," said Aubrey.

She looked to Lindsey, who smiled kindly down at her. A small smile of her own appeared, and she threaded her arm through Lindsey's.

"Thank you," she said to Aubrey as they passed by.

"Think nothing of it," said Aubrey, following along behind.

Thanks to the delay in the drawing room, everyone else was seated by the time Aubrey arrived alone to the dining room. Lindsey sat at the head, then Graves, Halloway, and Lady Pelham down one side, with Miss

Althorp at the foot. Emmeline sat on the opposing side, with an empty seat between her and Lindsey.

Aubrey stopped on the threshold, not quite believing his good fortune. Emmeline gave him a fluttering wave, which drew Lindsey's attention. The second he spotted Aubrey, Lindsey stood up and pulled out the empty chair. Even Aubrey couldn't misinterpret such an invitation. He crossed the room to sit beside his Lindsey, a stupid grin tugging at his scars.

Thrilled by the seating arrangements, Aubrey would've been content to be as ignored as he'd been at his last party. But he quickly realised that wouldn't be the case tonight. With Clarence absent, Emmeline had no qualms about speaking up. She alternated between society news with the ladies and engineering discussions with Aubrey. Nor was she alone in encouraging his conversation. Halloway, though less learned than Emmeline, was just as interested in the sciences. Between the two of them, Aubrey felt almost at home.

Graves occupied most of Lindsey's attention talking theatre and literature, but in a lull between courses, Lindsey's hand found Aubrey's underneath the table, and Aubrey knew he'd not been forgotten.

After dessert, Aubrey cast a wary glance at Graves. But his lordship kept his lips sealed as the ladies withdrew, giving a nervous look of his own to Lindsey. Lindsey, however, had eyes only for Aubrey, and laid his palm on Aubrey's thigh. Aubrey relaxed and returned his smile.

Mr Hudson brought the port and departed, leaving the four men alone. Lindsey poured Aubrey's glass first. Graves appeared perturbed by the favouritism. Aubrey couldn't resist smirking as he sipped. Graves got his revenge by taking up all Lindsey's attention with a rousing debate on Henry James, but since Lindsey's hand soon rejoined Aubrey's—over the table, rather than under it—Aubrey found it difficult to care. The gentle pressure of Lindsey's fingers distracted him from noticing Halloway circumnavigating the table. He only realised Halloway'd sat down beside him when he spoke.

"Do forgive the intrusion," Halloway said after Aubrey jumped. "But I've an impertinent question."

"Oh?" Aubrey took a fortifying gulp of port.

"What sort of painting would you be willing to sit for? I thought perhaps Icarus after his fall. It'd be a reclining pose, simple enough on your end. Though I might need you to remove your shirt."

Aubrey made a mental note to ask Lindsey what Icarus was. "What else did you have in mind?"

"Haphaestus," Halloway replied as though it were the most natural conclusion. "Working at his forge. Which would require a raised hammer. Bit heavy. But I sketch quick, and we could rig up a pulley system."

"Icarus sounds safer," said Aubrey.

"Icarus, then," Halloway echoed with a satisfied nod.

Perhaps it was his good mood, or perhaps it was the wine, but as Halloway looked back towards Graves and Lindsey, Aubrey found himself voicing a question that'd puzzled him for months.

"How did you and Lord Graves...?" he began, then thought better of it. At least he'd had the presence of mind to speak in a low tone. Graves and Lindsey, wrapped up in their own conversation, didn't seem to have heard him. But Halloway did.

"...meet?" Halloway finished for him.

Aubrey nodded.

Halloway grinned. "He wanted a portrait done. One of his friends recommended me."

"And ever since...?"

"He had to seduce me first. That took some doing."

Aubrey could imagine. "What won you over?"

"Truthfully?" Halloway glanced at Graves, determined he wasn't listening, then leaned in to answer. "He's rich, hilarious, and sucks cock like a French sailor. What's not to love?"

Aubrey stifled his laugh behind his hand. Halloway joined him with a chuckle.

"What's so funny?" Graves demanded.

"Nothing, darling," said Halloway. "I was just telling Warren about Mrs Bellingham's portrait."

Graves laughed and turned to relay the tale to a puzzled Lindsey. It involved an unfortunate pug, an oblivious husband, and a request to "make the red more red."

"It was straight out of the bloody tube!" Halloway insisted for a third time, over the other men's mirth. "It doesn't come any redder than that! Hadn't even started painting, and she's already criticising my palette! If she'd just let me slap together some greens—"

Lindsey, still laughing, stood from the table. "We should probably rejoin the ladies."

"And tell them of Mrs Bellingham's portrait?" Aubrey asked, affecting an innocent air.

"Perhaps," Lindsey replied, eyes twinkling.

Back in the drawing room, the ladies paused their conversation so the gentlemen could join in. Graves and Halloway did so. Lindsey hung back, arm-in-arm with Aubrey, apparently content to watch the party from afar.

As much as Aubrey liked having Lindsey to himself, he thought there were probably better times and places for it. Particularly when the conversation across the room appeared to exclude Emmeline. A polite smile remained on her face, but with an air of confusion about it, and her eyes flicked away from the knot of people towards the room's corners.

Aubrey turned to Lindsey. "Have you spoken to Emmeline?"

"What about?" Lindsey asked.

"Anything," said Aubrey. "She's your *fiancée*. You're going to be married, for God's sake. Talk to her!"

"Yes, but—what should I say? You know her better than I."

A wry half-smile appeared on Aubrey's face. He never thought he'd see the day Lindsey came to him for advice on conversation. "Ask her about the London-Paris telephone line."

Lindsey echoed the advice in a mumble, then turned to Emmeline's side of the room with grim determination.

"And smile!" Aubrey whispered after him.

Lindsey looked back, his sheepish grin outshining the sun, then hurried on to fulfill his quest. Aubrey watched him approach the ladies, saw Emmeline's nervousness turn to delight as the words Aubrey'd suggested dropped from Lindsey's lips; then she was off, grabbing Lindsey's hand to pull him down beside her. Lindsey appeared startled, but relaxed as Emmeline's enthusiasm washed over him. Soon Lindsey returned to his good-natured self, asking all the right questions to keep her talking and happy. Aubrey ignored the pang in his chest as he watched them get on.

"May I?"

Aubrey gave a start. Lady Pelham stood before him, indicating the seat Lindsey had vacated.

"Of course," said Aubrey.

He made to stand up out of respect for her rank, but she seated herself before he could do more than shift uncomfortably. An awkward silence settled in.

"Forgive me," said Aubrey when it grew too much to bear. "I haven't the first notion how to converse with a highborn lady."

Lady Pelham smiled. "Then it might comfort you to learn I wasn't born as such."

Aubrey blinked. "Then, how...?"

"Did I come to be Lady Pelham? Quite simply, I married Sir Arthur Pelham. Before that I was merely the third daughter of the Reverend Mr Evans. The Althorps have controlled the parish for generations."

"And the Pelhams?" said Aubrey.

Her expression grew wistful. "My husband was the last of that line."

Aubrey offered his condolences for her loss. She accepted them and continued.

"He lived in Yorkshire all his life. I haven't the faintest idea how Rowena met him. She seems to know everyone."

"She introduced you, then?"

Lady Pelham gave him a considering look, seemed to decide something, and spoke on. "The marriage was her idea. My father wished me to spend the rest of my life as his faithful secretary."

"What did Miss Althorp wish?" The evening had removed many of Aubrey's suspicions regarding his hostess, but he couldn't quite banish his wary nature.

Lady Pelham smiled on. "She wished for my happiness. She thought marriage to a respectable bachelor might do the trick."

Aubrey thought he might be catching on to something. "When you say 'bachelor'..."

"I mean confirmed."

"Ah," said Aubrey. "And... did it make you happy?"

"Oh, very. Sir Arthur was kind, charming, quite funny. Not a bit wicked. Much less trouble than most husbands, or so I gather. Truth told, it was more of an adjustment for him, having a woman about. But he grew accustomed to me as I made myself useful—reading to him, playing piano, and so forth. For all his worldly wealth, he was lonely. He didn't speak of it often, but he'd had a particular friend long ago, before I was ever born, and I'm afraid their parting broke his heart. He couldn't bear to seek out anyone else until Rowena suggested what I suitable wife I might be."

Aubrey had a feeling Miss Althorp had done a bit more than "suggest" the arrangement, but another thought superseded it. He worded it carefully. "As the daughter of a man of God, did you not find your husband's proclivities objectionable?"

Perhaps her husband's status as a celibate sodomite had improved her opinion of him, but Aubrey didn't want to jump to such conclusions lightly. She seemed comfortable enough with Lindsey, Graves, Halloway, and himself. Still, he couldn't relax until he heard her opinion on such matters from her own lips.

Lady Pelham replied in a soothing, even tone. "When David had finished speaking to Saul, the soul of Jonathan was bound to the soul of David, and Jonathan loved him as his own soul."

No syllable gave her pause. She'd evidently recited it many times before. Possibly during the same argument.

Yet Aubrey couldn't rest easy. He'd spurned his chaplain over this very point. He opened his mouth to argue it.

"Really, Charity?" Miss Althorp appeared in front of them, one eyebrow cocked. "Religion? At a dinner party? You'll be posing Parliament questions next."

Lady Pelham smiled coquettishly. "Surely by now you know what to expect when you invite me to dine. You can take the lady out of the church, but..."

Miss Althorp rolled her eyes. "Spare me."

Aubrey recalled how the two women had gone down to dinner together—an occurrence he'd attributed to allowing the partnership of Graves with Halloway, and Emmeline with Lindsey or himself. Now, he thought Miss Althorp might've served her own needs as well as her friend's when she ensured Lady Pelham married a man unlikely to touch her. Which would explain Lady Pelham's passionate Scriptural defence of inverts.

"Aha," said Aubrey to no one in particular.

Lady Pelham and Miss Althorp, who'd continued conversing in his absence from the discussion, both turned towards him with curious looks.

Aubrey's cheeks grew hot under their scrutiny. He coughed. "May I have a word, Miss Althorp?"

She continued to look skeptical, but followed him away from the general crush nonetheless. They ended up by a mahogany bookcase in the north-west corner.

"How might I be of service, Mr Warren?" she asked once they'd arrived.

"Forgive me," said Aubrey. "I don't know the proper society way to say this, but—thank you."

Miss Althorp's eyebrows came very near her hairline.

Aubrey continued before his courage could fail him. "I realise it must've taken considerable effort to put this dinner together, and I appreciate your sacrifice. I've had a marvellous time. I wanted to be sure to tell you."

Her eyes remained round and her eyebrows high, but her lips widened farther than Aubrey'd ever seen. Gone was the petulant smirk he'd come to expect from her. In its place came a broad grin. She'd never looked more like her brother. She suppressed it in a flash, but Aubrey could still see traces of it in her eyes.

"You're quite welcome, Mr Warren," she said, her arch tone gone. "Or... Aubrey, if I may?"

Aubrey smiled in return. "Of course, Miss Althorp."

"Please, call me Rowena."

A burst of laughter from the centre of the room drowned out Aubrey's response. Both Aubrey and Rowena looked over to see Emmeline with one hand over her mouth and the other arm wrapped around her waist to contain her mirth. Graves, Halloway, and Lady Pelham were more composed, but no less amused. Lindsey wore the satisfied expression of a storyteller whose tale was well-received.

"What's so funny?" Rowena asked, approaching the group with Aubrey close behind.

Emmeline removed her hand from her mouth, gasping, but couldn't compose herself enough to reply. It was up to Graves to turn and say, "Miss Althorp, you never told me you were a playwright!"

"Oh," said Rowena. "That."

"Pardon?" said Aubrey.

Lindsey caught his wrist and gently tugged him closer. "I was just telling Emmeline about Rowena's early dramatic efforts."

"Very early," said Rowena. "I was eleven."

"I particularly liked the one where the hero survives a house fire, an avalanche, and a hanging," said Graves, "only to die of a broken heart."

"His true love had run off to marry a highwayman!" said Lindsey. "It was very distressing."

"Yes," said Rowena. "And you acted the part to perfection."

"Did you, now?" asked Aubrey, struggling to withhold a smile as he turned to Lindsey.

"I did," Lindsey replied with a grin. "Quite well, I thought, since I had to play both the hero and the highwayman."

"And the lady," said Rowena. "He flung himself about the nursery in the throes of Romantic anguish for the better part of an hour. Most convincing."

"Mother liked it," said Lindsey. "The writing and acting both. In another life, we might've made quite a name for ourselves on the stage."

"I'm sure of it," Graves snorted.

Lindsey put an arm around Aubrey's shoulders and launched into the highlights of his dramatic career, with Rowena interrupting to correct details or add commentary. Aubrey hadn't laughed so hard in years.

Then Charles appeared in the doorway.

Aubrey, ever alert, noticed him first and brought his presence to Lindsey's attention.

"Yes?" said Lindsey, still laughing. "What is it, Charles?"

Charles approached and bent down to drop a few quiet words into Lindsey's ear. Lindsey's expression sobered.

"What's wrong?" asked Aubrey as Lindsey stood.

Lindsey paused his exit to look down at Aubrey, then to Emmeline, and Rowena sitting beyond her. He swallowed and spoke.

"Clarence is here."

CHAPTER THIRTY-FOUR

EMMELINE'S FACE DRAINED of blood. Her hands clenched in her skirts. Her lips parted, but no sound escaped.

Before Lindsey could comfort her, Rowena flew to her side. Lady Pelham followed, and Aubrey likewise.

Graves and Halloway appeared confused. Graves opened his mouth.

Lindsey rushed to cut him off. "I'll get rid of him."

All eyes fixed upon him. He'd intended to speak in a perfunctory yet reassuring tone, but the words came out with a hard edge that brooked no argument. Either way, it sufficed to shut Graves up. Or perhaps Halloway's hand on his elbow took credit for that.

Lindsey followed Charles out to the hall.

"He's in the foyer, sir," Charles explained along the way. "I didn't suppose you wanted him any further."

"Good," said Lindsey. "Tell Mr Hudson to have two robust footmen stand guard outside the drawing room." He didn't think Clarence would try anything drastic, but then again, he'd never suspected Clarence capable of any villainy before now.

"And for yourself, sir?" asked Charles.

"You'll prove sufficient reinforcement. Though, if you've a pistol...?"

"I'm afraid not, sir. Though I do have a pen-knife."

"That'll have to do."

They arrived at the top of the stair. In the foyer below stood Clarence. Lindsey sent Charles on his way with a nod, then descended the stair alone.

Clarence smiled up at him. "You might want to see to your man. He absolutely refused me further entry. Shall we retire to the library?"

"We shall not," said Lindsey as he alighted on the ground floor. He kept one hand on the banister, drumming his fingers on the polished oak.

Clarence glanced at Lindsey's hand, then back to his face, apparently unimpressed. "I'd feel more comfortable discussing our business in private."

"I don't give a damn about your comfort," Lindsey snapped.

"Careful," said Clarence, stepping closer. "It wouldn't do to offend me. Not with so much at stake."

Lindsey endeavoured to reign himself in. "My apologies. What the devil do you want?"

Clarence stopped short in his approach, eyebrows raised. "Very well. I require funds."

"How much?"

"Five hundred pounds," said Clarence. Before Lindsey could protest, he added, "I'll need a new suit for the wedding."

"What wedding?" Lindsey asked.

Clarence laughed. "Yours, of course!"

"You won't need a new suit for that."

Clarence kept smiling. "Really now, Lindsey! The marriage of my darling little sister and my dearest friend? It wouldn't do to have me show up in something shabby."

"It wouldn't do for you to show up at all," said Lindsey, "as you're not invited."

Clarence dropped his smile in confusion. Lindsey stood firm, his knuckles turning white against the banister.

"Oh," Clarence said at last, his crocodilian grin returning. "I'd still like the five hundred pounds, if it's all the same to you."

Lindsey looked back up the stair to Charles, who'd reappeared in the interim, and dispatched him to fetch his cheque-book.

An uneasy silence settled in the foyer. Lindsey endured it. If Clarence expected to be invited in to the party, he was sorely mistaken.

"I heard you saw Miller," said Clarence.

Lindsey looked at him sharply. "Why shouldn't I? He's my friend."

"Not according to the word in the clubs. And it was my understanding that this particular visit was for business, not pleasure."

Lindsey had no retort.

Clarence continued. "I suppose you've learned your lesson, then."

"And what lesson would that be?" Lindsey asked, affecting an airy tone.

"The one about telling all and sundry of our private arrangement."

Lindsey scoffed. "Miller is hardly all and sundry."

"Yet I heard of it, didn't I?"

"From the man himself, most likely."

"Which should tell you how much you can trust him," said Clarence, unfazed. "Or anyone else."

Lindsey, no longer able to bear the sight of Clarence's smug face, glared down at the gleaming marble floor.

Clarence inclined his head to get into Lindsey's line of sight. When he spoke again, his voice was hushed and gentle. "It's in your own best interest to keep quiet about all this, you know."

Lindsey said nothing.

Clarence waited almost a full minute, then added conversationally, "You might want to reconsider your stance on inviting me to the wedding."

"There's nothing to consider," said Lindsey.

"On the contrary! Such a momentous occasion requires careful consideration indeed. Particularly the guest list. I do hope you don't intend to invite your clerk."

Lindsey's jaw clenched. "And if I do?"

"I'd strongly advise against it. What will the other guests say when they discover a mary-ann in their midst? The uproar will rival Cleveland Street."

A chill swept over Lindsey's frame. "I don't know what you're talking about."

Clarence chuckled. "He hasn't told you? How else do you think such a wretch made his way from workhouse to office? Not through legitimate means, certainly."

"You—!"

The clearing of a throat interrupted Lindsey's retort. Both men turned to find Charles at the base of the stair, Lindsey's cheque-book in hand.

Lindsey wrote out the cheque on a marble-topped end table. It took considerable effort to tear it out of the book and hand it to Clarence with anything resembling decorum. Lindsey would've much rather crumpled it up and thrown it in Clarence's face.

"See him out, Charles," Lindsey said the instant the cheque left his fingers, pinched in Clarence's grip.

Clarence raised an eyebrow. If he made any further protest, Lindsey didn't stay to hear it. He turned on his heel and marched back upstairs.

The whole affair had taken little more than a quarter-hour. Per Lindsey's request, two footmen stood guard outside the drawing room. Inside, Rowena had taken charge. Upon entering, Lindsey saw Emmeline sitting quiet with a steaming cup of tea, Aubrey on one side of her, Lady Pelham on the other. Rowena shook hands with Graves, and Mr Hudson handed Halloway their coats.

"Is he gone?" Rowena asked Lindsey, her sharp look suggesting that if Clarence hadn't gone, she'd happily help him on his way—perhaps with violence.

"Yes," said Lindsey. His eyes avoided her cold fury and met Graves beside her.

"Nasty business," Graves said in response to Lindsey's inquiring look. "I'd like to say I never expected it of him, but... well." He fiddled with his cuff links. "Best of luck with it, then."

Halloway, who'd retrieved his hat from Mr Hudson, tipped it to Lindsey. Lindsey nodded in return. Rage at Clarence still surged through his veins, leaving his hands trembling and his throat unable to utter even the smallest niceties.

Graves and Halloway took their leave. Lindsey tried to compose himself. He focused on the ceiling, then the hearth, then the cluster surrounding Emmeline. Emmeline herself stared into her tea. Lady Pelham had an arm wrapped around her shoulders. Aubrey, holding Emmeline's hand, caught Lindsey's eye with a sympathetic look. Lindsey relaxed with a ghostly sigh.

"What did he want?" Rowena asked, her hand alighting on Lindsey's elbow. She spoke quietly, likely so as not to disturb Emmeline further.

Lindsey followed her lead, replying, "Five hundred pounds."

"The nerve of that devil!" Rowena hissed.

Lindsey thought himself the only one close enough to hear her, but Lady Pelham's suddenly-raised head proved him wrong.

"Perhaps it'd be best if we retired for the evening," she suggested.

Everyone else agreed, though it took a few repetitions for the concept to reach Emmeline. When it did, she nodded dumbly, her eyes downcast. Aubrey and Lindsey helped her up from the sofa. Her white hand clenched the black sleeve of Aubrey's jacket. He patted it, and she looked up at him.

"See?" Aubrey murmured. "What did we tell you? Lindsey threw him out, just like Rowena said. He'll not come near you again. We won't let him."

Emmeline stared at Aubrey, then threw her arms around him and buried her face in his chest.

Aubrey shot a panicked glance at Lindsey over her shoulder, but it was Rowena who stepped in to rescue him.

"Come away, dearest," she said, taking Emmeline by the arm.

Emmeline disentangled from Aubrey and let herself be lead away, Rowena on one side and Lady Pelham on the other, like a pair of elegant bookends.

Lindsey and Aubrey remained in the drawing room. Apart from the crackling hearth, all was silence. Aubrey stared at the flames with his hands thrust into his pockets. Lindsey watched him for some time.

"You made me out to be rather heroic," Lindsey said at last.

Aubrey looked up. "You are."

Lindsey scoffed.

Aubrey went to him, removing his hands from his pockets to wrap one arm around Lindsey's waist and brush through Lindsey's curls with the other.

"I don't feel heroic," said Lindsey, embracing Aubrey in turn. "I feel useless." He heard the beginnings of a protest in Aubrey's throat, but went on regardless. "It's just as you said. He'll never be satisfied. Five hundred pounds tonight, a thousand pounds tomorrow—"

Aubrey flinched. Lindsey paused to press a kiss to his brow.

"It's not the money I mind," Lindsey continued, though he knew how ridiculous it must sound to Aubrey's ears. "But he'll bleed the mill dry; they won't stand a chance. To say nothing of what he's done to Emmeline. He ought to be banished to the Antipodes. Or Australia, at least. I'd happily send his money there."

Lindsey, half-joking, expected Aubrey to laugh—bitterly, perhaps, but laugh all the same. He didn't expect Aubrey to pull away to look him soberly in the eyes.

"What is it?" asked Lindsey.

Aubrey hesitated, then said, "I have an idea."

CHAPTER THIRTY-FIVE

LINDSEY TOOK ROWENA aside after breakfast to explain Aubrey's plan. He'd prepared an eloquent defence for it. To his surprise, Rowena readily agreed to the scheme, leaving him to stumble over arguments that no longer applied.

By noon, Aubrey was on a train to his lodging-house in Manchester. Lindsey, Rowena, Emmeline, and Lady Pelham departed for the Wiltshire house later that evening. Aubrey joined them the morning after—his Manchester journey merely a diversion to allay suspicion. Together, they began to plot.

Once they'd settled on a course of action, Lady Pelham whisked Emmeline off to York. Aubrey and Rowena remained to drill Lindsey on his role. After a week of gruelling rehearsals, Lindsey invited Clarence over for an afternoon's shooting.

As he awaited Clarence's arrival, Lindsey hovered by the morning room window, peering between the drawn curtains to watch for the family carriage returning from the train station. He cleared his parched throat a hundred times if he cleared it once, but he'd given the drinks cabinet key to Aubrey for a reason. He needed his wits about him for the challenge ahead.

The grey clouds darkened as the hours passed. Leaves turned over in the garden. Then, at two o'clock, carriage wheels crunched on the drive, bringing Clarence to the front door.

The moment Clarence stepped down from the carriage, Lindsey released the curtain and went to his mark. He'd settled on the study as the stage for the coming confrontation. Aubrey'd suggested the library, thinking Lindsey would feel more at ease surrounded by books, but Lindsey knew of no place more suitable than where he'd first learned to keep his cards close to his chest. He sat at his father's desk, assumed his father's pose, and waited.

Rowena remained in her own chambers, Aubrey in the library. Lindsey wasn't truly alone in his quest. He reminded himself of this over and again as the minutes crept by. As slowly as the hands of his pocket-watch moved, he wished they'd moved slower still when Charles appeared on the threshold and announced Mr Clarence Rook.

Clarence stepped in with a wide, bemused smile as Charles retreated down the hall. Lindsey didn't return it.

"I'd thought to meet you at the stables," said Clarence. "But you're hardly attired for shooting. The threat of a little rain hasn't scared you off, has it?"

No threat would scare Lindsey off. He was determined. "I've called you here to renegotiate the terms of our agreement."

Clarence blinked. "That sounds... rehearsed."

Lindsey refused to let on how close to the mark Clarence had hit, though his heart jumped in his throat. "And your confessions weren't?"

"Touché." Clarence seated himself in one of the leather chairs before the desk, casually throwing one knee over the other. He glanced at the drinks cabinet over Lindsey's shoulder.

Lindsey kept his own gaze burning into Clarence's forehead.

Clarence sighed. "What terms would you prefer?"

"You've asked me to take your sister as my wife, in exchange for which I shall give you Rook Mill, and you shall not turn me over to the police," said Lindsey. "My counter-proposal is as follows: I take your sister as my wife, keep Rook Mill, and have your solemn vow of silence regarding my private business. In exchange, you may have your pick of the Colonies. Anywhere you care to start your new life, I will happily book your passage and provide you with enough funds to sustain yourself for one month— on the condition that you never return to English soil, or contact myself or any member of my household ever again."

Maintaining an even tone took immense concentration on Lindsey's part. By the end of it, he felt ready to collapse atop the desk. Yet he kept his spine straight and his hands still.

Clarence's smile had steadily dimmed throughout Lindsey's speech until it disappeared entirely. "And if I should refuse your generous offer?"

"Then you will meet me on the Continent."

Clarence's eyes widened. Lindsey couldn't blame him. He'd suggested the idea to Rowena and Aubrey thoroughly expecting to be brushed off. Duelling hadn't been legal for over a century, and had been out of fashion for almost as long. To his surprise, both his sister and his dear friend had agreed to the notion. Theatrical, impractical, and bizarre as it was, as Aubrey had put it, "It's also very you." Lindsey chose to take it as a compliment. Aubrey'd confirmed his choice with a kiss.

At present, Clarence snorted. "Preposterous."

"Those are your options."

"I'm not going to duel you, Lindsey." Clarence laughed. Perhaps it was only Lindsey's wishful thinking, but he thought it sounded forced.

"I offer you the opportunity of a meeting out of respect for our long friendship," Lindsey continued, careful to keep his face stone. "And your status as a gentleman. However, if you decline the invitation, I will have no choice but to shoot you like the dog you've proved yourself to be."

Rowena had authored that particular line. Lindsey thought it unfair to dogs.

It seemed Clarence was of Rowena's mind, judging by his pallor. He stared at Lindsey for what seemed a full minute. "You can't be serious."

"I am."

"You couldn't shoot me, Lindsey."

"A pheasant is a far smaller target than you."

"There's a bit more to it than that!" Clarence snapped. "For God's sake, Lindsey, we're old friends. I know you, you couldn't—you couldn't *murder* me. You'd never be able to live with yourself."

"You underestimate the extent to which you have angered me of late, Mr Rook."

Clarence's mouth, opened for further protest, shut with a click. Lindsey let him stew in silence, as Rowena had recommended, until Clarence burst out with, "You'll never get away with it."

"Who knows you're here?"

Clarence's brow furrowed in confusion. "My maid—"

"—hates you, and will be happy to join Rowena's household once you're gone."

"—and your staff—"

"My loyal staff, as you've no doubt discovered by your failed attempts to infiltrate their ranks with your own agents." Rowena had brought up that horrifying fact during the planning stages. Lindsey could only thank God she was so thorough in vetting potential staff. "All conveniently out of the room. No one to say otherwise should I be forced to kill you in self-defence."

Clarence's second laugh was even more strained than his first. "Self-defence!?"

"Yes. I've just asked your sister to marry me. Clearly we've been desperately in love behind your back without your approval for many, many years, and have only recently found the courage to openly defy your wishes. People will naturally assume you've attempted to throw one final obstacle into the path of our happiness."

That was all Lindsey's own invention. He'd been rather proud of it, especially the looks on Rowena and Aubrey's faces when it rolled off his tongue for the first time.

Clarence wore a similar look now.

Lindsey, never once taking his eyes from Clarence's, opened the desk drawer and pulled out a pistol. He laid it atop the desk, pointed at Clarence, keeping his fingertips balanced on the handle. "Your father's, I believe. Purchased when *Mary Barton* made unions seem a mortal threat. It will be very clear to the police that you brought it here to use against me."

That had been Emmeline's contribution to the plan.

Clarence stared at it a moment longer, then glared up at Lindsey. "I don't believe you. You're not capable. You couldn't carry it through."

The slight tremor in his tone gave Lindsey more confidence than a hundred rehearsals. "You've no idea. I've seen your corpse laid out on this floor every night for weeks, in my fondest dreams. I've felt the weight of the pistol in my hand. I've relished its recoil. The scent of gunpowder fills my lungs. Your blood pools on the carpet, a magnificent vermilion. All my troubles are ended. I've waited too long for this moment, Clarence. I'd be more than happy to show you its beauty."

Composing the speech had been excruciating. Rehearsing it had nauseated him. Reciting it now made his stomach and throat clench. Lindsey channelled his disgust with himself into rage at Clarence, and prayed his performance seemed convincing.

Muted expressions flicked across Clarence's countenance— shock, disgust, confusion, rage—and left him sneering as he made his announcement. "Canada."

Lindsey smiled and put the pistol away. "An excellent choice. Let us shake hands on it. A gentleman's agreement."

Clarence looked as though he'd rather break the hand Lindsey offered him, but shook it all the same.

With their show of peace ended, Lindsey rang for Charles. "It'd be best if you left today. I'll send some of my men along to help you pack. Your maid is overworked as it is."

Clarence's jaw clenched, but he nodded his agreement. He stared silently into the cold, empty hearth as they waited.

Charles arrived with two brawny footmen and escorted Clarence from the room. Clarence offered no word of good-bye. Lindsey didn't miss it.

Lindsey listened as their footsteps echoed away down the hall, then crept back to his post in the morning room to watch their departure. The footmen flanked Clarence like prison guards. As a consequence of what Rowena had assumed Lindsey's standards of attraction would be, they stood just as tall as Clarence, and their muscled shoulders strained the sleeves of their uniforms. Clarence wouldn't escape them easily.

Still, Lindsey would breathe far easier when he received Charles's telegram announcing Clarence had boarded the steamship to his new home.

The carriage trotted off. Lindsey sagged, his forehead thudding against the windowpane. He very much wanted to slump to the floor, but not here. He had news to deliver first. He shoved off from the window and dragged himself upstairs to the library.

Unlike the cold, dark study, the library bloomed with light from a dozen lamps and a roaring hearth fire. But what warmed Lindsey's heart better than any flame was the presence of his Aubrey.

Aubrey stood at the window, looking down at the road winding away from the house and the black carriage rumbling along it. He turned as Lindsey opened the door.

"It's finished?" he asked.

Lindsey coughed to clear the lump from his throat. "Yes. He'll be at sea before the night is out."

"Good riddance."

Lindsey nodded, and having done so, found he couldn't raise his head again. He stared down at the carpet.

Aubrey's shoes entered his field of vision. Lindsey looked up and saw his own misery mirrored in Aubrey's eyes.

"Come here," said Aubrey.

His arms opened. Lindsey rushed to fill the space. He buried his face in Aubrey's collar. Aubrey rubbed his quaking shoulder blades.

"I'm sorry," Aubrey murmured in his ear, and, "It's all right."

Lindsey couldn't do more than breathe in reply. But with Aubrey's arms around him and Aubrey's lips pressed against his skin, it felt like enough.

CHAPTER THIRTY-SIX

THE SELF-ACTING MULE completed its final rotation. Miss Brewster lifted her hands from the machine and stepped back. Two girls hurried in to hold up the finished bobbins for the gathered mill hands to see.

Aubrey applauded with all the strength his newly-healed arm could muster. Mr Jennings did the same beside him. The rest of the crowd joined in.

Miss Brewster caught Aubrey's eye with a wry smile. Then she turned to the opposite side of the room, where Lindsey stood beside Emmeline, and curtsied in her new mule-spinning apron. Lindsey clapped as loudly and enthusiastically as any of the mill hands.

Six months past the boiler explosion, and Rook Mill was repaired. It wasn't yet electric, much to Emmeline's chagrin, but it would be—Lindsey had promised it as an engagement gift. The wedding was some months off yet. Rowena needed time to plan what she glibly called "the social event of the century."

Having completed her demonstration of the new equipment, Miss Brewster rejoined her union girls. Or tried to. Emmeline rushed forward to shake her hand. Aubrey couldn't hear their conversation across the bustling floor, but he guessed Emmeline had introduced herself and begun peppering Miss Brewster with technical questions. Lindsey followed her with an indulgent smile.

Aubrey looked away. It no longer pained him to see Lindsey and Emmeline together, but it wouldn't do for anyone present to catch him staring. In Rowena's eyes, it would rather defeat the purpose of bringing Emmeline along in the first place. Rowena had suggested showing Emmeline off to the mill hands to prove Lindsey's *fiancée* was a real woman and not a flight of fancy to cover up his and Aubrey's secret. Lindsey agreed to the notion as a means of showing off the new mill to Emmeline.

Emmeline herself, with her breathless delight at everything the mill had to offer, certainly made an impression. Aubrey hid his smile and turned to depart.

"May I walk with you?" asked Mr Jennings.

The question startled Aubrey. He nodded nonetheless, and they entered the stairwell together.

"The day finds you well, I hope?" Mr Jennings asked as they began their descent.

"Better than I was," said Aubrey. "And you?"

Mr Jennings didn't answer the question. Nor did he look Aubrey in the eye. Even half a year later, he still couldn't bring himself to behold Aubrey's new face. The other mill workers had no such qualms; as they'd gathered for the demonstration, most had occupied themselves by staring at Aubrey's scars. Aubrey bore it stoically. Lindsey's entrance with his chartreuse-clad bride-to-be had distracted them all soon enough.

"I don't suppose you could be convinced to return?" asked Mr Jennings.

A wistful smile tugged at Aubrey's list. "I'm afraid it'd be difficult to balance clerking or coal-passing with my studies."

"Oh!" said Mr Jennings. "Congratulations, my dear boy! Engineering, I presume?"

"Yes, sir," said Aubrey. "Thank you, sir."

They reached the bottom of the stair. Mr Jennings turned to Aubrey and, for an instant, managed to meet both his eyes. Aubrey stuck out his hand. Mr Jennings clasped it with both his own and shook it warmly.

"It'll be nigh-impossible to replace you," said Mr Jennings. He looked as if he wished to say more, but his eyes were rimmed with red, and the best he could do was cough.

"I'm sure you'll find someone suitable," said Aubrey. "Particularly now that you can offer a living wage."

Mr Jennings chuckled. "You'll be sorely missed, my dear boy."

"And you, Edward."

Mr Jennings coughed again and let Aubrey go, holding the door open for him. Aubrey tipped his hat and went.

Prior to meeting at the mill, Aubrey and Lindsey had agreed to leave separately. Lindsey would take Emmeline to meet Rowena at Manchester Central, from whence they'd return to the London townhouse. London was safe now, ever since Clarence's last letter, postmarked from Toronto.

Aubrey, meanwhile, would go alone to the house in Chorlton-cum-Hardy and await Lindsey's return.

As he rode the train, Aubrey allowed himself to feel some small measure of pride at attending the demonstration without collapsing. He'd had a moment when he first heard the machines' rumble and saw the rising steam, but the sight of the central mill building repaired and whole did much to calm his nerves. The demonstration had gone beautifully smoothly. Miss Brewster would excel in her new post. Emmeline would ensure electrical efficiency. Mr Jennings would manage the rest. All would be well. Aubrey could leave it in peace.

Upon his arrival at the Chorlton-cum-Hardy house, Aubrey headed to the library. He'd spent the last few months taking notes from his collection of *The Engineer* and a dozen books he'd acquired since. Developments in electrical engineering came as quick as their ancestral lightning. He had much to catch up on before he started at the Manchester Technical School.

Aubrey settled in to work and didn't look up from the desk until hours later, when the rattle of the door knob attracted his attention.

"Yes?" he said, only half-turned from his work in expectation of Charles telling him tea was ready.

"That went well, don't you think?"

Aubrey dropped his pencil and whirled around. Lindsey stood in the doorway, beaming, with one hand behind his back.

"I have something for you," he said, stepping into the room.

A smile twisted Aubrey's mouth to one side as he stood. "You didn't have to."

"I know. But I wanted to." From behind his back, Lindsey brought out a brown-paper package the size and shape of a book.

Aubrey came closer than was strictly necessary to retrieve the package, close enough to feel the heat radiating from Lindsey's heart, and inhale his masculine scent. He untied the twine and pulled off the paper. Underneath it lay *Experimental Engineering and Manual for Testing*.

"I meant to give it to you earlier," Lindsey explained, "but between rebuilding the mill and the business with Clarence..."

Aubrey set the book down on the table and tangled his fingers in Lindsey's curls as he kissed him. He manoeuvred Lindsey towards the couch. When they reached it, Lindsey took Aubrey by the waist to spin him around. Aubrey fell back onto the couch willingly, laughing. Lindsey straddled him with an eager grin.

Aubrey sat up. "Do you want me to...?"

But Lindsey shook his head. "Just lie back, and I'll take care of everything."

Aubrey's confused frown became a smirk. He leaned in to kiss Lindsey out of spite.

Lindsey laughed into his mouth. Then he pulled back to kiss Aubrey's throat, collarbone, shoulder... and on down his burned arm. Aubrey tensed. Lindsey paused and looked up, his gaze offering reassurance and asking permission. Aubrey nodded, and Lindsey's mouth closed over his scar.

Aubrey could imagine how the burns felt on Lindsey's lips—rough, jagged, unyielding—but Lindsey never flinched from them. He kissed them with reverence from elbow to wrist.

Then he nipped at the base of Aubrey's thumb, sending sparks flying up Aubrey's spine and down to his groin. Aubrey gasped. Lindsey grinned and moved on to take two of Aubrey's fingers into his mouth. Aubrey's hips jerked up of their own accord.

Taking the hint, Lindsey drew back to wrestle Aubrey's trousers off his hips. Aubrey twisted to get out of his clothes faster. Lindsey left him to it and undid his own fly. Not a minute later, jackets, waistcoats, and shoes tumbled into piles on the carpet. Aubrey tore open Lindsey's shirt and clutched Lindsey to him. The heat of their bare chests together was matched only by that of Lindsey's hands dipping into Aubrey's drawers.

Lindsey caressed Aubrey's rigid cock, teasing its length, trailing his fingers down the shaft and up Aubrey's inner thigh. Aubrey writhed beneath him, panting, cursing, and finally snatching a fistful of Lindsey's open collar before devouring his mouth in a desperate kiss. Lindsey's own prick stood stiff from his trousers, bobbing against his belly.

With Lindsey distracted by his kiss, Aubrey took the opportunity to grab Lindsey's cock. It throbbed in his hand as Lindsey yelped into his mouth, hot blood pulsing under velveteen skin.

Aubrey ran his thumb across the head, a drop of seed easing the way. Lindsey bit back a moan and pulled out Aubrey's cock. Their hips aligned, and their pricks slid together between their bellies.

As he'd promised, Lindsey did most of the work, rolling his hips in response to Aubrey's bidding. A breathy "harder," a gasp of "faster," the clench of Aubrey's fingers on Lindsey's arse—Lindsey matched them all, with additional sucking kisses to Aubrey's throat, and nipping at his ear.

"Close," Aubrey gasped. "I'm so close—"

Lindsey groaned in reply, his thrusts growing erratic.

Aubrey slipped a hand between them. "I want you to spend with me."

328

"—Christ!" Lindsey cried, burying his face in Aubrey's shoulder.

Aubrey took them both in hand, slick with sweat and seed alike, clenched tight in his fist. With merciless pulls, he brought himself over the edge, and Lindsey with him. Lindsey ecstatic cries rang in his ear. His own crisis choked him with pleasure until his vision spotted with stars.

Lindsey collapsed beside him. They lay panting for some time. Then Lindsey wrapped Aubrey in his long, lean arms. Aubrey let himself be pulled to Lindsey's chest, admiring the strength of his shoulders despite his semiconscious state.

Aubrey supposed he could drift off as well. There could be no safer place than in his Lindsey's arms, with the mill repaired and Clarence gone. And yet a dangerous thought lingered in his mind. Gazing down at Lindsey, half-asleep, he felt brave enough to voice it.

"I love you," he murmured.

"What?" Lindsey mumbled, his eyelids fluttering.

"I love you," said Aubrey, louder.

Lindsey's eyes flew wide. He lifted his head. "What did you say?"

Perhaps Aubrey should've taken that as his cue to stop, but once the floodgates opened, he found they couldn't be shut. "I love you, I love you, I love—"

Lindsey kissed his lips, his cheek, his neck, every part of Aubrey he could reach, and echoed his own phrasing back at him, filling his ears with it. Aubrey couldn't help laughing—he knew not why—until tears stung his eyes, closed his throat, stopped his speech, leaving him mute. His mouth was good for nothing but kissing Lindsey, clenched in his trembling arms. Lindsey laughed enough for both of them, holding Aubrey tight in return.

"I love you," Aubrey managed to mumble one last time into Lindsey's collar.

To his infinite joy, Lindsey replied, "I love you, too."

THE END

ABOUT THE AUTHOR

Sebastian Nothwell writes same-sex romance. When he is not writing, he is counting down the minutes until he is permitted to return to writing. He is absolutely not a ghost and definitely did not die in 1895.

If you enjoyed this book, you may also enjoy:

THROW HIS HEART OVER (AUBREY & LINDSEY)

HOLD FAST

THE HAUNTING OF HEATHERHURST HALL

sebastiannothwell.com
nothwellsebastian@gmail.com

CPSIA information can be obtained
at www.ICGtesting.com
Printed in the USA
LVHW090342020222
710044LV00003B/92